Biographical Theatre

Biographical Theatre

Re-Presenting Real People?

Ursula Canton

First published 2011 by
PALGRAVE MACMILLAN

Palgrave Macmillan in the UK is an imprint of Macmillan Publishers Limited, registered in England, company number 785998, of Houndmills, Basingstoke, Hampshire RG21 6XS.

Palgrave Macmillan in the US is a division of St Martin's Press LLC, 175 Fifth Avenue, New York, NY 10010.

Palgrave Macmillan is the global academic imprint of the above companies and has companies and representatives throughout the world.

Palgrave® and Macmillan® are registered trademarks in the United States, the United Kingdom, Europe and other countries.

ISBN 978–0–230–25277–6   hardback

This book is printed on paper suitable for recycling and made from fully managed and sustained forest sources. Logging, pulping and manufacturing processes are expected to conform to the environmental regulations of the country of origin.

A catalogue record for this book is available from the British Library.

A catalog record for this book is available from the Library of Congress.

10   9   8   7   6   5   4   3   2   1
20   19   18   17   16   15   14   13   12   11

Printed and bound in Great Britain by
CPI Antony Rowe, Chippenham and Eastbourne

Für meine Eltern

Contents

Acknowledgements

Much of the material in this book is based on my PhD research, and I would like to thank the University of Sheffield and my PhD supervisor, Steve Nicholson, for their support at this stage.

If theatre studies wants to engage with the way theatre is made and received, it cannot ignore the views of those who make and see performances. I am greatly indebted to the practitioners who gave me their time to tell me about their experiences of working on the biographical performances discussed in this book (and many others I interviewed about different plays), as well as the students who participated in the interview study and audience members at Warwick Arts Centre who filled in my questionnaires.

Many other people whose views shaped this book are not cited explicitly in the text, but they were no less important and I am very grateful to all of them. Through Dee Heddon at Glasgow University I met Hannah Goddard, Sunniva Ramsay and Lisa Dawn Varty, undergraduate students from the Department of Theatre, Film and Television Studies, who offered very helpful feedback about the reader-friendliness of the text. Paola Botham and Sarah Bell, my friends and colleagues, accompanied me from my first academic conference to the publication of this book. Our interesting discussions and their insightful comments on papers, articles and chapters helped me greatly to develop my ideas about biographical theatre. As important as their academic input was, however, their friendship was invaluable. Another friend who shared the journey into academia with me is Katsura Sako, and her moral support was equally significant.

Finally, those who were closest to me, encouraged me, shared the moments of joy that followed progress and kept me sane when things did not work out were my family: my parents who gave me the same loving and unconditional support from my first attempts at holding a pen to academic research in an area and a language foreign to them; my husband for great patience and listening skills even after years of hearing about the same topic, and finally my sister whose multiple talents meant she was a great sounding board for new ideas, my most merciless critical reader, a sympathetic listener to PhD worries and even the best babysitter our daughter could have had while I finished the book.

U.C.

1
Introduction

Outline

British stages have increasingly become host to the famous. While an evening with one of the growing number of Hollywood stars who grace productions in the West End is relatively costly, other encounters do not depend on famous actors and a small number of high profile theatres. The subsidised houses, small fringe venues, regional theatres, and even touring companies, all attract their audiences with the promise of sharing a few hours with well-known personalities from different professions who have gained their fame through their artistic achievement, their political careers, their pioneer work as women in formerly male areas of public life or through their advances in science. They include Vincent van Gogh, Mozart and the Brontë sisters, the former German Chancellor Willy Brandt and Queen Christina of Sweden, the first actresses on the London stage and the Victorian traveller Isabelle Eberhardt, Darwin, Einstein and Freud. These and other figures from ancient to contemporary history are brought back to life as historical characters in a surprising number of plays. Sometimes the performances speculate about short, decisive moments, such as Oscar Wilde's visit to a palm reader in *In Extremis* (Bartlett, 2000) on the day of his arrest; more often they offer a chronological view of longer periods, as in *Marlene* (Gems, 1996a) or *Thatcher – the Musical!* (Foursight Theatre, 2005), sometimes in the form of seemingly autobiographical retrospectives, where the historical characters themselves lead the audiences through the events of the past. Pam Gems' play presents Marlene Dietrich's reminiscences before a concert and in Foursight's production Maggie comments on her political life from a cosy living room inside a giant handbag.

The use of characters based on historical figures in the last three decades of the twentieth century is by no means new, as famous predecessors such as Shakespeare and Schiller show. Palmer (1998, p. 21) even suggests that from the sixteenth century, the 'principal case of historical drama was biographical'. What is surprising, however, is the increasing number of plays that use this device.

This high level of current interest can be partly explained through a heightened interest in history, which, according to Jerome de Groot, has become 'the new rock'n'roll, the new gardening or the new cookery' (de Groot, 2009, p. i). Nevertheless, this development seems to be part of a wider phenomenon, the omnipresence or seemingly un- or little mediated representation of reality in nearly all media.

Traditional forms such as documentaries experienced a boom in the 1990s and became more present not only on television but also in hitherto unusual contexts, such as cinemas or a growing number of film festivals specifically dedicated to them (Rosenthal, 2005, p. 171). In the UK, the launch of News 24 (today BBC News) made round-the-clock-news available to 'Freeview' audiences in 1997 (BBC, 2010), and internet news pages further expanded this offer. At the same time, new forms that promised a direct, mainly entertaining, glimpse of the world arose, including Reality TV, 'a catch-all category that includes a wide range of entertainment programmes about real people' (Hill, 2005, p. 2) and, at the beginning of the new millennium, a growing number of internet applications that gave users more and more possibilities of representing their everyday life online through written descriptions and photographs (blogs), videos (YouTube) and real-time communication that includes all of these forms (social networking sites).

The widespread use of these sources of information and entertainment shows that the increased availability of mediatised windows onto the world has not yet led to a saturation of interest. On the contrary, new opportunities seem to fuel further curiosity. In this sense, biographical, and particularly documentary, theatre clearly benefits from these developments. Nonetheless, one might wonder what its special attraction is, since it cannot rival the media described above in terms of immediacy, both in the sense that historical and contemporary figures are represented by actors and with regard to the time difference between original event and representation.

Recent articles about documentary theatre tend to attribute its popularity to a growing dissatisfaction with traditional forms of documenting current affairs (Bottoms, 2006, p. 57), which has led to a growing interest in alternative views on events presented in an apparently more trustworthy medium. Both a general desire for authenticity in an increasingly mediatised world, and the perception that official media are restricted to politically opportune representations have led to a search for untainted, more authentic perspectives on reality (see for example Forsyth, 2009; Megson, 2006). The liveness and frequent political opposition of theatre thus answers the wish that, in a world that 'seems to have become a more serious place, [...] our theatre [can] help us understand it' (Hammond and Steward, 2008).

For activist theatre the presence of human beings on stage, albeit not the original ones, also offers the promise of an antidote to the danger of desensitisation to the concerns of others known to us only through media reports. Their 'live' representation on stage is hoped to evoke empathy that existing presentations in mainstream dominated media cannot achieve (see Hesford, 2006; Jeffers, 2009). Interestingly, one could assume that the same hope underlies the continuing popularity of plays about the famous despite their omnipresence in a culture obsessed with celebrity. Perhaps a credible live representation on stage can create the illusion of co-presence better than articles in magazines or video clips.

As the variety of explanations demonstrates, the current popularity of biographical forms arises from a complex interplay of changes in the world outside the theatre. Similarly, no single event or cause can account for the development of this form, but it is possible to identify some contributing factors and decisive moments (see Appendix 1 for timeline of plays).

Abolition of Censorship

The abolition of censorship through the Lord Chamberlain's Office in 1968, which lifted the ban from representing 'on stage in an invidious manner a living person or any person recently dead' (Lord Chamberlain's report 1909 cited in Shellard et al., 2004, p. 63), is certainly one of the most important. Nonetheless, literature on theatre censorship shows that this restriction was not the one most frequently enforced: a list of plays that were refused licence (partly or wholly) between 1945 and 1968 suggests references to sexuality in the form of nudity, prostitution or overly explicit mentions of sexual acts led to the refusal of 22 licences. An additional 19 were deemed unsuitable as a result of references to homosexuality. In comparison, only three plays were censored for breach of the rule on living persons and another six for unfavourable representations of Queen Victoria (Shellard et al., 2004).[1]

Although such precedents of censorship related to the representation of contemporary figures might have had a deterrent effect, as could the fact that the ban of 'living persons' allows less room for argument than, for example, references to sexual acts, the number of plays refused licence suggests that censorship did not wholly discourage the use of biographical material. It still allowed the representation of historical figures from a more remote past, such as Thomas More in Eliot's *Murder in the Cathedral* (1935), or characters based loosely on relatively unknown figures as in *The Winslow Boy* (1946) by Terence Rattigan. Censorship was thus aimed primarily at performances that countered the interpretation of historical figures held by those the Lord Chamberlain represented: in his report on *Our Ladies Meet*, the reader suggests that it is not generally unacceptable to represent 'the great queen', Victoria, on stage, but that this should be restricted to 'strictly accurate historical' versions (Reader's Report cited in Shellard, 2000, p. 12). As Tynan (cited in Shellard, 2000, p. 137) remarked, the censor's recruitment 'from the peerage' suggests that the definition of historical accuracy is based on the version of history promoted by this small social elite. Rather than an absolute ban on the representation of figures from the life world, it is thus possible to regard censorship primarily as a way of avoiding inopportune representations of famous figures.

Another aspect that puts the importance of formalised theatre censorship into perspective is the fact that it is not the only way of restricting the use of biographical, historical or documentary material. States can use other judicial means to prevent performances that clash with their interest; for instance, in 1936 Arthur Arendt's documentary play *Ethiopia* was banned before its first night by US authorities, as they feared that the use of verbatim quotation from Mussolini and the British Foreign Minister at the time 'might have a negative effect on American foreign relations' and that 'the impersonation of foreign dignitaries was "particularly dangerous"' (Sova, 2004, p. 92).

Even where state security is not considered to be at stake, 'ethical and juridical considerations' still apply to the representation of 'living figures' (Barton, 1987, p. 17; transl. UC), or those who are still part of living memories.

Influences: Left-Wing Theatre

The abolition of censorship therefore did not necessarily open up a completely new era for biographical performances, but it marked the beginning of a period in which other perspectives on historical figures could find their place on the stage. This change opened British stages to a long tradition of left-wing theatre that made use of biographical representations. The first famous example of documentary theatre from a left-wing perspective is often considered to be Piscator's work in Weimar Germany, especially *Trotz Alledem* (*In Spite of Everything*, 1925), which was based on an understanding of history as systemic and deindividualised, and which 'rejected the emphasis on the clash of personalities'. In terms of its theatrical style it moved from 'psychological drama in realistic idiom' (Favorini, 1995, p. xviii) towards a highly theatricalised montage that used the new technical possibilities of the theatre to create a sequence of scenes without close links through temporal or spatial proximity. Projection allowed the inclusion of original documents such as photographs, film or texts taken from newspapers or historical sources that could be spoken on stage, as well as a combination of a variety of styles, including pantomime, slapstick, song and other forms borrowed from music hall rather than naturalist theatre. The references to historical and contemporary events often led to the use of biographical characters (Irmer, 2006), albeit not in the 'serious accurate historical' fashion advocated by the Lord Chamberlain.

The most prominent continuation in the English speaking world of Piscator's documentary theatre and of similar forms created by workers' theatres in the USSR was the Living Newspaper in the US (Meserve, 1965, p. 257). Nonetheless, some workers' theatres in the UK used similar strategies. Although Unity, an amateur workers' theatre formed in London in 1936, did not reject realism and Stanislavskian acting entirely, it used the format of the Living Newspaper, for example in *Crisis* (1938). The performance combined a politically radical agitprop with a documentary approach, including a representation of Hitler delivering a diatribe about Nazi aims (Chambers, 1989, p. 163). Its most famous take on current political events, however, made recourse to a traditional British form of entertainment to convey its criticism of the UK's appeasement policy. *Babes in the Wood* (1938) used the association with the stock characters of a pantomime to explain their view of appeasement. Thus Austria and Czechoslovakia's role as victims was shown through their association with the babes, and Hitler and Mussolini's role as perpetrators in their part as the robber accomplices of the wicked uncle. This allowed Unity to present a left-wing perspective on current events in a highly entertaining manner. It is noteworthy that such an alternative view on living historical figures, including a clearly recognisable rendering of Neville Chamberlain as 'a bedraggled yet evil figure reminiscent of the Low cartoons in the *Evening Standard*' (Chambers, 1989, p. 173), was only possible for an amateur theatre organised as a theatre club, which there-fore operated outwith the reach of the Lord Chamberlain.

In the 1960s, however, the Piscatorian tradition gained new momen-tum in the UK through the production of various German documentary plays, including Rolf Hochhut's *The Deputy* (1963), Peter Weiss's *The Investigation* (1965) and Heiner Kipphardt's *In the Matter of J. Oppenheimer* (1964). The Marxist view of history underlying these plays had already been prepared by a visit Brecht made to London in 1956 with his com-pany, the Berliner Ensemble. This had aroused great interest, which was further reinforced by the publication of John Willett's translation of Brecht's *Little Organon for a Theatre* (Willett, 1964). In the UK, many of these ideas were also used in the work of Joan Littlewood's Theatre Workshop, whose aims included the creation of a theatrical space for a working class perspective, which was usually 'debarred from expres-sion in the present day theatre' (Papers related to H.M. Tennet quoted in Shellard, 2000, p. 61). The success of *Oh, What a Lovely War!* in 1963 meant that Littlewood's work and her understanding of history became recognised by a wider circle of audiences. The increasing engagement with a Marxist perspective demonstrates a development away from the 'poetic drama and the theatre of the absurd which were dominant dur-ing the 1950s to the overtly political theatre of the 1960s' (Irmer, 2006, p. 17), and reflected the political forces that made alternative views of society and history more acceptable.

In addition to the reinforcement of this explicitly left-wing tradi-tion, individual authors experimented with new theatrical forms of bio-graphical theatre without a clear political agenda. With Thomas More and Martin Luther, Robert Bolt and John Osborne both placed famous historical figures at the heart of plays performed in the early 1960s. Although Bolt's play, *A Man for All Seasons* (1960), is particularly influ-enced by Brecht's theatrical style, neither of the two playwrights presents a Marxist view of history: Osborne's *Luther: A Play* (1961), as well as Bolt's play, focus on 'great', outstanding historical figures and are thus closer to the conventional history play. Even though the men are portrayed as rebels against an established system of belief, the plays' interest in these systems is limited. Instead they focus on the individuality of the characters. The emphasis on the psychological dilemma of the main character in *Luther* has prompted Richard H. Palmer (1998, p. 42) to cite the play as a prime example of 'psychobiography'. Similarly Robert Bolt includes domestic scenes, such as a family visit to Thomas More in prison, combining the traditional focus on great deed and ideas with an emphasis on personality. Despite some formal innovations, the plays could thus be seen as a continuation of the more traditional representations of historical figures.

The ongoing influence of traditional history on biographical plays can also be seen in its combinations with spectacle inspired by the idea of total theatre that stimulates different senses in Peter Shaffer's *Royal Hunt of the Sun* (1964). The play's main characters, the conqueror Pizarro and the Incan leader Atahuallpa, are based on historical figures of the same name, and the concentration on the conflict between these two great men follows the conventional approach to history as made by great men. Nevertheless, detailed psychological development of these characters would not suit the presentation of historical events through spectacular stage imagery, monumental crowd scenes and music. Christopher Hampton's *Total Eclipse* (1968), in contrast, focuses on the life of two famous historical figures, but combines this with a close examination of a specific topic, the role of artistic inspiration and the artist's relationship to his art. Tracing Verlaine's love for Rimbaud, it presents their different concepts of art and its place in the world. Although clearly centring on the two poets, it uses biography to examine other concepts. The combination of traditional forms and new elements shows that the end of the Lord Chamberlain's reign is not the starting point for biographical theatre in the UK. Instead it allows the existing traditions of both conventional history plays that use biographical characters and left-wing documentary theatre to blossom without legal restrictions.

Biographical Elements in Political Theatre after 1968

The new freedom to use biographical elements could suggest that biographical and documentary traditions blossomed after 1968. Yet, biographical elements remain relatively rare in British political theatre after the 1960s. This may partly be due to a development away from 'agit-prop groups such as CAST, Agit-Prop (later Red Ladder) or 7:48' (Bull, 1984) towards an avant garde that resorted less and less to the tradition of Piscator and workers' theatres. Although many of them follow in Brecht's footsteps and present historical events and situations, only a small number includes historical characters or original documents. Joint Stock's work, for example, involves the actors in extensive research that is shared in the rehearsal process, but uses this information merely as a starting point. It is then transformed into a performance text whose roots are not directly visible any more. The direct inclusion of 'raw' biographical materials, whether in the form of documents or historical figures, is mainly abandoned. Some notable exceptions that use biographical material follow Brecht's tradition rather than Piscator's: the representation of Lord Nelson in *The Hero Rises Up* (Arden and D'Arcy, 1969), for instance, is clearly mediated by the playwrights. They examine the grounds on which his claim for national fame is based, allowing greater space to the 'forgotten figures' around him, such as his lover Emma Hamilton, an aspect that is not recorded in original documents. This re-examination also introduces a relatively high degree of psychological realism, despite the clearly Brechtian structure of montage scenes and interspersed songs.

In Brenton's *The Churchill Play* (1974) the re-examination of the former Prime Minister's role as 'an enemy of the working class who created an illusionary sense of liberty' (Billington, 2007, p. 221) is embedded into the frame of a theatre performance by a group of prisoners. Here the re-imagination of a historical figure is explicitly used to interrogate the present, directly echoing Brecht's concept of *Verfremdung* (alienation). Rather than resorting to the representation of biographical characters and original documents in the tradition of Piscator and workers' theatres, theatre practitioners thus used the liberty after the abolition of censorship to 'adapt [mainly historical events and situation, but on occasion also] biographical histories for Marxist purposes' (Palmer, 1998, p. 102). Despite the limited popularity of biographical theatre, the rise of left-wing theatre and political changes meant that the establishment's control over the perspectives from which history could be presented was threatened, and a Marxist view of the past was the first to gain greater acceptance in addition to the 'strictly accurate' forms advocated by conservative empiricism.

The Impact of Postmodernist Thought

During the 1970s, however, the advent of Postmodernist reflection on the hidden assumptions that underlie our understanding of the past extended the binary structure of conservative and Marxist history into a greater variety of perspectives. The interrogation of the principles underlying the Empiricist concept of history can be seen as part of a wider epistemological shift from modern certainties to the increased recognition of relativity in Postmodernism. Although it would be hard to determine whether practice preceded theory, or the other way round, it is safe to argue that this shift is observable in nearly all areas of artistic expression. It is also reflected in academic publications in almost all areas of the humanities and social sciences from the 1970s, including early theorists such as Derrida (1967) or Baudrillard (1970) and Hayden

White's (1973) seminal challenge to the Empiricist concept of history. At the same time theatrical practice is marked by increased self-reflexivity and interrogation of its own condition, as well as a great deal of experimentation as accepted forms were challenged. As Michael Billington (2007, p. 240) observes, the theatre rejected the binding nature of master discourses in favour of 'pluralistic, questioning, fragmented and diverse' practice.

In terms of biographical theatre, the challenge to Empiricist history and to the belief in a clear dichotomy of factual Truth and fiction was expressed in the playful use of historical and biographical references. One could argue that the way for these forms had been paved by the growing popularity of satire that engaged with contemporary events and figures, but was not supported by an explicit political agenda. For example, *Beyond the Fringe* (Bennett, 1960), described by Michael Frayn as a watershed in British revue and satire (Frayn in Bennett, 2003), did not endorse a clearly confined political agenda and pursued its aim of wittiness without a strong commitment to 'factual' or 'empirically supported' material.

Similarly, Tom Stoppard's *Travesties* (1974) draws on a wealth of biographical information about James Joyce, Tristan Tzara and Lenin and combines them freely with intertextual references to *The Importance of Being Earnest*, whose main character Algernon exists here alongside the artistic and political dignitaries. The play has the potential to raise questions about the status of 'factual' and 'fictional' sources of information, but above all, the unexpected situations, such as the intercalation of Joyce's writing and Lenin's dialogue with his wife, or Joyce's speeches in limericks (Stoppard, 1974, p. 20), endow *Travesties* with great wit and comic moments. The playful undermining of the Empiricist tradition proves to be a great source of humour.

A few years before Stoppard, Anthony Mitchell had employed biographical material in a similar format in *Tyger* (1971), which presents William Blake and his contemporaries at his birthday party where a controversial crowd consisting of Chaucer, Shakespeare, Alan Ginsberg and the Beatles gathers. Here the meeting of pop and established culture provided a source of entertainment. In contrast to the success of *Travesties*, *Tyger* was widely decried as 'a populist musical about William Blake' (Billington, 2007, p. 237). Nonetheless, both plays indicate that the dominance of Empiricist history or the politically motivated opposition between Conservative, Empiricist and Marxist history no longer restricted the presentation of biography on British stages. The delight in the playful departure from historical accuracy for its own sake continued over the next decade, both in lesser known productions, such as David Pownall's *An Audience Called Edouard* (1979) or Terry Eagleton's *Saint Oscar* (1989), and in plays whose authors are often counted among the contemporary classics of British playwriting, including Alan Bennett (*Kafka's Dick*, 1986) and Terry Johnson (*Insignificance*, 1982, and *Hysteria*, 1993).

In addition to its comic potential, the reversal or interrogation of the conventions and assumptions on which Empiricist history is based can itself take centre stage in the form of meta-biography, i.e. narratives that interrogate the process of representing past lives through the presence of biographer figures or structural devices that direct the audience's attention to the way in which the past is evoked. This development began to show itself much later than the first, playful Postmodernist interrogations described above. In 1989, Howard Brenton and Brian Friel placed the reconstruction of past lives at the heart of their, albeit very different, plays. At first sight Friel's *Making History* (1989) is a rather conventional biographical play that follows Hugh O'Neill's life from his marriage to Mabel Beganal to his political decline. The presence of Peter Lombard as Hugh O'Neill's biographer, a position loosely based on the idea that Lombard did indeed collect information for O'Faoláin's *The Great O'Neill* (Moran, 2000), however, provides an opportunity for Friel to make the biographer's agenda explicit, thus destroying the idea of a disinterested historian. Although he does not explicitly negate the possibility of such a neutral presence, as Hayden White (1973) did in his examination of the narrative elements in history, the act of raising such questions on stage can be seen as a clear step towards a more self-reflexive position in biographical theatre. Brenton in *H.I.D.* (1989) chooses a less rational and explicit way of raising questions about the reliability of historical memories, the impact of the media in which historical documents are preserved and the biographers' ability to approach these with a neutral eye. A journalist finds his interview partner in a Swiss sanatorium for patients with mental health difficulties. Charity Luber uses a range of different forms, including dance and videotapes, to support her deceased husband's conspiracy theory of Rudolf Hess's death. The supposedly neutral, factual medium of video, however, is shown to be no more reliable than the dance sequence, as the tapes change when they are replayed. Contrary to Friel's biographer figure, who poses questions about the factual nature of biographical narratives directly through his speeches, Brenton thus embeds his examination of this assumption in the structure and form of presentation of *H.I.D.*

The questions approached in *Making History* and *H.I.D.* are taken up in a great number of meta-biographical performances throughout the

1990s and in the first decade of this century. Meta-biographical performance, which will be discussed in greater depth in this volume, follows
both Friel's strategy of using a biographer-character who can explicitly
examine our concept of the past, as for example *After Darwin* (1998),
and Brenton's approach of combining the presentation of biographical
processes with implicit formal and structural means that raise questions
about its nature, as, for instance, *Marriage in Disguise* (Dromgoole, 2000).
Many other plays, including *Variations on a Theme by Clara Schumann*
(Yeger, 1991), *Arcadia* (Stoppard, 1993), *The Invention of Love* (Stoppard,
1997) and *Copenhagen* (Frayn, 2000), combine the two.

The temporal distance between the plays described as early, comic
expressions of Postmodernist suspicion of the master discourse of empiricism and these plays that contain a more explicit meta-level of reflection could be seen to echo the development of Postmodernism: from
the playful and seemingly inconsequential provocations of the tenets
on which our understanding of the past was based, theatre practice has
shifted towards a sustained inquiry into our concept of the past and
past lives. Forty years after the abolition of censorship, it is not only the
practical liberty that has enriched the landscape of biographical theatre,
but also an increasing conceptual diversity that allows the portrayal of
historical figures from a wider range of different perspectives.

Lives from the Margins: Community and Women's Biography

Although many aspects of Postmodernism are directly opposed to the
tenets of Marxism and socialism, both schools of thought share a commitment to challenging previous canons and master discourses, whether for
openly political or more philosophical reasons. For biographical left-wing,
political theatre, this shift often consists in the presentation of famous
historical figures from a working class perspective, as in Brenton's *The
Churchill Play* (1974). The presentation of the forgotten history of working class lives is less common in performances with explicit biographical
references, as historical documents on individuals from this group are
often scarce. Despite these difficulties, however, the opening of British
stages for a greater variety of histories and views from which they are
presented has also led to a growing body of work that moves away from
the canon of traditional biography towards the life stories of smaller or
marginalised groups.

An important advocate of de-centralised history on stage is Peter
Cheeseman, whose Stoke Documentaries have adapted the 'form of

living newspapers' (Shellard, 2000, p. 179) to discover neglected local histories and historical figures. Beginning in 1964, his work at the Victoria Theatre in Stoke on Trent has thus used 'actors as instruments to expose factual material' (Paget, 1990, p. 72). Even though the decline of industry in Staffordshire has often meant that the performances concentrate on workers and their stories, Cheeseman's should not only be seen as a continuation of the tradition of Piscator and workers' theatres, but as an expression of interest in community history that does not evolve around a canon of famous figures and events, but is made up of a mosaic of local histories. His belief that beyond the canon there are many stories that '"should" be told' on stage to allow the theatre to engage with its local audiences and that these are best through 'the re-creation of actual events' and people (Lipkin in Rosenthal, 1999, p. 370) is not shared by many other theatre makers. With the revival of documentary theatre in the late 1990s, however, some other examples of biographical productions based on community history can be found, such as April De Angelis's *A Warwickshire Testimony* (1999), Recorded Delivery's *Come Out Eli* (2003) about the hostage crisis of the Hackney Siege, or Hope Theatre's work on the gay community in Manchester, including *Village Voices* (2006).

Reans Girls (2003, Foursight Theatre) presents the stories of women immigrants in the Reans area of Wolverhampton and thus combines community history with women's history. The latter is arguably the most prolific strand of biographical theatre that represents marginal or forgotten lives, partly due to the ongoing popularity of explicitly feminist plays and plays about women in general which began in the 1970s, but also due to the high interest in biographical material among women playwrights. As Ryan Claycomb observes on his work as Literary Manager for The Theatre Conspiracy's Emerging Women Playwrights Series in 1998, from a good 50 scripts he read, 'at least fifteen were biographically oriented' (Claycomb, 2004, p. 526). Similar to left-wing theatre, women's biographical plays are often dedicated to the re-interpretation of famous lives, for example in *Queen Christina* (1982), *Piaf* (1985) and *Marlene* (1996) by Pam Gems, Liz Lochhead's *Blood and Ice* (1985), Sheila Yeger's *Variations on a Theme by Clara Schumann* (1991) or Polly Teale's *Brontë* (2005).

The second strand is the re-discovery of women whose achievements have been largely forgotten or ignored, in plays such as *The Bitches' Ball* (2007, Penny Dreadful Theatre Company) and *Self Portrait* (Sheila Yeger, 1990). Despite her fame as an actress and the scandal that followed her affair with the future George IV, 'Perdita' Mary Robinson is not often remembered in history books and Penny Dreadful Theatre Company use their production not only to revisit her life but also to give her poetry an airing (Dovreni, 2007). In *Self Portrait* the imbalance between the fame of Augustus John and his sister Gwen, also a painter, is addressed. Similar attempts to (re-)discover the lives of outstanding women are made, for instance, in Winsome Pinnock's *A Rock in the Water* (1989) about Claudia Jones, community activist and founder of the Notting Hill Carnival, or *Anywhere to Anywhere* (Joyce Holliday, 1985, publ. 1991), which traces the work of the RAF's women pilots who flew planes from one base to another, but were not allowed to participate in action and are hardly remembered today.

Although some of these 'herstories' question the belief in historical (or other forms of) representation, the majority do not take this aspect of Postmodernism on board. On the contrary, the idea of re-discovering forgotten lives indicates that many of these plays share the assumption that the past can be re-told, often from a traditional Empiricist perspective. They thus combine the suspicion against a canon of famous figures with more traditional forms of re-telling women's and community history on stage. Re-discovering the lives of people whose experience relates to our own is often seen as the basis for a new 'understanding of our own lives' (Schaff, 1992, p. 18).

The Continuation of Traditional Bio-Plays

Although performances that question the traditions of an Empiricist form of biography or the choice of 'great men' as subjects have characterised biographical theatre since the late 1960s, the panorama would not be complete without plays that continue the tradition of the 'serious history play' recommended by the Lord Chamberlain. Yet, even here a shift in interest can be noted: many of them focus more on the private lives of their subjects, especially on psychological conflict. *Breaking the Code* (Whitemore, 1987) presents both Alan Turing's success and his struggle with his sexual orientation. Similarly, *The Madness of George III* (Bennett, 1992) presents the king's illness as a threat both to his identity and the state, and *Albert Speer*'s (Edgar, 2000) controversial investigation of Speer's guilt juxtaposes public condemnation of his role in the Nazi regime with his own rejection of personal guilt. Others focus on personal relationships, such as *Judas Kiss* (Hare, 1998), which examines Oscar Wilde's separation from Bosie, or *Stanley* (Gems, 1996b), which follows Stanley Spencer's complicated relationship with two wives. In such plays about the private life of famous figures it is often hard to distinguish between the wish to re-interpret their stories and role in history, psychological interest and attraction of offering a 'secret' view into their private lives, similar to that of gossip magazines. While plays such as *The Madness of George III* can be wholeheartedly defended against accusations of voyeurism and the use of a famous name simply to draw in an audience, the higher aims of others, such as Michael Hasting's dissection of T.S. Eliot's domestic difficulties in *Tom and Viv* (Hastings, 1984), are harder to perceive. At the Edinburgh Fringe, the one-hander in which a biographical character, usually well known, delivers an hour-long monologue on his or her life has become a classic form in its own right. Mark Jenkins' plays about Orson Welles, Richard Burton (Jenkins, 2004) and others, or Andrew Dallmeyer's *Hello Dali* (2003), are just some of numerous examples. Although there are variations in the form and depth of this format, one might be forgiven for thinking that one of its main advantages is the use of a famous name in the title that helps it to stand out from hundreds of other performances in the Fringe programme.

Sometimes biographical material is used to explore ideas, in particular with regard to the role of art, as for example in *The Libertine* (1998), Stephen Jeffrey's portrayal of the Earl of Rochester's rebellion and decline, or Nick Dear's *The Art of Success* (1995, publ. 2000), in which William Hogarth's life helps to anchor debates about the nature of art, the role of censorship and the relationship between artist and model, men and women. In addition to this 'wave of *bio-plays*, in particular plays about famous artists' (Meyer-Dinkgräfe, 2003, p. 87) that explore ideas and concepts related to art, a number of performances also use biographical material to examine a broader range of concepts: in *Democracy* (2003) Michael Frayn explores the complexity of the reasons for human behaviour in the context of Willy Brandt's government and the infiltration of the German Chancellery by GDR spy Günther Guillaume. The focus on rationality as the origin of human actions, or often its absence, suggests that Michael Frayn indirectly questions one of the tenets of Empiricist biography. Even though this interpretation is not the first aspect many spectators would comment on, its possibility demonstrates that the forms of biographical theatre identified above are not to be seen as mutually exclusive categories. The plays have been grouped to demonstrate the variety of different forms, based on different concepts of history, a wide range of possible biographees and a range of different purposes of biographical theatre.

Documentary Theatre

This variety of biographical formats is partly based on the freedom brought by the abolition of theatre censorship in 1968. Nonetheless, the epistemological changes related to the advent of Postmodernism and the openness towards previously marginalised discourses have played an equally important role in providing the conceptual space for a wider range of approaches to past lives. The recent surge in documentary and biographical theatre could be seen as a reaction to some of the changes brought by this shift to the lack of a binding understanding of the past. While this has led to a great richness of forms, on the one hand, it has also led to the lack of a fixed point of orientation. Janelle Reinelt (2006, p. 82) confirms that the 'appeal of the old-fashioned documentary' could be its status of a 'public rehearsal of "facts" as one way of holding on to the very notion of facts and building a meaningful narrative around them'. Nicolas Kent's series of tribunal plays at the Tricycle Theatre, starting with *Half the Picture* (1994), *Nuremberg* (1996), *Srebenica* (1996) and *The Colour of Justice* (1999) in the 1990s, consisted only, or mainly in the case of *Half the Picture*, of excerpts from transcripts from judicial proceedings of the Scott Arms Into Iraq Enquiry, Nuremberg Trials, the UN Rule 61 Hearing and the Stephen Lawrence Inquiry, promising the audience 'raw information about public events' (Billington, 2007, p. 385). Later plays have extended the possibilities of documentary theatre beyond the re-enactment of tribunals, but the orientation towards politically relevant issues has remained in performances such as *The Permanent Way* (Hare, 2003) or *Guantanamo* (Brittain and Slovo, 2004). Common to all these documentary performances is the primacy of the word – characters are developed within the limits given by the words spoken by historical and contemporary figures. Other plays have tried to avoid this restriction by mixing verbatim sections with those written by a playwright in order to convey a fuller picture of the historical characters and their actions, as, for example, in *Stuff Happens* (Hare, 2004) or in *The Permanent Way* to a minor degree. Another recent development is the increasing use of documentary performances about specific communities, stable ones such as refugees in *Crocodile Seeking Refuge* (Linden, 2005), or specific members of such groups, for example in Zane's *Yesterday When I Was Young* (2007) about Josie Pickering, a member of Manchester's gay scene and dominatrix. While the early phase of documentary performances was mainly based on existing transcripts from highly formalised public situations, the latter are mainly based on recordings gathered specifically for the purpose of creating a performance and focus on the private life of the figures portrayed to a greater extent. These plays might lay claim to a high degree of authenticity based on the reconstruction of original words and characters, but many acknowledge the variety of perspectives and views the past can offer. Compared to the tribunal plays' focus on sources that allow us to reconstruct historical and political events, these perform-ances thus use documentary methods to represent lives and individual experiences on stage.

The variety of biographical references in documentary performances from the last 15 years thus reflects the diversity found in performances that have used biographical material since the late 1960s. Following the short historical outline of the development of biographical theatre and the many forms it has taken on British stages, the distinctions between different examples might seem to outweigh any similarities between them. The National Theatre's monumental production of *Albert Speer* (2000), involving a cast of nearly 30 performers directed by Trevor Nunn, and *Yesterday When I Was Young*, Adam Zane's verbatim one-woman show, could easily be considered as fundamentally different, as could Tom Stoppard's playful encounter between Lenin and Algernon in *Travesties* (1974) and the representation of court proceedings on Nazi crimes in *Nuremberg*. While awareness of these differences is essential for an insight-ful discussion of biographical performances, this book suggests that rec-ognition of biographical characters as a specific link between the world created in the performance and that surrounding it provides a point of departure for an analysis previously neglected.

Previous Research into Biographical Theatre

The lack of earlier recognition of historical characters as privileged links between the world outside the theatre and that created within the performance is particularly surprising if we take into account that the literal *incorporation* of a reference to a historical figure in the body of an actor can be seen as a uniquely theatrical feature, possible in this way only in the physical reality of live performance. Working from the simple premise that the creation of such a specific, visible, audible and, at least potentially, tangible connection to the world outside the theatre affects the way in which such plays are perceived, this book does not seek to establish biographical theatre as a category separate from related genres. Many of the performances discussed here could equally be des-cribed as historical or documentary theatre. Nonetheless, the focus is firmly placed on the presence of the human bodies that become the 'connecting link between here and now and past' (Rokem, 2000, p. 12), between the physical reality of the world and the imagined reality of the theatrical narrative. This choice of focus means that many other interesting aspects of the performances discussed in this book cannot be taken into account. While it is regrettable to leave aside such fascinating issues as the choice of biographical subjects, their impact on a play's potential to attract audiences, or their role among various discourses on a particular historical character, this limitation is necessary to provide a thorough description of their shared, defining element: characters based on historical figures.

In the 1980s Niloufer Harben (1988, p. 1) observed that, 'although the history play is a most popular genre among English playwrights of this century, very little research has been done in the field'. Since then a number of monographs and a variety of journal articles have filled this gap for history plays, but few of them have paid specific attention to the use of biographical material. Richard Palmer recognises the importance of historical characters, observing that 'of the eight new plays by British writers running in London theatres in 1997, all were biographies' (Palmer, 1998, p. 53), and devotes, as Harben did, a chapter to this phenomenon. Nonetheless, only a small number of other authors have followed his example. Sometimes the phenomenon has been recognised in connection with labels, such as bio-play (Meyer-Dinkgräfe, 2003, p. 87), biographical drama (Spencer, 1994) or biodrama (Bassett, 2003), but the lack of a unified term in itself suggests that it has not often been discussed as the most characteristic feature of a performance. This is also visible in a range of journal articles that are often restricted to the discussion of individual performances, or mix theatre and other media (Moog-Grünewald, 1991; Huber and Middeke, 1995; Kramer, 1998; Mergenthal, 1999; Reitz, 1999). Three monographs offer more comparative studies of plays with biographical material, but two of them limit their discussion to the representation of artists (Schaff, 1992; Meyer-Dinkgräfe, 2003) and one to women's lives (Kramer, 2000) and only one of them is available in English.

The resurgence of documentary theatre has meant that another area closely related to the use of biographical material has received greater academic attention. Over the past years an increasing number of journal articles has appeared, and Alison Forsyth's and Chris Megson's (2009a) collection of articles has added the first new monograph since Derek Paget's *True Stories?* (1990). Another monograph will conclude the Acting with Facts Project (University of Reading, 2010) which focuses on the role of actors in documentary forms of theatre and film. It is interesting to note that many of these publications see documentary theatre as a place where different perspectives on events can be heard. Chris Megson (2007) suggests that it promotes an assessment of 'the state we're in'. Melissa Salz (quoted in Claycomb, 2003, p. 96) confirms its power to scrutinise our political and social, as well as personal, experiences, adding that documentary theatre 'often represents multiple points of view', 'focussing less on "what happened" than on the discourse that surrounds' (Claycomb, 2003, p. 110) the events that are represented.

This focus on the use of documentary material also means that, overall, the literature on documentary theatre is of more interest in terms of the conceptual framework chosen, as it is more compatible with Postmodern views. Many publications on historical theatre concentrate on the plays' 'relationship to the external historical reality it purports to imitate' (Lindenberger, 1975, p. 3), and even relatively recent publications, such as Berninger (2006), adhere to the modernist dichotomy of fact and fiction. Although this juxtaposition of a fiction and a 'non-fiction mode' in which 'the characters are seen as human beings in our daily life' (Schoenmakers, 1992, p. 49) can be found in individual publications on documentary theatre as well, for instance in Gary Fisher Dawson's view of performances as 'documented reality' (Dawson, 1999, p. 61), it is more prevalent in the discussion of historical theatre, where it is often applied, whether openly or in disguised forms. In most cases the continued use of the fact–fiction dichotomy is not based on convincing arguments that counter their deconstruction in Postmodern theory.

Structure and Theoretical Approach of this Book

The lack of engagement with the tenets of a theoretical development that has dominated the humanities over the last three decades in this literature is rather unsatisfying. At the same time, the adoption of a radical Postmodernist perspective that treats all discourses as equal and discusses biographical references in the same way as intertextuality is also problematic, as spectators' reactions to biographical theatre counter the idea that they perceive performances in the same way they would see those without any references to historical figures. Their intuitive notion that historical characters differ from entirely fictional ones can be witnessed in anecdotal observations of spectators' reactions to performances: positive comments of my fellow theatre goers often related to the truthfulness of a performance or its power to give them new insights into lives they knew little about. Negative ones, on the other hand, were regularly justified by the perception that a play's representation of a life or of a historical figure did not tally with my companions' understanding of it. Similarly, reviews of biographical performances tend to focus as much on their relationship to the world outside the theatre as they do on aspects such as acting, direction or scenography.

The paradox between this intuitive belief in representation and the relativity of different discourses in current philosophical and conceptual approaches strongly suggests that a new theoretical framework is needed in order to gain a better insight into the theatrical use of biographical references. This will be the first challenge of this book. Chapter 2 begins to address it with an examination of other fields in which references to past events or lives are prominent, particularly historiography. These discourses influence the perception of biographical, documentary or historical plays, as they provide the 'structures that determine the perception of the past and the way in which it is communicated in the relevant texts and genres' (Breuer, 2005, p. 52), or in other modes of representing the past. In these fields a similar division between Postmodern theories of history and historical practice that is largely untouched by such criticism of its underlying premises can be observed. In order to solve the apparent paradox between the two, I suggest a functional approach that concentrates on describing the way in which people differentiate between different worlds and observes how they attribute different degrees of truthfulness to them, instead of anchoring these uses in a system of absolute ontological categories.

This distinction between the world of the play and that of the audience can offer a very satisfactory theoretical approach, but terminologically it often touches difficult, if not dangerous, territory. The difference between the concepts of Reality, Fact and Fiction as absolute entities in contrast to the notion that they are merely 'working definitions' does not seem to be expressed sufficiently by the use of capital and small letters or quotation marks around them, as seems to be the standard practice in academic literature. The situation is further complicated by the fact that the everyday use of such terms often reflects a continuing belief in their universal nature. In order to avoid interferences from other usage, I prefer to follow Willmar Sauter's (2000, p. 10) terminology that establishes a contrast between the world outside the theatre, the everyday context of the spectators called the 'life world', and the one that is created on stage, the 'world of the play'. The degree of similarities between the two could then be indicated on a spectrum between the (only theoretically possible) poles of extra- and intra-theatricality, where the two worlds are identical or do not share any common features, respectively. The suggested terms acknowledge the fact that most adult spectators have learnt the rules of make believe and distinguish between the life world and the world of the play, in contrast to many children who fear that the actors might really be 'hurt' when they suffer injuries on stage. At the same time it does not impose any view on the way in which they perceive one or another as more or less 'real'. Used in the singular the term 'life world' does not explicitly convey the great potential of variation between the spectators' different life worlds, or indeed that in their perception of the world of the play, yet it seems to have a less unifying quality than the notion of 'reality'.

The functional approach developed in Chapter 2 informs the discussion of biographical performances in the further chapters of the book. For readers who are mainly interested in the discussion of plays, it is possible to read these chapters without detailed study of the theoretical perspective. Its approach to theatre as a cultural *practice*, only realised completely in the 'joint act of understanding' in which 'the meaning of a performance is created by the performers and the spectators together' (Sauter, 2000, p. 2), leads to the division into two parts that concentrate on production and reception, respectively. Through detailed analyses of selected performances and interviews with theatre practitioners the first part (Chapters 3 to 5) evaluates how relevant the theories discussed in Chapter 2 are for theatrical practice; the second part (Chapters 6 and 7) focuses on the perspective of audiences, collected through interviews and a survey. The selection of plays discussed cannot claim to be exhaustive, nor can it concentrate on well-known or highly applauded plays; instead plays were chosen to represent typical uses of biographical material.[2]

Chapters 3 to 5 are structured around common patterns of biographical references in performances. In each chapter the analysis of case studies begins with an examination of the collection and selection of biographical material in scripts or performance guidelines and writers' or editors' views of this process. On this basis they consider the contributions of others involved in the collective creation of theatrical productions, including actors' representations of historical characters through their movement, gestures, voice and physical appearance, and scenographers' work on the environment of these characters. Finally the effect of accompanying materials, such as publicity material and programmes, and the directors' influence on the overall relationship between the world of the play and the life world is explored.

The theatre's potential to create a sense of authenticity on stage is explored in Chapter 3. It explores how the use of verbatim quotation and a highly extra-theatrical presentation can indicate a close relationship between plays and the life world. While *Rendition Monologues* (2008) by Ice and Fire develops its truth claim almost entirely through the use of original documents, *Gladiator Games* (2005) combines this approach with scenes scripted by its author, Tanika Gupta. The impact of content and presentation for the creation of a representation is examined with the help of *Vincent in Brixton* (2003), a play based entirely on the playwright's conjecture about a gap in our knowledge of the painter's life, which is nevertheless performed in such a highly extra-theatrical form that the imagined scenes seem to offer a vivid reconstruction of moments in his life.

This sense of authenticity is undermined by performances like *Insignificance* (1982), in which an implausible encounter between Marilyn Monroe, Albert Einstein, Joe DiMaggio and Senator McCarthy clashes with the audience's previous knowledge about these historical figures. *Thatcher – the Musical!* (2006) by Foursight Theatre, the second performance analysed in Chapter 4, on the other hand demonstrates that the use of highly theatrical means of presentation does not necessarily undermine its potential to engage closely with the life world.

The discussion in Chapter 5, finally, focuses entirely on self-reflexivity in biographical performance, investigating the use of biographer-characters and performance structures in *Copenhagen* (1998) and *Mary Queen of Scots Got Her Head Chopped Off* (1987) that implicitly challenge the assumptions hidden behind Empiricist biography.

The second part of the book introduces a shift in focus towards the reception of biographical performances. It thus complements the first part, as the two processes cannot be neatly separated from one another: they occur at the same time and those involved in them participate, to a certain extent, in both; practitioners also see and hear the show, and spectators are actively involved in creating meaning. Similarly, the first part on the production of biographical performances could not exist in isolation from my perception as a researcher, a perspective that is not always acknowledged in performance analysis. Since the conceptual tenets of a functional approach suggest that a single spectatorial perspective is not sufficient to allow a thorough examination of the impact of biographical material, the second part of the book thus presents a range of voices that complement those of the researcher and theatre practitioners in the first part.

Chapters 6 and 7 concentrate on the perspective of general theatre audiences, introducing a methodological framework for the study of spectators' views and presenting the results from an interview study and a survey, respectively. A long-term interview study offered an insight into the reception of *Vincent in Brixton* and *Insignificance* by a small group of spectators and a survey of audiences of *Thatcher – the Musical!* was used to test the results obtained on a bigger scale and to explore aspects of reception specific to this production. Both endeavour to answer questions about elements that can trigger, maintain or counter a biographical or documentary mode of understanding of a performance, as well as the consequences of this mode of spectating, particularly the possibility that spectators integrate information from the play into their knowledge of the world. Although the results presented allow greater insight into the impact of biographical material on spectators' approaches, it is important to remember that these findings cannot be easily generalised. Audiences with a different cultural background, for example, might perceive some of the theatrical events as non-biographical.

The concluding Chapter 8 returns to the theoretical approach developed in this book and examines whether it offers an appropriate way of studying biographical performances. It relates a summary of the findings and a question about the role of personal experience that arose in Chapter 7 to potential shortcomings in the theoretical background and identifies a potential addition to the approach that has explanatory power for the performances discussed in the book and other biographical plays that have provoked controversy. It thus acknowledges the contribution to the way in which biographical theatre can be conceptualised and indicates how a revised approach could be used for further research into similar kinds of performance.

2
Re-Framing the Discussion of Biographical Theatre: A Functional Approach

Introduction

As suggested in Chapter 1, the presence of either a recognisable subject of biography or the portrayal of the search for such a life story is seen as a defining feature of biographical theatre. Reflecting this emphasis on conceptual questions, the point of departure for this discussion is not a number of specific biographical plays, but theoretical concepts from related disciplines that are also concerned with the way in which historical material shapes the relationship between discourses, in the Foucaultian sense, and the past to which they refer. The first part of this chapter is therefore devoted to a presentation of theoretical approaches to history and biography that address this relationship. It will present the changes from a Modernist approach to history as a factual science to Postmodern claims that every narrative is dependent on the perspective from which it is told and the medium in which it is conveyed. While these models enrich our discussion of biographical theatre, it has to be remembered that the necessary brevity of such a discussion means that the theories presented here cannot reflect the variety and complexity of these fields.

The lack of a clear differentiation between historiography and biography is the result of such limitations and has to be understood as such. Although the latter is often regarded as history's younger brother, adopting many of the characteristics and working methods from its sibling, its concentration on 'creat[ing] a portrait of [a] man's life', as Plutarch puts it, has led many historians to think of 'good biography [as] bad history' (Carr, 1962, p. 42). In comparison to the shared assumptions and beliefs in the two disciplines, however, such 'discord between historians and biographers' (Raulff, 2002, p. 55) might appear negligible.

The same need for brevity applies to the choice of different theories and their presentation. Presenting a closer reading of some theories that have either acquired the status of (modern) classics in their field or been particularly influential for the study of historical novels or plays, the chapter charts the development from an empiricist, scientific view of history and life writing towards a new concept that is characterised by increasing self-reflexivity. Although overall this change of epistemes can be seen as an ongoing process, beginning with nineteenth-century positivism up to Postmodernist ideas of the late twentieth century, the present situation is best described as a competition of different positions. Placed on a scale between the two extremes, many of them can be seen as variations of partly modernised defences of post-Enlightenment empiricist, rationalist thought, here referred to as 'Modern'. At the other end of the spectrum there are departures from this tradition which are influenced by post-Modern criticism of language as a 'neutral' mirror to an objectively perceivable 'Reality'. This focus reflects the most profound changes in the way in which the relationship between the past and descriptions of it are understood in historiography and biography, and thus seems suitable for the present purpose.

The emphasis on the role of language in these theories also leads to difficulties when they are applied to performances. Written historical accounts in academic publications seem at first an unsuitable comparison to theatre's 'almost magical power of resurrecting historical personages from their graves' (Peacock, 1991, p. 11), but at second glance the role of language in the production of biographical theatre alongside other systems of discourse cannot be denied; unless a performance is based on an actor's direct imitation of another person, the documents used to gain information about the historical figure are likely to contain written and spoken language, at least in the form of comments on photographs or video recordings. Nevertheless, the impact of differences introduced through the mode of presentation, i.e. the use of direct presentation, different generic traditions and collective authorship, is acknowledged and discussed in the context of their relevance for the theories presented below. The theories are thus applicable, but have to be discussed in the light of the differences introduced by direct presentation on stage.

Referentiality in Theories of History and Biography

An understanding of history as categorically different from other kinds of literature developed in the eighteenth century, when the study of the past was first considered to be a scientific endeavour. As such it adopted the working methods and ideology of the natural sciences, aiming at 'first, ascertaining facts; secondly, framing laws' (Collingwood, 1946, p. 127). Although the idea of searching for universal laws that govern history in the same way that laws of gravity govern the behaviour of physical bodies was soon abandoned (see for example Carr, 1962, p. 82), a Fact-based Empiricist approach continues to be the basis for the work of numerous present-day historians.

Comparing our physical reality with the statements made about it, empiricist history defines Truth[1] as 'a relation of correspondence between the contents of our thoughts and reality, or between our judgements and facts' (Engel, 2002, p. 14). Lyotard's analysis of different forms of knowledge in *The Postmodern Condition* (1979) states that this comparison is made possible by exteriorising the referent of an enunciation – history thus defines itself clearly as a subject that is concerned with 'the past as something exterior to language existing irrespective of what we think they [past events] are like' (Buckingham and Saunders, 2004, p. 12). Our descriptions of them are based on our direct, or in the case of history, indirect experience of them and are also measured against these observations – where the description matches the experience it can be ascertained as Fact. Epstein defines Facts as the result of a procedure in which 'a track of natural occurrence in the concrete world can be [...] folded into narrative' (Epstein, 1987, p. 33). In this folding process it is important that, although the form of the original occurrence is changed in order to make it possible to represent the event in a text, this must not affect its nature; it must continue to be recognisable as essentially the same event. This concept of 'the past as it actually was' (Ranke quoted from Powell, 1990, p. xv) is echoed in many European languages, including English, where the word 'history' is used to refer to both remote times and texts that describe them.

In order to achieve its goal, empiricist historiography has developed an intricate system of methodologies designed to establish the correspondence between past events and the historians' account of them, thus creating Facts. Contrary to the variety of publications that discuss the validity of the research methods used in their field, however, many historians and biographers have produced little reflection on the underlying assumptions of their empirical work. For a long time its prevalence was uncontested and doubts are still met with suspicion by some of them: comparing the work of biographers to the gait of a centipede, Robert Blake observes in 1998 that the progress of both is merely made slow and painstaking by unnecessary reflection (Blake, 1998, p. 75).

The Opposition between Fact and Fiction and the Hybrid Nature of Biography

The predominance of Empiricism in historiography is further endorsed by the association of literature with Fiction, which results from the division between literature and history during the Enlightenment. Defining Fiction partly in opposition to Fact, the opposition between True and symbolic representation set the two fields further apart from each other. Their opposition is also central to the definition of fictional discourse, which has rarely been described in its own terms – neither of the two lines of thought that dominate the discourse on Fiction explains the concept without reference to the juxtaposition of the two concepts. Iser (1989, p. 164) ascribes this not to a lack of interest but suggests that this reluctance may result from the difficulties inherent in a concept rooted more in its use for 'purposes of cognition' than a clear ontological basis.

The first theory suggests that fictional discourse cannot avoid the referential qualities of language. Instead of referring to a physical world, however, reference is established to an object of a different ontological quality, an object that only exists as a conceptual possibility, in other words in thoughts and is *'unreal* [...] created by using language in the ways practiced by authors and storytellers' (Crittenden, 1991, p. 62). Nonetheless these 'unreal', 'ficticious' and 'imaginary' objects are different to others that had a clear, physical correspondence before they died or became extinct (Crittenden, 1991, p. 67), as traces of their previous existence demonstrate. Whereas factual discourse is verified by the physical traces of real objects of references, or at least the possibility of finding these, Fictions have their only antecedents in other linguistic constructs. Their truth status is thus not determined by correspondence to external objects, but merely through their consistency 'with the linguistic usages current in a given social context, at a given moment in time' (Riffaterre, 1990, p. vii). Applied to theatre one could say that fictional characters exist only in the play. The basis on which historical characters are built, on the other hand, points beyond the world of the play.[2]

The second approach opposes the 'real' reference in factual discourse to a more playful, 'as if' form of reference in Fiction. Rather than stating a Fact that we know to correspond with reality, the speaker or writer introduces a reference 'as if' it was true in the full knowledge that this is or may be not the case. Linguists have struggled to explain how the different intention can be recognised by the reader or listener, since in linguistic analysis no differences can be observed between fictional and factual discourses; nor are Fiction and intentional lying clearly distinguished by linguistic markers. The most popular solution to this dilemma has been offered by Searle, who suggests that a conceptual mode of 'as if' can be activated by 'extralinguistic, non-semantic conventions' (Searle, 1979). By putting 'the world represented into brackets', Iser (1989, p. 16) suggests, the reader, spectator or listener is asked to adopt a different conceptual attitude towards it. For theatrical discourses elements such as the theatrical space, the use of props and other scenographic elements or, especially, the actors' appearance in character rather than themselves could be seen as signals to understand the performance in a mode of 'as if'.

In both theories of Fiction the introduction of an element of unreality is regarded as an inherent characteristic of the discourse, constitutive of a Modern understanding of literature (see Ronen, 1994, p. 1). Fictionality functions as a signal to the spectator or reader to receive a piece of artistic expression on its own terms rather than in direct comparison to their experience of the life world. Here the form of expression, the perspective of the artist and the means s/he uses in the process of creation are seen as an integral part of the discourse rather than something that has to be overcome in order to guarantee a neutral reflection of the world. Similarly, fictional discourse is seen to establish a different kind of knowledge. Analysing Francis Bacon's position on fiction, Iser (1989, p. 107) suggests that fictions 'arise out of the need to make incursions into what appears impenetrable'. With the growing emphasis on Empiricism following the Enlightenment, accompanied by a rapidly growing body of scientific knowledge, such narrative explanations of the world have often been assigned a place that is secondary to factual, 'provable' discourses. Fictions may be seen to explain elements of our world that elude scientific understanding, a position that implies the understanding that they can be substituted and overruled by empirically gained explanations once these become available. In literature, on the other hand, they are often attributed with a playfulness similar to the 'as if' found in child's play, as worlds of discourse that are devoid of consequences (Vaihinger quoted in Iser, 1989, p. 13). In a Modern framework, the dichotomy of Fact and Fiction is not a balanced juxtaposition, as the latter is seen to be less relevant for our understanding of the external physical world.

While history is clearly rooted in factual discourse, biography is often regarded as a hybrid that exists between these two poles. Its formal closeness to the novel leads to a situation in which different degrees of poetic licence are allowed. Unlike the differentiation between academic history and the historical novel, genres that have long been analysed in different disciplines, the term biography covers texts written by scholars in 'plain scientific language' which rigorously apply academic standards for historical writing, as well as others in which writers present a narrative that includes a considerable amount of speculation understood to belong to the realm of 'as if'. The co-existence of such a diversity of forms under one term gives rise to a differentiation within its boundaries, and many scholars differentiate between analytic vs. narrative, fictional vs. historical or academic vs. popular biography (Frank, 1980, p. 507; Charmley and Homberger, 1988, p. xii; Clifford, 1970, p. 168).

As a result of this variety within the genre of life writing, biographical discourses are not always subject to the same standards as historical writing. Although it is mainly regarded as factual writing, the format allows a greater degree of divergence from the ideal of objectivity. In addition to the generic traditions, this phenomenon can be explained by the existence of a potential conflict between different realms in which a truthful account is expected. Whereas in history, this translation of the past into text has to preserve the identity of events, in biography it should also lead to 'a record, in words, of something as mercurial and as flowing, as compact of temperament and emotions, as the human spirit itself' (Edel, 1973, p. 1). As Edel's position indicates, human character or personality is generally regarded as something that cannot be expressed in its entirety through an account of the actions of a person. While these can often build the basis for judgements of character, it seems to be the subject of general agreement that underlying motivations for human actions are of equal or even greater importance, and the empirically oriented search for Facts in historiography is not often regarded as an appropriate tool to establish the Truth about someone's personality.[3] The call for alternative working methods, which allow intuitive insight into 'the other as a full person [in order to] make up for these limitations characteristic of factual biography' (Schabert, 1990, p. 4), distances some forms of biography even further from the strict adherence to historical evidence. While this can be regarded as an emancipation of narrative forms of knowledge, however, it does not undermine the difference between the two forms; it merely diminishes the claim that scientific, fact-oriented forms of knowledge can provide the only valid representation of the past. Establishing other methods as equally valid, they are nevertheless not seen to be the same. In some cases, the decision to concentrate on personality and internal developments of biographical subjects is prompted not by a rejection of empiricist, reconstructive history, but by the choice of biographee.

Linda Wagner-Martin (1994, p. 7), for example, states that the outward lack of eventfulness found in many women's lives requires biographers to work with alternative methods and structures in life writing. Her ardent defence of reconstructive biography on the other hand demonstrates that this decision cannot be necessarily linked to criticism of this approach.

The generic differences between written biography and biographical performances offer further ground for the use of poetic licence. First of all this can be explained by the differences in generic traditions: while prose has a long history of being employed equally for fictional and non-fictional texts, theatrical performances are predominantly classified as Fiction, as can be seen in most bookshops, for example. As a result, the classification of written discourses as either prose or fiction is made on the basis of individual cases, whereas theatrical performances are mostly considered to be fictional. Where factual material is introduced, they can be seen as hybrids, but the lack of a factual performance tradition, or perhaps the sheer contradiction of the ideas of performance and fact, mean that they are rarely seen as entirely factual.

The use of direct presentation in theatre is of even greater impact on performed biography: Niloufer Harben (1988, p. 256) points out that historical theatre is characterised by the 're-enactment, resurrection, of [...] historical material in a vital, immediate way', working 'not with bloodless abstractions, but with people on a stage who are required to move and be'. Obvious though it may be, this distinction deserves closer analysis as it profoundly changes the way in which references to the past can be established. As Hegel suggests with regard to plot, theatre deals with the specific, not the abstract, an observation that applies not only to the recommended choice of plot, but also to the need for specificity in the presentation. While a biographer can choose abstract terms for the description of a historical figure and his or her surroundings, theatrical presentation requires a greater amount of detail. Where the generalising effect of purely linguistic expression is abandoned, it is no longer possible to avoid unknown elements; in other words, a historical character on stage cannot be played without a head because the hair colour of the historical person in question has not been established beyond reasonable doubt. The consequences that arise from such a need for specificity depend partly on the style of individual performances, as a certain degree of abstraction can also be gained from the use of intra-theatrical forms (see Chapter 3), while a highly extra-theatrical style would have more difficulties in accommodating events such as accidents or the process of aging.

Regarded as a hybrid form in a Modern theoretical framework, bio-graphical theatre integrates aspects of fictional and factual references to the life world. On this basis the discussion of biographical plays is dominated by questions concerning the dominance of one aspect or the other, as well as complaints about their mutual incompatibility. The advent of Postmodern theories, in particular the linguistic turn in historiography, however, undermine this definition.

From Empiricism to Postmodernism

Although Modern concepts of history are still the basis for the work of some historians today, others have questioned it on the basis of its ties 'with a set of challenged cultural and social assumptions', includ-ing issues of 'logic and reason, consciousness and human nature, progress and fate, representation and truth [...] linearity and continuity' (J.H. Miller, 1974, pp. 460–1 quoted in Hutcheon, 1988, p. 87). Similar to the development of Postmodern theories in related subjects, theorists have challenged the assumptions underlying the dichotomy of Fact and Fiction and have exposed the hidden perspectives behind the apparent neutrality of historical texts. The basis for such new approaches is a growing interest in the difference between the two meanings of history and the observation that the *historia rerum gestarum*, the past as written, cannot correspond to the *res gestae*, the past in itself, as language can merely arbitrarily refer to, but never correspond to, the physical reality it describes. Facing the question of 'how well [...] language [can] incar-nate reality' (Nadel, 1984, p. 155), historians have shown themselves to be slightly more reluctant in their answer, but some nevertheless agree that the inherent cultural relativism of language cannot be over-come. As Munslow suggests, 'narrative interpretations can only signify the past. They can not correspond to it' (Munslow, 2000, p. 83). In Keith Jenkins' words, the past can be compared to a landscape that we may be able to see, but only through the glass of language (Jenkins, 1991, p. 8). The gap between the two is further aggravated by temporal distance and problems related to the quantity of information that is available at any specific point in history. These problems had been recognised by Modern historians as well who devoted many publications to the dis-cussion of ways to overcome them. For Postmodern thinkers, however, the difference in ontological status makes it theoretically impossible to find a description that corresponds to the events or the figure in the past. Without this possibility, however, the notion of historical Truth also loses its absolute character – if language is culturally dependent, so are the statements made with its help. In other words: 'truth in this sense is always a floating currency; and the exchange rates alter through history' (Holmes, 1995, p. 18).

Hayden White's *Metahistory* is the most influential exponent of the linguistic turn in historiography. Distancing himself from the empiricist tradition of placing history among the sciences that produce objective knowledge, he argues in favour of treating 'the historical work as what it most manifestly is: a verbal structure in the form of a narrative prose discourse' (White, 1973, p. x). Establishing the 'ineluctably poetic nature of the historical work' (White, 1973, p. xi), his work predicts Lyotard's observation that the Postmodern condition implies a 'return of narrative into the non-narrative' (Lyotard, 1979, p. 49; transl. UC). The work of White and other historians who adopt a Postmodern theoretical framework has presented a great challenge to a discipline that saw its objectives in the search for content. Acknowledging the narrative character of linguistic descriptions, however, it cannot deny that form also generates content (Munslow, 2000, p. 226) and that the validity and authority of these descriptions can only be measured within the boundaries introduced by the choice of language and of the forms of discourse. The idea that a universal Truth cannot be established through language, as the encoding of events in words inevitably 'provide[s] sets of events with different meanings' (Nadel, 1984, p. 103), has severely challenged the definition of historiography. Consequently few historians have paid more than lip service to it in their working practices. The work of those who advocate radical departures from the empiricist search for objective knowledge, on the other hand, is often limited to the development of theoretical reflections without wider application. Postmodern thought has thus deeply unsettled the discipline's understanding of its objectives and methodologies, but has not yet provided an alternative modus operandi. This development also has severe consequences for the definition of biographical theatre, as the emphasis on narrative elements in the supposedly factual elements leads to the erosion of the idea of hybridity. Before this is discussed in detail, however, the effect of this epistemological change on the role of historical authors is examined.

Changes in the Role of the Author

Here again the clear distinction between the tasks of historians and writers, who are not committed to the accurate description of an external reality, has been replaced by an emphasis on the similarities between them. For a long time, however, historians saw themselves not as writers, but rather collectors of Facts about the past. This view can cause slight bewilderment, even in the eyes of later empiricist historians, such as Edward H. Carr, as his description of positivist historians suggests: 'the facts are available to [them] in documents, inscriptions and so on, like on the fishmonger's slab. The historian collects them, takes them home, cooks and serves them in whatever style appeals to him' (Carr, 1962, p. 3). The concept of a passive collector of Facts is soon abandoned in favour of that of a judge who evaluates the evidence and reaches conclusions that 'display the standard judicial quality of balance and even-handedness' (Jenkins, 1997, p. 1). Despite this admission of the historian's active role in the process, Modern historiography often maintains the ideal of objective accounts created by disinterested, unbiased historians that do not depend on the point of view of the speaker. The potential contradiction between this aim and the historian's selecting presence is solved through the existence of a strict methodology designed to neutralise his or her influence, substituting subjectivity with supposedly universal assumptions like Rationality, Logic and the relationship of Cause and Effect. Interpreting historical evidence on the basis of these principles, an individual historian can reach the same conclusion that would be reached by any other human being with the same information. Regardless of their crucial role in Modern historiography, these guiding principles are rarely spelled out in detail, a phenomenon that might be explained exactly by the fact that they are all-pervasive: as an innate part of human thought, they are felt to need no explanation. Instead their application is seen to obey 'common sense'; in David Ellis's words biographers merely need '*intelligence* and *human understanding* to draw correct inferences from our information' (Ellis, 2000, pp. 18–19; italics UC).

The belief in the neutralising force of methodology has, for a long time, led to a focus on the best methods to avoid unnecessary bias, while the question of whether this is or is not possible *per se* has been avoided. Some authors, for example E.H. Carr, have asked questions about the degree to which historical authors can remain neutral. Acknowledging that historians are not positioned outside the flow of history, he argues that all history is necessarily written from a particular point within 'the procession of history' (Carr, 1962, p. 30) and that, as a result, 'the history we read, though based on facts [may] strictly speaking, not [be] factual' (Carr, 1962, p. 8) in an absolute sense. Nonetheless, the advocates of such a moderate version of Empiricism, including Carr, still maintain that this positioning within the subject matter does not lead to relativism or arbitrariness: being aware of their position, historians can rise above and thus overcome it.

Postmodernist thought suggests that perspective cannot be overcome through such compensation tactics. Based on the idea that all persons are necessarily influenced by their social context and their own position in it, the existence of a privileged position outside discourse for a historian or a biographer is inevitably denied. 'For the biographer and the autobiographer, postmodernity means understanding that there is no secure external vantage point from which one can see clearly and objectively, from where one can "realize" the subject', according to Marjorie Garber (1996, p. 175; see also Stanley, 1992), and the same assumption is made for historians. Their perspective is created by a mixture of both cultural and historical forces, as well as circumstances directly related to the authors, such as the sociological parameters of sex, age and race, and more individual personal characteristics and past experience. Most of these factors do not depend upon the will of the author, and the Postmodern focus on the author is directed at inevitable and often unconscious positions different from the conscious intentions that were studied before the idea of the intentional fallacy. In this respect, the review of the role of the historian or biographer is closely related to epistemological questions. Texts produced by an author who is clearly located are declared to 'have little to do with the "truth" *per se*, but a great deal to do with prevailing moral discourses and perceptions' (Evans, 1999, p. 141). The new understanding of the role of the author thus confirms the doubts about the concept of an absolute Truth raised through the criticism of language. Where texts are created by positioned authors in a relative language, it becomes important to ask 'whose truth' is being told 'by whom and for what purpose?' (Paget, 1990, p. 172).

This development of the author's role in the theory of history and biography acquires additional interest and complexity in the discussion of biographical performances, due to the phenomenon of collective authorship found in most theatrical practices. Although the practitioners who contribute to performances have different fields and degrees of influence over the production, all of them can be seen as creators of it. Where productions are based on written scripts, the playwright's freedom to choose material and to determine the information given through language certainly gives him outstanding power to shape the final result. Similarly the director's overall responsibility for the production offers him or her a great deal of influence on it, while scenographers are often limited to shaping the environment of a historical character. The impact of actors, while highly dependent on the degree of creative intervention granted to them by the script and the director, demonstrates clearly that unavoidable factors, such as their own bodies, influence their presentation of the historical figure. Collective author-ship thus means that theatre productions are the result of a combina-tion, and in a certain way also a negotiation, of the perspectives of all the located authors that contribute to it.

The premise that authors are necessarily located has also led to a re-reading of historical discourses whose authors claimed to be disin-terested, neutral conveyors of Facts. Their apparent absence in Modern history or biography is exposed as a hidden presence and influence. In order to create the impression of neutrality, authors working in a Modern framework are now seen to use a Realist mode of writing in which they cover their authorial voice under apparently neutral for-mulations in order to create the illusion of the unfiltered presentation of Reality. Paula Backscheider analyses the writer's 'magisterial voice' (Backscheider, 1999, p. 18) in life writing, and comes to the conclu-sion that the popular combination in biographies, where an author writes from the hidden position of a historian but adopts the vivid style of a novelist, is most successful in convincing the reader of the Truthfulness of an account. 'The more invisible interpretation and even judgement are, the better the book reads – and the more subversive it is' (Backscheider, 1999, p. 3), as the reader is not aware of the influence exerted by the writer. In written history and biography linguistic and discursive structures are thus used to cover the authorial presence and to create 'truth effects' (see Zimmermann, 2000, p. 5).

The observation of the authors' hidden presence can be applied to playwrights who produce biographical scripts with minor alterations: instead of using only an impersonal style of writing, they can hide behind the apparently life-like existence of their characters and plot (see Chapter 3). Chronologically presented actions, carried out by psy-chologically motivated characters who exist in a recognisable social set-ting, in biographical plays can thus be regarded as achieving an effect similar to that of prose writing in the third person singular in written historical accounts. The three-dimensional nature of the theatre offers further opportunities to create the impressions of life-likeness through the use of stylistic means. In his book on documentary drama, Derek Paget observes that realist costumes and designs, as well as continuity in the action, also create 'an "authentic" background [that] helps to vali-date the view of history being put up by the makers' (Paget, 1990, p. 26) of films or plays that deal with historical events. An extra-theatrical acting style that diminishes the visible gap between actor and charac-ter, for example, can help to convey the impression that the historical character is 'resurrected' rather than represented on stage. While the means with which such an impression of an immediate experience, rather than a mediated representation, can be created are discussed in further detail in later chapters, the current examples should suffice to demonstrate the relevance that these developments in the field of historiography and biography hold for the discussion of biographical theatre.

Acknowledging the impact of form and the medium of communication on the presentation of events and figures, 'Post-empiricist history, written by a positioned author' (Munslow, 2000, p. 19), also allows ways of presentation that would have been rejected by rationalist, Modern history. The structures which before this epistemological change were perceived as inherent and universal can now be shown to depend on underlying assumptions. Similar to language, these can be found behind apparent objectivity. As indicated above, the idea of Logic and Reason as principles that govern all human behaviour in a similar way are no longer regarded as universal and all-encompassing. In this context the idea of a linearity, given by a strict order of cause and effect, is also questioned. In the first instance this affects the role of the biographical author, whose task changes from discovering inherent structures in the biographical material to that of actively creating them. A certain variation in the structures found in human lives is also recognised by advocates of empiricist biography and history: according to Bernard Crick (1980, p. 15), the 'kind of biography' one writes depends on the 'kind of man' at its centre. In a Postmodernist framework, however, the kind of biography depends to the same extent on the kind of person who writes and chooses its structures. This change in attitude is particularly visible in the use of chronology, which used to be *de rigueur* for academic biographies. Its abolition in more literary forms was seen as a sign of a higher degree of author intervention and thus fictionality; from a postmodern perspective chronology has lost its claim to measurable objectivity (Lowenthal, 1985, pp. 220–4), and is instead regarded as an imposition by an author who wants to efface his or her presence. Both in biographical writing and in performance, this new freedom has been used extensively, and theorists have identified various tendencies in these experiments, such as 'spiralling narratives' (Nadel, 1984, p. 4), or structures that follow cognitive and affective patterns (Scheuer, 1979, p. 88). The variety of different frameworks that can be used for biographical explanation (or the conscious lack of it) has not only created variety, but also offers an interesting insight into the way in which creators of biographical performance want to establish a reference to the past.

The Role of Biographical Subject

Finally, the criticism of biographical writing also changes the understanding of the biographical subject in postmodern biography. The idea of agent intentionality, for example, depends strongly on the concepts of rationality and logic, since it indicates a clear connection between a mental state and the directed action that follows it. As with language, this concept is criticised on the basis of its cultural relativity. Behaviour that seems to be illogical to one observer might nevertheless stem from a rational decision and be logical for others. In addition to this objection, theorists also argue that it depends on a particular anthropological model that overemphasises the human faculty of reasoning, neglecting less rational aspects. Postmodernist criticism thus extends not only to the way in which the relationship between the object of description and the description itself is conceptualised and the ensuing conventions of biographical writing, it also challenges the Modern understanding of what is described in biography.

Often these two aspects are closely related. Assumptions regarding the concept of identity and the inner unity of human beings also have an impact on the potential roles of the biographical author. The influence of social environments on human lives (Nadel, 1984, pp. 190–200) has put the idea that the self has absolute boundaries into question, an aspect that is often more visible in theatrical rather than written biographies, since the latter tend to evolve more strongly around a single, outstanding individual. Sometimes this opening of the concept of identity towards influences from the outside even leads to doubts whether a coherent core of identity exists at all. Similarly to some of the concepts discussed above, the tenet of an essential, unified self that prevailed in anthropological humanism (Epstein, 1987, p. 82) has been questioned before, as the various facets of a life are often hard to place within a coherent frame of personality. Death, however, has been seen as a point of orientation at which the fluid nature of a life becomes fixed, and which 'does not allow any other version' (Frisch, 1972, p. 87; see also Backscheider, 1999, p. 91). Denying the existence of structures inherent to a life, whether they become visible after a person's death or before that event, postmodernists reject the idea of a unified personality and argue that it is merely produced by authors, who 'try to heal that sense of fragmentation [of the self] by embracing documentation and emphatically chronological narrative' (Evans, 1999, p. 26). Coherence is thus shifted from the level of the life itself to the level of discourse, underlining again the active role of the author. Where the impression that it is possible to perceive the biographical subject directly in an objective and absolutely true way is lost, the perceiving subject has again gained importance.

This change in the understanding of reference in historiography and biography has led to a growth in self-reflexive discourses about the past, both written and performed. Treating 'biography as a process' (Stanley, 1992), these texts and plays use the experience of the author(s)' attempts to reconstruct the past as their structural framework. The focus is then placed more on the way in which knowledge about historical figures is created than on the result. The three-dimensional nature of the theatre makes this medium particularly suitable for such endeavours. While some plays introduce biographer-characters whose work echoes that of the creation of the performance itself, others contrast language and non-linguistic visual and audible presentation in order to show alternatives to the predominant structures and explanations in Modern biography. The immediacy of the presentation also facilitates the representation of clashing perspectives that cannot be reconciled or seen as more or less true. The rise of meta-biographical elements in performances is probably the most notable consequence of the changing concept of references to the past, and areas such as literature and theatre seem to have incorporated this shift in focus more willingly than many historians into their practices. Nevertheless, the Modern dichotomies have not been abandoned entirely.

Developing a New Approach to the Representation of the Past

In contrast to the great openness towards experimentation in theatrical practice, these changes pose a theoretical problem. Unlike historiography, which feels threatened in its core by the new emphasis on narrativity, theatre as a traditionally fictional genre does not see the same dangers in the insight that it cannot offer an objective Truth about the past. On the contrary, the insight that human beings may only be able to 'comprehend both the past and the present only in the form of a narrative' (Maack, 1993, p. 170) even enhances the status of theatrical biography. A theoretical framework in which *all* representations of the past are seen as narrative constructions which are no longer distinguished by a, sometimes fuzzy but existing, dividing line between true and false versions, does, however, have difficulties explaining the difference between biographical and other narratives. It would be possible to argue that in a postmodern context such a distinction is an obsolete remnant of

Modern thought structures. Yet, this suggestion does not seem to offer a satisfactory solution, as it contradicts long-term empirical evidence that such categories structure the production and reception of performances. Despite the fact that Postmodernism has dominated the theoretical discourse in many disciplines for various decades, the discussion of biographical material continues to be influenced by the concepts of 'factual material' and different degrees of 'historical authenticity', as marketing material, reviews, interviews with practitioners and audiences reveal. Furthermore, a complete rejection of different degrees of truth in historical accounts entails a range of difficult ethical questions. In a radically relativist framework, where competing accounts cannot be evaluated according to their Truthfulness, responsibility for historical acts cannot be assigned. An often cited example of this dilemma is that of Holocaust deniers, whose position would be hard to counter in such a context. These points suggest that a Postmodernist framework cannot suffice for the discussion of these plays, as 'radical relativism does not take into account that cultures do differentiate between fiction and reality' (see Ronen, 1994, p. 24). It cannot explain why truth claims made by theatre makers, for example in verbatim theatre, imposes an obligation on dramatists to 'abide, like journalists, by some sort of ethical code if their work is to be taken seriously' (Hammond and Steward, 2008, p. 10).

The challenge for a new approach to biographical theatre therefore lies in combining the insights gained by Postmodernism with the need to describe the persistent differentiation between these and non-biographical forms of performance. Such an approach would have to acknowledge that Truth is no longer an uncontested concept without abandoning it altogether. Linda Hutcheon's own work, though firmly committed to Postmodernism, already contains an offer for such a framework when she points out that it is not necessary to deny that 'the real referent of their language once existed' in order to claim that it is only 'accessible to us today in textualised form'. Therefore it is not the concept of an external reality that is rejected, but 'our ability to (unproblematically) *know* that reality' (Hutcheon, 1988, pp. 93 and 119). Once we accept that we cannot perceive an external reality in a direct way, however, questions regarding the absolute Truth about an external reality become less important than the examination of how people interact with the help of an intersubjective construct of their shared social reality.

Further inspiration for such an approach can be found in the sociology of knowledge. Here Berger and Luckman see questions regarding the absolute ontological status of knowledge as outside their own discipline.

Instead they consider knowledge as a socially constructed concept and examine everything that 'passes for "knowledge" in a society, regardless of the ultimate validity or invalidity (by whatever criteria) of such "knowledge"' (Berger and Luckman, 1966, p. 15). The argument underlying this distinction in their and other authors' work in this particular field is twofold. First they argue that although there might be no 'non-question-begging argument for ER [*here* used for external realism]', this is not absolutely relevant as our everyday communications are based on the presupposition of external reality (Searle, 1995, p. 184). The possibility of relatively uncomplicated interaction on the basis of such constructs of reality, and the equally high intersubjective agreement on these, thus confirms that, although theoretically complicated, they are mostly used in a simple and straightforward way. In addition to a detailed analysis of their nature, attention to their function can thus give insight into the role they play in different cultural practices.

The second argument is based on the intersubjective validity of these concepts. Although the reality of social institutions is described by Berger and Luckman as 'a world that originates in [people's] thoughts and actions, and is maintained by these' (Berger and Luckman, 1966, p. 33), its temporal dimension transcends the thought processes of individual members of a society. The process of their construction and development may be continuous, but due to the fact that it is always already begun before human beings acquire the basic shared knowledge of their society, it is still 'experienced as an objective reality' (Berger and Luckman, 1966, p. 77). Echoing the ideas of social constructivism, they assert that '"Knowledge" comes to be socially established *as* reality' (Berger and Luckman, 1966, p. 15). The resolution of the apparent incompatibility between culturally dependent concepts and their perception as stable, or sometimes nearly absolute, is thus based on extended consideration of the position of the speaker: Postmodernism postulates that we cannot speak from outside the discourse, but sometimes one cannot help thinking that insistence on their own position betrays the assumption that, as a Postmodernist thinker, one can choose to *receive* other discourses from a neutral position. A functional view challenges this position, suggesting that we cannot understand discourse unless we follow its rules either. The impact of its conventions and restrictions imposed by the medium chosen cannot be avoided; 'language is epistemically indispensable' (Searle, 1995, p. 76).

Even where individuals can choose between different linguistic or cultural frameworks, it is merely a change in underlying assumptions and structuring principles; abandoning them altogether is impossible.

Furthermore it is not possible to change or abandon them single-handedly; over time the discourse of knowledge in a society might change, but it is not up to individual members of it to do so at their will. Despite their relative status, these concepts are intersubjective and maintain a coercive effect.

In this context, questions about the absolute status of any Fact or Fiction expressed by a located author and through a medium of discourse cannot provide satisfactory answers. Although we may choose to adopt a framework that rejects this dichotomy, we cannot deny the fact that many aspects of our culture are organised on the basis of these distinctions – receiving a discourse in a manner that respects the communicative intentions of others, on the other hand, implies adopting at least similar underlying assumptions. Therefore Berger and Luckman's shift of focus from the nature of knowledge in its absolute sense to an interrogation of the function of knowledge in a society does not have to be regarded as an evasion of the postmodern insight into the relativity of these contexts. Concentrating on the way in which the concept of Facts structures a culture's experience of the world could also be seen as an acceptance of the Postmodernist tenet that perspectivity is unavoidable, and an attempt to find more meaningful explanations within this framework. Rather than looking for absolute Facts in historiography and biography, one could concentrate one's attention on the level of man-made historical facts, investigating the ways in which they interrelate with each other and how they are created and used. Against the fears of many historians, such an integration of Postmodernist thought would not mean the end of the discipline as we know it, even though it does entail a change in focus away from the past as it was towards our understandings of the past. Then, however, as Breuer suggests in his book about documentary theatre, history exists 'as long as there is a belief in a real or artificially created memory of the past, or something that is believed to be the past' (Breuer, 2005, p. 3).

As knowledge in general, according to Berger and Luckman, man-made intersubjective knowledge about the past cannot be changed at will and counter-versions will not be accepted readily. The adherence to a preferred version, however, cannot be explained by radical relativism either. This opens up a new problem: if the empiricist view that one version is 'truer' than another is no longer tenable, but our culture continues to prefer one over another, an alternative criterion for their evaluation is needed. This need is already indicated in Hayden White's argument in favour of narrative history, where he suggests that 'the only grounds for preferring one [version of history] over another are *moral* or *aesthetic* ones' (White, 1973, p. 433), but to date this approach has not been developed significantly in the area of historiography or biography.

As Engel suggests, however, the concept of more or less ethical versions could prove very fruitful since the fact that 'truth could be a minimal concept, with no hidden essence, does not by itself imply that there is no *point* in using this concept, [...] that it does not carry with it certain constitutive commitments' (Engel, 2002, pp. 7–8). This insight offers a promising framework for a discussion of biographical plays. Instead of asking whether the elements in a production are factual or fictional, we have to ask how the distinction is made and why it matters. Studying everything that passes for 'biographical knowledge', and the ways in which it infuses theatre, makes it possible to demonstrate how ideas about past lives, even if they cannot be proven to be true, influence the thinking of those who produce, as well as of those who receive, the plays in question. It would allow us to explain better why, despite Postmodernism, the sense remains that biographical and documentary theatre are somewhat more 'real' than other plays.

Such a new framework also requires new methodologies. In a first step, it substitutes the division between factual and fictional elements in a performance in favour of a comparison between plays and other discourses about a historical figure. The different labels attached to the discourses in the life world are still taken into account, though not as inherent textual properties. Instead they are seen as an assigned characteristic that leads to the application of 'conventions dictating the status and proper interpretation' of discourses (Ronen, 1994, p. 11). On the basis of such a comparison we can evaluate to what degree a specific performance refers to the life world and becomes extra- rather than intra-theatrical. Such an investigation into these modes of interpretation cannot only be applied to the performances; in addition we can identify self-reflexive elements that make the 'uncertainty about the validity of its representations' a topic within these plays, revealing an increasing and 'pervasive insecurity about the relationship of [theatre as a] fiction[al form] to reality' (Waugh, 1984, p. 2). Questions about reference are thus not only a key distinguishing feature of the reception and production of biographical theatre, but increasingly form part of the performances themselves. As such, reference should take a prominent place in the discussion of the genre, not as an absolute and permanent feature of a discourse, but as a relationship between two shifting and fluid entities: that of shared, intersubjective discourses about the life world and the performance.

The focus on the way in which biographical theatre functions rather than its ontological status leads to a further expansion of the context in which it is discussed. In addition to the comparison with other discourses about the historical figures represented, the role of those involved in the performance has to be examined in further detail. While it may be possible to make predictions about the way in which a representation will be perceived on the basis of the performances themselves, the dominance of the view of the researcher in this approach has to be countered by the inclusion of the perspective of other audience members. Given the lack of universal and objective standards in a Postmodernist framework, such a plurality of voices is paramount, and the inclusion of interviews with practitioners and empirical audience studies in this book tries to take this necessity into account.

The methodology of this analysis is thus born out of the theoretical difficulties associated with the object of inquiry. In practice the inclusion of a greater number of perspectives poses a challenge, but despite potential shortcomings in its application it is hoped that this framework will offer a view of biographical theatre that overcomes the dead end of Postmodernist Relativism without returning to the false certainties of a 'Modern' understanding of the world. Beyond a better understanding of the use of biographical material, this could offer more general insight into the way in which performance relates to the world surrounding it.

3
Re-Living the Past: Authenticity on Stage

Introduction and Terminology

The 'strictly accurate historical' manner (Reader's Report cited in Shellard, 2000, p. 12) stipulated by the Lord Chamberlain for plays about Queen Victoria has had a profound impact on British biographical theatre to this date. A great number of plays performed after the abolition of censorship, perhaps even the majority, follow this model, grounding the presentation of past lives in discourses that are considered to be 'historically accurate', such as historical, biographical, journalistic or legal texts. Although centred around a great variety of biographical subjects, plays like *The Madness of George III* (Alan Bennett, 1992), *The General from America* (Richard Nelson, 1996) about General Benedict Arnold's role in the American Civil War, *Total Eclipse* (Christopher Hampton, 1983) about the relationship between Rimbaud and Verlaine, and Dusty Hughes' group portrayal of Russian poets under the Soviet regime in *Futurists* (1986) all promise to portray their central figures in a way that echoes generally accepted interpretations of their lives. In Aristotelian terms this means that they are not seen to show 'what is *likely to happen* according to the rule of probability or necessity' (Aristotle, 1970, p. 33; italics UC). Instead they promise to present what has actually happened or what they assume happened given the personal circumstances of their biographical subjects. Other plays, including *Piaf* (Pam Gems, 1978, publ. 1985) or *Blood and Ice* (Liz Lochhead, 1982, publ. 1985), challenge established interpretations of the lives and loves of Edith Piaf and of Mary and Percy Bysshe Shelley and Lord Byron, respectively, offering their versions as more truth- or insightful.

The promise of authenticity is not solely based on the choice of material that is (partly) familiar to audiences from other discourses. This can be demonstrated by another group of plays, which endeavour to save forgotten lives from oblivion: audiences will be less likely to have previous information about biographical characters like Claudia Jones, the founder of the Notting Hill Carnival, whose life is presented in Winsome Pinnock's *A Rock in the Water* (1989), or the women pilots portrayed in *Anywhere to Anywhere* (Joyce Holliday, 1991). Nonetheless, the explicit claims of factuality made in advertising material and programmes have high credibility as the plays do not counter the audience's general knowledge about the historical period, place or people. Beyond these thematic links, the style of presentation is important to support their truth claims. These performances contain few or no elements that have the potential to draw the audience's attention to the differences between them and the material world which they purport to imitate: their characters are psychologically motivated, their time structure is progressive and linear (albeit with some interruptions), they rely on the sequence of cause and effect and are set in places that imitate, often with conventional means, places that exist in the world. In short, all of these elements suggest that they faithfully reflect the world outside the theatre, and hence the past.

Before exploring the combination of information taken from biographical discourses and the form of theatrical presentation used to create such an impression of authenticity, this chapter provides a short note on terminology and the parallels between the seemingly neutral, factual style of writing prevalent in traditional biography (see Chapter 2) and its equivalent theatrical style. The main part then illustrates these general observations through a detailed analysis of three performances and the views of practitioners involved in them. The first production's claim to authenticity is based mainly on its selection of material: *Rendition Monologues* (Christine Bacon, 2009a) consists in its entirety of quotations from materials used in courts of law and journalism. In *Gladiator Games* (Tanika Gupta, 2005) the use of verbatim material is combined with speeches written by the author and theatrical realism. *Vincent in Brixton* (Nicholas Wright, 2002) finally generates its truth claim mainly through its form of presentation, as it dramatises an undocumented period in Vincent van Gogh's life.

The most common term to describe a performance style that suggests a faithful imitation of the world outside the theatre is probably 'theatrical realism'. In a broad definition by Ruby Cohn (1992, p. 815), it refers to any formal means that make a performance resemble a 'slice of life', rather than a carefully constructed, aesthetic experience, describing 'the dominant style of modern drama'. Although the term is widely used and probably familiar to readers, in the following I would like to replace it with Sauter's concept of extra- and intra-theatricality for various reasons. The first is the ideological baggage the 'aesthetic philosophies of Realism and Naturalism' inherited from 'Positivism in the sciences' (Postlewait, 2003, p. 1114). This association was intentional at the beginning of the twentieth century, when Realist and Naturalist artists felt close observation and the portrayal of minute details could indeed turn literature, paintings or the theatre into truthful reflections of social life. The 'particular aesthetics' of this historical period have been abandoned since, but the term is still used for any style of presentation that seemed to give a truthful depiction of the world according to the audience's idea of 'reality' of the world, as well as their familiarity with different forms of representation (Armstrong, 2005, pp. ix–x). As long as theatrical experience looks familiar enough to 'slide through the mind without difficulty' (Paget, 1990, p. 23), spectators are willing to interpret events on stage in the same way they would see the world around them, merely through an invisible fourth wall.[1] The image of such a transparent wall will remind readers of Keith Jenkins' description of empiricist history, where historians claim that they can see the past through an untainted glass window (see Chapter 2). Jenkins observed that the temporal distance, just as the apparently invisible glass window, does not allow historians direct access to the past, and that any methodology used to gain indirect access will always have an impact on their understanding of it. Similarly we can claim that the world created in performances cannot reflect the world outside them without any mediation from the theatrical means employed to create it. For a functional analysis that aims at avoiding the concept of absolute ontological categories, such as 'Reality', this insight is vital. The term 'Realism', on the other hand, can distract attention from it by suggesting that some performances can be more 'real' than others.

The terms extra- and intra-theatricality, on the other hand, avoid such tacit associations, as they do not make any claims about the ontological status of a performance. Instead they merely indicate 'different ways of perceiving styles of performing' (Sauter, 2000, p. 62) between the (only theoretically possible) poles of absolute life-likeness or extra-theatricality (0) and entire artifice or intra-theatricality that does not share any similarities with the world in which the spectator lives (10).

0	1	2	3	4	5	6	7	8	9	10

extra-theatrical　　　　　　　　　　　　　　　　　　intra-theatrical

He maintains the notion that any evaluation of a play's relationship to the world is relative, emphasising that its place on the scale depends on contextual parameters such as conventions, performative genre, codes of everyday behaviour 'in typical and significant national patterns (such as verbal and gestural expressions, movement patterns, proxemic relationships, dress codes, and colour codes)' (Sauter, 2000, p. 62) and the social context of performer and spectator. Accepting the impact of these factors, but abandoning implicit ontological evaluation, this approach is similar to the functional framework suggested here.

Sauter's terminology can be developed further to distinguish between thematic and formal extra-theatricality, in order to reflect the two aspects introduced above: its content, or the selection of material and information given in the play (e.g. naming a character who will become a famous painter Vincent van Gogh) on the one hand, and the chosen form of presentation (e.g. the detailed imitation of a kitchen in *Vincent in Brixton*) on the other. It thus has the further advantage of avoiding the confusion of content and form, two entities that interact, but are not inter-dependent (Pavis, 1985, p. 172).

Both formal and thematic extra-theatricality can support the apparently invisible translation of figures in the life world into stage characters. Whereas the theoretical texts discussed in the previous chapter have analysed the linguistic means used to support the concept of reconstructing the past in a different medium, their theatrical equivalents have rarely been examined, even though an increasing number of plays has endeavoured to portray contemporary and historical events and figures on stage. The following sections are therefore dedicated to identifying the means that are used to create authenticity in three different biographical productions. The analysis relies on the perception of practitioners involved in the productions, as well as my own comparison of these performances to other discourses about the same figures. The relative nature of the ideas of extra- and intra-theatricality means that these perspectives merely suggest that the elements discussed here are likely to create truth effects for a wider audience. Whether they can indeed do this will be explored in the second part of the book.

Rendition Monologues

Rendition Monologues is a good example of a production with a strong claim to authenticity. Dedication to the life world is one of the key features of Ice and Fire Theatre Company, whose mission is to 'explore human rights stories through performance' and to 'creatively respond to key issues affecting our society and the world beyond' (Ice and Fire, 2010a). Based on the success of their early full scale productions *I Have Before Me a Remarkable Document Given To Me by a Young Lady From Rwanda* and *Crocodile Seeking Refuge* (Sonja Linden; first produced at the Finborough Theatre in London in 2003 and the Lyric Hammersmith in 2005, respectively), the company set up the outreach network 'Actors for Human Rights'. Collaboration with Amnesty International, the voluntary participation of actors and the self-imposed restriction to produce only rehearsed readings of 'documentary plays [that] can go anywhere at any time' (Ice and Fire, 2010b) show that the network's primary interest is human rights work, i.e. activism in the world outside the theatre that uses the potential of documentary theatre to 'catalyse public engagement and activism' (Reinelt, 2009, p. 12). As professional theatre practitioners, the full time members of staff and actor-volunteers involved describe their task as using their skills (Nzaramba, 2009) to create wider awareness for a range of different issues, including the situation of asylum seekers (*Asylum Monologues, Asylum Dialogues, The Illegals*) and the role of human rights in the war on terror in *Rendition Monologues* (Ice and Fire, 2010c). Their self-definition as an activists' network is also visible in the funding they receive, which stems mainly from organisations that fund projects 'for social justice and sustainability' (Network for Social Change, 2010), or 'change for the better' (Esmee Fairbairn Foundation, 2010).

Creating Authenticity through Original Documents

Actors for Human Rights' ambition to engage directly with the world outside the theatre is reflected in their choice, or rejection some might argue, of theatrical means of presentation. As all of their plays, the script of *Rendition Monologues* is based entirely on verbatim quotation from other sources, limiting Christine Bacon's role as a playwright to the selection and arrangement of existing text. While this format was unusual when Nicholas Kent and Richard Norton-Taylor re-discovered it for the tribunal plays at the Tricycle Theatre (see Chapter 1), it has since become a popular format on British stages, often referred to as verbatim or documentary theatre. The second name already implies the strength of its truth claim, as it promises nearly unmediated access to historical or contemporary 'documents' that record statements and conversations from the world outside the theatre. The performances can thus be seen as an alternative format to disseminate discourses to audiences who would not necessarily have access to them; in the words of Christine Bacon, writer and director of *Rendition Monologues*, Ice and Fire produced the play because they felt that these stories 'have got to be told' (Bacon, 2009b).

Frequent involvement of journalists who have published articles in national newspapers on similar issues, such as Richard Norton-Taylor at the Tricycle Theatre or Katharine Viner who co-scripted *Rachel Corrie* for the Royal Court, has further helped to place this genre in the realm of highly extra-theatrical performances. In *Rendition Monologues* the connection to journalism is only indirect, as some of the documents the author used stem originally from journalistic sources, such as newspaper interviews or documentaries with victims of extraordinary rendition (Ice and Fire, 2009). Instead it has a strong association with the legal system through the involvement of Reprieve, a charity that provides legal support to victims of extraordinary rendition. Christine Bacon received materials from them and relied on 'the lawyers [...] to check for factual accuracy, or whether [she] had overstated the point or understated it' (Bacon, 2009b). This collaboration suggests that the information in the play has been approved by experts from the life world.

In addition, various speeches in the play show their origin in legal discourse through the kind of information that is given and the terminology used: the first presentation of one of the four victims, Binyam Mohamed, for example, establishes his identity in terms of his legal status as 'a British resident of Ethiopian origin' and suggests that he will 'testify as follows' (Bacon, 2009a, p. 2), thus emphasising the legal value of his statement over that of his personal experience. This proximity indicates that the play also inherits the legal system's unbroken belief in language's power to adequately capture events. Some of the documents cited in the script were produced under a legal oath, as for example a *Sworn Affidavit of* Marwan Ibrahim Mahmoud Jabour; in other words, these speakers have sworn to 'tell the truth' and society reserves the right to punish those who do not comply with this requirement. Questions about ontological differences between life and language are rarely considered in the everyday operation of this system.

References to the origin of speeches and documents produced by specific individuals, especially politicians and governmental bodies, are often mentioned in the script itself. The script marks, for example, that the definition of extraordinary rendition in it follows 'the words of the European Parliament' (Bacon, 2009a, p. 3). In addition the company provides a list of sources they consulted for *Rendition Monologues* on their website (Ice and Fire, 2009). The practice of citing sources reflects the conventions of academic texts, where transparency regarding the origin of information is regarded as a vital marker of its scientific quality. Through its use of verbatim quotation *Rendition Monologues* thus establishes its closeness to three realms of the life world – journalism, the judiciary system and scholarship – which use elaborate systems such as legal oaths and citation systems to indicate discourses that accurately reflect the life world.

Beyond the claim that the information given in the speeches is valid outside the theatre, the use of verbatim material also influences the perception of characters. Although not all the people whose statements are quoted are named, the assertion that 'all language used in the scripts is recorded *from real life*' (Ice and Fire, 2010c; italics UC) implies that all speeches were originally uttered by *real people*. Although not all of them are mentioned by name and the audience will be unlikely to recognise even some of the victims who are named, this gives a different quality to the characters portrayed: hearing the testimony of people 'like them', people made of flesh and blood, the audience are more likely to transfer basic human qualities, such as the capacity to feel pain, onto them. As a result the distance between spectators and characters will be reduced and the effect of dehumanisation, found not only in abstract descriptions of torture but also in fictional formats such as drawn cartoons, where characters suffer all kinds of physical accidents and even abuse much to the delight of audiences, becomes minimal. The descriptions of torture will thus have a higher impact.

The empathy created could even outweigh the impact of the juridical texts on characterisation. In their first speeches, the four victims of extraordinary rendition give their names, but associate them with the legal characteristics attached to them rather than any sign of their individuality: Binyam Mohamed is 'a British resident of Ethiopian origin' (Bacon, 2009a, p. 2), and Marwan Jabour is identified both by name and his 'identification number 953103207', an administrative reference that clearly places his role in a system above his dignity as an individual human being. Although this tendency is countered by the inclusion of the men's background and the events that led to their abduction, taken mainly from interviews and legal declarations, the high degree of formality of the language means that it is still characterised by the relative absence of personality or the raw emotions triggered through torture. A good example for this tendency is a statement by Khaled el Masri, in which he is 'protesting [...] the inhuman conditions of [his] confinement' (Bacon, 2009a, p. 18): the language chosen is restrained, carefully chosen and fits abstract political discourse about human rights. Psychological and physical pain are not spelled out. The assertion that the events presented in *Rendition Monologues* took place in the life world, however, can heighten the spectators' empathy for the people behind this formal, juridical discourse.

Conflict between Authenticity and the Theatrical Format

Despite its strong reliance on the truth claim introduced by the use of verbatim quotation from authoritative legal and journalistic documents material, the practitioners affirm that they wish to 'effectively communicate' in order to encourage audiences to 'think about these issues' (Bacon, 2009b). This desire guides the development of both script and production. Thus Christine Bacon suggests that the selection of materials takes into account the audience's concentration span and juridically relevant information is cut to avoid loss of interest. Instead she often uses summative statements, such as 'this circle of torture was to last another 18 months' (Bacon, 2009a, p. 14), to combine descriptions of individual moments of intense experience with a larger narrative and overall development. While her choice does not alter any speeches, it demonstrates that their selection is made mainly from a theatrical perspective.

Another potential area of conflict between the authenticity of the materials and the need for effective communication on stage is given by the form of presentation of these discourses: while the texts are mainly written as narrative and indirect speech, direct presentation in the form of dialogue can be seen as the standard form of presentation in theatre and is often perceived as easier to process. (see Chapter 3). Compared to this conversational structure, long speeches require more sustained concentration to follow. In *Rendition Monologues* this potential dilemma is addressed in various ways: the most popular is to use sections of remembered dialogue in victims' testimonies to create a conversation among various actors, often with very short interactions as these create a welcome change in pace from longer narrative speeches:

Actor 2: Where you live, are there any mosques?
Actor 4: How many people attend the services there?
Actor 2: What are their nationalities?
Actor 4: Have you ever invited someone to Islamic activities at the mosque?
Actor 2: Has anyone invited you? (Bacon, 2009a, p. 7)

In the absence of longer dialogues, the change from descriptive narrative to direct interaction can take place within the same line to quicken the pace of the performance: 'One day I asked the guard – (noise gets louder) [actor turns to another actor; comment UC] Please, stop this noise' (Bacon, 2009a, p. 2). Alternatively, vocal monotony is avoided by intercalating short extracts from different documents. In addition to aiding the audience's concentration, these create a mosaic of individual experiences spoken by various actors that constitute the systematic human rights abuse:

> *Khaled:* I was beaten severely from both sides.
> *Binyam:* They stripped me naked...
> *B/K:* took photos
> *Binyam:* put fingers up my anus
> *Khaled:* I felt a stick being forced into my anus.
> *Marwan:* They dressed me in a
> *Khaled:* Dark blue
> *K/B/M:* Tracksuit
> *Khaled:* I was dressed in a diaper
> *Marwan:* They put diapers under my pants...
> *Binyam:* I was shackled.
> *B/K/M:* and blindfolded. (Bacon, 2009a)

It is interesting to observe that such interference with the original documents, which points to the fact that unmediated access to the events in the life world is not possible as the medium in which they are retold or re-presented, is explained by theatre practitioners as a necessary step to communicate these events most effectively. Without at least some concessions to the medium of theatre, the promise of thematic extra-theatricality is not sufficient to achieve this aim: the practitioners involved in *Rendition Monologues* explain that they consciously employ the potential of theatrical means, such as 'the voice, the visual, the lightening, a bit of staging [...] to keep [the audience's] focus sharp' (Bacon, 2009b), to engage people.

At first sight, these statements might appear to be surprising, as the production's minimalist staging confirms Ice and Fire's view that it is a 'staged reading' (Ice and Fire, 2010c) rather than a fully staged production: all actors, dressed in uniform black with minimal make-up, read from scripts, as rehearsal times tend to be very short. Although the one-week run in Edinburgh allowed a full day's rehearsal, preparation time for individual readings sometimes amounts to only three hours (Bacon, 2009b). Scenography is also subject to the company's ethos of activism and their decision to put 'practicality before anything else [in order to] get the stuff out there' (Bacon, 2009b). Boxes that function variably as chairs or lecterns are the only items on an otherwise empty stage and the lighting rig is restricted to the equipment the venues can offer to them.

In front of this rather empty physical performance space, references to existing geographical locations in the script, such as Ethiopia, Lebanon

Rehearsal for *Rendition Monologues* (Ben Chessell)

or Germany, or descriptions of specific spaces like 'the cells in Karachi [that] were small, each perhaps eight by ten feet' (Bacon, 2009a, pp. 3, 6 and 5), are the only means to evoke the physical environment of the characters. In contrast to more fully staged performances, this 'spoken scenery' is not supported by generic visual references to the places mentioned, but is indeed the only way in which specific spaces are evoked. In the first minutes of the performance, this lack of visual clues about space is partly compensated by sounds from original places, such as the 'faint sound of [a] jet engine' or 'the now familiar atmos sounds connected with the 9/11 attack' (Bacon, 2009a, pp. 1 and 2), but such additions remain sporadic. Overall theatrical presentation is again subordinate to the power of the quoted word. The scarcity of theatrical artifice in *Rendition Monologues* could thus suggest that the production uses hardly any elements of formal extra-theatricality. Yet, the fact that even a company as dedicated to the verbatim presentation of human experience as Ice and Fire relies on theatrical means to communicate their concerns demonstrates their vital role even in highly extra-theatrical formats. It can therefore be of interest to discuss *Rendition Monologues* as an example of a minimum level of stylistic intervention necessary in any form of biographical performance.

In the performance the use of space, light and music also indicates this for effective presentation and is often used to control the pace of the performance. Thus lighting and actors' movements serve to focus attention on their speeches: actors gather in more brightly lit areas in changing constellations. In addition music links different sections of the script, such as different sequences of torture, interrupting monotony and offering the audience 'the chance to [...] take a little break before [the play] goes on' (Bacon, 2009b). These elements are, however, also used to create additional layers of symbolic meaning. Colder colours of light can create a threatening atmosphere during torture scenes, and the musical underscoring of these moments further contributes to their emotional intensity. Here meaning is not created through visual or audible similarities between the world of the play and the life world, but through conventional associations between sensory impressions (cold light) and emotions (threat, discomfort). In the actors' movement both imitation and symbolic associations are combined when hierarchical relationships are represented visually: during interrogations, for example, those in the role of CIA agents stand at either side of the rendition victim who is interviewed (Bacon, 2009a, p. 6). On the one hand, this demonstration can be regarded as a direct imitation of human behaviour in the life world; on the other, it represents metaphorical expressions about high and low positions in hierarchies. This duplicity can remind us that our perception of the life world is often structured by the different media we have at our disposal to communicate it to others.

As in all forms of biographical theatre, the actors as the embodiment of individuals from the life world provide the strongest link to the life world. The practitioners involved in *Rendition Monologues* emphasise their ability to 'give faces and voices to the marginalised, demonised and hidden', thus creating a basis of understanding that is guided less by an analysis of their situation, but rather by 'compassion and understanding' (Ice and Fire, 2010a). Through the presence of a body on stage, whose visible, audible, olfactory and – though rarely tested – tangible here and now is shared with the audience, biographical characters will almost invariably provoke more of a sense of shared humanity and empathy than an intangible text, which exists merely in the form of shapes on a page.

The Actors' Role: Impersonation or Witness?

At the same time, however, the difference between the individual human being from the life world and the actors who repeat their words on stage is more visible than the transfer of text from one context to another. The aim of reconstruction as an invisible folding of the past into discourse (see Chapter 2) is harder to achieve in a three-dimensional medium which has to show the concrete and cannot resort to generalisations as linguistic systems do. The presence of actors' bodies serves as a more noticeable reminder of the authors of a biographical performance; even though they can embody a role, their own unique physical identity remains visible. The actors who take on the role of the rendition victims then have to decide whether they want to minimise their presence as creators of the role and, in the words of Ery Nzaramba (2009), the actor who played the role of Binyam Mohammed a number of times, 'interpret, act' them, or whether they merely want to be a witness to the victims' words and 'read the testimonies [...] because it is not going to be anywhere near the real person anyway'.

An analysis of *Rendition Monologues* seems to confirm Ery Nzaramba's (2009) impression that in 'these plays [his] work is always a hybrid of both'. Although the use of biographical characters introduces a strong extra-theatrical element, the lack of identity between actors and biographees demonstrates that the pole of absolute extra-theatricality is only possible in theory. Actual performances always oscillate between the two extremes of the scale. The popular understanding of acting based on actors' emotional investment into creating a character *as if* it was real (Stanislavski, 1980) has a clear impact on this production. Christine Bacon (2009b) confirms that the aim of the outreach programme is to 'offer [...] the next best thing to the person being there', or to present the material *as if* the person were there. Ery Nzaramba (2009) echoes this wish to bridge the gap between him and the rendition victim through getting to 'know the person [...] to put a face and a body and a voice behind his these words'. This intention seems to be closely linked to the individuality granted to these biographical characters; the people behind smaller roles of perpetrators, such as CIA officers, torturers or secret service personnel, are rarely portrayed as human beings with a unique character. In contrast to the responsibility the actor feels when 'you have characters who are like real characters in a play', a less psychological acting approach is required for those who merely represent their (negative) professional role: 'it's simply switching on the stereotype bad guy and say it aloud like that' (Nzaramba, 2009).

Despite this desire to 'invest emotionally' (Bacon, 2009b) and to present these characters in a way that does the people and stories behind them justice, *Rendition Monologues* rejects many elements of formal intra-theatricality that could hide the difference between the original figure and the actor. The most obvious of these means is physical similarity – cross-racial casting means that although audiences are not necessarily familiar with the appearance of the five men whose stories are told, they will not imagine that Khaled Al Masri, German citizen of Syrian origin, will look like the white actor Simon Tait. The same is true for more widely known figures, such as Condoleezza Rice, who was played by Nora Wardell. Similarly there are moments of cross-gender casting. Although the script stipulates that there should be one actress, who takes over the roles of women in the testimonies, including Condoleezza Rice, this actress also interprets the role of officials, who in countries such as Pakistan would be more likely to be male. Casting against or ignoring these relatively stable features of a person's identity is thus a clear departure from formal extra-theatricality and could counteract the similarities between the life world and the production.

Christine Bacon (2009b) declares that this aspect is partly due to practical limitations: 'we do not generally cast for type unless we're in a position where you can and you are paying people. It is just quality of the acting'. It could, however, also be argued that this decision demonstrates the wish to create authenticity not through the actor's resemblance with the character, but through their credibility and authenticity in relation to the issues that affect the life of these figures.[2] Similarly the actors' willingness to give their time to *Rendition Monologues* contributes to the play's authenticity in a sense unlike that of successful impersonation.

Extra-theatricality is thus created by a range of different means: on a thematic level, the choice of verbatim material and the knowledge that all the speeches were first uttered by individuals who exist in the life world is reinforced by associations with forms of discourse that are based on the belief that language can capture the world, such as judicial or academic discourse. This element is further reinforced by the actors' volunteer status, which demonstrates that beyond their professional skills they attach great value to the issues discussed. Formal means can contribute to the close relationship between the life world and the production. In this performance this is mainly done through symbolic links, rather than surface similarity, which can interfere with the apparently unmediated access to legal documents. In *Rendition Monologues*, however, this potential discrepancy between formal and thematic extra-theatricality is clearly decided in favour of thematic extra-theatricality and the audience's knowledge that the speeches presented originate in their life world. For Ice and Fire the sense that 'this is real' (Langton, 2009) entails an obligation to transfer the information they received into the context of their life world. In the words of their regional coordinator, the audience should not 'go away thinking "I feel really moved by that" but then head straight for their beer' (Langton, 2009). This demand is endorsed in both the text and the context of this production: the appellative function of

Binyam Mohamed's declaration that he merely asks 'that the truth should be made known, so that nobody in the future should have to endure what I have endured' (Bacon, 2009a, p. 2) remains when the words are spoken by an actor. Similarly, the addition of post show talks immediately after the performance conveys the idea that spectators should consider 'what they, as individuals, can do' (Bacon, 2009b). Finally their website explicitly confirms their aim of changing their audiences' views on the issues presented: 'If anyone doubts the shocking reality of rendition, they should see this performance' (Clive Stafford-Smith on Ice and Fire, 2010d).

Gladiator Games

While the knowledge that the speeches in *Rendition Monologues* are based on the experiences of specific people from the life world creates a strong truth claim, the lack of insight into the personalities of the figures portrayed means that an important aspect of biography is neglected in these plays. The growing impact of psychology on our understanding of human identity during the twentieth century means that insights into someone's self-concept, motivations and individual personality traits have become an important aspect of our understanding of human life. This development is reflected in life writing, where a subject's inner life has become more important than their great deeds, and in theatre, where the notion of Realist characters who are influenced by their social environment was introduced in the early twentieth century. Today the idea of extra-theatrical characters refers to roles that mirror our anthropological concept and presents figures whose actions and words are based on a unique personality. The result of these related developments means that a majority of plays pursues a reconstruction not only of events, but also of personality (see Chapter 2), or 'psychobiography' (Palmer, 1998, p. 42). *Gladiator Games* combines the use of verbatim quotation from sources associated with a high truth value and the wish to portray the figures involved as unique individuals. Both elements carry a different form of truth claim, and the following section discusses how the two strategies interact and shape the performance as a whole.

Nonetheless, the similarities between *Gladiator Games* and *Rendition Monologues* seem to outweigh the differences at first sight: both plays centre around legal inquiries, in this case the investigation into the murder of Zahid Mubarek by his cellmate Robert Stewart while he was imprisoned in Feltham in March 2000 (Home Office, 2006). Charlotte Westenra, the director of the production, states that her initial interest was sparked by media suggestions that institutional racism had led to a lack of care on the part of the institution. Seeing the 'prison system [...] and the way we treat our prisoners [as] symptomatic for the way society is' (Westenra, 2009), she felt that the inquiry into the accusations deserved to be brought to the attention of a wider audience. Her wish to use theatre as a means to create publicity for, and thus indirectly fight, a specific injustice, is shared by the playwright, Tanika Gupta, who saw the events as 'politically important', and two of the actors involved: Tom McKay, who plays Robert Stewart, agrees that 'the infinite list of failings within the prison service' constituted a 'story that badly needed to be told' (Tom McKay, 2009; also Panthaki, 2009).

Through the inquiry and press coverage the production team had a lot of material at their disposal, whose origin would have offered a basis for a strong truth claim, similar to that of *Rendition Monologues*. Although they used verbatim quotation from these sources for some scenes, they nevertheless decided to go beyond the limitations associated with it in order to avoid the 'dryness' of inquiry plays (Gardner, 2006) in which 'in terms of theatre, [...] nothing really happens' (Sierz, 2009). Their second reason for their decision seems to be partly related to the nature of theatre. For Tanika Gupta (2009), verbatim theatre 'where you don't see the victims of the story [is] a cold medium', as it ignores the need to give the issues it addresses a specific human face. Charlotte Westenra (2009) shares this concern to 'bring the man to the fore of the play', partly as a theatrical experiment 'to see what happened if [she] mixed the academic, the verbatim, with the narrative', partly as a testimony towards the young man who had become the victim. Beyond Zahid's mere presence on stage, which contrasted already with the tribunal plays at the Tricyle Theatre, they wanted to ensure that he was shown the way 'he was really like' (Westenra, 2009), i.e. as a complex, unique human being. Their intention to include an insight into his personality thus goes beyond verbatim plays like *Rendition Monologues*, where the victims appear on stage, but mainly in a reactive or passive role, reporting what their torturers did *to them*: '*They* put me into a room. *They* took my stuff. *They* took my wallet' (Gupta, 2005, p. 2; italics UC).

Whose Truth Should be Presented?

Their approach has direct consequences for the format of the play. Despite Tanika Gupta's affirmation that 'official documents [were the] most helpful material for writing the play' (Gupta, 2009) and the references to a 'List of Sources' (Gupta, 2005, p. 32) in the published playtext, the production strongly relies on a range of less official sources. In order to gain an insight into the personal element of the story, they sought interviews with those involved. Zahid's death and Robert Stewart's status as a mentally ill prisoner meant that the informants who were most closely involved in the events were Zahid's family and their representatives. Their descriptions of Zahid helped to ensure that 'this boy took on shape for' them (Westenra, 2009). In other words, the presentation of one of the central characters of the play was thus mediated not only by the production team as authors of the performance, but further through the perspective of their informants. As such, performances that do not use verbatim material resemble our expectations shaped by narrative life writing to a higher degree.

Their involvement also leads to a change in the practitioners' responsibilities. Whereas Christine Bacon's recurrence to the lawyers of rendition victims demonstrates her sense that the choice of verbatim material and its associated claim to factual truth obliges her to subject *Rendition Monologues* to approval of subject experts, the involvement of Zahid Mubarek's family in the production of *Gladiator Games* means that a more personal sense of responsibility is created. Tanika Gupta (2009) explains that both empathy for their 'pain and loss [that are] desperately sad' and the sense that 'as a fellow Asian, [she thinks] they trusted [her] more' meant that she and Charlotte Westenra were very conscious of their need for approval. Placing a stronger emphasis on the biographee's personality, especially following his death in 'such a personal and painfully recent tragedy' for his family (Amin, 2005), means that a more personal and private discourse becomes a point of comparison for the performance, which equals the importance of the professional ones evoked through the use of verbatim material.

Creating Authenticity Without Documentary Evidence

Although the two kinds of material are combined, the truth claim each of them generates is thus very different, and they can potentially challenge each other. The system of reference used to mark verbatim quotation in the printed text allows the company to clearly differentiate between the two, but in a live presentation on stage, this is not possible to the same extent. Charlotte Westenra (2009) acknowledges this difficulty, but asserts that the audience should decide whether they 'just come and watch the play', or whether they wish to embed this experience in additional information the company offers through the playtext, which she sees as 'mini booklets about the events themselves' and post show talks. For her, the inclusion of material from the life world creates a responsibility to 'allow [...] people the opportunity to see how much of it came from actual sources', but ultimately each spectator has to decide to which extent they grant truth value to the performance.

Although this possibility exists theoretically, it remains questionable whether a detailed differentiation between verbatim and non-verbatim scenes is made by most audience members, and indeed the practitioners involved. The actor Ray Panthaki (2009), for example, suggested his outrage about the treatment of the Mubarek family was greatly enhanced by 'knowing that the play was verbatim'. It could thus be argued that reactions to the play are not necessarily dependent on a detailed differentiation between two distinct ways of relating the performance to the life world, but a closer analysis reveals that the thematic extra-theatricality created by the choice of material is very different from the elements that support this close relationship on a formal level.

At first sight, many of these elements even seem to lower the authenticity created by verbatim quotation, as gaps in the company's and even family's knowledge about the events before the murder meant that they 'had to use artistic licence to bring [these events] onto the stage' (Westenra, 2009). In other words, the process of adding the physical elements of performance to a skeleton of factual discourse is inverted. Based on information from the family, for example their indication that Zahid 'got into a playfight with Bernie James when they started throwing his radio around with Robert Stewart', the company improvised scenes, which Tanika Gupta then incorporated into the script. Here character is not inferred solely from existing words, but a verbal summary provides the basis for a more elaborate 'physical and verbal construct' that is 'a theatrical character' (Richardson, 1997, p. 91).

The scenes created from family information rely to a far greater degree on the direct presentation of dialogue and interaction between characters than documentary theatre, where narrative dominates. Echoing our experience of the life world, where, at least in the here and now, direct interaction usually outweighs narrative, this form of presentation adds to the impression of 'naturalness and authenticity' (McConachie, 2001, p. 592), where the spectators can 'see with their own eyes' what 'really happened'. Their perception of the characters can thus follow the same patterns they would use to interpret someone else's behaviour in the life world, and it could be assumed that this parallel heightens their sense of similarity between the two different realms. The director confirms that this choice supported her intention to 'keep the audience in the experience the whole way through' (Westenra, 2009), rather than bringing them out of it.

The director's intention could be compared to that of narrative biographers who hide their 'magisterial voice' to render their personal interpretation of a life 'invisible' and therefore highly 'convincing' (Backscheider, 1999, p. 18). Compared to written narrative, which is characterised by physical absence, the physicality of actors and their presence in the here and now, shared with the audience, could further reinforce the perceived absence of mediation. The possibility of guiding the audience's perception without raising awareness of the author's interpretative intervention is used to reinforce the company's emphasis on the human side to the inquiry. Zahid and his fellow inmates are presented as mainly likeable, three-dimensional characters in scenes that formally resemble the audience's experience of interaction in the life world. The official nature of statements from the Home Office and Feltham prison, on the other hand, differ from everyday speech, in terms of both their formality and their narrative structure. It could be expected that at first glance, at least, the audience will perceive the first, formally more extra-theatrical scenes as a more direct, unmediated version of these events. Their potential privilege is particularly important where the officers' and the prisoners' memory of the events contradict each other:

> JAMIE: I asked about moving cells again. ZAHID: Any luck? JAMIE: Said he was 'too busy'. ZAHID: Ask again. JAMIE: Alright. *SKINNER* [prison official] *steps forward.* [...] I knew Zahid from working on Swallow Unit. He used to come over and chat to the officers working on the unit when it was association time. During these conversations with Zahid he never expressed any concern about his safety or indeed his cellmate. (Gupta, 2005, pp. 78–9)

If direct presentation privileges the view presented through its immediacy, it endorses Zahid's story rather than the version propagated by the prison services. Although the company juxtaposes them to allow audiences the opportunity to arrive at their own conclusions, the form of presentation is likely to influence this decision.

Another area in which the potential discrepancies between formal and thematic extra-theatricality can be clearly observed is scenography. For the designer of *Gladiator Games*, Paul Wills, the knowledge that the events and characters presented in the play closely resemble situations and figures from the life world leads to the wish to make the design 'as real and authentic as possible' (Wills, 2009). The wish to create formal resemblance between the two worlds is, however, complicated by the differences between the stage and the original places which are represented.

A high degree of formal extra-similarity is hard to achieve unless a play is set in a single, indoors location, and Paul Wills confirms that 'multiple location changes' were one of his biggest challenges. His solution was to 'keep things as simple as possible [...] and strip design back to its elemental elements' to merely support the stories and the actors. This decision echoes the development of scenography away from the nineteenth-century belief that by 'putting the "real thing" on stage', practitioners could 'somehow shock an audience into a greater understanding of the truth' (Baugh, 2005, p. 30). Although the idea of physical imitation of the life world can 'still find [...] a place within the ambitions of some theatre and performance of the twenty-first century' (Baugh, 2005, p. 30), today's audiences would not expect a detailed reproduction of 'a real space' (Ubersfeld, 1982, p. 143). Instead the idea of a restricted realism, i.e. 'a style which stops short of nature and emphasises only those essential details that are acquired to establish the effect of reality' (Wolfe, 1977, p. 46), is sufficient to support the impression of extra-theatricality.

The choices made by Paul Wills and Hartley TA Kemp, the lighting designer, illustrate this approach: it uses token elements, such as the harsh neon light for the scenes set in prison cells or bars that separate the upper level from the empty space below, reminiscent of the galleries around the ground floor in many prison buildings. These are combined with a few pieces of furniture necessary to support the actions presented on stage, such as beds or the table, whose leg becomes Stewart's murderous weapon. In addition it allows symbolic interpretations of space: the differentiation between the lower and upper level represents the opposition between the scenes from Zahid's life and the comments on these events from the inquiry (Wills, 2009). Nonetheless, these symbolic readings never interfere with the idea of representation of specific or generic spaces, and it could be argued that they are not shared by all members of the audience: the association of the prison cells with 'bear pits' and the link to the gladiator games to which the title alludes, for example, escaped me until it was suggested by Paul Wills (2009). One could argue that the focus on their physical resemblance rather than associative closeness to the life world supports the idea that even the sparse use of token and functional elements in scenography can support the impression of formal extra-theatricality established through other elements of the performance.

Life-like Biographical Characters

Formal extra-theatricality is finally supported by the development of biographical characters and their embodiment by actors. On the most basic level, characters can share the same physical abilities and be sub-jected to the same biological restraints as human beings. In *Gladiator Games* this aspect is introduced at the very beginning: the first stage image shows Zahid's 'body on a stretcher', and at the end of the scene he is declared dead before '*The* DOCTOR *pulls a sheet over* ZAHID'*s body*' (Gupta, 2005, pp. 35 and 42). It is thus clear from the outset that the characters in the play are subject to mortality in the same way as the audience members are.[3]

More important, however, is the creation of psychologically credible characters, i.e. of characters who mirror the features considered to be essential to human psychology: they are conscious of their own existence and its limitations, endowed with the capacity to think in a rational way; they accumulate experience and use it in order to give their behaviour and opinions coherence, and they interact with other people in a way that allows successful communication. The latter means, for example, that their speeches follow patterns familiar to the audience from every-day communication, for example by adhering to Grice's Cooperative Principles (1989, p. 26), implicit rules which most speakers obey uncon-sciously, and which allow conversations to take place in a clear, precise and ordered way. Since most theatrical performances build characters in parallel to our understanding of human beings, their behaviour and use of language in the life world, the consistent absence of these features, as for example in the theatre of the absurd, is often more notable than their presence. In *Gladiator Games* the extra-theatricality of characters is confirmed by the existence of a character who is singled out for his devi-ance from expected behaviour. Robert Stewart's first appearance is pre-ceded and accompanied by an expert's comment on his state of mind. Marked as a case for forensic psychiatry, Robert's irrational acts, such as setting fire to things or himself 'for fun', eating things that damage him and smearing himself with faeces (Gupta, 2005, pp. 49, 61, 51 and 50), are no longer a challenge to the impression that characters resemble our idea of normal human beings. On the contrary, his abnormality confirms the parallels between human beings and the other theatrical characters.

Finally, highly extra-theatrical characters are multi-faceted figures, whose numerous and sometimes conflicting characteristics imitate the complexity of human beings and, as Forster (1974, p. 81) observed in the context of the novel, the 'incalculability of life'. Ray Panthaki con-firms that his portrayal of Zahid, for example, was guided by the wish to overcome a common, stereotypical perception of prisoners as 'bad guys' and to give him more complexity by bringing out his positive role as a 'good, loving 19 year old', without slipping into another one-dimensional portrayal of 'a good angel' (Panthaki, 2009).

For biographical drama, an extra-theatrical approach to characters is a basic requirement if a play is intended to provide the impression of a truthful reconstruction of a historical life. Yet, a generic similarity is insufficient to establish a parallel between a character and a specific figure from the life world. In order to create such a unique reference, *Gladiator Games* combines the structural elements that make scenes involving Zahid resemble the audience's expectations of the life world with the idea of thematic similarity, provided by feedback from those who knew the figures presented. Even though these scenes are not directly based on evidence, they are thus tested for consistency with existing discourses and perceptions. Often the point of comparison is given by the family, especially Zahid's cousin Imtiaz, who was present at rehearsals and gave 'feedback [...] he would initiate changes, saying that it wasn't really like this' (Westenra, 2009). The need to create similarity between character and life world figure that goes beyond generic human features becomes especially apparent in a potential conflict of interest between the family and the company. Although Charlotte Westenra confirms that the company knew about Zahid's drug use, which they alluded to in the play, they did not know that he had a previous conviction for this matter. When they found out they felt obliged to raise this matter with the family to ensure that if the production was revived, they 'would have to show that side of Zahid as well' (Westenra, 2009). For a biographical character the concept of extra-theatricality has to be based both on formal similarities to human beings, and on an overlap with previous discourses about this figure. As we will see further on in the book, some discrepancies can be excused as concessions to theatrical conventions, but other deviations can provoke criticism and accusations of deliberate falsification (Highfield, 2005).

The wish to create extra-theatrical characters who bear specific resemblance to models in the life world both through formal means and through comparison with other information available about them is shared by the actors. The first aspect leads to the adoption of a Stanislavskian acting approach, as this is based on the assumption that acting has to 'create the life of a human spirit' and therefore has to be based on 'true feelings' (Stanislavski, 1980, p. 15). Actors interpret the given circumstances in order to react 'as if' they were faced with them; in other words, Stanislavski assumes that the behaviour of theatrical characters should follow the same patterns as human behaviour in the life world. Although Ray Panthaki (2009) does not use Stanislavskian terminology, he describes the process for his work on Imtiaz. In a similar way the character's circumstances as 'a relatively young man who had to grow up very quickly to represent his family', he relates to 'experiences from [his] own life [which] although not completely similar [gave] him a little understanding of the burden that Imtiaz carried during the time' and thus helped him to create the role on the basis of 'sincere emotions' (Stanislavski, 1980, p. 52). The actors thus make an important contribution to the invisibility of their mediation as they are hiding their own identity behind their characters instead of making the difference explicit.

Beyond this formal extra-theatricality of their performance, the actors are also actively engaged in creating specific references to figures from the life world. For some characters, such as Suresh and Imtiaz, the actors had access to a wealth of information through direct contact with the figures on whom their roles were based. For Ray Panthaki the possibility of working from a live model and observing the person closely gives him the chance to build his interpretation of his personality, or 'what makes him tick', and to include some of these observable signs, such as facial expression, use of voice or gestures, in his performance. At the same time talking to Imtiaz offered feedback on his interpretation from the person he represents on stage. Although Panthaki (2009) suggests that 'with Zahid it was obviously a lot harder' because he did not have direct access to him, the process of creating the character follows a similar pattern of creating a psychologically credible character who also resembles the 'Zahid that all his friends and family knew and loved'. Finally his wish to 'meet some of Zahid's friends from Feltham' echoes the idea that the resemblance to a specific person places him under the obligation to take into account all sources of information available to him. Instead of relying solely on the family's perspective he feels that it would have benefited his work had he been able to '*know* what [Zahid] was like while in that awful place' (Panthaki, 2009; italics UC) instead of relying on inference from official witness statements.

The company's attempts to create extra-theatrical, individual characters even extends to the figures who are mainly present as representatives of the prison system in the text, such as Nigel Herring, the Branch Chairman of the Prison Officers' Association. Charlotte Westenra (2009) reports that his interpretation was based not only on the script, but also on Imtiaz Mubarek's description of him as 'always jingling coins in the pocket of [his] coat', a detail that the company 'could take hold of to give [...] an energy to the character and that [made] him quite distinct from the others'. The limitations of the information available in the inquiry transcript means, however, that these parallels often rely on external details, such as Herring's hand movements, or visual details, for instance Robert Stewart's tattoo, which is also mentioned in the text: 'you must be mad or sick to tattoo "RIP" on your forehead' (Panthaki, 2009). The actor confirms that the company used such external features to draw conclusions about the person's personality and thoughts, even where the script does not indicate this: the fact that 'Robert Stewart actually had a tattoo of "Bob Marley" shocked me immensely. What had changed in him in just a few years that made him such a hardened racist? It was information like this that would change how we looked at [the characters]' (Panthaki, 2009). Nonetheless, a few critical voices suggest that these working methods do not guarantee that the characters will be perceived as highly extra-theatrical: 'the rest of the cast all work wonders with a full gallery of family, prisoners and representatives of the system, though [...] they are playing types rather than characters' (Highfield, 2005).

While a physio-psychosocial approach to Stanislavskian acting plays an important part in creating extra-theatrical characters by modelling them on our understanding of the inner life of human beings, external aspects can add to this impression. Physical resemblance between the character and the figure from the life world is probably the most important one. The degree of resemblance required, however, depends on the images to which the actor on stage can be compared. Few spectators of *Gladiator Games* would have been very familiar with any of the figures portrayed; their only visual point of comparison would have been the press coverage of the inquiry, in which only two different photographs of Zahid and Robert Stewart were used. Robert's tattoo featured prominently in one of these photographs, and its unusual choice of letters and location (on his forehead) makes it a very distinct image, one that audience members who followed the news probably couldn't forget any more than actor Ray Panthaki (2009) could. Similarly the two photographs released of Zahid showed him in the same, green jacket. Panthaki suggests that the decision to 'dress in the same costume' at the end of the play was a form of tribute as 'apparently Zahid loved that jacket', but the reproduction of one of the images on the marketing material for the play and the programme's cover suggests that it also helped to strengthen the link between the character and the figure in the life world.

The previous paragraphs show that the degree to which characters are developed not only as credible representations of human beings, but as specific persons from the life world depends partly on the information available about them. The representation of Robert Stewart, however, demonstrates that ethical considerations can also have an impact on these decisions. On the one hand his position as highly dangerous prison inmate (Gupta, 2009) and his family's personal difficulties (Westenra, 2009) meant that their co-operation would have been more difficult to obtain than that of the Mubarek family. On the other hand, the actor, playwright and director explain that they did not have the same desire to understand his motivations and feelings as part of his unique individuality. Instead, Tom McKay (2009) explains that although he was committed to creating a 'unique and above all truthful representation of him', he focused strongly on 'captur[ing] the essence of who he is in order to [understand] how he came to [...] commit the crime that he did'. In other words, his mental illness becomes the most defining personality trait: 'There was enough on his mental illness [...] to understand who he was' (Gupta, 2009). Regarding his role as representative of a medical condition weakens the link to a specific human being and allows the actor to work with images of similar people, especially an image from a documentary on young prisoners, to create a higher degree of generic similarity. Their lack of motivation to 'honour' Robert Stewart with a unique representation is closely related to ethical concerns and the disgust evoked by 'the horror of his crime' (Tom McKay). Beyond their responsibility to portray him as a very troubled and sick human being, who did not receive the support he needed (Westenra, 2009), he does not inspire the same feelings of solidarity and responsibility as Zahid. The company's perception of the figures in the life world thus clearly influences the development of the biographical characters in the play.

In addition, the director saw the danger of 'fuelling' Robert's 'wish to become a star, in some kind of ill way' (Westenra, 2009), thus recognising that the performance, in turn, can influence the audience's views on the persons portrayed. Similar to Ice and Fire who see themselves as activists who use the medium of theatre to raise the public's awareness of human rights issues, the production team of *Gladiator Games* acknowledges that the use of biographical characters is a powerful tool to blur the habitual distinction between stage and life world, especially when spectators witness the characters, in this case Imtiaz, on stage and shortly afterwards see 'the man the play was about' in a panel discussion and the theatre bar (Westenra, 2009). For Charlotte Westenra (2009) this offers the chance to overcome Boal's concept that theatre should 'show how things really are' and show 'how real things are' at the same time. Despite the different ways in which they create the proximity between the life and the stage world, formal- and thematic extra-theatricality thus support the same aim. Their combination might require a number of compromises, as the discussion of *Gladiator Games* has shown, but their combined effect can create a strong truth claim. The final play discussed in this chapter demonstrates that the role of formal similarity can be extended even further.

Vincent in Brixton

First performed under Richard Eyre's direction at the Cottlesloe in 2002, Nicholas Wright's play soon transferred to London's West End and went on an extensive tour. A year later, Jochum ten Haaf and Clare Higgins played their parts as the young Vincent van Gogh and his London land-lady, Ursula Loyer, once more in a film screened on BBC4. The success of the original production sparked further interest in the play, and in 2004 it was revived at the Library Theatre, Manchester. The discussion in this book is based on these two stage performances, as they closely resemble each other: no changes were made to the script for the second production and both create the biographical link in a similar way (and even use the same interview in the programme to establish this). Most importantly, however, both chose a highly extra-theatrical form of pres-entation in terms of acting and scenography, despite the fact that the story is not based on a well-documented reconstruction of the artist's London days. The last section of this chapter thus concentrates on the use of formal means to create a sense of authenticity that is 'so richly compelling that one completely accepts Wright's imaginative view of the events as the greater truth' (Thaxter, 2002, p. 551).

The analysis of non-verbatim scenes in *Gladiator Games* has demon-strated that the mode of direct presentation rather than narrative on stage requires playwrights and theatre practitioners to add to the infor-mation drawn from documentary evidence, but the scarceness of docu-ments about van Gogh's stay in London means that the plot is mainly made up of Wright's 'imagined and intimate portrait' (Anon., 2004c) of a gap in the young painter's biography. Thematic extra-theatricality is thus reduced to very few pieces of information from historical documents about the artist's time as a lodger in the Loyer household: his family's observation that he experienced an atmosphere of 'secrets [that] has done him no good' (van Gogh Bonger, 1913), a short visit to Mrs Loyer on the occasion of her birthday after he had moved away, and his familiarity with a quotation by Michelet.

Nicholas Wright suggests that it was this 'gap in his letters to [his brother] Theo', and the potential that any further hints were destroyed on purpose by Theo van Gogh's widow (Wright, 2009), that inspired his interest. The lack of historical confirmation allowed the playwright to combine this loose biographical link with his other interests, for example life in London at the time, or the development of young artists: how did the young van Gogh turn into an artist although at that time painting was not one of his interests, whereas others, such as his fellow lodger, 'had ambitions to being a painter' but never realised them (Wright, 2009).

While he explores these interests through his development of characters and situations, this does not lower his sense that the use of a biographical link places a responsibility on him to provide at least a likely version of the unknown events in the artist's life: 'My pattern for this is the famous example of Schiller's invention of a meeting between Elizabeth I and Mary Stuart. It didn't happen, but it might have done and it's not belittling anyone to suggest that it did' (Wright, 2009). For this purpose, his research into the period included visits to the van Gogh Museum in Amsterdam to acquaint himself with the surviving letters, and extensive reading of biographies, especially Martin Bailey's *Young Vincent* and other historical books on art and life in Victorian London. As a result he can support the biographical link by integrating even minor known details into the play, such as Vincent's addition of a Michelet quote underneath a drawing: 'A woman is not old as long as she loves and is loved' (National Theatre, 2002, p. 5 and Wright, 2002, p. 49), and by avoiding elements that would counter the thin layer of extra-theatricality.

Elements that Support Plausibility

Wright's emphasis on plausibility and the intention to emphasise the biographical link are echoed in the marketing material and programmes of both productions. Both productions used a well-known picture by van Gogh on their poster in order to disambiguate the use of the first name 'Vincent' in the title,[4] and the National Theatre announced its production as an examination of 'the transforming effect of love, sex and artistic adventure on unformed talent [...] based on the true facts of Vincent van Gogh's early life in London' (National Theatre, 2003). In the programme the Library Theatre offers a slightly more differentiated picture, even though it clearly endorses the biographical connection as well. This is mainly done through the inclusion of texts that are strongly associated with historical truth claims, either through their format, such as the chronology of key dates in van Gogh's life, or through the expertise of their authors, for example Martin Bailey, who authored a biography of *Young Vincent* in which he includes the re-discovery of the Loyer's house (National Theatre, 2002, pp. 25 and 10–11). Furthermore, original documents from van Gogh's life are included in the form of excerpts from his correspondence with his brother Theo (Library Theatre, 2004a, pp. 12–13), or a photograph of the young van Gogh, whose well-educated, formal appearance counters the famous image of his self portraits (National Theatre, 2002, p. 9). Although the interview transcript, reproduced with permission from the first production, clarifies the limited parallels between the performance and other discourses about the young painter, there is no detailed reference system to mark elements of the performance that are directly based on historical evidence. Nicholas Wright explains that this is a consequence of the 'complicated mix of fact and speculation' (Wright, 2009) of the theatrical medium, in which referencing conventions, such as footnotes, would seem alien.

The programme's impact on the reception of the Library Theatre production is thus interesting for two reasons: firstly, it could be examined to what extent audience members rely on the programme as part of the 'sphere of theatrical activity that circulates around the performance and in which the performance itself circulates' (Rebellato, 1999, p. 115) to inform their perception, and also how far this sphere can influence their understanding of the connection between the performance and the life world. Secondly, it would be interesting to know whether audiences see the connections between performance and life world as outweighing the uncertainties that are implicitly acknowledged in it. Reviewers' comments and anecdotal evidence, including my own reaction and that of practitioners (such as Peter Mumford, the lighting designer of the National Theatre production), suggest that despite the small overlap between other biographical discourses the biographical link is strong: 'I've always liked Vincent van Gogh's work and also been fascinated by his life although *I did not previously know about* his time in Brixton' (Mumford, 2009; italics UC). While a closer examination of audience reactions to the play will be conducted in the second part of this book, the current chapter concentrates on the way formal extra-theatricality, or 'acutely observed domestic realism' (Bassett, 2002), compensates for the small number of thematic links.

Creating Authenticity through Scenography and Characters

Although the degree of formal intra-theatricality is greatly determined by the choices made for each production, Nicholas Wright's script provides the structural foundation for it. He sets the play in a kitchen, a closed, indoor space whose dimensions are similar to those of many stages, and suggests that the space should be used in the same way audiences would use its equivalent in the life world: for the preparation of a meal and other everyday activities. All four scenes of the play are set in the same space, and although the time in the play exceeds its running time, the gaps between the scenes are unlikely to attract attention or induce disbelief: they pass in chronological order[5], contain references to the length of time that has passed and events that happened in the meantime, and are framed by black-outs and music. The audience's experience of the linear procession of time is also reflected in its physical effect on the characters: the pregnancy of Ursula's daughter Eugenie is first mentioned in scene 3, followed by a comment about the advancing age of her children in scene 4 (Wright, 2002, p. 61). The presentation of gaps between the scenes, on the other hand, follows widely accepted conventions, which means that any discrepancies in the passing of time in the theatre and in the life world can pass almost unnoticed.

In both productions the spatial and temporal structure in the script is used as the basis for highly extra-theatrical scenography, almost reminiscent of early twentieth-century Naturalism. The kitchens not only imitate spaces from the life world in great visual detail, they are also fully functional, serving the on-stage preparation of a meal. Georgina Brown observes at the National Theatre that 'everything [in this design] is for real' (Brown, 2002, p. 547). At the Library Theatre, the sounds and even smells of cooking also heighten this sense of authenticity. At the same time, sound and further visual elements hint at the world beyond the kitchen. In scene 4 rain can be heard off-stage and becomes visible when the door opens and a character enters in a drenched costume. This dedication to precise imitation seems to be shared by few contemporary scenographers. Partly this can be explained by practical concerns – frequent changes in location mean that such a wealth of detail can only be achieved with a high amount of technical effort, such as the use of projected photographs to imitate the Austrian palace interiors where Mozart works in Peter Shaffer's *Amadeus* (1979), for instance. Nonetheless, the changes in attitudes towards imitation in design and current prevalence of a restricted realism, or extra-theatricality achieved through symbolic and tokenistic similarities rather than detailed imitation, has had a strong impact on expectations. As a result, *Vincent in Brixton* is likely to stand out as an exceptionally extra-theatrical production – a formal characteristic that can be interpreted as an indication of a close resemblance between the world of the play and the life world overall.

In contrast to the specific link created by a biographical character, scenographic extra-theatricality mainly works on a generic level in the production. Although in the script Nicholas Wright (2002) refers to '87 Hackford Road', the house where van Gogh is known to have lived as a lodger, the lack of information on the property's interior at the time means that this thematic link could not be transported into the production. Nor would this have had a strong effect on the audience, as they would be highly unlikely to be familiar with this specific space in any case. *Vincent in Brixton* is thus typical of the majority of plays where a concrete biographical link is supported by more generic scenographic similarities.[6] This difference between the presentation of biographical characters and their environment can remind us that extra-theatricality is a highly relative concept that does not rely on an objectively determinable degree of similarity between the world of the play and the life world, but is largely determined by practitioners' and audiences' familiarity with them, as well as the importance granted to each of these elements.

Whereas *Vincent in Brixton* demonstrates the first aspect, the latter can be seen in a little thought experiment: David Edgar's *Albert Speer* was highly controversial for its portrayal of the Nazi architect, but criticism concentrated entirely on the presentation of the central character – no one would have deemed it necessary to point out any discrepancies in its design, such as inaccuracies in the reproduction of Hitler's new Chancellery. Scenography's contribution to formal extra-theatricality is thus little influenced by the historical standard of exact correspondence, but it is an essential element of a style of presentation highly dependent on conventions.

Although visual similarities are likely to contribute most strongly to the impression of extra-theatricality, the National Theatre production adds a more specific link to the biographee through an 'additional semantisation of space' (Schaff, 1992, p. 105). In other words, they integrate symbolic references to van Gogh's work into the scenography. Peter Mumford explains that the inclusion of specific objects that reference his paintings, such as 'chairs – the huge kitchen table – a pair of boots', the imitation of 'his rich use of colour' in the design and 'the shadows reminiscent of Van Gogh's work' were used by the design team to create 'naturalistic images with a hint of "expressionism"' (Mumford, 2009). As in *Gladiator Games*, this symbolic level is not intended to lessen the 'naturalistic [design] where everything in the kitchen/dining room [is] functional right through to the stove'; instead it adds a layer of meaning, heightening its intensity (Stratton, 2002) and tightening the thematic link to the biographee. This thematic connection is typical of plays about painters or figures whose work gives practitioners a visual reference, such as *Stanley* (Pam Gems, 1996b about Stanley Spencer) or *The Art of Success* (Nick Dear, 2000 about William Hogarth). Nevertheless few of them integrate these references so fully into an extra-theatrical, functional design. As a result, the strong link to the life world that is provided by formal means is further underlined.

Similarly, the development of biographical characters in *Vincent in Brixton* could not exist without a high level of formal extra-theatricality. In addition to the creation of an inner life that governs the characters' actions, mainly on a basis of emotions and rational thought, discussed in the context of *Gladiator Games*, the creation of multi-dimensional characters suggests that they resemble human beings. Nicholas Wright achieves this effect through comments about the characters' off-stage activities that complement those witnessed by the audience, presenting them in a range of different social roles and emotional states. Thus Ursula Loyer's observation that van Gogh's tobacco reminds her of her father who also used to smoke an unusual blend (Wright, 2002, p. 25) suggests that her perception is shaped by her former role as a daughter, as well as the current ones of mother and lover; her commitment to her school (Wright, 2002, p. 6) adds a role outside the confines of the household to this impression. At the same time, it shows her social commitment, which contrasts the egocentricity inherent in her depression.

The creation of 'pseudo-real characters' (Schaff, 1992, p. 29) can also be furthered through language. Although dramatic language is a highly artificial construct, as any comparison of a well-written play and a non-script based reality TV show will demonstrate, the impression that characters' speeches mirror the communication between individuals in the life world can be conveyed through conventional means. These include syntactic features, such as the use of unfinished sentences, morphemic aspects, such as shortened verb forms (isn't instead of is not), and vocabulary choice, particularly the inclusion of colloquialisms; all of these elements are present in *Vincent in Brixton*. In addition, Wright individualises speech, imitating the idiolect every human being possesses. His characters' speech thus varies according to their place of origin, for example when Vincent's sister introduces Dutch words into her speeches (Wright, 2002, p. 48), and specific situations: following the beginning of their love affair, the private exchanges between Vincent and his landlady take on a more intimate tone than their previous conversations. Through their speeches, the playwright thus endeavours to endow all his characters with a multi-faceted, individual personality.

Despite his emphasis that not only Vincent, but the other characters, 'Sam, Ursula, Eugenie and Anna all existed' (Wright, 2009), our limited knowledge of these historical figures from historical evidence means that most elements of their presentation are based on inferences about their personalities, circumstances and actions, both in the script and in the productions. Gus Gallagher (2005), who played Vincent at the Library Theatre, confirms this in his differentiation between 'a young man named Vincent' and 'the great artist Van Gogh', implying that his knowledge about the latter could even compromise his portrayal of the first, as it would give his character insights that would not fit the stage of his life presented in the play.

Nonetheless both productions build on the specific biographical references provided in the script wherever possible. The difference between his self portraits and the young van Gogh is brought to the audience's attention through the inclusion of an unconfirmed photograph from his youth in the programme. Although neither Gus Gallagher nor Jochum ten Haaf, who both played van Gogh, resemble the painter's iconic self portraits, both of them bear some similarity to the young man in the photograph. The casting can thus be seen as an important step in establishing the biographical link, despite the fact that none of the characters 'lives in the memory' (Wu, 2000, p. 64; for a discussion of such characters, see Chapter 4). The effect of supplying additional information on the biographee's visual appearance to create an additional point of reference for spectators depends on their study of the programme, but it does not seem to be lost: one reviewer combines it with his existing knowledge, declaring that ten Haaf's 'uncanny resemblance to the tortured artist [made him] worry that he might actually cut his ear off!' (Young, 2002, p. 551).

Fulfilling the audience's visual expectations could, however, be only a secondary effect of the National Theatre's decision to cast 'a real ginger Dutchman' (Coveney, 2002) as the protagonist. His natural accent might have been of equal or greater importance, as there seems to be a particularly close relationship between identity and speech patterns. Their affinity is considered in very few scripts (e.g. Gems, 1996a), but directors and actors often go to great length to recreate the accent of a historical figure. Few go as far as Richard Eyre in casting an actor whose natural accent fits the role, but both regional accents of English and foreign accents are taken into account in the majority of biographical productions. Although not entirely representative of the genre as a whole, the plays discussed in this volume are a good indicator of this tendency: pronunciation, vocal quality and intonation are based either on the specific historical model, as in *Thatcher – the Musical!* or *Insignificance* where Marilyn Monroe's voice is recognisable before the actress appears on stage (see Chapter 4), or generic differences, such as Gus Gallagher's imitation of a Dutch accent, Heisenberg's German accent in the Lyceum's production of *Copenhagen* or Mary's French Scots in Liz Lochhead's *Mary Queen of Scots Got Her Head Chopped Off*. The importance of accent is underlined by actors' commitment to it even in circumstances where audience members are unfamiliar with the language spoken by a biographical character: in David Pownall's *Master Class*, a play not discussed in more detail in this book, Timothy West (2005) studied the particulars of Georgian and Central Russian speech to differentiate Stalin's Georgian accent from that of other characters. Such efforts seem worthwhile, as reactions to biographical performances show that unsuitable accents are often a reason for complaints, as numerous comments on an Irish speaking Kafka in reviews of *Kafka's Dick* at Derby Playhouse demonstrate (see for example Brown, 1998, p. 1573; Macauly, 1998a, p. 1575; Anon., 2004b, p. 23).

However, a close imitation of a biographee's voice and visual appearance alone is also unlikely to suggest a high degree of extra-theatricality. Impersonators use these means to great comic effect, but few of them can be credited with creating an impression of a figure credible. In combination with the formal means employed in *Vincent in Brixton*, on the other hand, a biographical link that extends to little more than a name and some basic biographical facts, such as van Gogh's fame as an artist, can give the impression of a pronounced similarity between the play and the life world.

The discussion in this chapter thus supports the claim that truth is less an intrinsic property of discourses, including performances, but rather an effect created by them. This effect can be based on different combinations of extra- and intra-theatrical means, i.e. on both congruence between the performance and other discourses about the life world and on structural means that create similarities between the life world and a performance. While *Rendition Monologues* and *Vincent in Brixton* suggest that these combinations can lean quite strongly towards one side, a more thorough exploration of the way in which formal and thematic extra-theatricality interact in biographical plays has to take into account their perception by wider audiences. Before this is undertaken in the second part of this book, however, the next chapter examines productions in which biographical information and the form of presentation seem to counter, rather than complement, each other.

4
Creating and Undermining Expectations: Forms versus Content

Introduction

Although the productions discussed in Chapter 3 differ significantly in terms of the means used, all of them strive to create a strong link to life stories in the world outside the theatre. The exclusive or partial reliance on thematic extra-theatricality in *Rendition Monologues* and *Gladiator Games* is more strongly associated with the intention to reconstruct events from the life world and its inhabitants on stage, but *Vincent in Brixton* demonstrates that formal intra-theatricality can also be used to heighten the impression that a performance is very *likely* to reflect a past life. In many performances thematic and formal similarities between the world on stage and the life world of the audience thus pursue the same goal, and potential conflict between them (see Chapter 3) is often played down in order to maintain a high level of overall extra-theatricality.

The current chapter, on the other hand, concentrates on performances that emphasise and exploit discrepancies between form and content. As the first part of the title suggests, the main character of *Thatcher – the Musical!* by Foursight Theatre (2006) is a former Conservative Prime Minister, and the events and speeches presented in the production closely resemble her life story and British politics in the 1970s and 1980s. These are, however, presented in the highly intra-theatrical format of a musical with song, dance and glamorous costumes. A detailed discussion of the production describes the means with which this discrepancy is created and examines its entertaining and often comic effect. Interviews with the practitioners involved demonstrate that it is clearly desired, but does not diminish their wish to 'do justice' to their biographee, even if she was far from being a particularly cherished figure for them. It could also be argued that the stylised form of presentation is unlikely to entirely undermine a strong sense of thematic extra-theatricality among audiences, a question that is explored in further detail in the second part of the book dedicated to the reception of biographical performances (Chapters 6 and 7).

The second production discussed in this chapter establishes a contrast the other way round. Samuel West's production of Terry Johnson's *Insignificance* at the Lyceum in Sheffield presents an unlikely encounter between four American icons from the fifties in a highly extra-theatrical style: the hotel room shows no differences from countless rooms in hotel chains across the world, the linear flow of time is interrupted only between the two scenes, and although unusual, their interaction does not present many elements that are entirely impossible according to the rules that govern the world outside theatre. Implausible plot elements, such as Marilyn Monroe's attempt to seduce Albert Einstein, and some aspects of the recognisable yet stereotyped characters, however, clash with all other sources of information about their real life counterparts. The chapter explores the playful mode of 'as if' that is created by the fine balance between formal (and a few but essential thematic) similarities to the life world and clear thematic deviations from it, and describes its comic potential.

Although the contrast between form and content in these two plays serves different purposes, both pay tribute to the theatre's potential for a more playful engagement with the life world compared to the high degree of commitment and earnestness towards specific lives and issues found in *Rendition Monologues*, *Gladiator Games* and, to a lesser degree, *Vincent in Brixton*.

Thatcher – the Musical!

Thatcher – the Musical! was devised and first performed by Foursight Theatre at Warwick Arts Centre in 2006. After a highly successful first run a slightly changed revival of the production went on a national tour in 2007. Its combination of biographical references on the one hand and a highly visual, theatrical style including song and dance on the other continue Foursight's tradition of 'creating both devised and text-based theatre which places the actor at the centre of the process, combining word, movement and music' (Foursight Theatre, No Year). At the same time it continues the company's dedication to the exploration of women's lives established in performances about immigrants living in Wolverhampton's Reans area (Cooke, 2003; O'Reilly, 2006), the wives of King Henry VIII (Barnard et al., 1999) and Hitler's wife Eva Braun

(Cooke et al., 1989). The title clearly introduces this double orientation of biographical elements. On the one hand it is unlikely that anyone in the theatre would not expect it to focus on the former Prime Minister (PM), particularly since the marketing material features a photograph of Margaret Thatcher as well. On the other it is presented in a form that thrives on its open theatricality.

At the same time it demonstrates that the discrepancy between the two can create a comic effect: the sense of bemused surprise and wonder as to what can be expected from this performance cannot be explained by its structure; the combination of a proper name and a genre title, such as *Sherlock Holmes – the Musical* (Bricusse, 1988) or *The Buddy Holly Story* (Mansfield, 1989), is highly popular in contemporary theatre circles. Yet, only life world knowledge about the former PM suggests that she is an unlikely heroine of a conventional stage musical and can account for its comic effect. The marketing material echoes this again: while the choice of blue, red and white can create a symbolic link to Thatcher's UK-centric stance, the bright pink background introduces a rather un-Thatcherite colour. From their first point of contact audiences are thus prepared for the contrast between thematic extra-theatricality and intra-theatrical presentation. The following discussion will examine the way in which this discrepancy is continued throughout the performance, identifying elements that contribute or put into question the link to the life world, and discuss the potential effect of such a combination.

For the co-directors of the production, the comic effect created by the title is an important part of the play's appeal. The sense that it 'sounded so wrong, it had to be right' (Barnard, 2009) promised to be 'fun [and to] make people come and see it' (Cooke, 2006). This was deemed to be especially true due to the choice of a controversial protagonist. Indicating that they would approach the former PM's life with the 'tongue in cheek humour' Naomi Cooke (2006) regards as typical of Foursight Theatre, they felt that the title would help to attract audiences who would appreciate the 'delightfully risky' undertaking of presenting a controversial protagonist on stage. At the same time, Deb Barnard (2009) admits that the mere choice of a famous figure would help to attract audiences, regardless of the way the play is presented, as 'people like to see their heroine or arch enemy on stage'.

Despite this emphasis on entertainment, the directors confirm their dedication to extra-theatricality and the wish to explore the former PM's life, as it offers the 'fascinating story' of a woman who made her way from 'humble beginnings to one of the most powerful people in the world' (Cooke, 2006). Their view is echoed by Kath Burlinson (2009), who played Britannia Maggie: asked about the reasons for her interest in the production she affirms that it was 'intriguing to consider *researching* and devising a show about MT'. The emphasis on research involved in the devising process is thus comparable to that described in the context of the productions in Chapter 3, despite the different choice regarding the style of presentation.

Nonetheless, two interesting differences can be identified. Naomi Cooke (2006) explains that the company used two main sources of information, namely other discourses about Margaret Thatcher, partly compiled and prepared for them by a research assistant hired for this purpose, and their own memories of the time. Cooke confirmed that this research was important to know 'what happened here exactly and go into much more detail', but she emphasises that they used their own memory as a starting point. As this helped them to imagine 'what it was like not to have done the research', it put them into 'the position in which many of our audience would be'. Foursight thus acknowledges that our perception of the past is highly dependent on perspective. For figures from the recent past our own experience of these figures, or perhaps more likely the press coverage in their time, is an important point of comparison for new discourses about them.

The second difference is also related to perception: in contrast to performances written by playwrights, Foursight devises their shows together with the actors. Hence they are more fully involved in the process of finding, sharing and selecting material that contributes to the script.[1] In addition to the general reading most company members did, every actress was given 'a two-year period that they had to become an expert on' (Cooke, 2006). Kath Burlinson (2009) explains that she prepared for her period of expertise, the years from 1983 to 1985, by reading 'Thatcher's autobiography, other biographies of her, investigative journalism from the period, political histories and analysis', listening to 'a lot of speeches' and looking at photographs and videos. Using sources very similar to those used by many playwrights, the actresses involved in *Thatcher – the Musical!* became co-authors not only of the physicality and interpretation of a character, but of the information on which this character is based as well. As a result, the influence of a great number of contemporary perspectives on the biographical character became visible in the heated debates that took place during the rehearsal period (Cooke, 2006). The involvement of the actors in the devising process thus underlines the fact that the different Maggies are the result of negotiation between different points of view rather than a neutral reconstruction.

This alone, however, does not distinguish it from the performances discussed previously, as *Gladiator Games*, for example, combines the acknowledgement that the perspective of Zahid Mubarek's family was more important than that of Robert Stewart, his murderer, with the claim to use the performance to draw attention to these events in the life world. Similarly, Naomi Cooke (2006) claims that the motivation behind their intense research was to achieve 'accuracy in terms of what happened when and [...] what she said about certain things. We really wanted to get that right'. As a result, the degree of thematic extra-theatricality is high: the events in the play echo key events in Margaret Thatcher's political and, to some extent, private life: her upbringing in Grantham, the beginning of her political commitment at Oxford, her first campaigns to become an MP, the controversy over school milk while she was Secretary of Education, her election victories and events during her reign as PM, from the controversy of the poll tax to the Falklands War, are presented in chronological order. The overlap of the life story that will be, at least partly, familiar to the majority of British audiences thus confirms and extends the biographical reference of the title, suggesting a biographical reading.

The way in which these events are presented, however, is highly intra-theatrical and Naomi Cooke (2006) confirms that their research was mainly 'a starting point' for their work. In terms of character, they did not aim at capturing the full complexity of Margaret Thatcher's thoughts and actions, but worked in archetypes that represent different phases of her life instead. The result is 'different manifestations of Margaret Thatcher', simplified characters who represent specific roles she played, such as the Grocer's Daughter, whose values are shaped by her father's attitudes to business and life, or Military Maggie, who leads the UK into the Falklands War, using her demonstration of military strength to deflect from the controversy of internal affairs. Contrary to many biographical plays Foursight does not attempt to draw a detailed and credible interpretation of the PM's personality, but focuses more on her public role. Only the portrayal of a frail, widowed Margaret who mourns her husband and misses public attention, as well as a sense of power, extends slightly beyond her overtly public image. In Naomi Cooke's (2006) words, 'this is the nearest we get to the essential person who can feel'.

The emphasis on archetypes rather than complex, psychologically credible personality is reflected by the use of images and sound. Appropriating the material they obtained through research and translating it into three-dimensional, theatrical action through games (Cooke, 2006), the company creates a highly stylised form that departs clearly from the idea of an 'invisible translation' from the life world onto the stage. One of the most obvious examples is the main character: even a basic, biological similarity between the character and human beings in the life world such as advancing age is reflected in a visibly theatrical way. Although some aspects of her aging process, such as her greying hair, her choice of clothes and her curbed posture and frailty in old age, directly imitate the way humans change over time, the fact that a different actress plays her role at each stage of her life undermines these references. This violation of the convention that the coherence and unity of the biographical subject is echoed in the use of a single body to represent her is not mitigated by any attempt to hide the differences between the various actresses: no make-up is used to hide their facial features, and the different body shapes of the performers are not hidden but rather emphasised through the use of similarly cut dresses.

Thatcher – the Musical! by Foursight Theatre (David Finchett)

Instead continuity is created through a number of outstanding features: all Maggies sport a similar hairstyle, most wear twin sets, and most importantly, all carry the same style of handbag as their trademark. These similarities indicate that the different actresses represent aspects of someone who is normally considered a single physiological and psychological unity. In the style of caricatures that choose outstanding elements of a person's visual appearance and exaggerate them, they can also help to establish the link to the historical figure. Whereas caricatures often use size to emphasise these elements, Foursight uses materials, colours, patterns and context: the haircut might mirror that of Margaret Thatcher, but the use of plastic wigs undermines the effect of a simple reconstruction. Similarly some of the twin sets might echo the cut preferred by the PM, but the use of a purplish colour and slightly reflective material instead of her sober royal blue wool crepe suit, or even a shiny grey twin set with a Union Jack at the back, emphasise the gap between the life world and the stage. The handbag is the most interesting item in this context: all the handbags carried by the different Maggies are very similar to the ones Thatcher used. The element of exaggeration is introduced in the first scene, in which a giant handbag is rolled onto the stage and opens to reveal Narrator Maggie in her living room. Following this introduction, the smaller handbags are unlikely to be considered merely as a faithful imitation of the original ones – the constant presence of the giant handbag cum living room serves as a continuing reminder of the gap between the life world and the performance. Whether these intra-theatrical elements outweigh the biographical references and prompt a less extra-theatrical understanding remains to be seen and will be discussed in Chapter 7.

In addition to these visual links between the different Maggies, all actresses adapt their diction in a similar way, echoing that of the middle-aged Thatcher in her speeches. It is interesting to observe that this auditory connection between the characters is less stylised than the visual ones. The development of diction and tone of voice from one Maggie to another can even be seen as a highly extra-theatrical imitation of these changes over the course of Thatcher's life: while the speech of the Grocer's Daughter is still characterised by some regional features of pronunciation, especially in terms of vowels ('I wasn't lucky, I deserved it'; Foursight Theatre, 2005, p. 5), the Twin Set Maggie who attended Oxford now speaks immaculate RP. Furthermore the successful politician who is elected PM abandons her high-pitched voice for a deeper tone that is clearly reminiscent of the one Margaret Thatcher used for her most famous speeches. Although the production draws attention to these changes and uses them as a source of humour – most clearly when young Margaret Thatcher practises a more genteel pronunciation, repeating the same sentence over and over again like Eliza Doolittle in *My Fair Lady* (Foursight Theatre, 2005, p. 5) – these moments are less likely to challenge the impression of extra-theatricality than, for example, the use of rubber wigs or a giant handbag. This could confirm an observation made in Chapter 3: voice is essential for biographical references and most productions strive to imitate diction and tone of voice to heighten extra-theatricality.

Other historical characters are identified mainly through visual means due to Foursight's emphasis on physicality. This and their lower importance means that the simplifying effect of caricature is even stronger than it is for Margaret Thatcher. As Kath Burlinson (2009) who 'played Denis Thatcher, Alan Clark and miscellaneous others' points out, 'all were researched', and identifying them as historical characters is important to support the production's thematic extra-theatricality. The need for brevity, however, means that they are reduced to a very small number of token features, which are greatly exaggerated and, therefore, highly intra-theatrical in their presentation. As one reviewer observes, in addition to his name and family situation, Denis Thatcher is identifiable through two visual cues: 'a big grin and glasses' (Glover, 2006, p. 147). Ronald Reagan is not even introduced by his full name, but through the exploration of general clichés about US presidents and their security entourage, as well as his past as a film star: preceded by an army of security personnel who push their way onto the stage in an aggressive manner and followed by an army of photographers, his entrance in a cowboy hat and Maggie's friendly greeting identify 'Ronnie' without much further doubt. For other characters, for example members of her Cabinet, such visual cues may be insufficient. Here the closeness of the biographical link might vary, depending on the audience's familiarity with the events in the life world.

The intra-theatricality of the characters is increased further by the fact that all of them sing and dance. The good relationship between Thatcher and Reagan, for example, is represented by a dance number that shows them cheek to cheek, stopping occasionally to discuss policy decisions. Maggie's own political actions are also translated into musical form, for instance in the song 'No, no, no' that presents her anti-European stance when a mature Thatcher rejects 'cooking up a European Superstate' (Foursight Theatre, 2005, p. 24) in the manner of a singer in a punk rock band. For Foursight's artistic director, 'Music has always been a key element in all [their] work [as] it is a great communicator', but similar to the visual appearance of the characters, it presents extra-theatrical references in a notably theatrical style.

Physicality is as important for Foursight's style as music, and images, lyrics and speeches interact closely. Naomi Cooke (2006) explains that 'the starting point is almost always physical', something that 'illustrate[s]' events or characteristics, 'not necessarily in an obvious way'. A good example is a scene in which Maggie becomes captain of a ship, travelling in a stormy sea of resistance to the poll tax and other political decisions she has taken. On the one hand this emphasises the difference between the actions on stage and those in the life world: it is unlikely that any audience member will assume that Margaret Thatcher once stood on the steps of 10 Downing Street, swaying wildly while holding an imaginary stirring wheel, shouting 'The trade winds will carry us through' (Foursight Theatre, 2005, p. 16). On the other hand, the continuation of these images in speeches and lyrics shows that metaphorical images are essential in discourses that are thought to reflect our life world more neutrally. Lines from this scene, such as the instruction to her Cabinet to 'stay on course' or 'avoid collision' or the warning 'Recession ahead!' (Foursight Theatre, 2005, p. 16), could also be part of everyday conversations or newspaper articles, respectively. As the translation of such metaphorical, but common, use of language into images on the stage is less commonly found, audiences are more likely to pay attention to the process of mediation between the life world and the stage. Yet, at the same time the comparison indicates that all discourses shape and mediate our perception of the life world.

Another aspect in which the form of presentation is likely to heighten the play's perceived intra-theatricality is the presentation of space. In addition to textual references to places in the life world, which are very common in highly extra-theatrical performances, such links are established through acting. Their recognition depends on the audience's background knowledge, but once they have identified the symbolic references, the highly theatrical form of presentation could become less important than the thematic extra-theatricality established by them. A good example is a scene in which all actresses adopt the movements of penguins, but no further information is given. Theoretically this scene could be interpreted in a great variety of ways – one might assume that Maggie visits a zoo or takes a family holiday to Antarctica, but familiarity with Margaret Thatcher's life story gives audiences a wealth of specific information that can help them to understand this as a reference to Margaret Thatcher's controversial decision to go to war with Argentina over a dispute concerning the Falkland Islands. Even though waddling human beings are not a daily sight on the Falkland Islands or a characteristic occurrence of the British–Argentine war, this image can thus reinforce the connection between the performance and the life world.

Another example of such highly intra-theatrical references to specific places in the life world is the Cabinet shuffle, but here a metaphorical level of interpretation is added. The presentation of a parliamentary speech in front of two rows of actresses, kneeling in the same formation as the benches in the Chambers of the House of Commons, creates the link to this specific location. An additional comment on the relationship between Margaret Thatcher and her Cabinet is made when the actresses adopt the behaviour of dogs to indicate that 'she treats them like dogs and that they are servile like dogs, but that they are also vicious, and that a dog can turn' (Cooke, 2006). Although Foursight's intention is to make a comment on a situation in the life world, the formal differences between the images from Parliament that audience members will have seen, probably on televised news, and those on stage creates additional distance between the two. Here again, it remains to be seen whether the form or the thematic link outweigh the other in the audience's perception.

Compared to the performances discussed in Chapter 3, where the scenography mainly evoked a general idea of place that supports, or in the case of *Vincent in Brixton* heightens, their extra-theatricality, *Thatcher – the Musical!* contains more visual references to specific places, not only in the stage action, but also in the design.

The black door to 10 Downing Street is clearly recognisable for an audience familiar with television news. The strong reference to the life world is, however, accompanied by a range of other elements that emphasise the production's theatricality: the stairs leading away from the door and the central position of the piano are reminiscent of the sets often used for dance scenes in MGM musicals. In the final scene, these formal differences become even more pronounced when Diva Thatcher, played by a black actress in a decidedly un-Thatcherite, glittery costume, enters through the door of No. 10. For this last Maggie the corrugated iron above has turned into a blinking disco decoration and the opening door reveals a glittering curtain.

The design used to introduce Narrator Maggie, whose reminiscences provide a frame for the presentation of her life, is also particularly intra-theatrical: although her living room does not contain any particularly unusual items, its location within a giant handbag suggests that in this section of the performance formal intra-theatricality might also outweigh thematic references. This scenographic decision reflects the

Thatcher – the Musical! by Foursight Theatre (David Finchett)

role of Narrator Maggie, just as the glittery costume with a feather boa supports the intra-theatricality of Diva Maggie: in the same way that few spectators will interpret the appearance of Diva Maggie as a revelation that the PM had unknown hobbies and pursued a secret career as a singer, the narrator is clearly not intended to replicate the way in which Margaret Thatcher is likely to look back on her life. The inclusion of her as a narrator figure is similar to an apparently autobiographical situation created in many plays, for example *The Bitches' Ball* by Penny Dreadful Theatre (2007) or *Marlene* by Pam Gems (1996), where an older character re-tells his or her life with hindsight, but apparently from the biographee's own point of view. Narrator Maggie, however, is not endowed with characteristics likely to be shared by her life world model. Instead her comments on her actions and words demonstrate a detachment from her actions that resemble the perspective of the company, and potentially many members of the audience. The quotation that socialism was comparable to 'trying to cure leukaemia with leeches' is accompanied by the comment, 'I really said that' (Foursight, 2005, p. 21), suggesting that Narrator Maggie is fully aware that this view could be seen as highly offensive or even ridiculous. It is equally unimaginable that the PM would make the following comment on her relationship with Ronald Reagan: 'If it wasn't for Denis and dear old Nancy, the story would have played out in a different way, know what I mean' (Foursight, 2005, p. 22). But endowing Narrator Maggie with such views that Margaret Thatcher did *not* utter greatly adds to the humour of the play. At the same time it emphasises the fact that Foursight Theatre do not attempt to reconstruct her life, but rather provide their comment on it, at times through the speeches of Narrator Maggie.

In the autobiographical frame the emphasis on humour and commentary might outweigh concerns about historical accuracy, but in other parts of the production the biographical reference and formal intra-theatricality are more equal, as the previous pages have shown. Maintaining this delicate balance is essential to both purposes, as the comic effect depends on the discrepancy between the audience's knowledge about the historical figure and the images and comments made on stage by a character based on her. Similarly the political comment would lose its poignancy if the link to the life world, and thus its potential to be understood as a comment on this world, was interrupted entirely. These effects can only be achieved if the audience's knowledge of the world beyond the stage is activated and they interpret the information from the play in that context (see Chapter 7).

Co-director Naomi Cooke (2006) confirms the twofold orientation of *Thatcher – the Musical!* which tries to 'tell a story accurately about a woman from our living history and it also comments on her politics' and explains that they used the biographical link as a 'tool' to 'comment on today's political machine, how that works, what the priorities are in politics, not only in policy, but actually how politics is played out in this country'. Her comment indicates their commitment to the present, rather than a focus on the past for past's sake. This is made explicit in the company's insistence that 'it is significant that she is still alive' (Cooke, 2006): acknowledging that 'she is very much in people's minds', or in other words recognising the importance of the audience's knowledge and perspective, she emphasises the impact of the present on our understanding of the past.

Just as the audience's memories of Margaret Thatcher and her government will influence the spectators' understanding of the play, Foursight also acknowledges that the production could have an impact on their views about the life world. This potential impact on the life world, or 'educational value' in Naomi Cooke's (2006) words, leads to a sense of obligation towards various people or groups that extends beyond the abstract notion of historical accuracy as a value in itself. Their feeling of responsibility towards the biographees is perhaps most plausible if one assumes that the production can alter the audience's perception of them (for a more detailed discussion of the ways in which their views changed, see Chapter 7). It is likely that the practitioners make such an assumption as they themselves admit that working on the production changed the way they think about the former PM. Kath Burlinson (2009) admits that despite her strong dislike she 'develop[ed] a grudging respect for her', an idea echoed in Deb Barnard's (2009) statement that she now had a 'different respect for Maggie'. Naomi Cooke (2006) reports that not only had her views on Thatcher as a person changed, but that revisiting Thatcher's time in government sometimes even made her 'question [her] own thinking' about political decisions. Although one could argue that those involved in the production also engaged with other discourses about the historical figure, it does not seem unreasonable for them to assume that the production based on these discourses can, in turn, change the spectator's thinking as well.

For a public figure like Mrs Thatcher this worry might be less pronounced, as she had been represented in a number of little-benevolent formats. Previous representations also offered the company a chance to make conjectures about her potential reaction, which in this case led to the encouraging observation that the PM had shown great tolerance towards satire made at her expense in television series such as *Spitting Image* (Cooke, 2006). On the other hand, their wish to respect their biographee is heightened by her 'frail stage in body and mind' (Cooke, 2006), which makes her more vulnerable and thus deserving of greater consideration than she did at the height of her power. This sense of a moral obligation extends to other people who had emotional ties with the central historical figure. Co-director Deb Barnard (2009) confirms that Carol Thatcher's attendance was 'a sensitive moment [as] it is her mother after all', and various practitioners report with great satisfaction that none of the audience members who were close to Margaret Thatcher objected to her portrayal. Their wish to deal respectfully with the figures represented in the play is thus guided by ethical considerations, but these are further accompanied by practical concerns: Foursight sought legal advice before the show's opening as they feared being 'sued left, right and centre' (Cooke, 2006). It is interesting to observe that the two practitioners who mentioned these concerns in interviews only did so after talking or writing about ethical ones. While legislation enshrines a person's right against 'words or matter containing an untrue imputation against his or her reputation' (Liberty, 2008), the moral obligation to avoid such conflicts seems to be predominant.

Their representation is thus influenced by the perception that Margaret Thatcher, as any human being, especially one who is in a frail state, deserves respect. On the other hand, her role as someone who used her power to the detriment of others demands consideration of their suffering as well. Since her political decisions affected the lives of many people in a fundamental way, the 'people who suffered under her' are of particular concern. Despite Naomi Cooke's (2006) insistence that *Thatcher – the Musical!* 'is a play about her [...] not about their [i.e. the victims'] voice', Foursight therefore addressed criticism 'that [they] did not give them long enough' in the first production by adding a scene in which the ghosts of her victims haunt Maggie. The concern expressed in these changes suggests that biographical performances can be regarded as comments on the life world to the extent that even figures from the life world who are not represented on stage are seen to hold a stake in the performance, as it indirectly affects them (see also Chapter 8).

The mutual influence between the two different worlds also leads to a sense of responsibility towards more abstract notions, in this case the practitioners' political views. The actress Kath Burlinson (2009) declares that she did 'not want to celebrate a person whose politics [she] abhor[s]' and Naomi Cooke (2006) feels that despite fair treatment it was important that 'the Tories [might] go away thinking "wasn't she fabulous"'. Her unease is shared by Burlinson, who had the impression that this has happened, as a 'group from a university Conservative society came and loved it'. Engaging with material from the life world, the practitioners seem to be concerned about maintaining their values from this context as well. This sense of obligation could be based both on the need to remain faithful to their own ideas and on social considerations. Naomi Cooke (2006) expresses satisfaction that 'on the whole the left really do get it' – the play then does not endanger Foursight's position among audiences who sympathise with the fact that 'none of the cast are Tories'.

The previous paragraphs show that for the practitioners involved in the production the intra-theatrical form does not diminish the production's extra-theatricality to such an extent that it reduces their sense of responsibility towards the people represented or violates a shared notion of what happens. Although they want to provide a commentary, they wish to do so within the limits of accepted discourses about

Margaret Thatcher. Many reviews suggest that despite the theatrical format, they achieve this aim: Michael Portillo (2006) describes the production as 'at times closer to a documentary than a musical'. Another reviewer uses language normally reserved for articles in the press: 'The story covers her era in power including the miners' strike, Falklands War and the Brighton bomb' (BBC, 2006). Nonetheless, a detailed examination of the way in which thematic extra-theatricality and formal intra-theatricality interact in *Thatcher – the Musical!* is necessary in order to establish whether audiences' reactions are similar to the views of the practitioners and many critics.

Insignificance

The discrepancy between intra- and extra-theatricality in *Insignificance* is likely to create fewer ethical dilemmas for theatre practitioners, mainly because Terry Johnson's play strengthens the link to the life world more through formal means than through the biographical link. As a result, it does not make a claim to present the historical characters 'as they really were'. For the practitioners the biographical link is not intended to indicate that the play provides information about the life world. Instead, its theatrical appeal is heightened by it. In other words, it does not make reference to Albert Einstein, Marilyn Monroe, Senator McCarthy and Joe DiMaggio to say something about the historical figures, but uses their celebrity to enhance its appeal as a play. The following paragraphs examine in more detail how rather spurious biographical links and formal extra-theatricality together with clearly intra-theatrical information about the characters can create a playful mode of 'as if'. Its balance between elements that are familiar from the life world and unexpected, and delightfully improbable, additions from Terry Johnson has made *Insignificance* a popular play that has been revived regularly since its first production at the Royal Court in 1982, and even led to a film recording released in 1985 (Roeg, 1985).

The discussion in this chapter is based on Samuel West's 2004 production at the Crucible (Sheffield). As with many other productions (e.g. Arkle Theatre, also 2004), the Crucible built on the indications of formal theatricality contained in Terry Johnson's script: the whole play is set in a hotel room, situated in New York as one of the characters informs the audience, and its duration is nearly identical to that of the performance. The continuous passing of time is only interrupted for the interval, a highly conventional element that is unlikely to draw attention to the play's status as theatre. While the specific time and place provided in the stage directions (Johnson, 1986, p. 3) are not available to spectators, the production team uses it for the basis of a strongly extra-theatrical stage and lighting design. The furniture of the hotel room echoes the uniformity of business hotels from the 1950s. Due to the sparseness of many hotel rooms, it is possible to create a space that resembles a stereotypical idea of such rooms in the life world in every detail bar the fourth wall. The impression that the audience is granted insight into the privacy of a room is enhanced further by lighting. As an inside location, the artificial light of the room is easy to recreate and its place in a wider context is suggested by the reflection of a neon advert outside the window and the orange light, imitating a sunrise towards the end of the play. Neil Austin (2009), the lighting designer, confirms that 'portraying the passing of time and other specific narrative elements' was their primary aim, even though the lighting additionally 'enhance[d] the story [...] through mood and atmosphere'. With the exception of the strobe lights used to indicate the explosion of an atomic bomb that haunts the Einstein-like physicist, these effects are so subtle, however, that they are unlikely to be perceived as noticeably theatrical by most audience members.

In this highly extra-theatrical setting the audience meets characters who bear close resemblance to four iconic figures from the 1950s: the Actress, a gorgeous blonde, who has her white, pleated skirt 'blown up around [her] goddam ears' while filming in New York (Johnson, 1986, p. 8), visits the Professor, a physicist who is called 'Daddy of the H bomb' and who had to avoid Dachau (Johnson, 1986, p. 6). They are later joined by her Ballplayer husband and the Senator whose job it is to scare those invited to talk to the Un-American Activities Committee (Johnson, 1986, p. 6) and who is interested in the Professor's political affiliations. In a programme note for the first production, Terry Johnson 'announce[d] that there are no impersonations in his new play' (Barber, 1982, p. 383), but the similarities above are sufficient to suggest that the characters are based on specific historical figures. Since Terry Johnson does not use the names of any historical figure (for more on the lack of names, see below), these similarities have to suffice to allow *readers* to identify them as biographical characters. Mostly, however, visual elements and sound are used to enhance these similarities. In the words of Frances Barber, who reviewed the first production at the Royal Court, 'everything is done to make us believe we are witnessing an encounter of Albert Einstein, Marilyn Monroe, her husband Joe DiMaggio and Senator Joe McCarthy' (Barber, 1982, p. 383).

The means of creating a visual resemblance between two of the characters and their famous counterparts seem to be similar in most productions of *Insignificance*, as they all use a small number of token elements to evoke iconic images of Einstein and Monroe. For the Professor the wild, grey hairstyle is sufficient to evoke Arthur Sasse's photograph of the scientist sticking out his tongue.[2] The Actress may enter with 1950s sunglasses and a headscarf, but shortly afterwards she reveals a head of blonde, curled hair and the famous white pleated dress from *The Seven Year Itch*, under which padding helps Mary Stockwell to recreate Monroe's fuller and curvy body. Although neither she nor Nicholas Prevost bear a strong natural resemblance to Marilyn or Einstein, these elements seem to be sufficient to create an association between them for the Sheffield audiences, as anecdotal evidence from the author's first visit to the Crucible shows: photographs of the actors were displayed in a corner of the foyer, and audiences used the names of Einstein and Monroe when referring to these pictures.[3] For McCarthy and Joe DiMaggio, on the other hand, no iconic images are available, so their recognition depends to a higher degree on the information given in the text, such as the Ballplayer's relationship to Marilyn Monroe or the Senator's fight against Communism.

Despite the lack of names, the impact of the association between these characters and their historical counterparts has the same effect on the practitioners' work as in more extra-theatrical productions where names are used. The director and the actors report that they did extensive research into the people and the period. For Sam West (2005), the amount of 'homework' for a director depends partly on the degree of fame – in preparing for *Insignificance*, he felt that there was an almost 'endless amount' of it related to Marilyn Monroe and to Albert Einstein. In addition to the extensive research for his own information, which included a visit to 'the New York public library photo library' from where he 'brought back about a hundred photocopies of everything from Einstein as a baby to the interiors of 1950's hotel rooms' (West, 2005), he also organised information sessions for the other people involved in the production and passed on insights from his research to them. His approach thus not only reflects his need to find further information, but also his wish to encourage other members of the production team.

As in the highly extra-theatrical productions discussed in the previous chapter, the results of this research are clearly audible in *Insignificance* as well. All actors adopt an accent; Einstein speaks American English with a strong German accent, for example, and Mary Stockwell also imitates Marilyn Monroe's tone of voice. This confirms the impression that the manner of speaking is regarded as a key aspect in establishing the bio-graphical link, and anecdotal evidence from this production indicates that audiences share this view: the imitation of a cooing greeting in Marilyn Monroe's voice before her first appearance on stage is greeted with laughter on many evenings. These references to specific features are further supported by a more generic extra-theatricality of the costumes. With the exception of the Actress's white dress all other costumes are held in a style reminiscent of the 1950s and are appropriate for the age and profession of the characters: the Senator wears a suit, in contrast to Joe DiMaggio who is wearing a t-shirt with less formal trousers.

Despite all these extra-theatrical elements the characters of *Insignificance* are fundamentally different from many of those discussed previously, as the specific and generic similarities are restricted to the elements discussed above. Unlike the highly extra-theatrical characters in *Vincent in Brixton*, they do not have the psychological complexity attributed to human beings in the life world. As the actor Patrick O'Kane confirms (2009), 'as long as you have the costume and the hairdo, that's all you need [for Marilyn Monroe] and then you have the liberty to do what you want to do. It's the same for the Einstein character: as long as you have the hair and the accent, you can do what you want'. Here the token elements are not the basis for the creation of a life-like character, but rather an opportunity to introduce an archetypal figure by referring to a person who incarnates many of the key aspects of such an archetype. In other words, it is highly economical to present a Marilyn Monroe-like char-acter, as the biographical reference automatically establishes the idea of a not necessarily highly intelligent but very attractive blonde. Through the link to this famous figure, these characteristics are evoked even before the character has her first appearance on stage, simply through the imitation of her voice.

The fact that the use of biographical figures serves the development of the plot, rather than the creation of a strong link to the life world, is underlined further by the absence of names. The script refers to them as representatives of archetypal images of their profession: the Actress, the Professor, the Senator and the Ballplayer. Although the similarities described above mean that audiences are likely to imagine a historical figure, these biographical links are evoked entirely through visual and vocal resemblance, as well as contextual information. With regard to the character of Joe DiMaggio, Patrick O'Kane (2009) even observes that Terry Johnson uses many character traits that contradict histori-cal sources and discourses about the historical baseball star on whom his character is modelled. He observes that the 'real Joe DiMaggio was a very elegant man, sophisticated, not as sophisticated as the Einsteins or Arthur Millers [...] Marilyn Monroe was genuinely attracted to, [but] he was reasonably articulate and intelligent'. Nevertheless, 'that is not how it was written in the play', where the Ballplayer is 'this New York, Italian bull character [because] that is his function' in order to emphasise the difference between the visceral Professor, whose brain attracts the Actress, and the Ballplayer's attraction through 'physical power, strength and the fact that he had a lot of spunk in him essentially' (O'Kane, 2009). In other words, the references to other discourses about the historical figures are abandoned as soon as they do not serve the plot or character constellation. This choice is supported by the actor, who emphasises that he 'would always choose what is theatrically useful above what is historically accurate, because it is about serving the story that you're telling' (O'Kane, 2009). For *Insignificance* the sense of obligation to the life world is subordinate to the sense of obligation to the story.

Paradoxically, the story nevertheless relies to a strong degree on the audience's knowledge about the life world. The biographical material might be used to provide a shorthand for the references to stereotypes, but its comic elements rely extensively on a comparison between the life world and the play. As Geoff King observes in the context of film, 'comedy tends to involve a departure [...] from what are considered the "normal" routines of life' (King, 2002, p. 5) and many of the intra-theatrical elements gain their comic potential through a narrow, but delightful, discrepancy between the expectations raised by the biographical link and the events in the play. In part this is done on a more generic level by explicitly negating the rules that govern the life world, for example those of social interaction. When the Actress, the Senator and the Ballplayer invite themselves to the Professor's hotel room in the middle of the night, they ignore conventions that demand that the occupier be granted some privacy at such an hour. Similarly, the Actress's attempt to seduce the Professor, whose intellect she admires greatly, is only comic if seen as an inversion of the cliché that older, successful men try to seduce young, attractive women. Other elements of the plot use exaggeration of specific events in the life world to create a comic effect. Terry Johnson thus builds on discourses that suggest Einstein supported socialism – for example his article in the first edition of the Socialist journal *The Monthly Review* (No Year) and the suspicions this aroused – but exaggerates the consequences to a degree that most audience members will find improbable: in the play Senator McCarthy pursues Einstein into his hotel room in New York in the middle of the night to convince the scientist to give testimony. The comic effect created by the meeting of this character constellation is heightened further through condensation: suggesting that Marilyn's attempt at seducing Einstein with her understanding of relativity, McCarthy's efforts to convince the physicist to appear before the Committee for Un-American Activities, Joe DiMaggio's jealous pursuit of his wife and Marilyn Monroe's miscarriage all happen during a single night sets a fast, comic pace, but emphasises the theatricality of the situation further. With characters who are 'consistent with real people' but nevertheless 'use[d] to farcical effect', as Sam West (2005) points out, the plot subverts the rules governing the life world to create a highly intra-theatrical situation out of generic and specific extra-theatrical links.

As a result, the practitioners feel less responsibility towards the figures they portray compared to their obligation towards the audience and the play. Sam West confirms that it is important to 'embody the characters convincingly enough', but explains that this is necessary to 'put the audience at their ease', not necessarily to do justice to the historical figures who are represented. Patrick O'Kane (2009) echoes this idea, claiming that, as an actor, he feels obliged to fulfil 'an imaginative contract with the audience [...] make yourself, your character credible'. In *Insignificance*, credibility does not primarily arise from consistency with other discourses about the biographical characters, but also from consistency with the situation presented. As an example O'Kane refers to his character's costume. Although a 1950s suit might have reflected Joe DiMaggio's style, O'Kane (2009) insisted on playing him in 'a period shirt and high waisted trousers [that] emphasised [...] his personal energy and physical drive' as he felt this would support his character's 'dramatic function', i.e. the Actress's husband whose physicality is opposed to the Professor's intellectual attraction. *Insignificance* 'must be inspired by biography, not limited by it' (West, 2005). The evocation of biographical links facilitates telling the story, but the effect of *Insignificance* can only be achieved if they are then challenged through contradictory information.

One could argue that the idea of biographical reconstruction is mainly undermined with contradicting information, i.e. on a thematic level, while its presentation is mainly intra-theatrical. Nonetheless, there are a few moments in the Sheffield production when the style of action helps to interrupt theatrical illusion further. At various points the actors direct amusing lines that stem from their conversation with a fellow character towards the audience. In the words of Bert O. States, they abandon the convention of the audience as unacknowledged eavesdropper and a representational mode of acting and adopt a collective mode, in which they indirectly reveal themselves as individuals and recognise the presence of the audience (States, 1985). Acknowledging the audience in such a way is typical of comedies and other genres that recognise their status as theatre, but it contradicts the concept of reconstructionist historical plays that pretend to recreate a moment of the past on stage.

Unlike *Thatcher – the Musical!* where Reconstructionism is rejected mainly through formal means, the undermining of historical references through contradicting information in *Insignificance* creates a different effect. Lowering the link to the life world, the practitioners' – and presumably the audience's – interest is no longer sustained by their wish to explore an aspect of the life world. Where the actresses involved in Foursight's production declared that they were intrigued by the idea of making a play *about* the former PM, Patrick O'Kane (2009) cites the 'good story and interesting situation' as the main reason for his interest in the part of the Ballplayer. One of the main attractions of the story could be the humour that is borne from the constant shifting between extra- and intra-theatrical means described above. Although biographical material is not indispensable for creating a similar character constellation and plot, the specific link to the life world helps to emphasise the incongruity between the expectations this raises and the play, thus heightening the comic potential. At the same time the quick evocation of these archetypes through historical models allows the play to progress at a fast pace, facilitating comic timing.

The presentation of an unlikely, secret life of these four icons could provide the added appeal of a tongue-in-cheek glimpse behind the public façade of these celebrities. Director Sam West (2005) suggests that 'seeing someone you thought you knew go beyond your expectation' is one of the attractions of the play. For Patrick O'Kane (2009) this joy is heightened, as it decreases the distance many spectators will feel due to the achievements of these figures, which are unattainable to most people: 'They are both very famous people who are reduced to something [...] neurotic with everyday needs that you or I would have'. Presenting the characters without names places the spectators even closer to them, as it allows them the triumph of recognition, of feeling 'in the know'. The choice of an improbable situation, on the other hand, distances *Insignificance* from the openly voyeuristic nature of celebrity culture as practised in *Hello! Magazine* or similar publications. As it does not pretend to reveal any actual information about the historical models in the life world, it allows the audiences to revel in the playful pretence of revealing an unknown side to Einstein and Monroe while distancing themselves from the guilt of the voyeur.

Terry Johnson's play could thus be described as the opposite to *Thatcher – the Musical!*: where the latter uses intra-theatrical elements to provide an entertaining insight into the life and legacy of a famous figure in the life world, *Insignificance* employs extra-theatricality to 'revel in its own theatricality' (O'Kane, 2009). Without extensive meta-biographical elements the play could thus be considered as an example of post-modernist theatre that combines different types of discourses without respecting the labels, such as fact or fiction. Yet, it does this not to further a theoretical agenda or to challenge the way in which audiences engage with the life world openly, but to provide entertainment. The following chapter examines productions in which the postmodern challenge to Reconstructionism permeates their form to a greater extent, sustaining a meta-level throughout the plays.

5
Meta-Biography: Biographers on Stage and Non-Traditional Structures

Introduction

The creation and undermining of authenticity discussed in the previous two chapters demonstrates the continuing power of historical references to establish a close link between the world on stage and the life world, between theatrical characters and specific historical or contemporary figures. Although in the functional approach chosen this has been interpreted as an effect created by productions, not an intrinsic quality, the views of practitioners show that the idea of a trans-world identity of biographical characters (Ronen, 1994, p. 59), of their existence in the life and the stage world in a similar, recognisable form, remains at the heart of their work. The expectation that art depends on the life world or that it is usually defined as 'representation, likeness, imitation, resemblance and verisimilitude' (Postlewait, 2003, p. 1114) is confirmed by plays such as *Insignificance*: it undermines the notion of trans-world identity, but cannot obliterate it.[1] Through this it plays with the notions of fact and fiction, but it never explicitly questions these categories.

Other practitioners, however, have not only adopted the Postmodern liberty of a playful engagement with the tenets of Modernism, but have put their interrogation at the heart of performances themselves. This means that over the last 40 years biographical theatre has become increasingly self-reflexive and a variety of plays have undertaken an exploration of the process of biography, rather than presenting specific life stories. Similar to the theoretical texts discussed in Chapter 2, these plays use our expectation of biographical reconstruction as a starting point and then challenge the feasibility of biographical representation and the validity of the assumptions on which it is based.

Self-Reflexive Elements in Biographical Theatre

Apart from Stephanie Kramer (2000), few authors have recognised a wider trend to shift theoretical arguments about different ways of dealing with the past from secondary literature into the plays themselves, although many discussions of individual plays examine meta-biographical elements. This chapter thus begins with a short overview of different ways in which reflection on biographical representation can be integrated into performances, before proceeding to a discussion of two examples of theatrical meta-biography. As in previous chapters, the examples chosen cannot be considered to be representative, as the variety of content, forms and theoretical background in meta-biographical plays can almost rival that found in less self-reflexive performances. They can, however, give an insight into some of the variety of approaches outlined in the first part.

Here Stephanie Kramer's distinction between explicit and implicit meta-biography can introduce helpful terminology, creating an analogy to the differentiation between thematic and formal extra-theatricality that is made in the previous chapters. In parallel to the inclusion of biographical material, explicit meta-biography introduces reflection on the process of life writing by integrating biographical activity into the *plot* of a performance (Kramer, 2000, p. 127), often through the presence of a biographer. Showing their attempts at reconstructing past lives can then identify different reasons why these authors cannot comply with the idea of the disinterested, objective recorder of fact. In *Variations on a Theme by Clara Schumann* (Sheila Yeger, 1991) or *The Snow Palace* (Pam Gems, 1998), for example, the writers' own experiences clearly shape the way in which they perceive the subjects of their investigations. Louise in Yeger's play reads Clara Schumann's relationship with her father through her own experience of her abusive and dominating father. Similarly, the biographer in *The Snow Palace*, Stanislawa Przybyszewska, presents the protagonist of the French Revolution as reflections of her own experiences. Danton's pursuit of power reminds her of her selfish, abusive father, while she identifies with Robespierre's idealism. Their own painful experiences in the past thus overshadow their understanding of their biographical subjects. In *Arcadia* and *Making History* (Tom Stoppard, 1993; Brian Friel, 1989) the biographers have an equally strong, but more conscious, influence on the lives they write: the scholars in Tom Stoppard's play hope that sensational revelations about their subjects will further their career and Bishop Lombard openly declares that the aim of his work is to 'offer [the Irish] Hugh O'Neill as a national hero' (Friel, 1989, p. 67), and that his presentation of events is guided by this aim. In a comic variation of self-interested biographical zeal, Alan Bennett's *Kafka's Dick* (1986) presents an encounter between Kafka's father and Sydney, an ardent Kafka fan working in the insurance industry. Sensing a chance of being judged more favourably by posterity, Kafka senior tries to convince Sydney to write a new biography of his son with a positive, benign father image, suggesting that this would allow Sydney to escape his much-hated day job.

Mostly explicit references to biographical activities relate to writers – references to the representation of lives in theatre are relatively rare. Among the few exceptions are Timberlake Wertenbaker's *After Darwin* (1998), which alternates scenes from rehearsals for a play about Darwin's voyage and the play in the play, and Polly Teale's *Brontë* (2005), where the actresses take on the roles, costumes and accents of the Brontë sisters in front of the audience. The small number of plays that place the theatrical re-telling of lives at the centre could suggest that meta-biographical elements do not take into account the specific medium of performance, but merely echo self-reflexivity in narrative forms of life writing. This impression is countered by the second form of meta-biography, implicit references to its status as artefact rather than neutral reconstruction. Here the inherently theatrical nature of performances is emphasised with the help of thematic patterns (see Hawthorne, 1994, p. 117), intertextual references or elements that call attention to the mediating influence of language and the conventions behind the presentation of space, time and characters (see Kramer, 2000, pp. 130–1). Implicit self-reflexivity is not explained but produced (Kramer, 2000, p. 129: 'Inszenierung von Biographie'), leaving it to the spectators to translate the structural aspects into statements and ideas about biography. As such, implicit meta-biography makes wider use of the unique features of stage performance. This can take the form of alternative structures to substitute for chronology, based, for instance, on associations and memories, as in Sheila Yeger's *Variations on a Theme by Clara Schumann* (1991) or, at least partly, based on juxtaposition, as in Liz Lochhead's *Mary Queen of Scots Got Her Head Chopped Off*, which will be discussed later in this chapter. At the same time the two plays undermine modern assumptions about the unity of their characters: Liz Lochhead uses doubling to create visible parallels between Mary, Elizabeth and their maid servants and commoners, and Sheila Yeger introduces five characters whose costumes suggest that 'any of them could be Louise' (Yeger, 1991, p. 174), the biographer at the centre of the play. Instead of echoing the idea that human beings are unique individuals with a relatively coherent and continuous personality, this unity is visually deconstructed on stage. In Dominic Dromgoole's *Marriage in Disguise* this challenge to our assumptions about the nature of human beings is taken even further through the introduction of three different characters called Molière. Although each of them recognises his fellow Molières as earlier or later versions of himself, they reject any similarity and describe the transition from one phase to another as a process of killing the predecessor (see Dromgoole, 2000, p. 47). The script and the visual distinction between the characters thus denies the assumption that life writing can trace the way in which personality is shaped through the accumulation of experience and the belief in the unity of the biographical subject.

Finally, the mediating function of language is often exposed. This can take place through intertextual references, such as the parallels between the biographical characters of poet and scholar A.E. Housman and his fellow students at Oxford and the characters from Jerome K. Jerome's *Three Men in a Boat* in Tom Stoppard's *The Invention of Love* (1997) or the references to *The Importance of Being Earnest* in *Travesties* (1974), another Stoppard play about historical figures, in this case Lenin, James Joyce and the Dadaist poet Tristan Tzara. A similar effect is achieved by the combination of very different styles of language, including modern-day terminology for institutions such as the Home Office and William Blake's poetry in *Tyger* (Mitchell, 1971).

In the examples of implicit meta-biography mentioned above, the elements that undermine traditional structures are introduced in the plays' scripts. A similar effect of self-reflexivity can also be created in performances by introducing elements that create distance, freeing theatrical devices from 'the stamp of familiarity' (Brecht in Willett, 1978, p. 192). In the context of theatrical biography, Brecht's concept of alienation, of making well-known elements feel strange in order to draw attention to their artificiality, is not used to promote changes in contemporary society, but to question the way in which we see the past and past lives. Using a self-reflexive acting style that reveals the actors' presence as creator of a role rather than emphasising a representational mode where their presence seems to disappear behind the character (States, 1985) can be achieved in a variety of ways, including the overt acknowledgement of the audience's presence, costumes that emphasise the actors' bodies over those of the characters, especially modern-day dress that disrupts the impression of historical reconstruction, or the use of acting styles, such as music hall or comedy, that are traditionally associated with intra-theatrical modes of performance. A similar effect can be achieved with scenographic elements that underline the 'physical reality of the resources of the stage house, the lighting equipment, flying winches and associated machinery' (Baugh, 2005, p. 47), rather than creating a seemingly life-like, extra-theatrical world.

Although all of these self-reflexive elements in the performance or the playtext can promote reflection about biographical representation, none of them necessarily has this effect, especially in isolation. In fact, many of these theatrical devices were analysed in the previous chapters, i.e. in the context of plays that were not seen as overtly meta-biographical. The use of thematic intra-theatricality in *Insignificance*, for example, is complemented by formal aspects when the performers address comic lines to the audience rather than their fellow characters, thus breaking the illusion that the audience is an unacknowledged eavesdropper. In *Thatcher – the Musical!* the costumes and wigs, as well as the intense doubling of the main character, provide a strong visual challenge to the pretence that the past is recreated on stage. Nonetheless it can be assumed that the thematic parallels between the production and the audience's life world will balance these intra-theatrical elements and allow a biographical interpretation (see Chapter 7). Even in *Rendition Monologues* and *Gladiator Games*, the two plays discussed in the context of high extra-theatricality and a strong dedication to authenticity, the epic, narrative structures of the documents quoted in them could be regarded as potentially self-reflexive, as they are more likely to draw attention to language than everyday speech presented in dialogues. The discussion has shown, however, that such elements do not significantly disrupt the impression that the stage world closely echoes the life world if they are used in isolation or are balanced by highly extra-theatrical aspects.

Such isolated instances of self-reflexivity are, therefore, not discussed in this chapter. Instead it focuses on performances that 'systematically draw attention to [the plays'] status as [...] artefacts in order to pose questions about the relationship between fiction and reality' (Waugh, 1984, p. 2), specifically about the process of representing figures from the life world on stage, its possibilities and limitations and our expectations of it. Although some plays present a biographer at work without recourse to implicitly meta-biographical elements, most performances with such a sustained level of meta-biography combine structural elements typical of performance and the presentation of biographical activity. In other words, the distinction between implicit and explicit meta-biography made above is a useful analytical tool, but should not be misunderstood as a typology of plays. The combination of implicit and explicit references to the process of biography also balances the emphasis on writing and language introduced by the predominant presence of writers who pursue a life story, which does not necessarily differ greatly from meta-biography presented in a narrative format. As a result, plays that employ structural means specific to the theatrical medium to draw attention to their own nature as life *stories* are more interesting in terms of performance analysis as well.

The two performances discussed in this chapter fulfil the criterion of sustained self-reflexivity: in *Copenhagen* the characters are trying to reconstruct the story of a meeting, acting simultaneously as each others' biographer and narrator of their own interpretation of the events that occurred. At the same time, however, the presentation of different versions of the same moment helps to theatrically visualise their difficulties in agreeing on a single, shared version. In *Mary Queen of Scots Got Her Head Chopped Off* by Liz Lochhead self-reflexivity is not introduced through explicit references to the process of creating biography, but through implicit means. Here the narrator figure, La Corbie, who acts as a mediator between the events and the audience, co-exists with a structure that emphasises self-reflexivity, as it is mainly based on juxtaposition. Furthermore, the use of doubling to show different aspects of the central characters and the shift from historical characters to contemporary children in the last scene underline the impact of the specific perspective from which Mary's and Elizabeth's conflict is told. In the following the meta-biographical potential of these elements will be discussed in further detail.

Copenhagen

Michael Frayn's play stages a posthumous meeting of German nuclear physicist Werner Heisenberg with his former Danish friend and mentor, Niels Bohr, and his wife Margrethe. Together they try to reconstruct what happened during Heisenberg's visit to Copenhagen in 1941. Although they agree on the main events that happened during this meeting, the different roles imposed on them by war – Heisenberg as a citizen of Nazi Germany, which occupied Denmark at the time, and the Bohrs as Jewish citizens and later refugees in the US, where Niels Bohr was marginally involved in the allied nuclear programme – created a climate of distrust and a struggle to agree on a mutually acceptable version of their more minute actions and the intentions behind them. Due to these difficulties they are forced to start their attempt at reconstruction again and again, only to find that detailed analysis of their reasons seems to blur them rather than making them clearer. Following the first production by the National Theatre, directed by Michael Blakemore (1998),

Copenhagen has been revived many times. In this chapter, the original production and a revival at the Edinburgh Lyceum in 2009 are discussed together as they strongly resemble each other, perhaps as a consequence of a similar directorial approach that 'serves the play' rather than imposing a recognisable directorial style on it (Frayn, 2004).[2]

In addition to the directorial approach, the similarities between many productions of *Copenhagen* could also be attributed to the complexity of the script. Michael Frayn emphasises the ethical conflicts connected to the physicists' work on nuclear fission as citizens of enemy factions competing to produce an atomic weapon. He also uses the physical theories they formulated, including indeterminacy and complementarity, to describe their difficulties in recovering the past. The result is a highly complex script that works on different levels, and consequently allows a variety of interpretative approaches. Many reviewers suggest a biographical reading that focuses on the 'portrait of a relationship disintegrating' (Anon., 2002a, p. 29), and this understanding could be seen as the basis for the controversy that followed its first production. Donna Soto-Morettini's (2002) article overcomes this concentration on the accurate and justified representation of the two men and relates their discussion to different historiographical theories instead. While this approach stands out from the straightforward interpretation as a life story, it has not often been adopted by academics. In this context the presentation of science in the play (Stewart, 1999; Shepherd-Barr, 2002, 2006) has raised more interest, and some reviewers agreed that its philosophical inquiry and its ability to 'settle on an abstract notion [and] embod[y it] in characters' (Clapp, 2004) was its main achievement. The short introduction to the range of interpretative approaches shows that the meta-biographical reading suggested here cannot only address one aspect of such a multi-faceted performance. Concentrating on performances, rather than the scripts, and including the voices of the author and some of the actors involved in the two productions, it can, nevertheless shed new light on this particular aspect.

Posthumous Reflection

The illusion of biographical reconstruction is rejected from the beginning of Michael Frayn's play when Heisenberg announces that 'now [they] are all dead and gone' he will 'make one more attempt' to explain the motives for his journey in 1941 (Frayn, 2000, p. 4). While the posthumous perspective on a life echoes the traditional biographical practice of re-examining a life after the subject's death, i.e. at a point where no alternatives are possible any more (see Chapter 2), the fact that the characters try to recapture a moment in their *own* past establishes clearly intra-theatrical circumstances, as one can safely assume that few figures from the life world will have the opportunity to review their own lives posthumously in the company of their fellow mortal beings. Michael Frayn regards this structure as a clear departure from plays where 'the events are presented as being actual events, happening in front of our eyes' (Wolf, 2003), explaining that it creates a situation where the 'real events that did occur' enter into a world of discourse where they can be 'endlessly disputed'. Apart from introducing a different ontological status, this situation also endows the characters with abilities that are different from those of their life world models at the time of their meeting in Copenhagen. As Tom Mannion (2009), who played Niels Bohr at the Lyceum Theatre, observes, the chat between Frayn's characters is marked by their ability 'to come out of time and comment' on their behaviour at that moment with the benefit of hindsight.

In both productions of *Copenhagen* the oneiric quality created by this 'dreamlike collapse of discrete time levels' (Barnett, 2005, p. 145) is supported by the creation of a neutral space that does not echo any specific type of location in the life world. Staged in the round in the original production by the National Theatre, one side of the stage is set apart from the audience by a curved, low, sand-coloured wall with a door that is not reminiscent of any specific door in the life world. The only elements on stage are three, relatively neutral, chairs that can be rearranged freely in different constellations. At the Lyceum, a proscenium stage was used, but the scenography was similarly neutral. The area upstage right is dominated by a sculpture consisting of three columns covered in letters and writing, which could at best evoke a symbolic reference to their work/the controversy. As in the first production, neutral chairs are the only element used to demarcate different areas of the stage in different scenes. In their neutrality, these spaces do not support the idea of a reconstruction, nor do they explicitly present the events as fictional.

At the same time the neutral spaces offer an extremely flexible environment in which the shifts from the characters' post mortem discussions to their memories and back can be seamlessly carried out. In both productions these changes are supported by the lighting design used. One reviewer suggests that the emptiness of the stage means that it is mainly 'transformed by John Comiskey's lighting, which sometimes creates the airy atmosphere of a city in springtime, at others the stifling claustrophobia of an interrogation chamber, as Heisenberg sits to defend his transgressions' (Anon., 2002a, p. 29). The effect of lighting in the Lyceum production is similar: with the help of spotlights and different colours the re-enactment of their memory is set apart from their posthumous conversation. The lighting design thus supports the differentiation of the two time levels and, at the same time, creates an environment in which every attempt at reconstruction can, through the varying arrangements of chairs and light, find its space and atmosphere. Michael Blakemore (cited in Wu, 2000), the director of the National Theatre production, suggests that the round stage emphasises the arbitrariness of their memories, but the Edinburgh production creates a similar effect on a proscenium stage. The limited, but effective, use of scenographic elements thus offers an appropriate setting for the self-reflexive presentation of the (auto-)biographical processes introduced in the plot.

Unreliable Memories and Intentions

The first lines of the play which introduce the idea that they will recapitulate what happened 'now that we're all dead and gone [when] no one can be hurt' (Frayn, 2000, p. 3) also draw immediate attention to these processes, as their shared attempt at reconstructing their meeting establishes the characters as biographers of their friends' and autobiographers of their own stories, and allows the presentation of the same event from three different perspectives. Unlike the academics in *Arcadia* or Bishop Lombard in *Making History*, Frayn's characters are not presented as openly manipulative. Nevertheless they are caught in their own perception that is influenced by their experience and identity. Niels' and Margrethe's memories of 1924 are a good example that demonstrates how the different circumstances under which they lived these moments lead to unavoidable differences. Niels remembers the time of Heisenberg's arrival in Copenhagen mainly in terms of their work. Only Margrethe's gentle reminder that she had just given birth to their fifth son a week earlier triggers any memories of family life for this time (Frayn, 2000, p. 57). Neglecting the contribution these lines make to the characterisation of the Bohrs and their comic effect, they demonstrate that their view of the past, at least initially, differs according to the intensity with which they experienced an event. This unintentional, even unavoidable, restriction of seeing the world from a specific position thus echoes postmodern criticism of the biographer's objectivity even more closely than the deliberate and calculating adoption of a specific position does in the plays mentioned above. As a result, the characters' roles in *Copenhagen* could be seen as particularly suited for stimulating reflection on the possibility of creating an accurate reconstruction of past events, as it demonstrates that no reconstruction can reflect all their memories at the same time.

In addition to the multiplicity of voices that raise questions about the possibility of an objective, i.e. interpersonal, reconstruction of the past, the characters in *Copenhagen* also undermine the assumptions made about human nature in empiricist biography (see Chapter 2). In contrast to plays that create highly intra-theatrical characters that subvert our expectation of human beings as rational, psychologically motivated individuals who possess a core feature of characteristics that give them a unified personality, the Bohrs and Werner Heisenberg are presented in a highly extra-theatrical way. Although no longer subject to biological constraints in their posthumous reminiscence, Frayn's speeches and the actors' approach create extra-theatrical characters: their interactions follow the basic principles of communication described in the analysis of *Vincent in Brixton* (see Chapter 3) and their speech patterns suggest that each of them possesses a specific idiolect, using specific phrases, such as Niels Bohr's 'not to criticise' (Frayn, 2000, p. 24), and adapts to different circumstances, for example when Bohr addresses his colleague Heisenberg, or his wife Margrethe. The commitment to extra-theatrical speech is also visible in the Lyceum's decision to mark their different cultural origin by asking Owen Oakshott to use a German accent.[3] In addition, the characters' behaviour echoes the descriptions of their character traits, suggesting that they possess unique personalities. Thus Niels Bohr tends to find more favourable interpretations for Heisenberg's behaviour than his wife, a benevolence that is echoed in his description of him as 'a good man from first to last' (Frayn, 2000, p. 91). Following our predominant concept of human psychology, these core features of their character are influenced both by individual differences and by the accumulation of experiences, an expectation that is made explicit in the play through the juxtaposition of the characters' experiences and insights had during their war-time meeting and the broader horizon they possess as commentators after the end of their life (see for example Frayn, 2000, p. 80). Paradoxically the extra-theatrical nature of the characters is thus supported by the very element that denies an interpretation of *Copenhagen* as a life-like reconstruction from the very beginning of the play.

On the basis of the characters' apparent extra-theatricality, *Copenhagen* proceeds to undermine one of the core assumptions about the nature of human beings on which empiricist biography is based, namely the belief in rationality and intentionality. At the beginning of the play, the characters voice the belief that their actions follow clearly identifiable intentions, and that these motives, not necessarily the actions themselves, are the basis on which they should be evaluated. Thus Margrethe initially objects to her husband's plan to continue their habit of 'invit[ing] an old friend to dinner' (Frayn, 2000, p. 9), as she fears that under the different circumstances, their hospitality towards a German citizen 'might appear to be collaborating' to their fellow Danes. Under different circumstances the same action might be misinterpreted as the expression of an attitude she is keen to reject. Believing that their behaviour can be seen as the outward display of their state of mind, the Bohrs and Heisenberg thus concentrate their efforts in reconstructing a shared memory of their fateful meeting in 1941 on identifying their motivations: 'Heisenberg, why did you come to Copenhagen in 1941' (Frayn, 2000, p. 53)? To their great dismay, they have to discover, however, that the reasons behind their actions cannot only be interpreted in very different ways according to different perspectives: while Heisenberg insists that he failed to calculate the quantity of plutonium needed to develop a bomb as he did not want to provide a bomb for the murderous regime that supported his research, the Bohrs are convinced that only genuine lack of understanding could have prevented such a brilliant mathematician as Heisenberg from carrying out a relatively simple calculation (Frayn, 2000, pp. 85 and 82). Their initial belief in reasonable behaviour is shaken even further when Heisenberg himself cannot remember his own intentions; in recollection, possible motivations appear to him as blurred as the faces of colleagues he might or might not have met during his visit to Copenhagen (Frayn, 2000, pp. 7 and 77). Niels Bohr even 'doubt[s] if [Heisenberg] ever really knew himself', an idea echoed by Margrethe who suggests that 'the person who wanted to know most of all [why he had come to Copenhagen] was Heisenberg himself' (Frayn, 2000, p. 35). The initial belief that discovering a person's rational intentions is a vital aspect of reconstructing their life story is thus eroded as the play progresses, introducing further doubt about the possibility of empiricist biography.

Indeterminacy in the Play's Structure

These explicit elements of criticism are reflected in the structure of the play: instead of a linear development that leads towards a solution, the same situations are repeated in various versions. Played out one after another, the attempts at reconstruction nevertheless do not progress towards a definite version. Just as the motivations behind the characters' actions cannot be evaluated according to any objective judgement and often seem equally plausible, so do the three different versions of the events during Heisenberg's visit. Although the characters can agree on some of the key moments of their encounter, such as the fact that they went for a walk after dinner but returned sooner than they, or Margrethe, expected, some of the smaller details and, crucially, the intentions attributed to their behaviour change in their different attempts to replay the evening. As indicated in the previous paragraph, their increasing doubt about the possibility of remembering one's own intentions, or even the existence of clearly identifiable motivations in the first place, means that none of these different versions seems more truthful than another. Similarly, their presentation in a neutral, flexible space means that their form of presentation does not guide the audience in their evaluation. While it is likely that the audience will follow the characters' attempts to choose among the three different versions offered, the play's suggestion that our interpretation always takes place from a specific perspective could be seen as an indication that the spectators are no more likely to overcome their own, inherent perspectivity than the characters in the play. One could thus regard the play as the basis for a multiplicity of different interpretations, rather than a definite reconstruction of the past.

This reading is further supported by the parallels to physical theories that are established in the play. The allusions to Einstein's physics call into mind the premise that everything is relative and that no phenomenon can be perceived independently from the position of the perceiver. In relation to the theory of indeterminacy, formulated by Heisenberg, Margrethe draws an explicit parallel between their unsuccessful attempts to re-discover their original intentions and the behaviour of particles: just as particles cannot be observed without being deflected, the attempt to identify their motivations seems to deflect and change them. The reasons for human behaviour are therefore ultimately indeterminate. Finally the theory of complementarity is linked to the idea that no version of the past is necessarily more credible than another: just as in his thought experiment on quantum physics Schrödinger's cat can be alive and dead at the same time, the past can exist in two different versions for a certain time (Frayn, 2000, p. 26). The explanation of the scientific theories to which Bohr and Heisenberg devoted their lives can in itself be intriguing and one of the major aspects of interest in the play; for example, Tom Mannion (2009) cited 'the science' as one of the main reasons he wanted to become involved in a production of *Copenhagen*. Providing images for the criticism of empiricist biography in the play, it can also be considered as further support for a meta-biographical interpretation.

Although Michael Frayn does not explicitly describe the play as meta-biographical, he affirms that philosophical questions, such as 'the difficulty of knowing why people do what they do' (Frayn, 2004), were at the heart of his endeavour. In contrast to performances such as *Rendition*

Monologues or *Gladiator Games* which are mainly interested in the specific experiences of their biographical characters, *Copenhagen* chooses historical lives mainly because the 'parallel between [the experiences represented] and the impossibility that Heisenberg established in physics, about ever knowing everything about the behaviour of physical objects [...] encapsulates something' (Frayn, 2004) about phenomenalism and the notion of complexity. Some reviewers echo his perspective, and perceive intentionality and our emphasis on reconstructing motivation as the core interest of the play (Macauly, 1999, p. 149). Similarly, Tom Mannion's observation that it is 'impossible to know [...] how Niels Bohr and Heisenberg would have that chat in hindsight' (Mannion, 2009) could be seen as the conclusion drawn in recognition of Frayn's doubts about reconstruction.

For audiences of the 2009 production in Edinburgh this interpretation is further supported by a programme note, a reprint of Michael Frayn's introduction to the published playtext, in which he emphasises his interest in the questions discussed above. Yet, reactions by other practitioners and the controversy that arose following the first production about Frayn's portrayal of Werner Heisenberg call into question whether a straightforward, biographical interpretation might not be more popular than the one suggested above: most of the critical reactions that considered Frayn's play as overly sympathetic to a Nazi physicist (see also Chapter 8) do not acknowledge the arguments against a definite reconstruction of the past put forward in the play. Similarly, David Burke, who played Niels Bohr in the National Theatre production, advocates an extra-theatrical interpretation of the characters that uses the '*common* humanity which connects us all' (Burke, 2009; italics UC) to bridge the gap between the life world and the characters in the play. Burke goes even further and rejects Frayn's suggestion that different versions of events can exist in parallel to the theory of complementarity in physics as 'confusion' (Burke, 2009). His view implies that this undesirable state of affairs needs to be resolved by a clear decision in our everyday life. As these reactions suggest, the potential of self-reflexivity might not be realised in many instances, but further investigation into reception would be necessary to establish to what extent meta-biographical elements are recognised.

Reconciling Self-Reflexive Elements and the Need to Engage with the Past

Interpretations that include self-reflexivity, on the other hand, do not deny the possibility of a biographical understanding. Victoria Stewart sets

Copenhagen apart from other plays about scientists, as 'Frayn chooses as his protagonists not fictional representatives of the scientific community but Werner Heisenberg and Niels Bohr, the architects of the uncertainty principle and complementarity' (Stewart, 1999) and historical figures. The same attitude can be observed among the practitioners involved in productions. Michael Frayn himself shows great commitment to transparency: even before the publication of critical comments he provided an overview of the sources he worked with and the extent to which he relied on them in his introduction to the playtext (Frayn, 2000), reiterating this position on various occasions, including a platform talk at the National Theatre (Wolf, 2003), and in answering to the accusations of sympathising with a Nazi scientist (Frayn, 2002a, 2002b, 2002c). Despite his doubts about the possibility of reconstruction, Michael Frayn thus recognises to what degree empiricism influences our thinking about the past and respects these rules by 'respect[ing] reality' (Frayn, 2004) where historical evidence allows him to justify his interpretation.

Other practitioners follow Frayn's example of respecting historical accounts: when asked to explain why the play repeatedly evokes the drowning of Niels Bohr's son Christian, Michael Blakemore (cited in Wu, 2000, p. 247) states that 'first of all it's true' before adding an alternative explanation that focuses on the scene's impact on characterisation. Similar respect for historical evidence underlies Tom Mannion's (2009) research activities in preparation for his role as Niels Bohr, although he recognises that, in the end, he had to leave behind his own interpretation 'to make it Michael Frayn's Niels Bohr'. His observation that 'Owen who played Heisenberg [...] read lots and lots of stuff about Heisenberg' supports their dedication researching the historical figures. His affirmation that his colleague became 'rather defensive' of his character as a result of his research, on the other hand, echoes the play's suggestion that we can only ever perceive the past from a specific perspective. In this case, the actor's empathy with the historical figure on whom his role was based seems to exert an important impact on his view of the past.

The playwright himself acknowledges this paradox. Frayn (cited in Wolf, 2003) admits that 'writ[ing] about people who actually existed' inhibited him. Although he felt that 'there was no way that [he] could get that right' (Wu, 2000, p. 141), he acknowledges that biographical performances perform 'a psychological trick [...] on people'. Spectators 'who knew the Bohrs or Heisenberg' approached him to assert 'that these are very good portraits of them: they were like this'. They often say, 'Even the actors are like Niels Bohr and Werner Heisenberg'. In spite of his own conviction that this is 'not possible that [he has] caught the actual tone of their voices just from reading letters and studying stuff about them [because] you can't do that!' (Wu, 2000, p. 124), Frayn feels that this effect bestows an additional responsibility on him to 'make it absolutely clear what [he is] claiming' (Frayn, 2004). Instead of rejecting the idea of life writing altogether, he advocates a more conciliatory approach that acknowledges its function in our interpretation of the world, but at the same time advocates transparency about its limitations, rather than absolute truth claims. The combination of criticism and insight into its function could be seen as a confirmation of the functional approach suggested in this book.

The play's ending could be read in a similar way: On the basis of the understanding that they will not find out the Truth about their meeting, the characters negotiate a version which allows their different perspectives to exist side by side. This decision means that they adopt the principle of complementarity in relation to physics and their past. Following this acceptance, they can once again embrace each other and each other's world as 'dear friend[s]' (Frayn, 2000, p. 93). In contrast to radical Postmodernism, the insight that no absolute historical or biographical Truth exists does not lead to a situation in which 'everything goes', but to a new possibility of seeing the truth in terms of the present, guided by the wish for mutual understanding. Reflecting the idea of ethically rather than historically correct versions (see Chapter 2), the characters' solution in Frayn's play could be regarded as an alternative to empiricist biography that is oriented towards its function rather than its ontological status. Such an interpretation would suggest that our attempts to reconstruct the past might be doomed to failure, but our wish to understand it can provide new insights.

Some of the testimonies of practitioners could support this interpretation. Tom Mannion (2009), for example, suggests that, although he was very conscious of playing 'Michael Frayn's Niels Bohr', he 'certainly [gained] a better understanding of Bohr the historical figure [...] after doing the play'. Yet, at the same time, his conclusion that 'the truth is [that] he couldn't, because he didn't have the maths, he didn't have the resources, there was no way he could have done it' contradicts my reading that the play convincingly argues that there is no definite version. This paradox, as well as the overwhelming number of voices in favour of a biographical reading, demonstrate that the inclusion of meta-biographical doubt in *Copenhagen* can challenge the role of biography. Similar to postmodernist historiographical theory, however, it is not at a stage where it could substitute reconstructionist representations of the past or past lives. As a play that offers an interpretation that goes beyond mere deconstruction, however, *Copenhagen* pushes the boundaries more than other discourses as it presents a positive example of postmodernist representation of past lives. Advocating an approach that evaluates versions of the past according to ethical concerns and their impact on the present, it suggests an alternative basis on which versions of the past can be evaluated.

Mary Queen of Scots Got Her Head Chopped Off

This emphasis on the present also underlies the meta-biographical elements in Liz Lochhead's play, but, in contrast to *Copenhagen*, it is less explicitly linked to philosophical questions; its meta-level is less prominent than it is in Michael Frayn's play. The presence of a narrator figure, La Corbie, still provides an explicit meta-biographical element, but the challenges to reconstructionist biography rely to a greater extent on structural aspects, including the visual negation of the concept of unique, historical individuals through doubling, and a structure that is based more on juxtaposition and a clear link to the present than linear chronology. This emphasis on playfulness and implicit meta-biography could be explained in terms of the play's historical background: *Mary Queen of Scots* was first performed in 1987, a time when postmodern experiments were widespread in artistic practice. Postmodernist theory had also begun to penetrate theoretical academic discourse, but had not yet become the predominant theoretical orientation it was when *Copenhagen* was first performed. As a result, the concepts and terminology to discuss it explicitly had permeated academic and artistic discourse to a lesser extent. It is equally plausible, however, to see reasons for these differences in the interests and working methods of Communicado Theatre, who commissioned the play from Liz Lochhead, or the playwright's personal preferences, as their epic style of performance had a strong impact on the play's form, according to the playwright.

In comparison to *Copenhagen*, the two productions of *Mary Queen of Scots* discussed here also differ to a greater extent in terms of the theatrical means of expression employed. The play was initially performed at the Little Lyceum in Edinburgh by Communicado Theatre under Gerry Mulgrew's direction in 1987 before it toured extensively throughout Scotland and was revived at the Royal Lyceum in 1998. It was written in close collaboration with the company in a process Liz Lochhead describes as 'writing almost in public' (Lochhead, 2009b), though not devising. Knowing the company's working methods, such as their emphasis on ensemble work that could be easily toured, had, according to the playwright, a profound impact on the shape the play took, particularly on the transitions between La Corbie's comments and the scenes in which the stories of Mary Queen of Scots and Elizabeth unfold, as well as the transitions between the Scottish and the English court. Although the revival staged by the National Theatre of Scotland (NTS) also toured extensively, and director Alison Peebles had performed as Elizabeth in the first production, it nevertheless introduced a number of differences. Those most notable at first sight include the exclusion of the fiddler and the dancer, which NTS substituted with recorded music and group choreographies, as well as the more complex requirements of the scenography: travelling with a complete lighting rig, including a ceiling installation of a Scottish flag and a more elaborate design, such as an illuminated St George's Cross, the 2009 production leaves a more elegant visual impression. Whereas Liz Lochhead describes the original as 'patchwork and cloth' that gave it the 'ragged glamour [...] from a charity shop' (Lochhead, 2009b), NTS announces their revival as 'bright, sensuou s [and] flamboyant' (NTS, 2009a).

A second notable change is the addition of a scene before Mary's death, showing her contemplating her situation in the company of her maid Bessie, which ends with the unequivocal sound of an axe (Lochhead, 2009a, p. 70). Although this scene had already been introduced in David McVicar's revival from 1994, Nick Hern Books used this opportunity to publish a revised version of the script in which it was included, together with minor changes in terms of scene divisions and stage directions. Although the latter mainly offer less explicit description of stage business than the original text based on Communicado's performance, they also introduce a more interpretative element, where characterisations, rather than a neutral description of specific actions or gestures, are described. John Knox's last speech before exiting is now preceded by the observation that he 'has to have the last word' (Lochhead, 2009a, p. 19). The more pronounced differences between the two productions introduce a stronger meta-dramatic element, as they emphasise the theatricality of each performance.

Narrating the Past to Comment on the Present

In addition to this, comments from practitioners and audiences suggest that a meta-biographical reading can also be supported by the productions' relationship to the context in which they are developed and performed. In an interview following the NTS revival Liz Lochhead makes this connection explicit, explaining that only in retrospect did she come to appreciate the degree to which the original conception

National Theatre of Scotland's production of *Mary Queen of Scots Got Her Head Chopped Off* (Peter Dibdin)

of the play was rooted in its time, 'personally, but also politically' (Lochhead, 2009b). With hindsight she identifies 'particular things in 1987 that influenced how we all felt about the project, how we all felt about women in power', as well as personal issues, such as the question of whether she or some of the other women involved in the production were 'going to have any children or not' (Lochhead, 2009b), that reso-nate the differences between Mary's and Elizabeth's lives. While she emphasises that these links do not 'limit the play in any way' and make it outdated today, her observation clearly recognises that past lives can only be represented from a specific historical and personal perspective. As Liz Lochhead (2009b) rightly observes, 'one would write it differently now'. Neil Cooper (2009) echoes this view in his remark that at the time of the '1987 premiere of [the] play [...] strong women were very much on the agenda'. The temporal distance between the original production and the NTS revival is thus sufficiently short for practitioners and audiences to remember the first production. Yet, at the same time it is long enough to allow them to identify differences between the contexts in which they were produced, and thus recognise the impact of the present on our perception of the past.

For the playwright, this orientation towards the present is reflected in the writing process. Despite the extensive research necessary for biographical plays, she affirms that 'any fictional character has to become quite mythical, quite archetypal' (Lochhead, 2009b). Decisions about characterisation mainly depend not on historical accuracy, but on the perspective that contemporary interpreters regard as particularly important and emphasise accordingly. If in *Mary Queen of Scots* the Scottish queen rejects the archetypal response 'to being a woman in power' adopted by Margaret Thatcher and Elizabeth I, i.e. to 'act like a man in women's clothing', her behaviour is not mainly based on historical evidence, but partly because 'that was what she and Gerry Mulgrew decided' (Lochhead, 2009b). A play born out of this process is necessarily 'far less concerned with the historic Mary than the mythic Mary [or] the mythic Elizabeth' (Lochhead, 2009b). As a result, the emphasis is placed more on 'this group of people telling that story' than a historical reconstruction, an impression supported by Communicado's style: the ensemble members remain on stage throughout the performance and make use of a variety of theatrical means reminiscent of Brecht's theatre, becoming visible as narrators of their characters' stories. It could also be regarded as a decision against the idea of studying the past for its own sake, and a conscious orientation towards evaluating its importance for the present. Communicado thus explored 'the correlation between that period of history and present day Scotland' (Mulgrew, 2010).

The potential for these links to contemporary Scotland is thus already present in the original production, but the opportunity to compare it with the NTS revival can give it greater prominence. For Alison Peebles (cited in McMillan, 2009), directing the revival allows her to take a fresh look at the play in a different context. Re-framing it 'feels like [...] discovering the play for the first time', as 'there is still something at the heart of it about where we are now, politically and in terms of sexual politics'. In other words, historical re-contextualisation leads to a new interpretation of the historical lives. Reviewers also commented more frequently on the play's portrayal of 'tensions over gender and religion that still haunt our society today', and its value in 'speaking to Scotland's past and present' on its sectarian wounds. In addition to chronological distance, the framing provided by geographical location can raise the prominence of meta-biographical aspects. Touring to communities all over the Highlands and Islands, Angela Darcy, the actress who played Elizabeth, was confronted with widely varying audience reactions to her character, depending on people's religious convictions. Playing the same historical character in places 'where [she] felt [audiences] were really with [her] and places where [she] knew they really hated [her] because [her character] was English' (Darcy, 2009) demonstrated the importance of current religious and national allegiances for their view of the past.

The element of comparison between two productions that originate in different historical contexts, or performances of the same production in different geographical and thus socio-cultural contexts, thus clearly supports the perception that the way *Mary Queen of Scots* is perceived depends on how and where the story is told, as much as it does on historical evidence. This double orientation is, nevertheless, insufficient to trigger a meta-biographical interpretation unless this is already suggested by elements in the productions themselves. The following paragraph therefore focuses on the productions themselves and identifies which elements of explicit and implicit self-reflexivity provide the basis for reflection on the nature of biography.

As observed above, Communicado's use of theatrical means often associated with epic theatre, such as the constant presence of the actors on stage or the use of banners to introduce scenes, emphasises the actors' role as storytellers who do not disappear behind their characters. Through the close collaboration between the playwright and the company some of these aspects have become permanent in the structure of the script. The NTS revival shows, however, that the degree to which these are played out depends partly on directorial decisions. In Alison Peebles' version, scene changes are still fluid and often a new dialogue starts while the actors involved in the previous scene are still present in the dark, but the constant presence of the company has been abandoned. Marc Brew, for example, is not present on stage before his first appearance as Riccio in the second act.

The use of a narrator figure is a more stable, explicit reference to the play's emphasis on telling, rather than reconstructing, a story. La Corbie's appearance already sets her apart from our notion of a biographer and places her in closer vicinity to fairytale creatures. Her opening speech, which establishes her as a narrator, begins accordingly with the traditional opening line of stories: 'Once upon a time there were twa queens on the wan green island' (Lochhead, 2009a, pp. 6 and 12 in Lochhead,

1989) and most of her speeches are written in the highly intra-theatrical form of rhymes. At the same time, however, she provides the geographical and contextual clues that allow the audience to connect this 'green island' with the 'country: Scotland' and the two cousin queens with Elizabeth and Mary; in other words she confirms the biographical link between the story and the life world.

Created by Liz Lochhead as 'the audience's friend to guide us through' the story (Lochhead, 2009b), La Corbie remains present throughout the play and her comments provide the connections between the different scenes and locations. Since most members of the audience will be familiar with at least the key events in the Scottish–English regal conflict, she is an interpreter rather than a chronicler of events: following Mary's thoughts on marriage, she concludes, for example, that 'oor queen, wha'd rul by gentleness, / Is but a pair fendless craiture' before announcing that Elizabeth's decisions in the next scene will demonstrate how 'An in Englan the Lass-Wha-Was-Born-To-Be-King / Maun dowse her womanische nature' (Lochhead, 2009a, p. 21). The clearly interpretative nature of her comments and the audience's likely familiarity with other versions of the story demonstrate that she guides spectators through this particular interpretation, speaking for their creators, not as a neutral document.

In the first production the presence of the fiddler, who 'charges up the space with eldritch tune', before La Corbie's first speech further highlights the aspect of storytelling by introducing another clearly intra-theatrical form of comment. Although the NTS production still uses recorded music, the musician is no longer a visible second narrator and the original balance where the 'poetic text, the live music and the choreography [...] had a similar status in the piece' (Mulgrew, 2010) is changed. The playtext compensates this with explicit instructions on La Corbie's role, which give further weight to her role as a narrator who 'drive[s] the story forward, as she must' (Lochhead, 2009a, p. 68) and two additional lines that explicitly refer to her role as narrator: 'I wish to Christ I could tell yez a Different Story!' (Lochhead, 2009a, p. 20). It could be argued, however, that the reduction of her to a single narrator slightly weakens the emphasis on storytelling.

Although the proximity to stories, rather than empiricist history, is promoted through the elements discussed above, it would be surprising if they were sufficient to trigger a meta-biographical understanding of the play. As *Thatcher – the Musical!* shows, the presence of a narrator and a highly theatrical format can also be regarded as a concession to theatricality – La Corbie could be seen as the extravagant proponent of an alternative re-interpretation of the past, rather than an element that challenges the possibility (and usefulness) of reconstructing the past on a broader level. Such an effect is likely to be achieved by the structural challenges to 'serious' history plays that reconstruct the past for its own sake.

Doubling

One of the most important visual challenges to reconstructionist biography is the fragmentation of its main subjects through extensive use of doubling. Liz Lochhead explains that the creation of the maids was partly inspired by a practical problem of creating opportunities for interaction between the two queens. Since the historical models for these two characters never met, she did not want to 'go down the Schiller route' and invent an encounter (Lochhead, 2009b). As doubling had been used by Communicado in previous productions, she decided to use the lead actresses in the role of maids who could act as confidantes to Mary and Elizabeth and thus allow them to formulate some of the thoughts they might have voiced in a personal conversation if this had ever taken place. While this pragmatic interpretation shows Lochhead's conviction that 'you always get your ideas out of your problems' (Lochhead, 2009b), it does not take into account the potential effect created by the similarities between these additional characters and the protagonists.

The additional characters are Bessie and Marian, the maids, as well as Mairn, 'a wee poor Scottish beggar lass', and Leezie, 'her tarty wee companion'. Embodied by the same actresses in the same costume as for their lead roles as queens, these characters already bear a strong visual resemblance to each other, which is further reinforced in the script through the choice of names and similar patterns of behaviour. Thus Marian echoes Mary's hopes that she can preserve her power, yet still marry for love, when she insists that her mistress can marry her lover, Lord Leicester, in secret, and thus gradually accustom her country to her choice (Lochhead, 2009a, pp. 14 and 22). Mary's servant Bessie, on the other hand, cautions her mistress against marriage: 'In good time. A guid man in guid time, madam' (Lochhead, 2009a, p. 13) – a sentence that echoes Elizabeth's affirmation that there is still time to produce an heir.

Similarly the encounter between Mairn, Leezie and John Knox reflects Mary's and Elizabeth's interaction with men: Leezie's visible enjoyment at the power she yields over Knox when she cheekily propositions him is reminiscent of Elizabeth's observation that 'there were no more *piquant* nights than those when [Leicester] were never sure if he were off to the *Tower* or to *Scotland* in the morning' (Lochhead, 2009a, p. 37). Mairn, on the other hand, tries to avoid open confrontation with him, similar to Mary's visible discomfort when she requests loyalty from the Earl of Bothwell (Lochhead, 2009a, p. 25). As both names and features of personality are commonly seen as strong indicators of a unique identity, their overlap between these different characters challenges this concept both visually and conceptually. As a result our expectations of characters as unique units that reflect our notion of individual identity in the life world are undermined.

The changes from one character to another further add to the meta-theatricality of this device. The first transformation from Elizabeth to Bessie is signalled when 'Corbie snaps her fingers' (Lochhead, 2009a, p. 11), but subsequent ones are no longer introduced. They take place in front of the audience, and are marked through a change in the actresses' posture, gestures, actions and accent. While their swiftness supports the impression of fluidity between the characters and thus the challenge to the concept of unique characters, their openness introduces a strong self-reflexive element. They are differentiated by external indicators that the actresses can adopt or abandon when the story requires it, for example of status when 'Elizabeth bobs a curtsy, immediately becoming Bessie' and origin, such as Mary's 'Braid Scots' vocabulary spoken with 'a French accent' (Lochhead, 2009a, pp. 11 and 4). As a result, the characters appear as deliberate creations of role play, not expressions of an inner self.

These swift changes bring challenges for the actresses who have to switch quickly from one body language to another or from Received Pronunciation, which Angela Darcy (2009) who plays Elizabeth in the NTS production finds 'quite difficult anyway', into a Scottish dialect that is not her own either. Liz Lochhead suggests that the absence of a specific costume and the bare stage of the first production were more successful in supporting these changes, but it could be argued that the more elaborate design of the NTS production also supports this differentiation, albeit in an alternative way. The light installation of a St George's Cross on the floor and the illuminated saltire above the stage clearly divide it into four different spaces. These structures thus help to mark opposite corners of the flags as the personal realm for each queen, and the crossing lines at the centre indicate clearly when the actresses move from one field into the other. As such, they provide a helpful indication of the exact moment at which they need to change from one role into another and for the lighting designer to cue any changes to indicate the transition from one court to another (Darcy, 2009). In addition to this practical aspect, the design adds symbolic value to these changes: linked closely to the structure of the two national flags, the spaces represent an abstract notion of nation, as well as a specific physical environment. Placed at the centre of these symbolic spaces the queens' role as head of these nations is emphasised over their individuality.

The emphasis on their official roles is continued in the publicity material, which shows a picture of the two lead actresses dressed in flags. Their poses express some of the traits that characterise their behaviour in the play: Elizabeth gazes straight into the camera and her folded arms seem to challenge the viewer, whereas Mary's elegance and haughtiness are underlined through emphasis on her tall, elegantly dressed figure and the angle of her head, chin firmly up, that allows her to look down at the camera. Their heavy, white make-up, however, hides their individual features, giving them the appearance of theatrical masks or shop mannequins. The flags thus become the most prominent aspect of their appearance and the clearest differences between them. In the NTS production costume and stage design reinforce the challenge to the idea of a unique self within a unique psychological body that was introduced by the extensive use of doubling.

The visual emphasis on their roles as queens is accompanied by a strong interest in the fact that they are women in such powerful roles. This question is raised explicitly in La Corbie's line preceding Elizabeth's first appearance as Bessie: 'when's a queen a queen / And when's a queen juist a wummin?' (Lochhead, 2009a, p. 11). The use of doubling can provide a possible answer. As Angela Darcy (2009) points out, Bessie 'gets to live out all the raunchy things that Elizabeth never gets to do' – adopting compromising poses in her second role is thus a way for her to explore the restrictions on her main character, Elizabeth. In other words, the differences between the queen, her maid and Leezie, the commoner, are mainly based on the boundaries imposed on them by their different social status. As Leezie suggests, the two wee commoners would also 'be braw in braw clothes' (Lochhead, 2009a, p. 31) and their impersonation by the same actress confirm this impression. The insight that their main distinctions originate in their social environment then confirm the criticism of a core personality. Doubling, which emphasises the visual continuity across characters and their dependence on external factors, such as their social status expressed in body language, thus reinforces the effect created by the use of national symbols in the design and the publicity photographs: it undermines the notion of a unique core personality on which most biographical accounts from the twentieth century rely. In *Mary Queen of Scots* criticism is directed at the elements that are reconstructed in biography, not only the process of reconstruction.

Similar to *Copenhagen* the challenge to Empiricism does not mean that re-telling the past is seen as a futile exercise. Instead it is possible to focus on the insights these characters allow us into our present. The fragmentation of characters, for example, can shed light on the questions Liz Lochhead asks about the decision she and the women in Communicado took about their lives at the time of the first production: on the one hand, the queens and maids are highly similar characters who, in different social circumstances, have a very different set of options at their disposal. On the other hand, we see Elizabeth and Mary who, in similar circumstances, take a radically different approach to these decisions. In these historical comparisons the external factors that influence personal decisions and the freedom we have to act according to personal belief and preference become clearly visible. Doubling can thus serve the epic function of making invisible factors in our own society visible.

Other Structural Elements that Encourage Self-Reflexivity

The element of comparison is further underlined by the play's structure. Although a basic chronology is preserved, juxtaposition is stronger than linear progression, as the scenes between the queens present their conflict over succession, power and marriage in a form of dialogue where the events at one court are followed by the reaction at the other, or opinions are compared directly. A good example of the latter are scenes 4 and 5 of the first act, where Mary explains her romantic notion of marriage to Bessie before Elizabeth decides against a love match (Lochhead, 2009a, p. 21). At the same time, the divergence from a simple, chronological progression highlights the playwright's impact on the form of presentation chosen, creating another link to the present, rather than the past.

The strongest negation of chronology is found in the last scene, set in a contemporary, Glaswegian playground. The time shift is clearly indicated by 'the more up-to-date Glaswegian slang' (Darcy, 2009), contemporary clothes and references to games and nursery rhymes familiar to contemporary Scottish audiences. Joyce Falconer (cited in English, 2009), who played Corbie in the NTS production, explicitly formulates the effect of this change, suggesting that the conflict between Wee Knoxy and Wee Mary shows how elements of the religious conflict between Mary and Knox are still part of, or, in her words 'still ingrained in[,] our society today, predominantly across the west coast of Scotland'. The children's rhymes demonstrate that they have firmly found their place in contemporary popular culture.

Originally it was conceived by Liz Lochhead as the initial scene that would show the actors as children who sang these songs before they became the 'grown up[s] that are telling the story' in the play. Its current position at the end of the play, however, changes this scene into a 'kind of parallel story' (Lochhead, 2009b). The play now finishes with a strong image that captures and identifies the links to the present, as it explicitly points to the way in which the story of Mary Queen of Scots is present in the audience's own childhood and cultural traditions, such as nursery rhymes. This ending thus provides strong support to the orientation towards the here and now already established through the emphasis on storytelling, the extensive use of doubling and its structure. In other words, the play ends with a final rejection of the notion of reconstructing the past for its own sake that has already been undermined by other explicit and implicitly meta-biographical elements.

The playfulness of the last scene, in relation both to its content and the way the actors of the NTS production 'played with it [and] in it, like children' (Darcy, 2009), also emphasises the differences between *Copenhagen*'s philosophical, more explicit challenge to empiricist biography and the more implicit, playful manner in which *Mary Queen of Scots* develops this potential. These differences should not overshadow their most important similarity, however: both plays deconstruct the notion that the past and past lives have to be reconstructed for their own sake. Yet, none of them adopts a radically postmodernist approach that denigrates the usefulness of stories about our life world: although this re-telling of Mary's story does not claim to tell *the* story as it really happened, it resonates with the present and raises questions that are important to the practitioners and spectators involved. Similarly, the attempts to remember the past in *Copenhagen* can be interpreted as an important aspect in understanding and negotiating different versions of the past to influence the present. Where the theory of history can provide concepts and terminology to explain meta-biographical criticism in theatre, these plays can perhaps suggest new directions for biographical and historical practice that overcomes the schism between modernist belief in absolute ontological categories and postmodern relativism.

6
Studying Reception: Theoretical Framework and Methodology

Introduction

As argued in Chapter 2, the function of biographical references in performances can only be analysed if their production and reception are taken into account. The analysis of productions in the previous chapters has identified different patterns of references and has sought to identify their impact on practitioners' work. This has allowed educated guesses to be made about the elements that can trigger, maintain or contradict a biographical mode of reception. The chapters also hypothesised about the potential consequences of conflicting signals about the play's relationship to the life world and the possible impact of biographical material on the spectators' expectations and evaluation of these productions. In the following chapters these questions will be pursued further through the discussion of feedback from audiences in order to overcome the emphasis on the scholar as sole spectator. Reception studies on specific plays in Chapter 7 are preceded by the presentation of a model of reception and an introduction to the methodological approach used for these studies. Such groundwork is important in order to predict at which points of the reception process biographical material is most likely to impact on audiences' reactions. Empirical studies can then be used to counter or confirm these differences in the context of specific productions 'in such a way that the theory is illuminated by the data, and the data take on greater significance through the lens of concepts and theory' (Barker, 2003, p. 327).

Finding a theoretical basis is, however, difficult, as audience research is an area that is often neglected in theatre studies, especially when compared to performance analysis. This chapter will review the main strands of audience research in theatre studies in order to develop a theoretical framework that can be used for empirical studies. In contrast to related disciplines such as media, film or television studies where audience research is such an integral element that an introduction to the topic is even included in textbooks (e.g. Stokes, 2003), this area is highly under-researched and hardly ever taught even in postgraduate courses.[1] Neither its proximity to fields such as film or media studies, nor the influence of reader response theories of the 1970s and 1980s (e.g. Iser, 1972) in the literature departments where this field originated, have led to a higher recognition of audiences and the reception process in the discipline. The contents of *Participations*, an 'International Journal for Audience Research', demonstrate the current lack of research: despite the editors' specific expression of interest in publishing articles on theatre, the majority of papers deal with film or television audiences.

The reticence to engage with theatre audiences can partly be explained by subject-specific difficulties. Unlike other media, theatre is an ephemeral event. Although other media, it could be argued, only acquire their meaning in an encounter with readers or audiences as well, the existence of durable copies in the form of printed or recorded material means that they can be accessed at different moments in time and in a range of different places. Theatre, on the other hand, is highly localised – despite the relatively high number of touring theatre companies in the UK, it does not have the same national and often international distribution as television programmes, films, printed material and, probably the least local, the internet. Lack of wider accessibility, however, leads to smaller audience numbers. Combined with less marked commercial interests (the money from ads in theatre programmes covers a negligible part of production costs, whereas television and magazines often have to fund themselves through ads or spots that are inserted into the main product) this reduces the instrumentally motivated studies of theatre audiences.[2] Its local, ephemeral nature and the smaller group of recipients thus contribute to the lack of interest in audience research.

Further complications arise from the traditional connection between drama and literature. Although some film scripts are published as books, their readership is mostly limited to those with a professional or at least highly developed interest in the medium. Where films are based on other text forms, such as novels, the success of the cinematic version fuels interest in the original, not in the script. Playscripts might not become bestsellers either, but classics especially are often regarded as versions in their own right. When asked whether they are familiar with Shakespeare's work, many people would reply that they had *read* one of his plays, rather than *watched* it. Today most theatre scholars agree that scripts are merely one part of the complete, performed piece, but the long-lasting discussions about the status of theatre texts and the continued association of some classics with literature departments means that audience research in this field has to choose between various possible recipients (see Chaudhuri, 1984 or Holland and Scolnicov, 1991 which is aptly entitled *Reading Plays*), a multiplicity that could be seen as another reason for the lower interest in reception shown by theatre scholars.

The complexity of studying theatre audiences itself is the topic of some publications in this field. Chaudhuri (1984) and Krauss (1993) base their observations on Iser's idea of implicit recipients in novels (Iser, 1972), and suggest different groups of such 'rhetorical audiences' that can be studied, including contemporary and historical, or even imaginary audiences. Nonetheless, they do not abandon the idea that scholars can base their assumptions about the way in which these audiences receive a production entirely on their own knowledge of the audiences and the production. The academic thus continues to act as the representative of actual spectators through inference about their possible reactions.

Audience Studies and Reception Research

The majority of studies on actual audiences choose a sociological approach, concentrating mainly on 'describing the features of existing or potential theatre audiences' (Sauter, 2002, p. 117). In an academic context audience research, as Sauter terms this tradition, often implies the reconstruction of historical audiences. Research into the composition of contemporary theatre audiences on the other hand is conducted primarily by theatres' marketing departments or companies or organisations that are dedicated to building audiences, such as Edinburgh's Audience Business (The Audience Business, 2008). These institutions have developed standard methodologies to profile their audiences, but these are mostly used to develop their marketing strategies or support funding applications. Commercially motivated, they are not often accessible to academics for research purposes. Some examples of studies in an academic context can be found, such as Caroline Gardiner's (1994) long-term study of West End audiences or P.H. Mann's (1966) examination of the effect of specific young people's performances on the make-up of the audiences for *Uncle Vanya* at Sheffield Playhouse. While these studies go beyond the direct practical uses of their results to build audiences and often include reflection on methodology, they tend to be small, and become outdated relatively quickly.

Another approach in this area looks at audiences not as made up of individuals but as a collective and examines their role as 'a cultural phenomenon' (Bennett, 1997, p. 1). Among them Susan Bennett's mono-graph *Theatre Audiences* offers a detailed discussion on the impact of audi-ences on decisions concerning the choice of plays and venues, as well as the importance of the physical arrangements in the theatre and of outer frames, such as interpretative communities, for the reception of plays. Bennett combines a review of relevant theories with her own observations to provide a thorough and wide-ranging discussion of theatre audiences in general and particular cultural constellations. A number of journal papers and book chapters apply a similar approach on a smaller scale: Paterson (1991), for example, examines the audiences of Canadian Fringe Festivals and Sinfield (1983) discusses the impact of *Look Back in Anger* on UK audi-ences. Nonetheless, the focus on audiences as collectives means that these studies cannot give a detailed insight into the process of reception.

For a study on the impact of biography on audiences' perceptions, however, understanding this process in more detail is essential; reception research, which focuses on the experience of real spectators and the 'way in which spectators perceive performances' (Sauter, 2002, p. 116), is there-fore an important source for both the theoretical model and methodology for empirical research developed here. Unfortunately, this area has been even more neglected than audience studies. 'Precisely *how* audiences pro-duce meaning in negotiation with the particular, local theatrical event, fully contextualised [...] has only rarely been analysed or modelled in any detail' (Knowles, 2004, p. 17). The scarcity of studies in this area might be partly explained by the need to focus on small groups of audi-ences to conduct meaningful research into such a complex phenomenon. Due to the lack of contemporary audience studies, which means that it is impossible to choose groups that are representative of wider audiences, reception research cannot deliver results that are easily generalisable. While some might argue that this reduces its value, this could, however, be considered to reflect the local and ephemeral nature of theatre. At the same time, preliminary research on small groups is the necessary prereq-uisite for an understanding of this process in a wider context as well.

Background for this Study

Smaller studies can also gain in interest if they are based on a detailed model of the reception process. Knowles (2004, p. 100) suggests a theo-retical framework that takes into account cultural context and semiotic analysis. His materialist semiotics establish theatrical communication as a triangle of these conditions and the performance and examine the systems that can be found at each corner of this triangle. Although his approach is of great interest, it is not sufficiently detailed for the purposes of this study, as it lacks concentration on individual reception. Its triangular nature can be regarded as an inheritance from the semiotic triangle. Pavis, a semiotician himself, built his description of performance as an autonomous sign on Saussure's definition of the linguistic sign. In order to overcome semiotics' traditional emphasis on production, Pavis treats production and reception not as isolated processes but as two aspects of the same sign. In a first step he equates the corners of his performative triangle to those that make up Saussure's linguistic sign (Saussure, 1979, p. 99), in which a concept, or a meaning (a signifié, SÉ), is matched to a linguistic sign, in most cases a sound pattern (the signifiant, SA). In theatre, the role of the signifiant is assigned to the performance on stage, or elements thereof. Confronted with this representation, the spectator endeavours to match it with a possible meaning (SÉ). The two elements then constitute the autonomous sign, or, in his words, the concretisation of the performance or part of it (Pavis, 1985, p. 146).

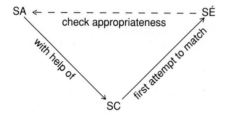

Unlike many other semioticians, Pavis rejects the idea of 'an artificial or pre-determined meaning' (see for example Aston and Savona, 1991, p. 99) and suggests that the social context (SC) is vital in the process of assigning the signifiant (SA) to the signifié (SE), as it helps the spectator to match the signifié with an appropriate signifiant. Perceiving the signifiant, the spectator refers back to the social context, which Pavis defines as 'the total context of social phenomena' (Pavis, 1985, p. 246), in order to connect his previous knowledge to the new reality of the performance and interpret the stage actions. This circle results in a tentative reading of the performance. Before the sign is complete, however, a second circle serves as a corrective mechanism: starting with the social context, spectators compare the potential signifié with the signifiant to check whether this tentative choice of signifié can be accommodated with their knowledge about the social context. If their tentative match is not confirmed, both of these processes can be repeated until a satisfactory concretisation has been reached. This final result depends on the nature of all individual elements that contribute to it. It can thus vary according to differences in the performance (the signifiant) and variations of the social context, both in time and for every individual member of the audience, which means that 'there are innumerable concretisations of one and the same text, but that they are nevertheless explicable due to the variations of the SA and the SC' (Pavis, 1985, p. 247).

Another theory of performance that includes both the presentation of the performers' actions and the reactions of the spectators who are present at the very moment of the creation is Willmar Sauter's concept of theatre as an event. The notion of the performative sign is thus rejected by a more dynamic concept of actions and reactions that take place between the performers and the spectators, but similar to Pavis, the theatrical event is not complete before this interaction has taken place. Sauter's conceptualisation of this process is, however, slightly more complex, as he differentiates between three levels of interaction: the sensory, the artistic and the symbolic levels. As the name suggests, the sensory level is the most immediate one, describing the performers' and spectators' awareness of each others' presence. When the performer exposes her or his body on stage, the audience can experience sensory reactions, although recognition is usually mutual.

The spectators' knowledge that this situation is different from everyday life leads to the next two levels of interaction. First of all, they will, cognitively or intuitively, judge the performers' actions as a form of artistic expression rather than everyday actions. This evaluation will be 'determined by individual and cultural conditions, but also by the aesthetic norms of the particular performance' (Sauter, 2000, p. 54), aesthetic norms that are defined for example by the genre. The spectators are therefore required to possess a certain competence in order to appreciate the performance on an artistic level. The 'artistic otherness of the event' (Sauter, 2000, p. 7) is also the basis for interaction on the symbolic level, as it leads spectators to assume that the actions that are presented on stage 'signify something beyond [their] directly perceivable appearance' (Sauter, 2000, pp. 55–6). On this level, spectators are thus called to transform the directly visible actions into symbolic or embodied ones, or, to use the example presented by Sauter, to complete the transition of the actor on stage into Hamlet. The creation of fictionality is thus explained by a mutual agreement between the performer and the audience.

Although Sauter's emphasis on interactions between performers and spectators differs from Pavis's focus on the sign as a result of the audience's interpretative activity, the concept of a symbolic interpretation of stage actions that goes beyond their immediate situation can be found in both of these models. They also agree that this interpretation is shaped by the audience's knowledge of life beyond the theatre. Sauter's description of this 'social context' (in Pavis's term) is, however, more detailed, as it is divided into five different levels:

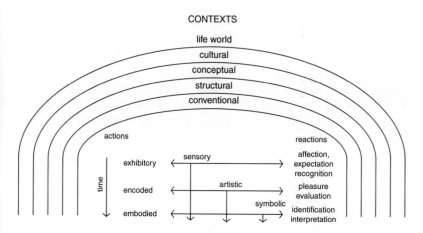

Sauter's description of the 'social context' (from Sauter, 2000, p. 8)

Those closest to the interaction taking place during the performance are related to the theatrical nature of the event. The conventional context, for example, contains 'attitudes towards genre, the tradition of perform-ance in a specific country at a given period, the artistic encoding of a performance, and the spectator's competence in understanding these codes' (Sauter, 2000, p. 34). The cultural context in turn looks at the role of theatre in a society in more general terms, for example the places where it is made and received, or whether it receives subsidies. The next two lev-els relate theatre to other forms of artistic expression, examining the ideo-logical and cultural contexts, which inform audiences about ideologies related to theatre and the interdependence of theatre and other art forms, respectively (Sauter, 2000, pp. 9–10). Although biographical material can have an impact on the way in which audiences use these four levels to interpret the performance, the fifth circle is the most important influence on the creation of a symbolic interpretation. The life world encompasses 'a vast range of things that we might consider important for the theatrical event' (Sauter, 2000, p. 10), including the audience's knowledge of other discourses about historical figures. Although Sauter does not explicitly state this in his book, I would argue that, as in Pavis's concept, these contexts have to be understood as individual ones that differ from one member of the audience to another. The theatrical event thus depends on the cultural and social factors identified by Sauter, as well as individual differences in the knowledge about the five different contextual areas.

A Combined Model of Theatrical Reception

Sauter and Pavis thus agree on three fundamental points: theatre, whether it is regarded as an event or a sign, only exists through the interaction between performer and spectator (see also Highberg, 2009). The result of this activity is a symbolic interpretation of the events on stage, and the 'meaning attributed to artistic actions' (Sauter, 2000, p. 7) is highly dependent on the spectators' knowledge of the contexts in which theatre takes place. These similarities demonstrate that Pavis's model overcomes semiotics' 'one-sided concentration on the production itself' that Sauter (2000, p. 24) bemoans and makes it possible to combine these two approaches into a model that benefits from their combined advantages. This model could be visualised as follows:

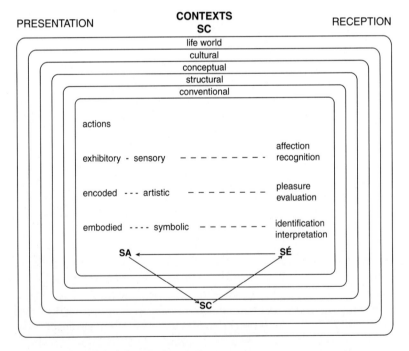

A combined model of theatrical reception

Pavis's search for an appropriate meaning for stage actions is situated on the symbolic level, where performers create the signifiant and spectators search for an appropriate signifié. In their search they match the material reality of the stage actions with potential meanings known to them from the social context (or the life world, to use Sauter's term) in which the performance takes place. The world on stage and the life world are therefore not separate entities but interact with each other. In Pavis's own words:

> the textual and dramatic theory of fiction insists on the inter-relatedness of these worlds and their complementarity. In fiction we recognise 'morceaux collés' or 'objets trouvés' of our own reality. The identification of a character or a situation can only take place on the basis of our previous experiences. (Pavis, 1985, p. 272)

Describing the creation of embodied actions on the symbolic level, Sauter echoes this idea, although he looks at this process in slightly less detail. Hamlet, a character carrying out embodied actions, thus exists only as a result of the interaction between the actor, who provides a material reality on stage, and the spectators who are willing to create 'Hamlet' in their minds, 'aided through the images presented by the performer' (Sauter, 2000, p. 9).

The collaboration of actors and spectators not only extends to the creation of symbolic actions, but usually includes agreement on the boundaries of the possible world they create. Although spectators need to activate contextual knowledge to complete the stage images, both they and the performers make the 'fundamental assumption [that] the discourse is only valid within a pre-determined space [...] and time' (Ubersfeld, 1982, p. 235; see also Sauter, 2000, p. 48). In other words, neither the audience nor the actor believe that the performer *becomes* Hamlet, but both agree to treat him as Hamlet. As Ben Chaim confirms, a minimum distance between the life world and the symbolic stage actions is a 'psychological phenomenon basic to art' (Ben Chaim, 1984, p. 70).

This tacit understanding between performers and spectators determines that the life and the stage world cannot be identical, or that the events on stage do not take place in the same way they do outside the theatre (Ben Chaim, 1984, p. 74). They are the result of two opposing tendencies: the knowledge that the status of embodied actions is different from that of actions in the life world and the need to refer to one's experience in the life world to create them. Engaging in a theatrical event 'always means to confront the spectator's own personal world with a suggested imaginary world' (Martin and Sauter, 1995, p. 84). The specific relationship between the two, the degree of intra- or extra-theatricality, then depends on the degree to which spectators 'supplement' the stage actions with knowledge from their life world 'before [the dramatic worlds] are fully constituted' (Elam, 1980, p. 92). Extra-theatricality can be re-defined as performances that encourage the spectator to refer extensively to their life world knowledge to create embodied actions; intra-theatricality, on the other hand, allows them to arrive at symbolic meaning with little recourse to the life world.

The audience's knowledge of other contextual circles, including general theatrical conventions, the performative genre, codes of everyday behaviour and the broader social context (Sauter, 2000, pp. 63ff.), can exert influence on the theatrical event they create with the performers (or the concretisation in Pavis's term). A good example of their potential effect is the presentation of death on stage: audiences familiar with basic theatrical conventions (Sauter's first circle) will have learnt that a body on stage might have to be regarded as dead on the symbolic level, even if the actor is visibly breathing. Although this interpretation contradicts their experience in the life world, acceptance of theatrical conventions means that this paradox does not have an impact on the symbolic interpretation of stage actions. Consequently, the audience's familiarity with discourses that are part of Sauter's contextual circles *and* detailed knowledge about the performance are necessary to predict their interaction with the performer and the way in which they translate stage actions into embodied actions.[3]

While the early chapters of this book concentrated on the similarities between the life world and the performance to predict the degree of reliance on contextual knowledge, these predictions might not provide a full and exhaustive explanation of the relationship between performances and the life world, since they are based on the perception of a single, specialised spectator, a scholar who 'cannot pretend to be an objective observer, since s/he has already been involved in the theatrical event' (Martin and Sauter, 1995, p. 16). As Sauter's and Pavis's model points to the active participation of audiences in the creation of the theatrical event, empirical research is needed to compare the predictions made with the reactions of actual audiences to examine the impact of biographical material in more detail. In the following my predictions about the impact of biographical material on reception are anchored in the model outlined above to guide the empirical studies outlined in the last section of this chapter.

The Impact of Biographical Material on Reception – Predictions

The analysis of productions suggests that biographical references are often used to increase the extra-theatricality of a performance. In terms of our model, this means that audiences rely on a greater amount of contextual information in order to assign symbolic meaning to the stage actions; even the contribution of references as short as a first and family name can activate a wealth of knowledge that supplements the information provided in the performance. In an apparent paradox, the dependence on more contextual material also leads to the use of a narrower social context: if the spectators' attempts to match an element of the material reality of the performance with a possible signifié are based on very little information from the play, this information has to be more precise. In the present process, precision means that it has to point clearly to a narrow range of contexts which can then complement the signifiant and lead to a signifié (see also Schaff, 1992, p. 19). *Insignificance* helps to explain how this process can be triggered by biographical information without the use of names. Here the Ballplayer is introduced as the husband of another character, who bears an uncanny resemblance (both physically and in her activities) to the actress Marilyn Monroe. The information given about this character, i.e. that he is the husband of the Marilyn Monroe-like actress and that he is a world famous baseball player, leads to a context that might be defined as 'sportspeople who at the same time were married to famous actors'. It is specific enough to allow the spectators to match the character with the 'concept' of the historical figure of Joe DiMaggio, a combination that subsequently can give them a wealth of contextual information about the historical baseball star.

With the help of such contextual knowledge, the limited information provided by the play can then be extended to a fuller picture of the character. A characterisation that does not allow the connection between the world of the characters with a specific and narrow context of the life world, on the other hand, means that the play itself would have to provide more information about the character in order to develop it to the same degree. Names mean that the information provided by the performance can be even scarcer. In *Thatcher – the Musical!*, for example, the reference to Thatcher's time as Education Minister is evoked by a single line: 'Maggie Thatcher, Milk Snatcher' (Foursight Theatre, 2005, p. 9). Here the name is sufficient to provide the context for the next two words, clarifying that they do not refer to a playground dispute between primary pupils, but to a political decision that caused an outrage in 1970s Britain.

The scarcity of information given in the performance, compared to the wealth of life world knowledge brought to it by audience members, also means that the embodied actions will vary to a higher degree, according to variations in the spectators' experiences in the life world. In the case of Margaret Thatcher, the different perspectives brought to the performance by an ardent admirer of the former Prime Minister and a left-wing opponent thus account for the fact that these two spectators would create a very different theatrical event. This is true not only for controversial figures from the recent past, but also for those in earlier times. Here the spectators' familiarity with different discourses about the historical figure is decisive, but the process cannot simply be equalled to the notion of historical accuracy. Popular beliefs might be more important than discourses based on thorough evaluation of original sources, since 'recognition does not occur because all recipients are familiar with the essential historiographic publications, but because they have notions of the past that are nourished by many, mainly non-academic sources' (Breuer, 2005, p. 53).

Once a biographical reading has been triggered, the embodied actions are likely to adopt a different status. While the audience's creation of a symbolic level continues to be based on their knowledge that this level is different from their life world, their 'willingness to "see as"' (Ben Chaim, 1984, p. 73) might mean that the information provided in the performance is not entirely limited to the theatrical event. In other words, few spectators are likely to believe that the figure on stage is indeed Margaret Thatcher,[4] but the similarity between the immaterial theatrical character and the material figure from the life world can blur the borders between the two entities. Recognising aspects of the figure of the past in the presentation of the performer, the practitioners might also expect that elements that were formerly unknown to them apply to both the fictional creation and the physically existing figure of the past. In other words, they could feel they had 'learnt' something about the historical figure, for example that Margaret Thatcher was Education Minister.

This new status of the fictional creation based on biographical elements in plays makes it possible for the transfer of information from the social context into the world of the play to potentially be converted into a two-way exchange. New elements of the fiction can be considered to be valid in the world outside the play as well, due to the close relationship between the fiction and the life world (see also Peacock, 1991, p. 13). In this case, the social context is not only used to build the fiction from embodied actions, but individual embodied actions may also be transferred to a person's contextual knowledge as well. The reception of biographical theatre can therefore be seen to result not only in a different status with regard to the fiction that is created, but also in a different way of dealing with a performance, as it can have a more direct and specific impact on the spectator's life world.

The difference in the creation and the consequences of embodied actions could be regarded as the most outstanding feature of biographical performance, but some minor changes can also be observed on the two other levels of communication established by Sauter. On the sensory level the possibility of recognition merely through sensory impressions exists: biographical characters with a distinctive visual appearance or voice, as for example Marilyn Monroe in *Insignificance*, can trigger almost immediate recognition in the audience. Although this effect might be mitigated by their cognitive awareness that due to the circumstances this cannot be the figure with whom they are familiar, this immediate sense of recognition can only be undermined, not undone. On the artistic level biographical material can introduce an additional criterion to evaluate the performance of the actors, according to the degree to which they achieve an imitation of the historical figure.

Just as the symbolic level is the level of communication most likely to be affected by biographical material, the life world is the contextual circle that gains most importance through such references. However, the recourse to other circles can also change to a minor degree. The conventional level, for example, can have a strong impact on the degree of extra-theatricality audiences attribute to a performance. Spectators who are familiar with a variety of theatrical traditions and style, for example, have a larger number of models at their disposal for the translation of stage actions into embodied actions. Their familiarity with different forms of expression might lead them to accept a wider range of stage actions as a 'natural' aspect of theatrical communication that does not decrease the extra-theatricality of biographical references. Audience members who have experienced few performances, on the other hand, might be reminded of the theatrical frame by theatrical conventions that are little known to them.[5]

Elements that Can Trigger a Biographical Reading

The elements that can trigger these potential consequences for theatrical reception can differ from one spectator to another. Many of those that fulfilled this function for me have been discussed in the preceding chapters, but before embarking on empirical research, it is helpful to review the range of aspects that could encourage spectators to choose a biographical mode of creating embodied actions on a more general level. Empirical research can then clarify which ones establish a biographical link for specific audience members or for groups of them. The following paragraphs therefore present the type of stage actions (and those found in accompanying material, such as posters, flyers or other publicity) that could potentially serve as the basis for embodied actions. In accordance with semiotic analysis of theatre, they are categorised into three different types of stage actions: language, visual aspects or non-linguistic auditory elements.

Language can be regarded as the most central among these, as it can be found in most plays, as well as in the other forms of material, i.e. the programme, the title and other accompanying texts.[6] It is also highly versatile in the way it creates references, for example through the use of proper nouns, mostly people's names but also those of buildings, institutions, etc. These are interesting from a linguistic point of view. Leaving aside many discussions about their status, which deal with questions such as whether they have a meaning and so forth, most linguists, however, agree on their function: they establish a direct reference. In order to do this, they 'replace deictic, or pointing gestures such that direct reference to that object or state of affairs is made' (Bussmann, 1996, p. 387). Another important aspect is their capacity to single out objects: 'A name is a word or a phrase that identifies a *specific* person, place or thing. We see the entity as an individual, and not as a member of a class' (Crystal, 1997, p. 112; italics UC). The reference to an individual object might be complicated if various entities bear the same name, but in the case of most biographees, this is clearly not the case. In some plays, names might not be given entirely from the beginning, such as for example *Vincent in Brixton*, where the Christian name of the title is completed with a surname in the play. Although not always part of the title, proper nouns are used in most biographical plays, particularly the names of the subjects of biography.

Insignificance is the exception to this rule, where none of the characters is ever given any name. Nevertheless they are clearly recognisable and thus demonstrate that despite their economy and convenience, proper names are not indispensable to establish a biographical name through language. Names are immensely powerful, however; once they are used, descriptions that counter a biographical link can, at best, undermine it, but not eliminate the expectations raised through the name. A good example of their impact on audience expectations is *Early Morning* by Edward Bond: without the use of proper names few spectators would associate the cannibalistic, lesbian monarch with a historical figure. Since the character is introduced as Victoria, wife to George and mother of Arthur and Albert, the link to a British queen can only be undermined by these characteristics. Few members of the audience will create the character without referring to their knowledge about Queen Victoria. In most productions the link created by proper names is supported by description provided in speeches, as well as visual and non-linguistic sound.

As suggested above, stunning similarities between an actor and the historical figure on whom a character is based can lead to a sensory reaction in the spectator comparable to the use of names. A person's visual appearance is so closely linked to personal identity (Bruce and Young, 1998, p. 97), however, that even the imitation of token features, such as Einstein's hair, is likely to be sufficient to establish an unequivocal reference to a single entity if they are widely known. In this case, a clear visual reference could be undermined by language, as Marilyn's attempt to seduce Einstein demonstrates. This example shows that visual appearance can be undermined by descriptions, but mostly visual elements complement descriptions or proper names, or vice versa. In contrast to comedians, such as Rory Bremner, whose acts rely on evoking famous people solely through the imitation of their voice and diction, few actors use this technique.[7] Instead smaller adjustments, such as a foreign accent, tend to accompany linguistic and visual references, mainly supporting them, but potentially undermining them as well.

If stage actions are perceived to undermine the biographical interpretation triggered by other elements in a performance, another important question for empirical research is raised: how do spectators integrate potentially contradictory elements into the embodied actions they create? The interaction between them will be a highly complex process and one could expect that some stage actions will have a stronger impact than others. Similarly, accompanying materials, such as programmes, might exert a different influence than stage actions do. It could also be assumed that the audience's understanding will be influenced not only by their perception of the life world, but also by their familiarity with conventional information and, potentially, structural and cultural knowledge. In addition their attitudes towards such combinations will be of interest.

In addition to examining the impact of biographical references on the process of creating embodied actions, questions about the consequences of these differences can be raised: do audiences attribute the same status to these embodied actions as they would if these were not built on biographical material? If the embodied actions are attributed a different value or status, it would seem likely that this could impact not only on the spectators' evaluation of the play, but also on the way in which they deal with the theatrical experience in their own life world. As such, biographical performances could be expected to exert a direct or indirect influence on the life world (see Upton, 2009, p. 191). Another aspect related to the relationship between the spectators' life world and biographical performances is meta-biography. In the terms used in our model of reception, a meta-level means that audiences would become aware of the process that turns stage actions into embodied actions and would reflect consciously on the meaning they attribute on the symbolic level and the way in which this is affected by their interaction with the performers and their own background knowledge. Here again empirical research could help to identify the elements that trigger such a thought process, the consequences this has and the audiences' attitudes to such reflexivity. Before these questions are investigated in the next chapter, the following paragraphs outline different methodologies that can be applied to pursue their study.

Methodology

Traditionally research in theatre studies relies mainly on academics' own reactions to performances and published reviews in order to analyse the embodied actions created in response to stage actions. The popularity of these sources of information is mainly based on their continuous accessibility: every researcher has access to his or her own experience of a performance and since the 1980s *London Theatre Record*, now *Theatre Record*, has provided a very convenient collection of reviews of contemporary performances. For historical performances written statements by spectators, whether professional theatre critics or others, are harder to locate, but are often the only window on spectators' experiences. Despite their usefulness, these sources cannot overcome various limitations. The first is given by their number: while they often present very detailed information, their small number cannot represent a wider audience.

More importantly, the background and purpose of these 'professional spectators' does not match that of the majority of theatre audiences. Scholars and critics bring more experience with performances and theoretical discourses about theatre than the average spectator. Their knowledge in the conventional and structural circle will therefore be broader. In addition, both write their impressions for a specific audience: critics are expected to combine description that informs their reader with a considered value judgement about the performance (in contrast to the rather crude form of stars granted to productions, their texts often have to defend this rating) and scholars need to relate their comments to current theoretical discourses. Finally their status as experts means that they will often conduct some form of research before or after witnessing a performance, which might affect their knowledge about the life world as well. While some spectators might pursue individual questions, either through research in published documents or through conversation with fellow members of the audience, the scope of their activities will be smaller than that of professional spectators.

Although some scholars acknowledge these limitations, not many studies attempt to overcome them by including the views of other, non-professional spectators. This can be partly explained by the inherently incomplete nature of such an endeavour. A detailed investigation of the questions outlined above would require empirical research on a scale that seems difficult to imagine even in theory. It would rely on a description of all the elements of a performance and the contextual material, as well as the spectators' entire contextual information, including their previous theatre experience, their experience with life stories, their knowledge about the historical figure and their familiarity with this period of history in general. Such a vast amount of information and the complexity of the interactions involved in such a process would be very difficult to consider, even for a single performance and a single spectator. In spite of these inevitable shortcomings, however, even relatively small studies can offer an insight into the way in which theatre or specific forms of theatrical performance function in our societies that cannot be attained when relying solely on the views of professional spectators.

The studies conducted on biographical theatre for this book are informed by previous publications. Although few publications on reception research explicitly develop their methodology, some helpful models are available in theatre studies, in particular Olsen (2000), Sauter (2000), Martin and Sauter (1995) and, to a lesser degree, Gourdon (1982). Willmar Sauter and his collaborators at Stockholm University (see Sauter, 2000, pp. 174–6) used informal group interviews after performances for an exploratory project that examined the perception of Swedish theatre audiences. Since their 'Theatre Talks' led to a number of highly interesting results, they could be used as a successful model for studies on biographical material in theatre. Their different basic premises, however, mean that they cannot be used without any adaptation. Most importantly, the lack of specific questions (Sauter, 2000, p. 160) leads to the danger of obtaining material that does not refer to the questions about reception established above. Another problem is related to organisation: a single group interview following a performance does not make it possible to examine the background knowledge about the historical figure or theatrical conventions of individual spectators. It is thus important to adapt the format sufficiently to consider the individual nature of such background knowledge and to inquire about it before spectators see a performance and have become familiar with the perspective on a historical life offered in it.

Such an adaptation could be informed by Jacqueline Martin's approach. Martin (Martin and Sauter, 1995, pp. 135–9) studied her students' reception of a production, combining a guided questionnaire, in which she tests her own perception against that of her students, with an essay-style question that allows her participants to develop their own reading. In other words, she combined questions that tested her predictions about their reaction with open questions to allow both the confirmation of her hypotheses and a more exploratory inquiry. Integrating this with Sauter's use of interviews, it would be possible to use semi-structured interviews that maintain the spontaneity of conversation but are sufficiently directed to maintain a focus on the use of biographical material.

The Studies Presented in this Book

The first study conducted for this book thus used semi-structured interviews with specific spectators before and after performances. This format enabled me to pursue the questions outlined above, i.e. to elicit information about their knowledge from different contextual circles and about the way in which the spectators employ this in the creation of symbolic meaning, and the consequences of this process. At the same time open questions allowed pursuing of the topics raised by the participants, especially since the immediacy of oral, rather than written, responses allowed more spontaneous, less developed responses from them. For practical reasons the participants were recruited from the undergraduate student body at Sheffield University, since homogeneity with regard to their age (18–27 years) and education (schooling in the UK) guaranteed some similarity in their cultural and social knowledge. Their familiarity with theatrical conventions, on the other hand, was deliberately varied in order to investigate whether this influenced their perception of the plays (see Appendix 2). The study was conducted over eight months and the participants were interviewed before and after four different performances of plays that were unknown to them to compare their perception of different ways in which biographical material was used.

The study included *Vincent in Brixton* and *Insignificance*, discussed in Chapters 3 and 4, as well as *Kafka's Dick* and *Letters Home*, but the latter will not be discussed in further detail as they are not included in the first part of the book.[8]

The main advantages of this setup – comparability between productions and spectators and depth of analysis – lead, however, to a number of disadvantages as well, particularly with regard to its limited applicability. A sample size of seven participants is appropriate for qualitative research – Kvale (1996) recommends a range of 15 ± 10 participants – but it means that the results cannot be generalised widely. As with theatre performances themselves, they are local and rooted in a specific situation. This problem can come to bear even more strongly as the study progresses and spectators become aware of its focus on biographical material, since their growing familiarity with the aspects discussed will influence their perception of the last performances. For an exploratory study that compares the experiences of non-professional spectators to the theoretical model based on scholarly predictions, this methodology is thus well suited, but further investigation could address these problems.

Martin's use of questionnaires shows that written answers can help to reach a wider number of participants. Olsen (2000) recommends a similar procedure in the form of a survey based on semiotic analysis. In contrast to the other two publications, he does not report whether he applied his questionnaire in empirical research, and its origins in scholarly theory contradict the emphasis on the experience of 'ordinary' spectators. Nonetheless his suggestions are interesting, as they offer an example of a structured questionnaire that tests hypotheses about theatrical reception. Substituting semiotic theory with the results from the interview study, Olsen could thus guide the preparation of a survey that tests our understanding of the impact of biographical material gained from the first phase of empirical research.

One of the aims of the survey conducted for this research project was thus to confirm or challenge the results from the interviews through closed questions based on our hypotheses. At the same time, the reference to a different play and production invariably adds a new aspect: focusing on *Thatcher – the Musical!*, the inquiry also provides an insight into the way in which audiences react to the highly intra-theatrical presentation of a performance with a very strong biographical link. The self-administered paper questionnaire (see Appendix 3) thus contains further open questions that explore this aspect. The questionnaire was distributed by the ushers before all six performances of *Thatcher – the Musical!* at Warwick Arts Centre (2006, Foursight Theatre); a total of

164 spectators participated, which meant that a software package (NVivo) had to be used to code and group the answers. The emphasis remains strongly on a qualitative interpretation, however, to reflect the complex nature of perception, and quotations from the questionnaire are included in the discussion.

Finally, the next chapter refers to reviews as one of the more traditional sources of information on reception. As the previous paragraphs have shown, the sources of information, such as different empirical methods or published material, automatically exert an impact on the information that can be gained from them. As a result transparency with regard to the basis of the discussion on reception presented in the next chapter is crucial. Having outlined in the current chapter the methods employed to investigate whether biographical material influences the reception process in the way predicted above, the following chapter concentrates on the discussion of reception without further references to methodology.

7
Audience Reactions to Biographical Performances

Introduction

This chapter presents the results of the empirical studies introduced in Chapter 6 and examines whether the predictions about differences in the reception process are supported by the reactions of actual audience members. Focusing on three productions, it also addresses questions specific to each of them. For *Insignificance* these aspects are the lack of names and the way in which biographical references are evoked solely through visual means, sounds and descriptions. In addition the discussion will examine whether the interviewees perceive the plot of this play as unlikely and if it can generate humour. In the context of *Vincent in Brixton* similar issues are raised. Chapter 3 suggests that the highly extra-theatrical form could convince audiences that Nicholas Wright's speculation is authentic, and the interviews can confirm or challenge this prediction. Furthermore, they can investigate the consequences of a more extra-theatrical reading. Finally, the reactions of spectators' views on *Thatcher – the Musical!* show whether audiences follow Foursight Theatre and see their highly intra-theatrical musical version of Margaret Thatcher's life as a contribution to the discourse about her political life and influence, or whether the form creates greater distance between the production and the life world. In this context the discussion can also give greater insight into the way conflicting signals can be negotiated. The results show that the appreciation of biographical material in theatre is more complex than the dichotomy of fact versus fiction would allow, but that the different degrees of proximity between events and figures on stage and in the life world have consequences for both of them.

Insignificance

The Use of Contextual Information Before the Performance

As detailed in Chapter 4, the Crucible production of *Insignificance* used neither the names of the historical figures, nor pictures of them or the actors in their roles in their publication material.[1] Nonetheless, the pre-show interviews were of great interest, as they revealed how expectations are formed without recourse to specific biographical links and thus offer a good point of comparison for the productions where names clarify the link beforehand. The interviewees connected the information from the title and the flyer to their knowledge about the life world, but did so on a much more generic level than they did for the biographical plays. Some participants used information about the period to establish visual expectations: '1950s, so, well 50s clothing obviously' (Canton, 2005a, participant 3). This is particularly interesting since the use on the poster of a plain blue background with the title in white does not give any clues about the images the interviewees are likely to see. This participant resists the neutrality created by this device and uses text to hypothesise about the images she is likely to see. Nonetheless, most participants concentrate on characters and plot elements, using their knowledge about the type of characters to guess that 'the Nobel Prize winning scientist *would* be very clever' (Canton, 2005a, participants 6 and 2; italics UC) or that 'the scientist is going to be really intelligent. The film star – they tend not to be. The baseball player might be all macho, I suppose' (Canton, 2005a, participant 6). As a consequence, this participant hoped that the conversations between an actress and a scientist '*might* be quite funny'. These quotations show that their generic expectations match those impersonated by the characters quite closely. The stereotypes can thus be evoked without biographical links, but recognition of historical figures who impersonate them in the play makes them more poignant, as the following paragraphs will demonstrate.

Recognition of the Biographical Characters

As suggested in Chapter 4, in *Insignificance* recognition of these figures is mainly created through visual means. The participants reported that especially the physical appearance of the Actress led to instant recognition: 'as soon as she walked in [I recognised her], because she's wearing the classic dress that she's always seen in in films and the hair and the make up' (Canton, 2005b, participant 3). This is echoed by two other participants who confirm that 'Marilyn Monroe was purely visual' (Canton, 2005b, participants 2 and 1). For another student the restriction of only a few token elements made this effect even more powerful, as it matched her previous image of Monroe and did not add any distracting elements: 'that dress, because that is all I really know about her, and the blonde hair' (Canton, 2005b, participant 7). Comments about the Professor and his similarity to Albert Einstein confirm that the imitation of some of his key features, such as 'the moustache and the crazy hair' (Canton, 2005b, participant 3; see also Canton, 2005b, participant 2), is sufficient to evoke the famous physicist, or in other words to establish a specific reference.

Compared to the powerful effect of the visual elements of the characters, the descriptions that help to establish biographical references become secondary. Nevertheless, most participants state that they help to confirm their impression. Whereas their reactions to the visual aspects are relatively comparable, the participants refer to a wider range of elements in the descriptions when explaining how they established the similarity between the Actress and Marilyn Monroe. Thus some participants picked up references to *The Seven Year Itch* (Canton, 2005b, participant 6; see also Canton, 2005b, participants 3 and 2), whereas others saw the Actress's marriage to a baseball player (Canton, 2005b, participant 5) or the idea that she was 'having affairs with people' (Canton, 2005b, participant 4) as evidence for her similarity to Marilyn Monroe. In the case of Einstein, there is less variation and most participants declare that references to 'his work and his theories' (Canton, 2005b, participant 5; see also Canton, 2005b, participant 4) or more specifically to 'the theory of relativity' (Canton, 2005b, participant 2) help to confirm his identity. The difference between the variety of connections they established to Marilyn Monroe and the limitation to one outstanding piece of information about Einstein demonstrates that the extent of their knowledge about the life world determines the process of recognition to the same extent as the play. Terry Johnson's script also contains further information about Einstein, such as his Jewish European origins or work at Princeton. Nonetheless, the students failed to pick these up as indications about the historical model, since they had less previous information on him (and potentially knew fewer famous physicists than actresses). This result reveals the difference from theatre critics as older and professional spectators, who referred to a wider range of characteristics that helped them to recognise Einstein. Nonetheless, there is significant overlap in terms of the features that support the biographical link. This can be seen in reviews that recreate the guessing game of the play, giving the following hints: the physical appearance and the work of the Actress and the Professor, her voice and her connection to a famous baseball player, and the political agenda of the Professor (see Cushman, 1982, p. 381; Armory, 1982, p. 384). Despite individual differences, a similar cultural background seems to allow some predictions about spectators' knowledge of the life world.

The interview study suggests that within a cultural group age is one of the factors that leads to differences in life world knowledge. While most reviews saw the reference to McCarthy's anti-Communist stance as unequivocal, the undergraduate students were too young to remember the fifties and apparently had not studied this aspect of the Cold War in any way. Although one participant recognised that the Senator was 'obviously very concerned with Communism and anti-American things' (Canton, 2005b, participant 3), for him this link was not sufficient to establish similarities with a specific historical figure.[2] The lack of an iconic image or further knowledge about the person McCarthy seems to have caused further difficulties, as one of them was informed about McCarthy's political role, but was not sure whether it was 'him or one of his side kicks' (Canton, 2005b, participant 6). In contrast to the two iconic figures, the characters based on less famous figures thus underline that predictions about the spectators' background knowledge are only possible for figures who have become part of popular and general knowledge in a specific cultural context. Outside these areas, audiences will use a variety of different ways to establish the relationship between a performance and the life world, characters and historical figures:

> The stage that I knew that it was McCarthy was when Einstein handed Marilyn Monroe a programme that was for the *Crucible* and then it all fell into place, because Marilyn Monroe was married to Arthur Miller who wrote *The Crucible* which uses the Salem witch trials in Massachusetts as a allegory for McCarthyism. (Canton, 2005b, participant 2)

The participants' lack of familiarity with McCarthy and Joe DiMaggio also demonstrates their expectation of uniformity in terms of the biographical links. One of the students who was not familiar with McCarthy and Joe DiMaggio explained that 'recognis[ing] two of them' made him wonder if he 'should [...] be able to recognise the others' (Canton, 2005b, participant 4), an impression echoed by participants 5 and 3. The latter explicitly gives lack of background knowledge as the reason for her conjecture: 'that is also *someone I don't know much about*' (Canton, 2005b, participant 3; italics UC). The biographical link to Marilyn Monroe and Albert Einstein is thus strong enough to be extended to other characters where contextual knowledge does not contradict this.

Against the predictions made in Chapter 4, however, the extra-theatrical form does not seem to reinforce the close link between the play and the life world to a high degree. None of the participants commented on the style of presentation, a lack of interest which could be explained by the fact that the degree of extra-theatricality in *Insignificance* is not as unusual as that of *Vincent in Brixton*. As a result, it might 'slide through the mind without difficulty', as Paget (1990, p. 23) suggested. Alternatively, it could also be explained with the fact that most of the participants regarded aspects of the plot as contradictory to their previous ideas about the historical figures represented. Participant 5 was the only one who was inclined to 'make assumptions that all the history and all the facts they are telling you were actual facts' on the basis that 'it was all so real' (Canton, 2005b, participant 5). For the others, the violation of their ideas about the historical figures outweighed the impact of presentation, as the following paragraphs demonstrate in more detail.

Aspects that Challenge a Biographical Reading

The counter indication to a biographical interpretation that is mentioned most often is contradictions between the character and the participants' knowledge about the historical figure. When asked about aspects that made them doubt that such a meeting had taken place, many participants gave examples of character traits and actions that did not fit with their concept of the historical figures. Participant 4 formulates his reasoning most explicitly: 'even if she was in a hotel room with Einstein' he believes that Marilyn Monroe 'wouldn't make a pass at him. [...] because it doesn't fit in with the image I had of her' (Canton, 2005b, participant 4). In some cases, even the fact that they have not heard about an event shown in the play is seen as sufficient reason to doubt its authenticity: 'I wouldn't imagine he would throw [his papers] out of a window, because that would be like a famous thing, [...] I would have remembered if he had done' (Canton, 2005b, participant 3). This judgement also demonstrates the students' certainty with which they believe in their life world knowledge about such a famous figure and event, as the impact of contradictions to their previous knowledge increases in proportion to their confidence in their previous contextual information. Such reasoning is confirmed by their use of generic knowledge in the absence of specific information about the historical characters. Although participant 1 applies his general ideas about the laws of sexual attraction to explain why he feels disinclined to believe that Marilyn Monroe should have tried to seduce Einstein, he precedes this with a disclaimer: although he does not know 'much about the history, it does seem an odd scenario'. She would be unlikely to choose him, as 'there were so many other men [and she] had the pick of everyone due to age difference' (Canton, 2005b, participant 1). Similarly, participant 5 accompanies her idea that they did not meet with an excuse: 'to my knowledge they didn't overlap. I'm completely wrong now, I'm sorry' (Canton, 2005b, participant 5).

Negotiating Contradictory Ideas about Biography

Uncertain about the degree of trust they could have in their own contextual knowledge, the participants also referred to the programme to clarify the relationship between the play and the world. Participant 1 uses it to confirm the name of Joe DiMaggio, since he 'wouldn't have been able to put a name on him until afterwards when [he] read the programme' (Canton, 2005b, participant 2). Two other participants explicitly mentioned that they wanted it to say 'a bit about each of the characters that were clearly represented on stage [...] It may have been good to mention that Marilyn Monroe did or did not have a higher than average IQ' (Canton, 2005b, participant 2) or to help 'fill the gap' (Canton, 2005b, participant 6). In contrast to the performance, they seem to expect the programme to offer a reliable indication about the status of the information given in the play, perhaps because written texts are more often used to convey knowledge about this world than performances.

Since the programme did not clarify their doubts, the participants had to rely on their own judgement about the probability of such a meeting, and just as contextual knowledge is used to reject ideas from the play, they also relied on it to accept some aspects of it: participant 7 believed in the 'rocky relationship between Marilyn Monroe and her husband because I think they did divorce' (Canton, 2005b, participant 7). In the same way she calculated that although 'most of his [Einstein's] important work was done before the second World War' (Canton, 2005b, participant 7), it made sense that in the 1950s he lived in the States. Without the opportunity to compare their impression to that of others, their conclusions varied to some extent. Thus participant 3 decides that her 'troubled personal life' and the fact that DiMaggio and Monroe 'were not getting on well' (Canton, 2005b, participant 3) made her attempt at seducing Einstein more plausible. It would be interesting to observe whether he integrated this aspect of his ideas about Monroe into his life world knowledge, or whether a comparison with other people would change his opinion, but the study did not allow for an assessment of the long-term impact the plays had on the participants' ideas about the life world.

The example demonstrates, however, that even in a play which the participants recognised as highly intra-theatrical, individual pieces of information are transferred into their life world knowledge if they are consistent with their previous ideas. For *Insignificance* this rarely applied to the events that make up the plot, but various participants felt that the play gave them a better idea of 'what the people were actually like' (Canton, 2005b, participant 7). While they separate the idea of 'truth of personality' in biographical writing (see Chapter 2) from the truth of events, they do so with certain caution. The previous quotation is preceded by participant 7's comment that she does 'not know how much of [*Insignificance*] was actual truth', and participant 1 explicitly observes that 'it probably sounds a bit contradictory if I can accept the characters for who they are so believably if it didn't happen' (Canton, 2005b, participant 1). While they recognise the potential to transfer information from the play into their knowledge about the life world, they remain cautious in view of the many elements that do not match their contextual knowledge.

Their reservations are confirmed by the overall judgement that the play appealed to them mainly on a theatrical level. Indirectly this is demonstrated in their comments about the actors. Although one participant applauded Mary Stockwell's imitation of Monroe as 'fitting' (Canton, 2005b, participant 2), most of them responded favourably to the comic, and thus intra-theatrical, elements of the characters: 'he was funny. The way he delivered the lines was very good and had comic timing' (Canton, 2005b, participant 3). They also explicitly formulated their appreciation of *Insignificance* as a 'clever combination of fact and fiction' (Canton, 2005b, participant 2) and recognised that the uncertainty and unexpectedness of these contrasting elements made the play attractive as it offered 'something that's a bit different' which made the audience 'listen more closely' (Canton, 2005b, participant 3). These answers show that the participants regarded it as a delightful piece of theatre, not a neutral window onto the life world. In the words of one of the students, he 'liked the fact that it was a very unbelievable scenario presented as a nice believable story' (Canton, 2005b, participant 2).

Participant 6 was the exception to this general view. She perceived the references to historical figures as confusing and felt upset and angry about the lack of clarity about them, considering that the meeting was unlikely to have happened this way. She nevertheless did not regard the contradictions as voluntary comic moments, since she could not imagine that 'the bloke who wrote it just made up these random things' (Canton, 2005b, participant 6). Her lack of appreciation of this sense of humour indicates that the playful 'as if' only works on the basis of complicity between the author and the audience; where spectators do not share the sense that the stage is an appropriate place for humorous alternative discourses about famous figures and instead expect a reconstruction of past lives, they reject the unbelievable elements: This participant declared that it could only make sense to her if 'it was something that had happened in history' (Canton, 2005b, participant 6).

The other participants, in contrast, report that even if they were not 'sure how much of [*Insignificance*] was actually based on facts or not, [...] it didn't really affect the way [they] perceived or enjoyed things' (Canton, 2005b, participant 4). Instead of confusion, they felt that the openness provided them with an opportunity to discuss the play with others to find out 'how everyone else came to guess who they were [and] if they had heard of the other two [DiMaggio and McCarthy]' (Canton, 2005b, participant 3). Whereas participant 6 assumes that there must be a definite signifié that she cannot access due to lack of knowledge about the social context, they are willing to negotiate it with others.

The other participants' greater flexibility to accept a fuzzy relationship between the world and the play might also be based on their analytical skills. Their comments demonstrate that some of them are able to consciously analyse the effect of Terry Johnson's play: participant 4, for example, identified the economy of using historical figures, observing that the biographical link 'prevents the playwright or the actors having to spend the first 15, 20 minutes of the play saying: we are the characters, this is our history' (Canton, 2005b, participant 4). Similarly, participant 7 acknowledges that *Insignificance* plays with the idea of voyeurism, suggesting that it gives audiences the impression of 'getting a look behind closed doors' (Canton, 2005b, participant 7). Even the applause for the author who had the 'very clever idea' (Canton, 2005b, participant 3) to bring these four figures together demonstrates their awareness of the theatrical artifice behind *Insignificance*. On this basis these participants might find it easier to accept the playful undermining of their expectations, as they appreciate how they are constructed. Participant 6 in contrast stated that the biographical link made the characters 'more like people, I suppose, three-dimensional as opposed to just characters on stage' (Canton, 2005b, participant 6); in other words, her lack of experience with theatrical performance, or familiarity with Sauter's conventional contextual circle, meant that she could not vary her approach to the play in the same way and felt that the only valid interpretation would be one that reflected events in the life world.

These reactions underline the impact of spectators' knowledge on their perception of biographical theatre, but the agreement among six of the seven interviewees suggests that the playful mode of 'as if' in *Insignificance* tends to be accepted by audiences. They establish bio-graphical links with the help of visual means and descriptions, but the contrast to their previous ideas about the two most famous figures is too strong to regard the performance as sufficiently extra-theatrical to estab-lish a significant bi-directional flow of information. Individual aspects of personality might be transferred, but overall they enjoy it for its the-atrical appeal. In the words of one of the spectators: 'it's just a nice piece to stand alone as a what if scenario' (Canton, 2005b, participant 7).

Vincent in Brixton

Expectations Before the Play

Due to the small overlap between other discourses about Vincent van Gogh and *Vincent in Brixton* it could be expected that the spectators' willingness to integrate the play's version of van Gogh's youth into their life world knowledge is even lower. On the other hand, the highly extra-theatrical presentation and the lack of contradicting elements could compensate for this aspect and lead to a higher acceptance of Nicholas Wright's speculations. This effect can indeed be observed in the inter-views conducted after the performance, but before discussing this in detail another factor deserves attention: in contrast to *Insignificance* the use of his first name and *La chambre de Van Gogh à Arles* (1889) by van Gogh in the publicity material for the Manchester production mean that audiences could establish the link to the painter before the performance.

The interviews confirm that proper nouns play an essential role in the formation of expectations about the play. Without seeing the picture, however, most of them used the more specific place name, concluding that 'Brixton [is] an area of London that is not so well kept [and that] is often associated with social problems, [...] it will be a story about a young guy' (Canton, 2004a, participant 2). The picture, however, helps them to clarify the name and establish the link to a specific person: 'The first thing I point out as I look at this flyer is that Vincent is Vincent Van Gogh' (Canton, 2004a, participant 2; see also Canton, 2004a, participants 1, 3, 4, 5, 6 and 7). The specification helps them to activate a slightly broader area of their life world knowledge: as a play about 'the *artist* Vincent Van Gogh' they conclude that this is 'more of an arty play' (Canton, 2004a, participant; italics UC) that will depict 'a picture of a young artist [who] eventually [...] is successful' (Canton, 2004a, participant 4). This addition is clearly dependent on their additional knowledge about the popularity of van Gogh's paintings today, as the flyer only hints at the possibility when it announces the 'story of the young Van Gogh on the brink of genius' (Library Theatre, 2004b). For one of the interviewees, contextual knowledge unexpectedly decreased the proximity between the play and the life world. Since he would not link van Gogh who 'was Dutch' with 'London, in Brixton' (Canton, 2004a, participant 2) the interviewee expected a performance that did not reflect the life of the painter. Although some of the other participants commented on this contradiction as well, he was the only one who perceived the contrast between the advertising material and his knowledge about the historical figure as sufficiently strong to contradict the biographical link that was evoked. While the combination of a first name and the visual link were strong enough to establish a biographical link, this exception shows that the effect can differ according to the spectators' confidence in the extent of their knowledge: unlike participant 2 the others felt that the gaps in their knowledge allowed them to integrate the reference to London into their concept of van Gogh's life.

In addition to their expectations based on their knowledge about the specific figure, the existence of this link leads to generic expectations about life stories. They expect the play to be 'about' someone: 'It sounds like a historical story about Vincent Van Gogh in Brixton' (Canton, 2004a, participant 1). As a consequence they have a clear idea about the plot structure based on their experience with other life narratives about artists: as the story of a 'young artist' the central character is expected to 'struggle and try to make a name for himself' (Canton, 2004a, participant 1), but his eventual success will be included in the play, as it will be 'about his work and life' (Canton, 2004a, participant 1). Although some participants emphasised his 'life around [his art] and who he meets and friends' (Canton, 2004a), others thought the primary focus would be 'Vincent's work as an artist' (Canton, 2004b, participant 4), but all of them expected to find a combination of these two elements in the plot. In retrospect they also reported their previous idea about the plot's time structure: 'I expected [...] more of his life [not just] like I think it was one year' (Canton, 2004b, participant 5). Their knowledge about the typical structure of artists' life stories (in Sauter's terms, the cultural contextual circle) is thus as important as their information about the specific historical figure at the heart of the play. Together these give them a relatively detailed idea about the narrative structures of the performance and suggest that the play will be of interest in terms of the information about the life world it provides: 'I'm quite interested in history. [Finding out about van Gogh] made me want to see it' (Canton, 2004b, participant 3).

The Influence of the Form on the Biographical Link

As suggested in Chapter 3, the unusually high degree of formal extra-theatricality reinforced the perception of *Vincent in Brixton* as a reconstruction of van Gogh's life. As the reviewer who observed that 'everything is for real' (Brown, 2002; see also Chapter 3), various participants explained that they were 'really impressed with the stage. They had running water and they're cooking because you see steam, and I thought, I felt I smelled the roast dinner at the beginning' (Canton, 2004b, participant 2). Similarly, participant 7 stated that the cooking included 'the things that don't usually happen in theatre'. She continued to explicitly link 'the fact that it was so real' to her inclination to 'make assumptions that all the history and all the facts that they are telling you were actual facts' (Canton, 2004b, participant 7). Another interviewee made a similar observation: 'The fact that it is one set, always in the kitchen, that made it more true, I think' (Canton, 2004b, participant 3). It remains unclear, however, whether he referred to the everyday nature of the setting, its naturalist detail or the continuity of one setting throughout the play. For participant 4, an amateur actor and active theatre goer, the symbolic links created through Vincent's sketching of 'a pair of boots on a newspaper on the table' that are similar to 'one of his famous paintings' (Canton, 2004b, participant 4) also reinforced the closeness between the performance and the life world. At least for someone with extensive experience of the theatrical conventions, symbolic links do not interrupt the extra-theatricality created through similarity between the life world and the scenography but reinforce them further.

Other participants confirmed that the style of acting and the aging process of the characters heightened their sense of extra-theatricality. Many of the participants found Vincent 'convincing', but only one of them specified her overall impression and identified 'his accent' and the 'subtlety' (Canton, 2004b, participant 7) and complexity of his character as the main reasons for his life-likeness. Furthermore, the 'way that he seemed to age a bit through the performance' (Canton, 2004b, participant 1) was important to indicate the passing of time and the changes this exerted on the protagonist in the same way as would happen in the life world. This evaluation does not only apply to the central historical character. Participant 5 felt that being able to 'imagine [Ursula Loyer] in her teacher role' (Canton, 2004b, participant 5) made her more like a human being.

For some of them the comic aspects of the performance countered this impression. Participant 4 commented most explicitly on this aspect: 'I wouldn't exactly say it was 100 per cent realist in its approach, we weren't there to have this like Stanislavskian belief in the characters; it was a funny play' (Canton, 2004b, participant 4). Similar to his recognition of symbolic links between the scenography and van Gogh's work, he compensated this interruption of a biographical reading with the recognition that peeling potatoes reinforced the link to van Gogh as 'in his early work he uses a lot of potatoes' (Canton, 2004b, participant 4). None of the other participants used such symbolic interpretations to the same degree to establish extra-theatricality, possibly because participant 4's theatre experience meant that he was able to use a wider range of aspects to inform the creation of embodied actions beyond surface similarity. Nonetheless, the other participant who reported the 'light hearted comedy' and comic acting at the beginning of the play made him wonder whether the play's version was 'actually what happened' (Canton, 2004b, participant 3). Other participants made use of similar mechanisms to translate stage actions into symbolic ones to maintain the biographical link. Observing that Vincent's sister was 'the most unrealistic, yet deeply comic of the characters in the play' (Canton, 2004b, participant 2), participant 2 nevertheless felt that her part 'shows the audience [...] the gap that had occurred between Van Gogh and his supportive family'. The participants' willingness to establish such a symbolic interpretation seems to be dependent on further support from contextual knowledge. The understanding shown above, for example, is further supported by the fact that this interviewee had 'heard that Van Gogh spent a lot of his life on his own, so [...] presume[d] there were rifts between him and his family' (Canton, 2004b, participant 2).

Evaluation of the Play's General Extra-Theatricality

The spectators' recourse to contextual knowledge demonstrates the main difference between *Vincent in Brixton* and *Insignificance*. Although some participants saw the comic moments as contradictory to their idea that van Gogh suffered from depression (Canton, 2004b, participant 5), few other aspects *counter* their previous knowledge. This might be partly due to their rather limited background knowledge, which meant that they were open to new ideas, as one participant explicitly stated: 'I was going pretty much open minded. I didn't really know much about Van Gogh anyway' (Canton, 2004b, participant 5). As a result they seem to be less inclined to question the authenticity of the events and to consult the programme to confirm the relationship between the play and the life world. Although one student read the programme note and decided that her assumption that 'he had written a diary or something' (Canton, 2004b, participant 2) was mistaken, two other participants failed to notice Nicholas Wright's reference to the gap in the official literature and concentrated on the chronology of his life, which, for them, 'filled in a lot of things' (Canton, 2004b, participants 5 and 6).

Their inclination to adopt the version of van Gogh's time in London is also reflected in their conclusions about the minor characters and their reactions to the ending. Echoing their reactions to *Insignificance* the spectators assume that a biographical protagonist means that the other characters are also based on life world models, but in *Vincent in Brixton* they apply this idea to a character who does not have any claim to fame himself. Wondering 'how much they found out about Sam' (Canton, 2004b, participant 3), a minor character based solely on a reference to another lodger in van Gogh's letters, participant 3 does not acknowledge the fact that detailed historical sources about a relatively unknown figure are unlikely to exist. In a similarly indirect way, the participants' reaction to the open ending provides an equally indirect indication of their belief that the play closely mirrors the life world. Many of them felt unhappy that 'it didn't give you anything [about] what happened afterwards' (Canton, 2004b, participant 2), and some of them specify that they wanted to know 'what he did in his life after' (Canton, 2004b, participant 6). Even though this formulation does not specifically clarify this aspect, another interviewee specifies that he 'wanted to like see what actually happened in his real life' (Canton, 2004b, participant 3).

The previous paragraphs have shown that their impression of a higher level of extra-theatricality is based to an equal extent on the use of formal extra-theatricality and the *absence* of contradictory signals. On this basis the interviewees incorporated information from the play into their perception of the historical figure, focusing again on personality rather than events: participant 6 claimed that her 'understanding of what he was like has changed' (Canton, 2004b, participant 6) and others provided specific examples of aspects of his personality they found believable, for instance the idea that van Gogh was 'quite set [...] once he decided to do something he'd do it' (Canton, 2004b, participant 5) or 'his strong faith' (Canton, 2004b, participant 1). Often the new aspects add 'things about Vincent Van Gogh that [they] didn't know before' (Canton, 2004b, participant 7). Sometimes, however, such bi-directional flow of information even occurs where the play contradicts their contextual information: although her image of van Gogh was of someone 'older, [who] looked a bit trampy and [...] a bit mad' (Canton, 2004b, participant 5), participant 5 accepts the idea that he might have been 'very smart, very intelligent' instead.

Balancing Fuzziness and Clarity

The participants' willingness to transfer information about the play into their life world knowledge is, however, accompanied by a number of disclaimers that they were 'not entirely sure whether every bit was all true' (Canton, 2004b, participant 3) and great eagerness to justify their assumptions. Participant 1, for example, hastens to add that van Gogh's religious fervour was probably 'another side of his character that isn't usually portrayed in a very maximised manner' (Canton, 2004b, participant 1) when he identifies this aspect as a believable one. Others use language structures to indicate remaining doubts, conceding that the play 'will have changed my opinion about how [he] thought Vincent was' only if it was 'meticulously researched' (Canton, 2004b, participant 4). Comparison with their reactions to a performance based entirely on verbatim material[3] shows that the participants used much stronger expressions to indicate that they integrated new information into their existing contextual knowledge. The reluctance to do so after *Vincent in Brixton* might be based on the lack of strong indications in favour of thematic extra-theatricality, or could be assumed to demonstrate their general disinclination to see performance as more than 'just a piece of fiction' (Canton, 2004b, participant 3) which, in Ben Chaim's words (see Chapter 6), is always placed at a minimum distance to the life world.

While further research would be necessary to clarify whether one of these explanations applies to a greater degree, the participants' apprehension about the potential consequences of misjudging the relationship between the play and the life world has an impact on their evaluation. With the exception of participant 4 who claimed that 'at the end of the day it doesn't really matter whether it was real or not, it was a good story' (Canton, 2004b, participant 4) and that he would not pursue the issue further, all participants expressed the wish to clarify this point, whether through conversation with other spectators they could 'ask whether it was actually all true' (Canton, 2004b, participant 3) or consultation of other discourses about van Gogh. Asked about the reasons why clarity on this point was important, participant 3 suggests that accepting a different version of van Gogh's life might be regarded as 'being stupid' (Canton, 2004b, participant 3). In other words, he feels that violating the shared and established concept of the historical figure could lead to social sanctions in the form of condescension. The interviewees' positive evaluation of a performance that combines 'an educational experience' with 'enjoyment' (Canton, 2004b, participant 5), or in other words provides information that can be transferred into the life world in a pleasant way, depends on the existence of a clear dividing line between extra- and intra-theatrical aspects. Without such a line they feel unprotected from the potentially negative consequences if they misjudge the similarities between the play and the life world. Their reactions thus echo participant 6's rejection of the invented events in *Insignificance* which confused her ideas about the life world. The fact that almost all of the students are willing to grant a higher degree of extra-theatricality to *Vincent in Brixton*, however, suggests that the form of presentation and the absence of elements that clearly violate their ideas about the life world strongly promote the impression of close proximity between the play and the life world.

Thatcher – the Musical!

The interview study thus suggests that biographical material had a strong impact on the spectators' expectations and perceptions of the performances. Where they concluded that the play closely reflected the life world, they transferred new information from it into their life world concepts. Their willingness to do so was mainly based on their perception that the representation on stage did not contradict their existing knowledge. The survey of *Thatcher – the Musical!* offered the opportunity to establish whether these observations would also apply to a higher number of spectators. At the same time, it explored whether the insight that formal extra-theatricality could greatly enhance the perceived proximity between the play and the life world in *Vincent in Brixton* implied that this mechanism worked both ways. The intra-theatrical presentation could then be expected to increase the distance. While this conclusion might be logical, this effect would counter the intentions of the practitioners, who hoped that the performance would engage the audience in reflection about the political legacy of Margaret Thatcher, in other words in reflection about the life world (see Chapter 4).

Expectations Before and Interest in the Production

In order to evaluate the impact of contextual knowledge on the audience's expectations and the way they translate stage actions into embodied ones, the study included questions that could give some indication about the respondents' life world concepts. Even though a survey does not allow a detailed exploration of individual background knowledge, questions about the participants' age and the time they had spent in the UK (see Appendix 3, questions 13 and 14) gave a rudimentary insight into their cultural background and hence their potential familiarity with the Prime Minister's work and life. This was deemed particularly important as the performances took place in Warwick Arts Centre, a venue attached to Warwick University. Although a significant percentage of the audience is not affiliated to the university, the presence of students who are too young to remember Margaret Thatcher, and even more international students who are not very familiar with political life in the UK, could have an impact on the results. Finally, the number of theatre performances the participants had attended over the last six months was elicited (see Appendix 3, question 15) to provide an indication of their familiarity with a range of theatrical means of expression, as this factor might also influence their evaluation of the performance.

In terms of their cultural background, the percentage of audience members who were between 10 and 29 years, or in other words too young to remember Thatcher's time in office, was lower than expected: only 27 spectators fell into this category, less than 20 per cent of the 164 who participated in the survey. A comparison of their expectations with those of older audience members also showed that their expectations did not differ significantly. Among the group who were 30 years or over, less than 10 per cent had been absent from the UK for a year or more, and less than 5 per cent had lived abroad for more than four years. Given Thatcher's long time in office, it could thus be assumed that the number of audience members who would not recognise the biographical reference in the title or the poster was negligible and most would be familiar with her political decisions. Since only four participants declared that they had been invited to see the play and were not aware of the title before seeing it, almost all of them could form their expectations around the reference to a famous name.

Although it is not possible to establish a definite connection between their familiarity with the title and their expectations about the play, their answers to the questions about their expectations about the play and their motivation to see it (see Appendix 3, questions 2 and 3) suggest that both the name and the reference to a genre have an impact on them. In addition, the open-ended formulation of the questions offers an insight into the aspects of the production the spectators choose to comment on without further priming from a researcher to include specific topics, such as the style of presentation or the content of the plot. About a third of the participants speculate about the plot and events that might be presented, predicting that the play would be concerned with 'historical events' (Canton, 2006, participant 21) or 'history' (Canton, 2006, participant 99). Others specify this expectation further and state that they expect the play to evolve around 'the life of Mrs. Thatcher' (Canton, 2006, participant 84). Among them only seven express the hope to see an 'unbiased production' (Canton, 2006, participant 63), in other words a biographical performance that reconstructs events from the life world on the stage without imposing a specific perspective on them. For this small number of spectators, the possibility of reconstructionist biography thus exists on stage. The majority, however, expect the play to convey a clear political opinion or a satirical view on the politician. This might be partly inspired by personal, political antagonism to Thatcher, but some of the answers suggest that it is related to the combination of her name and a genre usually associated with light entertainment. This connection is further supported by the fact that nearly a third of the spectators also hope to see a play infused with humour and wit, attributes that are rarely seen to favour neutrality. Although only a few explicitly comment on them, this expectation is likely to be based on the 'improbable' combination of Thatcher and the musical genre, the 'contradiction' of 'Maggie in a musical [that] was an amusing notion' in itself (Canton, 2006, participants 49, 132, 24 and 152).

These expectations seem to be derived mainly from the title, as no significant variation can be observed between the answers of the 160 spectators who were familiar with the title and the 63 who had seen the poster as well. Against the expectation that those who had seen additional marketing material could have interpreted the rather un-Thatcherite colour scheme in her photograph as an indication towards a view of her that is little concerned with historical accuracy, they were no more likely to expect a specific perspective or humour than those who had not seen this image. A small difference could be observed between the expectations of those who knew or did not know the company: those familiar with Foursight's work were (in relation to the overall number of answers in each category) slightly more inclined to expect humour and music. Their awareness of the theatrical conventions typical of this group made them receptive to the contradiction between reconstructionist biography and the indications of a more intra-theatrical format. For those who did not know the company's earlier work, this indication does not undermine the biographical reference, however; it merely changes their expectation about the presentation of this link.

For many of them the unexpected nature of this combination makes the play attractive. Asked about their reasons for attending the play, various participants explicitly name the 'intriguing title' (Canton, 2006, participant 43) or the promise of a 'combination of politics ("Thatcher") and 'light entertainment' ("the musical")' (Canton, 2006, participant 2). This attraction might be partly explained by curiosity: an audience member who apparently answered the questionnaire after the perform-ance declares that s/he 'thought [this] would be very difficult to portray – seems not' (Canton, 2006, participant 76). Nonetheless, their interest in the combination also testifies to their view that the play should offer more than a reconstruction of the life world. Four participants express a 'keen interest in politics' (Canton, 2006, participant 25), an answer that indicates their interest in political analysis. Nineteen respondents explain their motivation to attend the performance with their specific political sympathies, and against my and the company's expectations, these seem to be rather evenly distributed across the political spectrum, including nine spectators who feel 'admiration' for the former PM or are 'Margaret Thatcher supporter[s]' (Canton, 2006, participants 134 and 23), as well as ten who 'came to mock!', hoping to have their 'desire for abuse' fulfilled, as for them it is 'always good to see Maggie ridi-culed!' (Canton, 2006, participants 49, 21 and 59). At first glance, one could read these answers as an indication that they see the performance mainly in terms of the life world. If one assumes that their ideas about the kind of perspective they hope to see might vary, however, they are likely to, consciously or unconsciously, hope for a performance that replicates their own perspective.

Translating Theatrical Means into Life World Events

The frequent rejection of Reconstructionism before the performance is reflected in the respondents' perception of the production itself. Despite the use of highly theatrical means to present Margaret Thatcher – here the intensive use of doubling and the intra-theatricality of her recurring accessories, such as the hairstyle, the handbag and twin sets, are of par-ticular interest – and some of the events in her life, none of the audience members reported any difficulties in establishing this connection. The exploration of the way in which they related individual elements from the performance to their knowledge about the life world is based on two questions that asked participants to identify points of orientation in the development of the plot and the recognition of the protagonist (see Appendix 3, questions 5 and 6). Further specification of the types of elements that could establish this connection was avoided, since this would require the use of more technical terms which might counteract the intention to explore the perception of average audiences rather than my own perception.

In terms of the plot development the participants defied the expectation that the presentation might suggest a looser link and often named particularly intra-theatrical elements as those that helped them to interpret the stage action as references to specific events in the life world. The event that is named most frequently, for example, is the Falklands War, which is evoked in the production by a range of different means: the company huddles together as a group of Islanders surrounded by Argentinean forces, then imitates penguins and sheep. This is followed by Military Maggie who delivers Margaret Thatcher's speech to Parliament at the beginning of the war while standing on the piano that has been turned round to reveal a tank. Although none of these stage actions are likely to be mistaken for a neutral reconstruction, it is interesting that the participants who specified which of these elements they found most helpful did not name the original words of the speech or another more extra-theatrical aspect. Instead they recognised the actors' imitation of penguins (14 answers; for a more detailed discussion of the penguins, see Chapter 4) and sheep (10 answers), or the transformation of the piano into a tank (15 answers).

The elements that helped spectators to link the characters to the historical Margaret Thatcher offer a mixed picture. One of the most cited aspects is the characters' physical appearance, and the use of rubber wigs that imitate the perfectly styled hair of the PM, for example, demonstrates that here again audiences use a formally very intra-theatrical device to link the performance to the life world. The second element that is mentioned very often, however, is her voice – here again the natural voices of the different actresses who play the eight Maggies prevents them from becoming nearly identical to Thatcher's, but their attempts to imitate her tone of voice and her diction mean that this element is slightly less intra-theatrical than her physical appearance. One might assume that the recognition of people allows fewer departures from formal extra-theatricality, but the recognition of other historical figures counters this idea: some of the spectators felt that the representation of Thatcher's contemporaries helped them to anchor the plot in time and place. The figure that was recognised most frequently was Ronald Reagan, whose representation (see Chapter 4) could hardly be termed extra-theatrical. Even here the actress adopted an American accent for the few lines she speaks in this role. This suggests that similarities between biographical characters and the figures on whom they are modelled can be more diverse in terms of physical appearance than in terms of voice.

Overall Evaluation of the Relationship between the Play and Thatcher's Life

The audience members who participated not only demonstrated that the highly intra-theatrical form of presentation was no barrier to establishing a close link to the life world, they also evaluated this overwhelmingly positively when asked about the extensive doubling (see Appendix 3, questions 7 and 8). With the exception of six participants, all respondents affirm that they liked this device. In their explanations some of them declare that they regard the biggest advantage in its contribution to the clarity of the narrative, seeing it as 'the simplest solution to aging her convincingly' (Canton, 2006, participant 35) that shows 'change very graphically' (Canton, 2006, participant 36). For these respondents theatricality and referentiality seem to be two sides of the same coin rather than opposites. Others, however, appreciate the 'variety' of the play of 'various actresses' or its 'playful[ness]' (Canton, 2006, participants 123, 77 and 90), indicating that it enhanced the production's value as performance. A third group seems to combine the two aspects when they welcome the possibility of showing 'different facets of her personality' (Canton, 2006, participant 163), since 'all of [the actresses bring] a different perspective' (Canton, 2006, participant 119) to the interpretation of the historical character. Here the theatrical device is seen to enhance the link to the life world, but at the same time to reinforce Foursight's specific perspective on it.

The frequent use of intra-theatrical elements to link stage actions to specific figures and events in the life world and their positive evaluation is further confirmed by the participants' more general judgement of the relationship between the play and the life world. These were elicited through an open question that asked spectators to summarise their impression of the performance. Designed as a direct counterpart to question 2 about their expectations, question 4 did not include any further guidance, to allow a free choice of elements they wished to mention and to allow multiple comments. Although the formulations that related to the performance and its quality (mentioned in 89 comments) now slightly outweigh those that clearly refer to its relationship to the life world (Canton, 2006, participant 63), both aspects are still prominent in the answers. Interestingly, comments about the play's accuracy (five answers), its ability to 'capture the main events' (quoted from example in Canton, 2006, participant 77; similar formulations appear in nine answers) or state that it was 'informative' (quoted from example in Canton, 2006, participant 150; similar formulations appear in 14 answers) are more frequent than those that referred explicitly to the fact that the play presented a specific perspective or political comment (19 in total). The idea that the play might have been perceived as more balanced or neutral than expected echoes many reviews that emphasised this point (and suggests that the company achieved their aim of doing justice to Margaret Thatcher despite differing political opinions; see Chapter 4).

This conclusion has to be drawn with some caution, however, as it does not take into account the 44 participants who commented on the production's humour. If these are regarded as compliments on the presentation, this would suggest that twice as many spectators commented on it as *performance* as included a statement on its relation to the life world. If one chooses to conclude that the wittiness of its presentation depends on the discrepancy between Margaret Thatcher's usual appearance and the plastic wigs, on the other hand, this would indicate that these audience members wished to comment on the unusual perspective it takes. In order to clarify our understanding of this aspect, a more detailed examination of the origin and role of humour in the questionnaire would have been necessary. On the basis of the existing evidence, however, one might suggest that for these audiences, offering an unusual perspective on the past does not contradict the possibility of a balanced presentation. Perhaps the idea of capturing the past does not refer to reconstructing it 'as it really was' on the surface, but to offer a view of the breadth of interpretations of a material reality that existed at the time as well.

Such an interpretation would be further supported by the audiences' explicit evaluation of the degree to which the performance reflects Margaret Thatcher's life (see Appendix 3, questions 9 and 10). Surprisingly, only seven spectators declare that it reflects her life not very well or not well at all (options 1 and 2 on a scale of 5), 21 choose an average rating, and a clear majority of 125 think it reflects her life rather or very well (options 4 and 5 on the scale; 11 did not answer this question). Many of their answers refer to the quantity of references to events and figures with which they are familiar from the life world, rather than the way in which they are shown, stating that 'the major issues' or the 'most significant events were included' (Canton, 2006, participants 8 and 10). Thematic extra-theatricality thus seems to outweigh the form in which the similarities between the play and the performance are created. In other words, many spectators do not necessarily see the theatre as a place where the life world is reflected in a neutral, invisible translation, but in a range of different ways. The survey thus supports Reinelt's suggestion that audiences (in her case of documentary theatre) expect 'certain aspects of the performance [to be] directly linked to the reality they are trying to experience or understand' but that they do not 'expect unmediated access' (Reinelt, 2009, p. 9). In the interview study, the participant with most theatre experience expressed the greatest flexibility in terms of establishing a biographical reading from little extra-theatrical elements, whereas the participant who was least familiar with stage performances found this most difficult. This connectioñ is not upheld by the survey, as the respondents who had seen more than five plays in the last five months did not see it as a better reflection of the PM's life than those who had seen one play or less. Formal intra-theatricality then does not prevent a biographical reading for the audience of *Thatcher – the Musical!*, regardless of their familiarity with theatrical styles.

Can the Play Change Their Views on Maggie?

The respondents' impression that the performance reflects Thatcher's life well then suggests that, in parallel to the audiences of *Vincent in Brixton*, the respondents are willing to transfer information from the performance into their life world knowledge. Nonetheless, only very few of them, 26 of 164 respondents, reported that the performance had changed their concept of the historical Margaret Thatcher (see Appendix 3, questions 11 and 12). Despite the close relationship they perceived between the play and the life world 131 participants denied that it had changed their ideas about the historical figure in any way. Since the open question only inquired why they *had* their opinion, the survey does not clearly indicate the reasons for this apparent contradiction. While this demonstrates the limitations of this method of inquiry for more exploratory research as it cannot follow up unexpected results, it is possible to identify potential explanations. Among the spectators who answered the question, some felt that the play offered a more humanised image of Margaret Thatcher, a reaction that shows growing empathy following recognition of the human being behind the role of the politician. One could argue that the distance created by the visible role playing of eight actresses, rather than a highly extra-theatrical character embodied convincingly by the same actress throughout, makes this reaction more unlikely.

Alternatively to such a Brechtian interpretation, it could also be related to the fact that many of the spectators experienced Thatcher's time in government. The temporal and emotional distance over 15 years later might also open up the possibility of accepting a view that at the time would have been hard to accept – participant 47, for example, states that now s/he feels 'A degree of respect for her despite the horror she caused as we think of her in her current frail state' (Canton, 2006, participant 47). Further support for such an interpretation can be found in the answers to other questions, where the importance of personal experience and memory is also emphasised. In their evaluation of the degree to which the play reflects Margaret Thatcher's life, 26 participants explicitly compare the performance to their own memory rather than an abstract notion of 'historical truth'. While some spectators relativise this comparison, conceding that 'one does not know everything' but that 'the play echoed what one did know' (Canton, 2006, participant 74), others use it to make their evaluation more convincing: they know 'because we lived through the events' (Canton, 2006, participant 64). Whether they express such trust in first-hand experience or doubt the accuracy of memory, personal experience – or rather the impression of first-hand experience, since it stems mainly from the media – provides the most important basis for comparison.

The importance of personal memories to perception can perhaps not only offer an explanation for the tendency to see Maggie in a more humane way. It could also be argued that first-hand experience of her time in government explains why for many participants the play did not lead to a revision of their previous opinions: knowledge acquired from third parties might be more prone to be changed than that based on one's own experience. Such a hypothesis could be supported by a correlation between the spectators' age and their willingness to change their view, as older spectators are more likely to have stronger memories of Thatcher's time in government, but the data does not offer such a parallel. Instead the reasons why spectators felt that the play did or did not reflect the PM's life well can be seen to endorse this explanation: a significant number of respondents (Canton, 2006, participant 32) explained their evaluation with references to their own memories, suggesting that the play 'covered the main elements I remembered' (Canton, 2006, participant 124) or that 'It certainly seemed as I remembered it' (Canton, 2006, participant 89). Similarly, some see the origin for their uncertainty about the relationship between the play and the life world in their lack of personal memories – 'I can't say how well it reflected – being too young' (Canton, 2006, participant 138) – or their own doubts about them: 'I don't know whether my memories are accurate or biased' (Canton, 2006, participant 46). For these participants, personal recollections are the most important point of comparison, which either supports their evaluation or explains their hesitation when making one.

The last paragraphs clearly show that the relationship between the life world and the production is more complex than the dichotomy of fact and fiction would suggest. While it indicates that an intra-theatrical presentation does not necessarily increase the distance between the play and the life world, the perception that the two are closely connected in turn does not necessarily lead to a bi-directional flow of information. This result echoes the caution of the interviewees who watched *Vincent in Brixton* and the careful selection of information they accepted. In addition, aspects of personality, whether it is the painter's direct manners in *Vincent in Brixton* or Maggie's unexpected humanity in *Thatcher – the Musical!*, were most readily accepted in both plays. The fact that some spectators even reported that they gained a better insight into the personality of the American icons in *Insignificance*, despite their overall view that the play was a delightful theatrical fancy rather than a reflection of the life world, adds further complexity to the issue. Despite this varied picture, audiences' previous knowledge had the strongest impact on perception, since none of the participants in either study accepted a view that directly countered their previous ideas. The audience members who 'discovered' Maggie's humanity and the students who were happy to see the young Vincent as different from the image of the older painter were willing to fill gaps or fuzzy areas in their life world knowledge. Acceptance of information that directly countered it, on the other hand, was not found. The relation between new information and the participants' life world knowledge as the most important point of comparison might be decisive, and, as the reactions to *Thatcher* suggest, their own experiences might provide a particularly strong point of orientation. The concluding chapter will investigate this possibility in more detail while returning to the starting point of our investigation.

8
Conclusion and Review of the Theoretical Framework

Towards the end of this book, a return to the theoretical premises on which our discussion has been based can help to put the insights into the production and reception of biographical theatre into a broader context again. It can evaluate the insights that have been gained from a functional analysis and identify questions that remain to be examined, in particular the surprising result from the reception study of *Thatcher – the Musical!* presented in the previous chapter. At the outset I suggested that the disagreement over theoretical issues was one of the reasons for the lack of scholarly interest in the use of biographical material in performances: while a small number of authors discussed historical theatre in terms of its ability to reconstruct the past and its inhabitants on stage, many scholars seemed to reject this approach as theoretically unsatisfactory. The predominant postmodern emphasis on discourse, on the other hand, does not facilitate an inquiry into the way in which such performances engage with the world. In order to overcome the schism between the academy's resulting reluctance to engage with such forms of theatre and their popularity on British stages, I suggested a functional approach that could discuss the differences created by the use of biographical characters without relying on concepts such as fact and fiction. Similar to Wittgenstein's notion of a language game (Wittgenstein, 1978 cited in Gergen, 1999, p. 35), we assumed that biographical performances *were* not inherently different, but they *did* things in a different way. Practitioners and audiences would *see* and *interpret* biographical performances differently from performances that did not have such a close link to the life world through comparison with previous discourses about the historical characters. Echoing the idea of social constructivism, which recognises that 'individuals mentally construct the world [...] with categories proposed by social relationships' (Gergen, 1999, p. 237), this approach accepted the lack of absolute categories, as well as the constraints that were imposed by the social nature of discourses.

Consequently the discussion focused on everything that society, theatre practitioners and audiences specifically *regarded as* biographical material and the impact of this perception on the way they made and received performances. It thus included a comparison of the productions to other discourses about the historical figures on whom characters were based, identifying similarities and differences between them. In addition, interviews with practitioners revealed that they referred to these discourses and consciously used such a comparison to influence the production's relationship to the life world. Directors and performers who were very dedicated to create theatre that would give a credible reflection of the world reported using a variety of different means to ensure a high degree of overlapping information. Thus the writer of *Rendition Monologues* relied on juridical documents and the advice of experts, sources and people who exert a strong influence on the production of socially accepted discourses about the rights of individuals. Restricting herself to selecting, rather than changing, the quotations that were used in the play, the only differences between the performance and the original discourses were introduced by a changing context. Although few other performances strove to such a state of 'near identity' of discourses, it is remarkable that the practitioners' research and attempts to familiarise themselves with other sources of information about the historical characters was used extensively even for performances which later undermined the similarities established on this basis, such as *Insignificance*. The theatre practitioners whose views were included in this book thus appreciated the social constraints on the ways in which they could talk about the past and historical figures.

At the same time, some of them explicitly acknowledged the discursive nature of the 'knowledge' they gained about the past. This was particularly visible in the conversations with practitioners involved in meta-biographical plays. The emphasis on storytelling in *Mary Queen of Scots Got Her Head Chopped Off* reflects Liz Lochhead's statement that she was conscious that at some point the characters became *her* creation – the play could only offer one possible look at the myth of the two rivalling queens. The lack of a reception study on the meta-biographical performances discussed in this volume meant that it was not possible to elicit whether audiences recognised that all stories about the life world depend on the perspective from which they are told. The reactions to *Vincent in Brixton*, however, provided an indirect indication that form can create a 'sense of truth' (Gergen, 1999, p. 70), as the spectators' impression that the play was likely to echo other socially accepted discourses about the painter was based to a high degree on the use of typical narrative structures and an extra-theatrical form of presentation. In other words, Nicholas Wright's speculations about van Gogh's time in London were seen as probable versions mainly because they were presented in a way which the interviewees would associate with narratives about past lives. As Gergen suggests, we expect that 'in telling the truth, life should copy art' (Gergen, 1999, p. 70).

The discussion thus confirmed the postmodern notion of truth effects created by texts. At the same time, however, audience reactions demonstrate that these cannot be created at individual will. The participants rejected the meeting presented in *Insignificance* as it contradicted their existing ideas about the historical figures involved. Similarly, they remained cautious about the degree of authenticity in *Vincent in Brixton*, as the version of van Gogh's youth proposed by Nicholas Wright and the production team at the Library Theatre was indeed shared by others. The practitioners' efforts to manipulate the degree of thematic extra-theatricality, or the overlap of information between the plays and other discourses, through detailed research of these other discourses testify to their awareness of these social restrictions that shape our evaluation of discourses about the past and past lives. While biographical plays, as all other discourses, might not possess an absolute ontological status, those involved in making and perceiving them thus feel that they are limited by social agreement about their relationship to what we perceive as our life world. An approach that recognises both the lack of absolute status and these limitations can thus offer further insight into the way in which these two aspects are negotiated in the context of individual performances.

Audience reactions to *Thatcher – the Musical!*, however, could indicate that in its current form, the theoretical approach used cannot offer an exhaustive explanation of audience reactions. The high level of agreement among respondents that the performance reflected Margaret Thatcher's life rather or very well (see Chapter 7) suggests that Foursight Theatre's version was considered as a close reflection of a widely shared consensus about her life story. If, under these circumstances, only a very small minority of spectators states that the play changed their views on the former Prime Minister, does this suggest that the majority shared the same perspective? In the light of strong sentiments in favour of or against Thatcher expressed by the practitioners and in some questionnaires, this seems unlikely. In Chapter 7, I suggested that alternatively their reactions might be interpreted as a sign that for someone whose activities are part of spectators' living memories, bi-directional flow of information is rare, as their own memories provide a very strong point of comparison. In the remaining pages of this book, I would like to relate this hypothesis to observations about the reception of plays that fulfilled their potential for controversy and explain why this finding could point to the need for an addition to the theoretical approach outlined.

As the interviews with the company suggest, Foursight expected their production to be potentially controversial for various reasons. On the one hand they feared that an irreverent look at the former PM might provoke resistance from those who admired her and her work, on the other they worried that those who loved to hate her might feel betrayed by a kind portrayal. Since the questionnaires indicated that the respondents belonged to both ends of the political spectrum, the survey supports the impression given in most reviews: the potential for controversy was not fulfilled and Foursight's performance left sufficient space for both parties to accommodate their own interpretation of her work within this representation. While the frame of events mirrored their memories of what happened, only very few of them were willing to change their own interpretation of the main figure in them, seeing the PM in a more humane way.

Even though the study did not provide strong support for the idea that this reaction might be related to the role of personal memories of a past figure, one could argue that the impact of personal experience makes it particularly difficult to counter them. As the metaphorical expressions of 'first-hand' experience or 'seeing something with one's own eyes' show, our impression of the world around us is based on physical processes of perception before it is interpreted. Even though medical research suggests that the process of interpreting these impressions cannot be separated from the physical recognition of an external reality, and most of our impressions become mediated by language as soon as they enter our conscious memory, this does not seem to change our impression that direct experiences are more reliable than those mediated through written texts, for example. As a result, audiences who saw and heard Margaret Thatcher personally (or even through pictures on television news, whose mediating effect is often forgotten) could rely to a greater extent on their 'immediate' or seemingly 'unmediated' impression of her, and thus be disinclined to change this based on a visible mediated performance that presents these events in the shape of a musical. This might apply particularly to those who felt the consequences of her political decisions in a very immediate way: those who felt the effects of reduced spending on social issues, or on culture, and even more those who experienced cold, hunger or police batons during the Miners' Strike.

Such painful or even traumatic experiences also seem to be less prone to lose their immediacy once they are communicated to others and enter the social space. Although they have to be encoded in mutually understandable terms and have to compete with the way other people experienced the same moment, such experiences seem to resist smooth integration into discourse, as they are particularly tightly related to our physical existence. In his development of a corporeal turn in semantics, Horst Ruthrof (1997, p. 257) suggests that 'death, birth, survival, gravity and similar phenomena' are among the issues that provide such 'deep constraints' for the assignation of meaning: although the way in which cultures discuss them indicates cultural mediation, their existence in all cultures suggests that 'the universe and the limits of organic life' impose limits on all human communication.

In their article on Kenneth Burke's logology, Malhotra Benz and Kenny (1997, p. 89) present Burke's concept of 'body *as* the world (BAW)' as the origin of these constraints. Although our 'conscious intellect creates [...] metaphors through which it conceives itself, a body and a mind' this discursive activity nevertheless relies on the existence of our physical bodies. In other words, our textual memory is preceded by the physical traces in our body: for someone who has injured the tendons in his knee, the memory exists not only in textual form, but also through the 'pre-textual corollary of this in a tendency to collapse' when over-exercising this knee (Malhotra Benz and Kenny, 1997, p. 90). In most situations our 'rational-intellecting entity' detracts attention from our 'underlying BAW existence', but illness, death and other physical experiences act as reminders that the 'existential situation of a body in the world limits the range of freedom open to the dramatic and logological representations of ideas' (Malhotra Benz and Kenny, 1997, p. 90).

While only a small minority of the audience members who attended *Thatcher – the Musical!* at Warwick Arts Centre will have had experiences that fall under this category – very few of the mainly middle class audiences from Warwickshire are likely to have manned the picket lines during the Miners' Strike – the role of such experiences plays a more important part for other productions discussed in this volume. It could explain why the practitioners who worked on *Rendition Monologues* and *Gladiator Games* felt a great responsibility to portray the victims of torture and murder with respect, while the actors and writer of *Vincent in Brixton* felt less passionate about doing justice to van Gogh. Indirectly, such experiences also influence the reception of plays that proved highly controversial, as *Copenhagen* demonstrates. Despite its meta-biographical elements, discussed in Chapter 6, the portrayal of the past in Frayn's play was regarded to be sufficiently influential to provoke criticism of the specific *way* in which the historical figures were represented.

As in *Thatcher – the Musical!*, the concern over the representation of historical figures in *Copenhagen* is not related exclusively to concerns about slander or doing justice to those who are represented on stage, but more so about those whose lives were affected by the historical figures the play includes. Frayn's critics felt that the portrayal of Heisenberg did not sufficiently acknowledge him as an indirect supporter of a regime that subjected millions of people to horrific experiences that decry verbalisation. For Tom Paulin (2002, no page) 'Heisenberg was a Nazi sympathiser, his return to Germany proves that. His actions cannot be excused'. Since Michael Frayn's play does not offer a direct and outright condemnation of the physicist, he assumes that 'Frayn does not possess the ethical intelligence to see this'. At a conference about the Copenhagen meeting between the physicists, another critic even accuses Frayn of 'subtle revisionism ... more destructive than [David] Irving's self-evidently ridiculous assertions – more destructive of the integrity of art, of science, and of history' (Frayn, 2002c, p. 22; see also Anon., 2002a).

While Michael Frayn rejects the accusations, he implicitly accepts their basic premise: the idea that his presentation of Heisenberg cannot contradict or downplay historical sources that would demonstrate his involvement or indirect promotion of the Nazi regime (Frayn, 2002c). Despite the affirmation that the past cannot be reconstructed 'as it was' in the play, he thus accepts the fact that his writing is read as a historical document and answers his critics on the basis of the assumption that it can actually be read as such.

The fears of Frayn's critics that *Copenhagen* could change the way in which Heisenberg is viewed are confirmed by the events that followed its first production. Although the play does not promote a specific interpretation of Heisenberg's visit to the Bohrs in 1941, its appearance has rekindled the debate about this event. Previously held mainly among historians, the interest is extended to a more general public, for example in the form of newspaper articles that present the material on which the play is based (e.g. Anon., 2002b). It can also be observed in the number of symposia held on the meeting in Copenhagen,[1] which are often characterised by an interesting combination of speakers. At the University of New York, for example, a symposium called *Copenhagen* included presentations in the areas of science, history and theatre studies, thus bringing together the physicists' work, their biographies and the use of these biographies in productions of Michael Frayn's play (see Lustig and Schwartz, 2005). Furthermore, the play has led to new developments in the realm of biographical research. Finn Aaserud from the Bohr archives explains the decision to publish some letters written by Bohr as follows:

> In particular, the play has renewed and strengthened an already intense debate among historians of science about why Heisenberg came to Copenhagen and what transpired at the meeting. In the course of this debate, reference has been made to a draft of a letter to Heisenberg about the meeting that Bohr never sent. By making the documents accessible on the Internet we forgo the normal archival practice of making material available to scholars on application. This decision has been motivated by the high level of interest as well as the wish of the Bohr family to present the material as a whole. (Aaserud, 2002)

The play thus exercised a strong influence on the perception of the two physicists in the life world, and has nearly become a document in the historical debate in its own right: the bibliography that accompanies a biography of Niels Bohr in the form of a cartoon by Jim Ottaviani and Leland Purvis contains Frayn's play side by side with publications by historians (Ottaviani and Purvis, 2004).

Although few people agreed with Frayn's accusers and saw the play as an overly kind treatment of a perpetrator, the controversy over *Copenhagen* presents the conflict that underlies disagreement about various biographical plays. For David Edgar's *Albert Speer*, for example, almost all reviews pointed to the dangers of 'magnetic staging' (Clapp, 2000, p. 685), as this could create a degree of empathy for the Nazi architect that would promote empathy with Speer the perpetrator to the detriment of those who suffered from the regime he supported. One review explicitly confirmed this, suggesting that the danger of the play lay in the possibility that, 'rather than relying on the living eyewitness testimony of the participants, audiences trust film and theatre as the source of the truth' (Anon., 2000, p. 12), albeit one presented through the means of fiction. In the first place these debates underline the potential of biographical theatre to lead to a bi-directional flow of information, but the most interesting observation is their ethical dimension. Whereas no reviewer felt that the presentation of Marilyn Monroe's attempts to seduce Einstein on stage was objectionable, the fear that those involved with the Nazi regime could be represented too kindly is present in the discussion of almost all plays or films that include biographical characters based on such Nazis. Similarly, David Barnett suggests that *Copenhagen*'s potential for controversy is further increased through its link to the nuclear bomb. For him, the fact 'that Hiroshima is also mentioned substantiates the real historical stakes [in] the play. [It] is not an "easy" musing on postmodern epistemology' (Barnett, 2005, p. 146).

The controversy's connection to figures who were or might have been involved, directly or indirectly, in actions that subjected human beings to experiences related to extreme physical pain, or even the limits of organic existence (see Ruthrof cited above), suggests that a second limitation to postmodern relativity can be found in the body. Although such experiences cannot be communicated without mediation in discourse, they seem to be considered to be 'beyond' the possibilities of negotiated meaning. While those who criticise the presentation of perpetrators acknowledge the potential of performances to change social agreement on the possible interpretation of their life, they feel that positive interpretations would not be appropriate in Burke's terms, as they would contradict the existential history of the body as world of their victims. In other words, the representation of a Hitler figure who embraces his Jewish neighbours is not possible without disrespecting the millions of human beings he deprived of their physical existence, and thus any possibility to exist as a 'rational-intellecting entity' involved in discursive activities. Such a representation is not prevented by the textual boundaries but by the material ashes of those he murdered.

This insight has consequences for the functional approach suggested here: the first limitation to postmodern relativity, the social nature of knowledge, suggests that the theatre can become one of the places where the construction of our life world knowledge is negotiated. The second limitation, given by our bodily existence, on the other hand, is not negotiable while the existential histories of specific bodies have not been forgotten. Even though narrative is the only way of sharing such experiences, they do not lose their immediacy and exert a strong influence on the acceptability of discourses. Additional research will be needed to develop this notion further, but it has explanatory power in the context of the productions discussed in this book.

Developing a functional approach could also have benefits beyond the confines of biographical theatre. As the choice of theoretical texts that have inspired this theoretical perspective demonstrates, similar approaches have mainly been developed in other fields, particularly areas that have been challenged by the postmodern emphasis on discourse at the detriment of the physical world to a higher degree than theatre studies. Burke, as well as Berger and Luckman, worked in sociology, a discipline committed to the exploration of the social world. As Kohler Riessman (1993, p. 15) observed, retiring into 'textual practice' leads to a growing detachment between the academic middle classes and the experience of those whose social world they study. An increased 'concern with the embodiment of sociological analysis', on the other hand, helps to bring the discipline closer to 'the world of experience' of the majority of people. Similar dilemmas arise for postmodern psychology, since the reconstruction of life stories in psychoanalysis is subjected to the practical purpose of overcoming difficulties and not appreciated primarily for its literary value. Although the retreat into the world of postmodern relativity does not cause such immediate problems to theatre scholars, 'offering an account of bodies, sociology comes closer than it usually does to the experience of people outside the academy' (Kohler Riessman, 1993, p. 15).

Appendix 1: Timeline

1925
Piscator, Erwin. *In Spite of Everything*. Schauspielhaus, Berlin

1935
Eliot, T.S. *Murder in the Cathedral*. Canterbury Cathedral

1938
Unity Theatre. *Babes in the Wood*. Unity Theatre

1946
Rattigan, Terence. *The Winslow Boy*. London

1960
Bennett, Alan et al. *Beyond the Fringe*. Royal Lyceum, Edinburgh
Bolt, Robert. *A Man for All Seasons*. Globe Theatre

1961
Osborne, John. *Luther: A Play*. Royal Court

1963
Arendt, Arthur. *Ethiopia*. Living Newspaper
Hochhut, Rolf. *The Deputy (Der Stellvertreter)*. Freie Volksbühne, Berlin
Theatre Workshop. *Oh, What a Lovely War!* Theatre Royal Stratford East

1964
Kipphardt, Heiner. *In the Matter of J. Oppenheimer*. Hessischer Rundfunk (German Television) then Freie Volksbühne, Berlin
Shaffer, Peter. *Royal Hunt of the Sun*. National Theatre

1965
Weiss, Peter. *The Investigation (Die Ermittlung)*

1968
Bond, Edward. *Early Morning*. English Stage Society, Royal Court
Hampton, Christopher. *Total Eclipse*. Royal Court

1969
Arden, John and Margaretta D'Arcy. *The Hero Rises Up*. Institute of Contemporary Arts at the Round House, Chalk Farm

1971
Mitchell, Anthony. *Tyger*. National Theatre

1974
Brenton, Howard. *The Churchill Play*. Nottingham Playhouse
Stoppard, Tom. *Travesties*. RSC at Aldwych Theatre

1977
Gems, Pam. *Queen Christina*. RSC The Other Place

1978
Gems, Pam. *Piaf*. RSC The Other Place

1979
Pownall, David. *An Audience Called Edouard*. Greenwich Theatre
Shaffer, Peter. *Amadeus*. National Theatre

1981
Wertenbaker, Timberlake. *New Anatomies*. Women's Theatre Group at ICA

1982
Johnson, Terry. *Insignificance*. Royal Court
Lochhead, Liz. *Blood and Ice*. Belgrade Theatre, Coventry

1984
Hastings, Michael. *Tom and Viv*. Royal Court

1985
Holliday, Joyce. *Anywhere to Anywhere*. Derby Playhouse
Lochhead, Liz. *Blood and Ice*. Foco Theatre Company at Haymarket Theatre

1986
Bennett, Alan. *Kafka's Dick*. Royal Court Theatre

1987
Dear, Nick. *The Art of Success*. RSC The Other Place
Lochhead, Liz. *Mary Queen of Scots Got Her Head Chopped Off*. Royal Lyceum
    Studio, Edinburgh
Whitemore, Hugh. *Breaking the Code*. Theatre Royal Haymarket, London

1989
Brenton, Howard. *H.I.D.* RSC at the Almeida
Eagleton, Terry. *Saint Oscar*. Field Day Theatre Company at Guildhall, Derry
Friel, Brian. *Making History*. Field Day Theatre Company at Guildhall, Derry
Pinnock, Winsome. *A Rock in the Water*. Royal Court Young People's Theatre

1990
Yeger, Sheila. *Self Portrait*. Orange Tree Richmond

1991
Yeger, Sheila. *Variations on a Theme by Clara Schumann*. Dartington College of Arts

1992
Bennett, Alan. *The Madness of George III*. National Theatre

1993
Johnson, Terry. *Hysteria*. Royal Court
Stoppard, Tom. *Arcadia*. National Theatre

1994
Norton Taylor, Richard and John McGrath. *Half the Picture*. Tricycle Theatre

1995
Dear, Nick. *The Art of Success.* RSC

1996
Gems, Pam. *Marlene.* Oldham Coliseum
Gems, Pam. *Stanley.* National Theatre
Kent, Nicolas. *Srebrenica.* Tricycle Theatre
Nelson, Richard. *The General from America.* RSC
Norton Taylor, Richard. *Nuremberg.* Tricycle Theatre

1997
Stoppard, Tom. *The Invention of Love.* National Theatre

1998
Frayn, Michael. *Copenhagen.* National Theatre
Hare, David. *Judas Kiss.* Almeida Theatre Company at Playhouse Theatre, London
Jeffrey, Stephen. *The Libertine.* Out of Joint at Warwick Arts Centre
Wertenbaker, Timberlake. *After Darwin.* Hampstead Theatre

1999
De Angelis, April. *A Warwickshire Testimony.* RSC The Other Place

2000
Bartlett, Neil. *In Extremis*
Dromgoole, Dominic. *Marriage in Disguise.*
Edgar, David. *Albert Speer.* National Theatre

2003
Blythe, Alecky. *Come Out Eli.* Recorded Delivery at Arcola Theatre, London
Dallmeyer, Andrew. *Hello Dalí.* Edinburgh Festival
Foursight Theatre. *Reans Girls.* Newhampton Arts Centre, Wolverhampton
Frayn, Michael. *Democracy.* National Theatre
Hare, David. *The Permanent Way.* Out of Joint at Theatre Royal, York
Wright, Nicholas. *Vincent in Brixton.* National Theatre

2004
Brittain, Victoria and Gillian Slovo. *Guantanamo.* Tricycle Theatre
Hare, David. *Stuff Happens.* National Theatre

2005
Graham, James. *Albert's Boy.* Finborough Theatre, London
Gupta, Tanika. *Gladiator Games.* Theatre Royal Stratford East and Sheffield Theatres
Linden, Sonia. *Crocodile Seeking Refuge.* Ice and Fire at Lyric Hammersmith
Teale, Polly. *Brontë.* Shared Experience at Yvonne Arnaud Theatre, Guildford

2006
Foursight Theatre. *Thatcher – the Musical!* Foursight Theatre at Warwick Arts Centre
Zane, Adam. *Village Voices.* Hope Theatre Company at Taurus, Manchester

2007
Penny Dreadful Theatre Company. *The Bitches' Ball*. Edinburgh Festival and Tour
Zane, Adam. *Yesterday When I Was Young*. Hope Theatre Company at the Lowry,
  Manchester

2008
Bacon, Christine. *Rendition Monologues*. Ice and Fire Outreach, Bridewell Theatre,
  London

Appendix 2: Participants in the Interview Study

Participant 1 is a **female** student of the Faculty of **Architecture**, **19 years** old, and has **extensive experience of theatre** in various forms, both as a spectator and, to a certain extent, as a practitioner, both in an educational context as well as on the Edinburgh Fringe.

Participant 2 is a **23-year**-old, **male** student of Modern Languages at the Faculty of **Arts**, also with **extensive theatre experience** on both sides of the curtain. In addition to being an avid theatre goer, he participated in some professional productions in Scarborough.

Participant 3 is **male**, **20 years** old and a student at the Faculty of **Engineering**. He has not attended the theatre at all within the last year and had **little experience with theatre** before.

Participant 4 studies at the Faculty of **Law**. He is **27 years** old, and has **hardly any theatre experience** at all.

Participant 5 is a **27-year**-old, **female** student of the Faculty of **Medicine** with **some theatre experience** in the past.

Participant 6 also brings **some theatre experience**. She is **18 years** old and studies at the Faculty of **Science**.

Participant 7 is a **female** student of the Faculty of **Social Sciences** and has **hardly any experience** with theatre.

Appendix 3: *Thatcher – the Musical!* Survey

This survey is part of an ongoing PhD project about people's perception of different kinds of plays. Many questions therefore leave room for short answers in your own words. I am aware that this might require a little more of your time than simply ticking a box, but all your comments are greatly appreciated – without them it would be impossible to know what spectators really think! Please feel free to use complete sentences or just short notes, according to your own preference. **THANK YOU!**

Your Expectations

1) What information did you have about the play before coming to the theatre?
    (Please tick all appropriate answers)

    ☐ Information about the Company   ☐ Poster
    ☐ Title   ☐ Other, please specify:

2) Why did you choose to see this play? Please state the most important reason(s) for your visit.

3) Could you say what you expected from *Thatcher – the Musical!* in one line?

4) How would you sum up your impression of the play after watching it?

Your Reactions to the Play

5) Which elements helped you to locate when and where the action takes place?
    (Please list the ones you can remember)

6) Which elements were most important to recognise Margaret Thatcher?
      (Please describe the most important ones)

7) Do you like the fact that Margaret Thatcher is played by various actresses?

      ☐ yes   ☐ no

8) Could you explain why you did / did not like it?

9) How well do you think *Thatcher – the Musical!* reflects the life of the historical
      Mrs Thatcher?
      (Please circle the appropriate number on the following scale)

      not well at all   1   2   3   4   5   very well

10) Could you explain your answer to the previous question?

11) Do you think the play has changed your perception of the historical
      Mrs Thatcher?

      ☐ yes   ☐ no

12) If yes, can you explain how far your view of her has changed?

Some information about yourself

13) How old are you today?

            _____ years old

14) For how many years have you lived in the UK?
(Please specify absences of 6 months or longer within this time)

_____ years   absent from _____ to _____

15) How many plays have you seen in the last 6 months?

_____ plays

Thank you very much for your help!
Please hand the questionnaire to one of the stewards.

If you have any further questions regarding the survey or would like to know more about its outcome, please contact me by writing to Ursula Canton. ...

Notes

Chapter 1 – Introduction

1. In some cases the reasons for censorship overlap; thus John Osborne's *A Patriot for Me* (1964) was criticised for its references to homosexuality; 'whether Redl was a real person or not' seemed to be of little interest to the reader (Reader's Report cited in Shellard et al., 2004, p. 163). Similarly, the censorship of plays about Oscar Wilde was usually based on references to the author's homosexuality, not because he was a recently dead person (ibid., p. 137).
2. Another aspect that influenced the choice was the availability of performance documentation and interview partners. Though highly popular, biographical one-(wo)man shows, for example, are under-represented, as documents such as video or sound recordings or even scripts often do not exist. Where it was impossible to see live performances, video recordings were used.

Chapter 2 – Re-Framing the Discussion of Biographical Theatre: A Functional Approach

1. In the following, 'truth' will be capitalised when it refers to an absolute concept. The same will be done for similar concepts such as 'Reason', and the names of schools of thought, such as Empiricism. An exception is made for quotations.
2. Crittenden's example for this argument lays itself open to Postmodern criticism, as he suggests that information about Sherlock Holmes can only be gained through reading Conan Doyle's books, not 'by consulting histories of Victorian London, looking through the newspapers of that era, trying to locate his letters or personal belongings, searching for his relatives or visiting the place where he lived' (Crittenden, 1991, pp. 62–3). Including other narratives, albeit the ones labelled as factual, his argument becomes circular as he explains the difference between fact and fiction with examples of what we consider to be factual or fictional.
3. The same is true for other cultural practices, for instance the legal system, where character witnesses are explicitly included in the range of possible sources of information; see for example the government's official online information (UK Government, 2010).

Chapter 3 – Re-Living the Past: Authenticity on Stage

1. In this context it is interesting to remark that the idea of the exclusion of the audience from the 'life' on stage is not only important for the effect on the observer, but can also have an impact on the imagination of the actors. In Stanislavski's *An Actor Prepares* (1980), the director spends considerable time on training his students to concentrate their attention on stage, teaching

them to regard the proscenium aperture as a closed fourth wall through which they are not observed.

2. A similar decision was made for the New York run of *Guantanamo: Honor Bound to Defend Freedom* (Brittain and Slovo, 2004), where Bishop Desmond Tutu made a guest appearance as Lord Justice Steyn for two evenings (cf. Hattenstone, 2004). Although it is unlikely that he created a believable reconstruction of the famous judge in his appearance or demeanour, his history and activism contribute credibility to the play's political message contained in this character's speech.

3. It is interesting to note that these similarities only exist on the level of story and that audience members are able to differentiate between the representation of the character's dead body and the actor's living body. This aspect will be discussed in further detail in Chapter 6.

4. Since the play speculates about the artist's early life, neither *A Pair of Shoes* (National Theatre production) nor *The Bedroom* are related to any of the events in the play, although both productions attempt to create such a link, either by presenting a pair of boots on the kitchen table (National Theatre production) or by printing a small copy of the painting next to a quotation from Vincent's letters in which he praises his (bed-)room in London (National Theatre, 2002).

5. This is even more clearly visible in the printed text, where Wright indicates the time span of 1873–76 at the beginning of the play, specifying the exact setting of each scene according to the time of the year, day of the week and time of the day (Wright, 2002, p. 3). Indicating a particular moment rather than a general period of time once again evokes the notion of correspondence instead of probability.

6. An exception are performances set in or near famous landmarks, such as *Poet's Corner* (2009, Tea for Ten Theatre Company). Here the tombstones of Byron, Wilde and fellow poets reference a specific place.

Chapter 4 – Creating and Undermining Expectations: Forms versus Content

1. None of the actors involved in *Thatcher – the Musical!* commented explicitly on the difference between their role in the devising process and that of actors who perform a script researched and written by a playwright, but interviews with other actors show that they perceived this as a factor that limits their impact on the way in which biographical characters are developed. The need to 'play what is in the script and the character that is in the script' (Lloyd Pack, 2005 in an interview about *Kafka's Dick*), even if 'historical truth does not match what the playwright is saying about the character' (Timothy West, 2005 in an interview about playing Stalin in *Master Class* by David Pownall, 1983), is echoed by many practitioners.

2. The signature hairstyle is also used in other plays that feature characters based on Einstein, for example *Albert's Boy* (2005, Finborough Theatre).

3. Another good example of the power of token elements from iconic images is Brecht in Christopher Hampton's *Tales from Hollywood*. Journalist James Christopher remarks in an article about Phil Davis' Brecht in the first production

at the National Theatre (1983) that 'on paper it looks like a ghastly mistake by the director John Crowley. Brecht is one of the great theatrical revolutionaries; Davis is a walking mugshot who looks as if his career has depended on pleading guilty to every armed robbery since Dixon of Dock Green' (Christopher, 2001). Yet, a few elements, such as a pair of glasses, a cap and a cigar, all known from famous photographs of Brecht, are sufficient to make him recognisable for the audience.

Chapter 5 – Meta-Biography: Biographers on Stage and Non-Traditional Structures

1. Another powerful example of such plays is Edward Bond's *Early Morning*, where the similarities between the character of Queen Victoria and the historical figure of that name are restricted to her role as queen of England, wife of Albert and contemporary of Disraeli and Florence Nightingale. Other features of Bond's character, including the existence of Siamese twins among Victoria's offspring and her lesbian love affair with Florence Nightingale, can challenge this assumption, but not prevent its existence in the first place.
2. This seems to be true for most productions in the UK, where the play has been presented in further regional and student productions, and could be attributed to the complexity of Frayn's script. An amusing exception is the first German production, which Frayn witnessed 'because [he] cared very much about how it was received [...] particularly because Heisenberg was a German physicist'. To Frayn's dismay, the director chose a more intra-theatrical style that translated emotions and verbal action into physical expression, such as back somersaults that accompanied Heisenberg's rhetorical retreats (Frayn, 2004).
3. This decision allows for an observation about the role of conventions in the creation of extra-theatrical figures. While Tom Mannion, who played Niels Bohr at the Lyceum, reports that Michael Frayn seems to have welcomed this as an additional hint at 'the difference' between the characters' origins (and therefore perspective during the war), the actor remained sceptical, as he felt that it could evoke the concept of 'funny accents' from comedy, contradicting Heisenberg's use of very sophisticated vocabulary and the impression of a highly educated character. Both views are based on the wish to create an extra-theatrical character, but while Frayn's view values the indication of cultural origin as an important component of such a character, Mannion's reserve shows that he sees his membership of a specific social group as the more important defining feature of the character. These two aspects that would co-exist harmoniously in the life world are brought into conflict in the context of theatrical discourse that is marked by conventions that differ from the life world, such as the stock image of the funny foreigner.

Chapter 6 – Studying Reception: Theoretical Framework and Methodology

1. An exception is the MA in Audience and Reception Studies at the University of Wales Aberystwyth, which is, interestingly, taught by scholars from Theatre as well as Film and Television Studies.

2. Where funding bodies do require evidence of a company's success, critical reviews and audience numbers are often the only basis of evaluation, perhaps partly because the cost of more detailed research is out of proportion to the gain made by more detailed knowledge of spectators and their feedback.

3. One could establish a similar interaction between the stage actions and the spectators' knowledge about the life world on Sauter's other levels of performance, as sensory reactions to the performer's body and the spectator's perspective on artistic expression, for example an evaluation of the performer's acting skills, also depend on their experience of theatrical conventions, cultural conditions and the life world in general.

4. In the case of autobiographical plays, in which performers present their own life, this distance is abandoned and the relationship between the fiction created and the world would have to be described in different ways. Rosenthal confirms the audience's power to distinguish between their life world and others such as television or the theatre, stating that 'they are aware that what they see is only a producer's vague approximation of what actually happened' (Rosenthal, 1999, p. 10).

5. One could argue that this is especially true of audience members who are more familiar with cinematic conventions, as these tend to be based on a much higher degree of immediate similarity to the life world.

6. This does not mean that mimed biographical references, made explicit by visual similarities to a historical figure, are impossible, but such plays clearly are exceptions. A possible example is *Comedia Tempio* by Josef Nadj, presented at the London Mime Festival 2002, which is described by a critic from El Cultural as 'inspired by the life and work of Josef Brenner [...] who called himself Géza Csath' (Kumin, 2004).

7. Partly this may be due to the fact that the voices of historical characters who lived before the everyday use of radio and television are not very well known. The situation is different for biographical plays about singers, such as Pam Gems' *Marlene* or *Piaf* (1996 and 1978).

8. Their exclusion demonstrates the difficulties surrounding the local and ephemeral nature of theatre: *Kafka's Dick* was chosen as an example of metabiographical structures, but these were nearly obliterated in Cal McCrystal's production. *Letters Home*, based on verbatim quotation from Sylvia Plath's correspondence with her mother, offered an insight into the use of verbatim quotation, but as a student production would be of limited interest to a greater readership. Temporal and geographical restrictions, however, meant that the study could not be extended for another year with the same participants to include more productions.

Chapter 7 – Audience Reactions to Biographical Performances

1. The only exception were photographs displayed in the foyer. Since the participants visited the production as a group, I avoided this display on the way to the performance. One interviewee had arrived early and had discovered them; her comments about the recognition of the historical figures were therefore discarded.

2. A highly amusing example of such different frames of reference in terms of background knowledge was provided by one of the participants in the pre-show interview for *Kafka's Dick*. I had assumed that the proper name in the title would establish a link to the writer, but various participants did not recognise the name. Two of them did remember the imaginary book title of *Kafka's Motorbike* in *Bridget Jones's Diary*, however, and thus concluded that 'he's probably been travelling' (Canton, 2004c, participant 1). The interview thus demonstrated that frames of reference vary from one spectator to another, and that they are nourished as much by individual interpretations as they are by officially sanctioned discourses.
3. The participants were also interviewed about a student production of *Letters Home*, a performance based entirely on the correspondence between Sylvia Plath and her mother. Here they asserted that they 'didn't really know about Sylvia Plath beforehand, now [they] obviously do' (Canton, 2005c, participant 3).

Chapter 8 – Conclusion and Review of the Theoretical Framework

1. The New York University Graduate Center which devotes a website to the phenomenon gives a list of no fewer than seven symposia on the theme (University of New York, 2005).

Bibliography

Performances

Albert's Boy. By James Graham. Dir. Max Lewendel. Perf. Victor Spinetti, Gerard Monaco. Finborough Theatre. 13 August 2005

Arcadia. By Tom Stoppard. Dir. Rachel Kavanaugh. Birmingham Repertory Theatre Company and Bristol Old Vic at the Birmingham Rep. 30 October 2004

Arcadia. By Tom Stoppard. Dir. Trevor Nunn. Perf. Maria Miles, Alexander Hanson, July Legrand, Dearbhla Mollooy, Paul Shelley, etc. National Theatre transfer to the Haymarket Theatre. 24 May 1995

The Bitches' Ball. By Penny Dreadful Theatre. Assembly Hill Street Theatre. 13 August 2007

Brontë. By Polly Teale. Dir. Polly Teale. Perf. Diane Beck, Catherine Cusack, David Fielder, Natalia Tena, Matthew Thomas, Fenella Woolgar. Shared Experience at Warwick Arts Centre. 29 September 2005

Come Out Eli. By Alecky Blythe. Recorded Delivery at Arcole Theatre, London. 2003

Copenhagen. By Michael Frayn. Dir. Michael Blakemore. Perf. David Burke, Mark Henderson, Sarah Kestelman. National Theatre transfer to the Duchess Theatre. 27 July 1999

Copenhagen. By Michael Frayn. Dir. Tristan Moriarty. Sheffield University Theatre Company. 29 October 2003

Crocodile Seeking Refuge. By Sonia Linden. Ice and Fire at Lyric Hammersmith. 2005

Democracy. By Michael Frayn. Dir. Michael Blakemore. Perf. Roger Allam, Conleth Hill, David Ryall, etc. National Theatre transfer to Wyndham's Theatre. 7 May 2003

Gladiator Games. By Tanika Gupta. Dir. Charlotte Westenra. Sheffield Theatres with Theatre Royal Stratford East. 10 May 2005

Guantanamo. By Victoria Brittain and Gillian Slovo. Dir. Nicolas Kent, Sacha Wares. Perf. Badi Uzzaman, Aaron Neil, etc. Tricycle Theatre transfer to New Ambassador, London. 7 August 2004

Hello Dalí. By Andrew Dallmeyer. Perf. Tom Jude. ClubWest at the Edinburgh Theosophical Society Studio. 20 August 2004

Insignificance. By Terry Johnson. Dir. John Lally. Perf. Nick Cheales, John Mills, Alex Kinnear, Pat Hymers. Arkle Theatre Company at the Edinburgh Fringe Festival. 21 August 2004

Insignificance. By Terry Johnson. Dir. Samuel West. Perf. Nicholas LePrevost, Mary Stockwell, Patrick O'Kane, Gerard Horan. Lyceum Theatre Sheffield. 28 February 2005 and 7 March 2005

Insignificance. By Terry Johnson. Dir. Lee Waters. Perf. Ian McDiarmid, Judy Davis, William Hootkins, Larry Lamb. Royal Court Theatre. 1982

Kafka's Dick. By Alan Bennett. Dir. Cal McCrystal. Perf. Sarah Bracknell. Derby Playhouse. 17 November 2004 and 23 November 2004

191

Letters Home. By Rose Leiman Goldemberg. Dir. Sarah Bell, Ursula Canton. Sheffield Centenary Drama Festival. 19 May 2005

The Madness of George III. By Alan Bennett. Dir. Rachel Kavanaugh. Perf. Michael Pennington, etc. Birmingham Repertory Theatre Company and West Yorkshire Playhouse at the Birmingham Repertory Theatre. 25 October 2003

Marlene. By Pam Gems. Dir. Sian Mathias. Perf. Siân Philips. Oldham Coliseum. 2 October 1996

Mary Queen of Scots Got Her Head Chopped Off. By Liz Lochhead. Dir. Gerard Mulgrew. Communicado Theatre at the Edinburgh Lyceum Studio. 10 August 1987

Mary Queen of Scots Got Her Head Chopped Off. By Liz Lochhead. Dir. David McVicar. Royal Lyceum Edinburgh. 1994

Mary Queen of Scots Got Her Head Chopped Off. By Liz Lochhead. Dir. Alison Peebles. Perf. Angela Darcy, Jo Freer. Des. Kenny Miller. National Theatre of Scotland. Touring from 15 April to 6 June 2009

The Permanent Way. By David Hare. Dir. Max Stafford-Clark. Warwick Arts Centre. 2 February 2005

Poet's Corner. Tea for Ten Theatre Company at the Edinburgh Fringe. 2009

Queen Christina. By Pam Gems. Dir. Penny Cherns. Perf. Sheila Allen. Royal Shakespeare Company, The Other Place. October 1977

Reans Girls. Dev. Foursight Theatre. Adapt. Kate O'Reilly. BBC Radio 4. 12 December 2006

Tales from Hollywood. By Christopher Hampton. Dir. Peter Gill. National Theatre Olivier. 1 September 1983

Thatcher – the Musical! Dev. Foursight Theatre. Dir. Naomi Cooke, Deb Barnard. Warwick Arts Centre. 8 February 2006

Thatcher – the Musical! By Foursight Theatre. Dir. Naomi Cooke, Deb Barnard. Foursight Theatre at Warwick Arts Centre, Coventry. 31 October–4 November 2006

Village Voices. By Adam Zane. Hope Theatre Company at Taurus, Manchester. 2006

Vincent in Brixton. By Nicholas Wright. Dir. Richard Eyre. Perf. Clare Higgins, Jochum ten Haaf. National Theatre transfer to Wyndham's Theatre. August 2002

Vincent in Brixton. By Nicholas Wright. Dir. Roger Haines. Perf. Gus Gallagher. Library Theatre Manchester. 28 September 2004 and 11 October 2004

Yesterday When I Was Young. Josie Pickering: Her True Story. By and Dir. Adam Zane. Perf. Erin Shanagher. C Chambers Street. 22 August 2007

Secondary Literature

Aaserud, Finn. 2002. 'Release of documents relating to 1941 Bohr–Heisenberg meeting.' http://www.nbi.dk/NBA/papers/introduction.htm. Accessed 24 August 2005

Amin, Imtiaz. 2005. 'It Was Officers vs. Inmates.' *Guardian* [online]. Available from: http://www.guardian.co.uk/stage/2005/nov/14/theatre.prisonsandprobation. Accessed 12 April 2010

Anon. 2000. 'Humanising of Hitler: This Week our National Theatre Staged a Play that Questions the Evil of the Fuhrer's Leading Henchman, Albert Speer, in Murdering Countless Millions.' *Daily Mail*, 27 May 2000, p. 12

Anon. 2002a. 'Copenhagen.' *Sunday Times*, 28 April 2002. Eire Culture, p. 29

Anon. 2002b. 'Letter Casts Doubt on "Copenhagen" Theory.' *Independent*, 8 February 2002

Anon. 2004a. 'Amadeus, Derby Playhouse, 4/5.' *Guardian*, 13 September 2004

Anon. 2004b. 'Bennett Meets Kafka – Why Meddle With a Dream Team.' *Daily Telegraph*, 19 November 2004, p. 23

Anon. 2004c. 'Vincent in Brixton, Manchester.' *Guardian*, 18 September 2004

Arden, John and Margaretta D'Arcy. 1969. *The Hero Rises Up*. London: Methuen

Aristotle. 1970. *Poetics*, intr. and transl. Gerald F. Elise. Ann Arbor: University of Michigan Press

Armory, Mark. 1982. 'Spectator.' *Theatre Record*, 2(13): 384

Armstrong, Richard. 2005. *Understanding Realism*. London: British Film Institute

Aston, Elaine and George Savona. 1991. *Theatre as Sign-System: A Semiotics of Text and Performance*. London: Routledge

The Audience Business. 2008. *Homepage* [online]. Available from: http://www.tab.org.uk/. Accessed 15 April 2010

Austin, Neil. 2009. Unpublished Correspondence with Ursula Canton. Received 22 September 2009

Bacon, Christine. 2009a. *Rendition Monologues*. Unpublished Playscript

Bacon, Christine. 2009b. Unpublished Interview about *Rendition Monologues*. Conducted by Ursula Canton, Edinburgh, 19 August 2009

Backscheider, Paula R. 1999. *Reflections on Biography*. Oxford: Oxford University Press

Barber, John. 1982. 'Daily Telegraph.' *Theatre Record*, 2(13): 383

Barker, Martin. 2003. 'Assessing the "Quality" in Qualitative Research: The Case of Text–Audience Relations.' *European Journal of Communication*, 18(3): 315–35

Barnard, Deb. 2009. Unpublished Correspondence with Ursula Canton. Received 8 December 2009

Barnard, Deb, Naomi Cooke, Jill Dowse, Rachel Essex, Lisa Harrison, Frances Land, Toni Midlane and Lori Weidenhammer. 1999. *Six Dead Queens and an Inflatable Henry*. Unpublished Playscript

Barnett, David. 2005. 'Reading and Performing Uncertainty: Michael Frayn's *Copenhagen* and the Postdramatic Theatre.' *Theatre Research International*, 30(2): 139–49

Bartlett, Neil. 2000. *In Extremis*. London: Oberon

Barton, Brian. 1987. *Das Dokumentartheater*. Stuttgart: Metzler

Bassett, Kate. 2002. 'Independent on Sunday, 5 May 2002.' *Theatre Record*, 22(9): 54

Bassett, Kate. 2003. 'Independent on Sunday, 27 April 2003.' *Theatre Record*, 23(9): 535

Baudrillard, Jean. 1970. *La société de consummation*. Paris: SGPP

Baugh, Christopher. 2005. *Theatre, Performance and Technology*. Basingstoke: Macmillan

BBC. 2006. 'Iron Lady Musical Takes to the Stage.' *BBC Homepage* [online]. Available from: http://news.bbc.co.uk/1/hi/england/coventry_warwickshire/4688764.stm. Accessed 13 January 2011

BBC. 2010. 'The BBC Story.' *BBC Homepage* [online]. Available from: http://www.bbc.co.uk/historyofthebbc/innovation/index.shtml. Accessed 3 November 2010

Ben Chaim, Daphna. 1984. *Distance in the Theatre: The Aesthetics of Audience Response*. Ann Arbor & London: UMI Research Press

Bennett, Alan. 1986. *Kafka's Dick*. London: Faber

Bennett, Alan. 1992. *The Madness of George III*. London: Faber

Bennett, Alan. 2003. *The Complete Beyond the Fringe*. London: Methuen

Bennett, Susan, 1997. *Theatre Audiences*, 2nd edn. London & New York: Routledge

Berger, Peter L. and Thomas Luckman. 1966. *The Social Construction of Reality: A Treatise in the Sociology of Knowledge*. Harmondsworth: Penguin

Berninger, Mark. 2006. *Neue Formen des Geschichtsdramas in Großbritannien und Irland*. Trier: WVT

Billington, Michael. 2002. 'Vincent in Brixton.' *Guardian*, 2 May 2002

Billington, Michael. 2007. *State of the Nation: British Theatre since 1945*. London: Faber

Blake, Robert. 1998. 'The Art of Biography.' In: Homberger, Eric and John Charmley (eds) *The Troubled Face of Biography*. London: Macmillan, pp. 75–93

Bolt, Robert. 1991 [1960]. *A Man for All Seasons*. Oxford: Heinemann

Bond, Edward. 1987 [1980]. *The Fool. Plays One*. London: Methuen

Bond, Edward. 1993 [1974]. *Early Morning. Plays One*. London: Methuen

Bottoms, Stephen. 2006. 'Putting the Document into Documentary: An Unwelcome Corrective?' *The Drama Review*, 50:3(191): 56–68

Brenton, Howard. 1974. *The Churchill Play*. London: Methuen

Brenton, Howard. 1989. *H.I.D.* London: NHB

Breuer, Ingo. 2005. *Theatralität von Gedächtnis: Deutschsprachiges Geschichtsdrama seit Brecht*. Köln: Böhlau Verlag

Bricusse, Lesley. 1988. *Sherlock Holmes – the Musical*. Cambridge Theatre (London), 24 April–8 July 1989

Brittain, Victoria and Gillian Slovo. 2004. *Guantanamo: Honor Bound to Defend Freedom*. London: Oberon

Brown, Georgina. 1998. 'Mail on Sunday, 6 December 1998.' *Theatre Record*, 18(24): 1573

Brown, Georgina. 2002. 'Mail on Sunday, 5 May 2002.' *Theatre Record*, 22(9): 547–8

Bruce, V. and Andrew W. Young. 1998 [1986]. 'A Theoretical Perspective for Understanding Face Recognition.' In: Young, Andrew W. (ed.) *Face and Mind*. Oxford: Oxford University Press, pp. 96–130

Buckingham, Alan and Peter Saunders. 2004. *The Survey Methods Handbook*. Cambridge: Polity Press

Bull, John. 1984. *New British Political Dramatists: Howard Brenton, David Hare, Trevor Griffiths and David Edgar*. London: Macmillan

Burke, David. 2009. Unpublished Correspondence with Ursula Canton. Received 22 September 2009

Burlinson, Kath. 2009. Unpublished Correspondence with Ursula Canton. Received 10 December 2009

Bussmann, Hadumod. 1996. *Routledge Dictionary of Language and Linguistics*, transl. and ed. Gregory P. Trauth and Kerstin Kazzazi. London & New York: Routledge

Canton, Ursula. 2004a. Unpublished Interviews before *Vincent in Brixton* at Library Theatre Manchester. Participants 1–7

Canton, Ursula. 2004b. Unpublished Interviews after *Vincent in Brixton* at Library Theatre Manchester. Participants 1–7

Canton, Ursula. 2004c. Unpublished Interviews after *Kafka's Dick* at Derby Theatre. Participants 1–7

Canton, Ursula. 2005a. Unpublished Interviews before *Insignificance* at the Crucible Theatre Sheffield. Participants 1–7

Canton, Ursula. 2005b. Unpublished Interviews after *Insignificance* at the Crucible Theatre Sheffield. Participants 1–7

Canton, Ursula. 2005c. Unpublished Interviews after *Letters Home* at Sheffield University. Participants 1–7

Canton, Ursula. 2006. Unpublished Survey of Audiences of *Thatcher – the Musical!* at Warwick Arts Centre. Conducted 31 October–4 November 2006. Questionnaires 1–164

Carr, Edward Hallett. 1962. *What is History? The George Macauly Trevelyn Lectures delivered in the University of Cambridge January–March 1961*. London: Macmillan

Chambers, Colin. 1989. *The Story of Unity Theatre*. London: Lawrence and Wishart

Chambers, Colin. 2009. 'Unity Theatre and the Embrace of the "Real".' In: Forsyth, Alison and Chris Megson (eds) *Get Real: Documentary Theatre Past and Present*. Basingstoke: Palgrave Macmillan, pp. 38–54

Charmley, John and Eric Homberger (eds) 1988. *The Troubled Face of Biography*. London: Macmillan

Chaudhuri, Una. 1984. 'The Spectator in Drama.' *Modern Drama*, 27(3): 281–98

Christopher, James. 2001. 'A Hard Nut Cracked.' *Guardian*, 30 April 2001

Clapp, Susannah. 2000. 'The Observer, 28 May 2000.' *Theatre Record*, 20(11): 685

Clapp, Susannah. 2004. 'A Berlin Bug's Life.' *Guardian*, 14 September 2003 [online]. Available from: http://www.guardian.co.uk/theobserver/2003/sep/14/features.review107. Accessed 12 August 2010

Claycomb, Ryan M. 2003. '(Ch)oral History: Documentary Theatre, the Communal Subject and Progressive Politics.' *Journal of Dramatic Theory and Criticism*, 17(2): 95–122

Claycomb, Ryan M. 2004. 'Playing at Lives: Biography and Contemporary Feminist Drama.' *Modern Drama*, 47(3): 525–45

Clifford, James L. 1970. *From Puzzles to Portraits: Problems of a Literary Biographer*. Chapel Hill: University of North Carolina Press

Cohn, Ruby. 1992. 'Realism.' In: Banham, Martin (ed.) *The Cambridge Guide to the Theatre*. Cambridge: Cambridge University Press, p. 815

Collingwood, R.G. 1961 [1946]. *The Idea of History*. Oxford: Oxford University Press

Cooke, Naomi. 2003. *Reans Girls*. Newhampton Arts Centre Theatre, Whitmore Reans (Wolverhampton), 18–29 March 2003

Cooke, Naomi. 2006. Unpublished Interview about *Thatcher – the Musical!* Conducted by Ursula Canton, 15 October 2006

Cooke, Naomi, Jill Dowse and Kate Hale. 1989. *Hitler's Women*. Unpublished Playscript

Cooper, Neil. 2009. 'History Repeating for Queen Bee.' *The Herald* [online]. Available from: http://www.heraldscotland.com/history-repeating-for-queen-bee-1.838636. Accessed 15 April 2010

Coveney, Michael. 1982. 'Financial Times.' *Theatre Record*, 2(13): 382

Coveney, Michael. 2002. 'Daily Mail, 6 August 2002.' *Theatre Record*, 22(16): 1050

Crick, Bernard. 1980. *George Orwell: A Life*. Harmondsworth: Penguin

Criminal Justice System. No Date. *CJS Online* [online]. Available from: http://www. cjsonline.gov.uk/witness/walkthrough/index.html. Accessed 31 December 2008

Crittenden, Charles. 1991. *Unreality: The Metaphysics of Fictional Objects*. Ithaca & London: Cornell University Press

Crystal, David (ed.) 1997. *The Cambridge Encyclopaedia of Language*, 2nd edn. Cambridge: Cambridge University Press

Cushman, Robert. 1982. 'Observer.' *Theatre Record*, 2(13): 381–2

Dallmeyer, Andrew. 2003. *Hello Dalí*. Unpublished Manuscript

Darcy, Angela. 2009. Interview about *Mary Queen of Scots Got Her Head Chopped Off*. Conducted by Ursula Canton, 4 September 2009

Dawson, Gary Fisher. 1999. *Documentary Theatre in the US*. Westport, CT: Greenwood Press

De Angelis, April. 1999. *A Warwickshire Testimony*. London: Faber

De Groot, Jerome. 2009. *Consuming History: Historians and Heritage in Contemporary Popular Culture*. London: Routledge

De Jongh, Nicholas. 1993. 'Evening Standard, 17 September 1993.' *Theatre Record*, 23(19): 1051

Dear, Nick. 1986. 'Play Note.' *NT Programme, The Art of Success*

Dear, Nick. 2000. *The Art of Success. Plays One*. London: Faber

Derrida, Jacques. 1967. *L'écriture et la différence*. Paris: Éditions du Seuil

Dovreni, Mira. 2007. Unpublished Interview about *The Bitches' Ball*. Conducted by Ursula Canton, Edinburgh, 22 August 2007

Dromgoole, Nicholas. 2000. *Marriage in Disguise*. London: Oberon

Eagleton, Terry. 1989. *Saint Oscar*. Derry: Field Day

Edel, Leon. 1973 [1959]. *Literary Biography*. Bloomington & London: Indiana University Press

Edgar, David. 2000. *Albert Speer*. Based on *Albert Speer: His Battle with Truth* by Gitta Sereny. London: NHB

Edwardes, Jane. 1991. 'Time Out, 4 December 1991.' *Theatre Record*, 11(24): 1484

Elam, Keir. 1980. *The Semiotics of Theatre and Drama*. London: Methuen

Eliot, T.S. 1935. *Murder in the Cathedral*. London: Faber

Ellis, David. 2000. *Literary Lives: Biography and the Search for Understanding*. Edinburgh: Edinburgh University Press

Engel, Pascal. 2002. *Truth*. Chesham: Acumen

English, Paul. 2009. 'Theatre News.' *Daily Record*, 9 May 2009, p. 45

Epstein, William H. 1987. *Recognizing Biography*. Philadelphia: University of Pennsylvania Press

Esmee Fairbairn Foundation. 2010. *Homepage* [online]. Available from: http:// www.esmeefairbairn.org.uk/about-us.html. Accessed 12 April 2010

Evans, Mary. 1999. *Missing Persons: The Impossibility of Auto/Biography*. London & New York: Routledge

Eyre, Richard. 2003. *Vincent in Brixton*. By Nicholas Wright. BBC4. Screened 20 March 2003

Favorini, Attilo (ed. and intro.) 1995. *Voicings: 10 Plays from the Documentary Theatre*. Hopewell, NJ: Ecco Press

Forster, E.M. 1974 [1927]. *Aspects of the Novel*, ed. Oliver Stallybrass. London: Penguin

Forsyth, Alison. 2009. 'Performing Trauma: Race Riots and Beyond in the Work of Anna Deveare Smith.' In: Forsyth, Alison and Chris Megson (eds)

Get Real: Documentary Theatre Past and Present. Basingstoke: Palgrave Macmillan, pp. 140–50

Forsyth, Alison and Chris Megson (eds) 2009a. *Get Real: Documentary Theatre Past and Present.* Basingstoke: Palgrave Macmillan

Forsyth, Alison and Chris Megson. 2009b. 'Introduction.' In: Forsyth, Alison and Chris Megson (eds) *Get Real: Documentary Theatre Past and Present.* Basingstoke: Palgrave Macmillan, pp. 1–5

Foursight Theatre. 2005. *Thatcher – the Musical!* Unpublished Script

Foursight Theatre. No Year. 'About Us.' Foursight website. http://www.foursighttheatre.co.uk/The-Company/. Accessed 20 January 2010

Frank, Katherine. 1980. 'Writing Lives: Theory and Practices in Literary Biography.' *Genre*, 13: 499–516

Frayn, Michael. 2000. *Copenhagen.* London: Methuen

Frayn, Michael. 2002a. '"Copenhagen" Revisited.' *New York Review of Books*, 49(5): 22–4

Frayn, Michael. 2002b. 'Comment and Analysis. Letters: Heisenberg Mugging Does Not Fit the Facts.' *Guardian*, 15 April 2002

Frayn, Michael. 2002c. 'Letter: Tom Paulin's Woolly Thinking on Heisenberg.' *Guardian*, 5 April 2002

Frayn, Michael. 2003. *Democracy.* London: Methuen

Frayn, Michael. 2004. Interview with Ursula Canton. *The Theatre Archive Project* [online]. Available from: http://www.bl.uk/projects/theatrearchive/frayn.html. Accessed 15 April 2010

Friel, Brian. 1989. *Making History.* London: Faber

Frisch, Max. 1972. *Tagebuch 1966–1971.* Frankfurt/M: Suhrkamp

Gallagher, Gus. 2005. Unpublished Correspondence with Ursula Canton

Garber, Marjorie. 1996. 'Introduction to Part V.' In: Riehl, Mary and David Suchoff (eds) *The Seductions of Biography.* New York: Routledge, pp. 175–8

Gardiner, Caroline. 1994. 'From Bankside to the West End: A Comparative View of London Audiences.' *New Theatre Quarterly*, February, 10(37): 70–86

Gardner, Lyn. 2006. 'Write About an Arranged Marriage? No Way!' *Guardian*, 25 July 2006

Gems, Pam. 1982. *Queen Christina.* London: St Luke's Press

Gems, Pam. 1985. *Piaf. Three Plays.* Harmondsworth: Penguin

Gems, Pam. 1996a. *Marlene.* London: Oberon

Gems, Pam. 1996b. *Stanley.* London: NHB

Gems, Pam. 1996c. 'Why a Play About Stanley Spencer.' *NT Programme, Stanley*, pp. 11–12

Gems, Pam. 1998. *The Snow Palace.* London: Oberon

Gergen, Kenneth J. 1999. *An Invitation to Social Construction.* London: Sage

Glover, Julian. 2006. 'Thatcher – the Musical.' *Theatre Record*, 26(3): 147

Gourdon, Anne-Marie. 1982. *Théâtre, public, perception.* Paris: Éditions du Centre National de la Recherche Scientifique

Grice, Paul. 1989. *Studies in the Way of Words.* Cambridge, MA: Harvard University Press

Gupta, Tanika. 2005. *Gladiator Games.* London: Oberon

Gupta, Tanika. 2009. Unpublished Correspondence with Ursula Canton. Received 29 July 2009

Hammond, Will and Dan Steward (eds) 2008. *Verbatim Verbatim.* London: Oberon

Hampton, Christopher. 1983. *Tales from Hollywood*. London: Faber
Hampton, Christopher. 1991. *Total Eclipse: The Philanthropist and Other Plays*. London: Faber
Harben, Niloufer. 1988. *Twentieth-Century English History Plays: From Bond to Shaw*. Basingstoke: Macmillan
Hare, David. 1998. *Judas Kiss*. London: Faber
Hare, David. 2003. *The Permanent Way*. London: Faber
Hare, David. 2004. *Stuff Happens*. London: Faber
Hastings, Michael. 1984. *Tom and Viv*. Harmondsworth: Penguin
Hattenstone, Simon. 2004. 'My First Night in Guantanamo.' *Guardian* [online]. Available from: http://www.guardian.co.uk/stage/2004/oct/06/theatre.politicaltheatre. Accessed 12 August 2010
Hawthorne, Jeremy. 1994 [1992]. *A Concise Glossary of Contemporary Literary Theory*, 2nd edn. London: E. Arnold
Hesford, Wendy S. 2006. 'Staging Terror.' *The Drama Review*, 50:3(191): 29–41
Highberg, Nels P. 2009. 'When Heroes Fall: Doug Wright's *I Am My Own Wife* and the Challenge to Truth.' In: Forsyth, Alison and Chris Megson (eds) *Get Real: Documentary Theatre Past and Present*. Basingstoke: Palgrave Macmillan, pp. 166–78
Highfield, John. 2005. 'Gladiator Games.' http://www.thestage.co.uk/reviews/review.php/10178/gladiator-games. Accessed 8 January 2006
Hill, Annette. 2005. *Reality TV: Audience and Popular Television*. London: Routledge
Holland, Peter and Hanna Scolnicov. 1991. *Reading Plays: Interpretations and Reception*. Cambridge: Cambridge University Press
Holliday, Joyce. 1991. *Anywhere to Anywhere*. In: Griffiths, Gabriele and Elaine Aston (eds) *Herstory. Vol. 2*. Sheffield: Sheffield Academic Press
Holmes, Richard. 1995. 'Biography: Inventing the Truth.' In: Batchelor, John (ed.) *The Art of Literary Biography*. Oxford: Clarendon, pp. 15–26
Home Office. 2006. 'Zahid Mubarek Inquiry report published.' *Home Office Website* [online]. Available from: http://www.homeoffice.gov.uk/about-us/news/mubarek-Report. Accessed 16 October 2009
Huber, Werner and Martin Middeke. 1995. 'Biography in Contemporary Drama.' In: Reitz, Bernhard (ed.) *Contemporary Drama in English: Drama and Reality*. Trier: WVT, pp. 133–43
Hughes, Dusty. 1986. *Futurists and Commitments*. London: Faber
Hutcheon, Linda. 1988. *A Poetics of Postmodernism: History, Theory, Fiction*. London: Routledge
Ice and Fire. 2009. 'List of Sources for Rendition Monologues.' *Ice and Fire Homepage* [online]. Available from: http://iceandfire.co.uk/wp-content/uploads/2009/05/rendition-monologues-sources.pdf. Accessed 12 April 2010
Ice and Fire. 2010a. 'About Us.' *Ice and Fire Homepage* [online]. Available from: http://iceandfire.co.uk/index.php/about-us/. Accessed 12 April 2010
Ice and Fire. 2010b. 'Outreach Network About Us.' *Ice and Fire Homepage* [online]. Available from: http://iceandfire.co.uk/index.php/outreach/about-us/. Accessed 12 April 2010
Ice and Fire. 2010c. 'Outreach Network.' *Ice and Fire Homepage* [online]. Available from: http://iceandfire.co.uk/index.php/outreach/. Accessed 12 April 2010

Ice and Fire. 2010d. 'Rendition Monologues.' *Ice and Fire Homepage* [online]. Available from: http://iceandfire.co.uk/outreach/scripts/rendition-monologues/. Accessed 12 April 2010

Innes, Christopher. 1999. 'Elemental, My Dear Clare: The Case of the Missing Poet.' In: Huber, Werner and Martin Middeke (eds) *Biofictions: The Rewriting of Romantic Lives in Contemporary Fiction and Drama.* Rochester: Camden House, pp. 187–200

Irmer, Thomas. 2006. 'A Search for New Realities: Documentary Theatre in Germany.' *The Drama Review*, 50:3(191): 16–28

Iser, Wolfgang. 1972. *Der implizite Leser.* München: Fink

Iser, Wolfgang. 1989. *Prospecting: From Reader-Response to Literary Anthropology.* Baltimore: Johns Hopkins University Press

Jeffers, Alison. 2009. 'Looking at Esrafil: Witnessing "Refugitive" Bodies in *I've Got Something to Show You.'* In: Forsyth, Alison and Chris Megson (eds) *Get Real: Documentary Theatre Past and Present.* Basingstoke: Palgrave Macmillan, pp. 91–106

Jeffrey, Stephen. 1998. *The Libertine.* London: Nick Hern Books

Jenkins, Keith. 1991. *Re-Thinking History.* London & New York: Routledge

Jenkins, Keith (ed.) 1997. *The Postmodern History Reader.* London & New York: Routledge

Jenkins, Mark. 2004. *More Lives than One.* Cardigan: Parthian

Johns, Ian. 2002. 'The Times, 10 August 2002.' *Theatre Record*, 22(16): 1051

Johnson, Terry. 1986 [1982]. *Insignificance*, 2nd edn. London: Methuen

Johnson, Terry. 1993. *Hysteria.* London: Methuen

King, Geoff. 2002. *Film Comedy.* London: Wallflower Press

Knowles, Richard. 2004. *Reading the Material Theatre.* Cambridge: Cambridge University Press

Kohler Riessman, Catherine. 1993. *Narrative Analysis.* Qualitative Research Methods Series 30. London: Sage

Kramer, Stephanie. 1998. 'Imaging/Imagining Women's Lives: Biography in Contemporary Women's Drama.' In: Reitz, B. (ed.) *CDE: Anthropological Aspects.* Trier: WVT, pp. 69–82

Kramer, Stephanie. 2000. *Fiktionale Biographien: (Re-)Visionen und (Re-)Konstruktionen weiblicher Lebensentwürfe in Dramen britischer Autorinnen seit 1970. Ein Beitrag zur Typologie und Entwicklung des historischen Dramas.* Trier: WVT

Krauss, Kenneth. 1993. *Private Readings/Public Texts: Playreaders' Constructs of Theatre Audiences.* Rutherford: Fairleigh Dickinson University Press

Kumin, Laura. 2004. 'Teatro de la primera' [online]. Available from: http://www.elcultural.es/HTML/20041028/Teatro/TEATRO10552.asp. Accessed 15 June 2006

Kvale, Steinar. 1996. *InterViews: An Introduction to Qualitative Research Interviewing.* London: Sage

Lacey, Anne. 2005. Unpublished Correspondence with Ursula Canton

Langton, Clea. 2009. Unpublished Interview about *Rendition Monologues.* Conducted by Ursula Canton, Edinburgh, 19 August 2009

Liberty. 2008. 'Defamation.' *Your Rights Website* [online]. Available from: http://www.yourrights.org.uk/yourrights/right-of-free-expression/defamation/defamation-elements-of-a-claim.html. Accessed 3 March 2010

Library Theatre. 2004a. *Programme for Vincent in Brixton*. Manchester: Library Theatre

Library Theatre. 2004b. *Flyer for Vincent in Brixton*. Manchester: Library Theatre

Linden, Sonja. 2005. *Crocodile Seeking Refuge*, rev. edn. London: Aurora Metro Press

Lindenberger, Herbert. 1975. *Historical Drama: The Relation of Literature and Reality*. Chicago & London: University of Chicago Press

Lloyd Pack, Roger. 2005. Unpublished Correspondence with Ursula Canton

Lochhead, Liz. 1985. *Blood and Ice*. In: Wandor, Micheline (ed.) *Plays by Women 4*. London: Methuen

Lochhead, Liz. 1989. *Mary Queen of Scots Got Her Head Chopped Off & Dracula*. Harmondsworth: Penguin

Lochhead, Liz. 2009a. *Mary Queen of Scots Got Her Head Chopped Off*. London: Nick Hern Books

Lochhead, Liz. 2009b. Interview about *Mary Queen of Scots Got Her Head Chopped Off*. Conducted by Ursula Canton, 30 September 2009

Lowenthal, David. 1985. *The Past Is a Foreign Country*. Cambridge: Cambridge University Press

Lustig, Harry and Brian B. Schwartz. 2005. 'Copenhagen in New York.' http://web. gc.cuny.edu/ashp/nml/copenhagen/Lustig_Schwartz.htm. Accessed 24 August 2005

Lyotard, Jean-François. 1979. *La condition postmoderne*. Paris: Éditions de Minuit

Maack, Annegret. 1991. 'Charakter als Echo: Zur Poethologie fiktiver Biographien.' In: Brunkhorst, Martin, Gerd Rohnmann and Konrad Scholl (eds) *Klassiker-Renaissance: Modelle der Gegenwartsliteratur*. Tübingen: Stauffenburg, pp. 247–58

Maack, Annegret. 1993. 'Das Leben der toten Dichter: Fiktive Biographien.' In: Maack, Annegret and Rüdiger Imhof (eds) *Radikalität und Mäßigung*. Darmstadt: Wissenschaftliche Buchgesellschaft, pp. 169–88

Macauly, Alastair. 1998a. 'Financial Times, 21 November 1998.' *Theatre Record*, 18(24): 1575

Macauly, Alastair. 1998b. 'Financial Times, 15 July 1998.' *Theatre Record*, 18(14): 898

Macauly, Alastair. 1999. 'Financial Times, 10 February 1999.' *Theatre Record*, 19(3): 149

Malhotra Benz, Valerie and Wade Kenny. 1997. '"Body as World": Kenneth Burke's Answer to the Postmodernist Charges Against Sociology.' *Sociological Theory*, 15(1): 81–96

Mann, P.H. 1966. 'Surveying a Theatre Audience: Methodological Problems.' *British Journal of Sociology*, 17(4): 380–7

Mannion, Tom. 2009. Interview about *Copenhagen*. Conducted by Ursula Canton, 15 September 2009

Mansfield, Laurie. 1989. *The Buddy Holly Story*. Dir. Paul Bettinson. Perf. Paul Hip. Victoria Palace Theatre

Martin, Carol. 2009. 'Living Stimulations: The Use of Media in Documentary in the UK, Lebanon and Israel.' In: Forsyth, Alison and Chris Megson (eds) *Get Real: Documentary Theatre Past and Present*. Basingstoke: Palgrave Macmillan, pp. 74–90

Martin, Jacqueline and Willmar Sauter. 1995. *Understanding Theatre: Performance Analysis in Theory and Practice*. Stockholm: Almqvist and Wiksell Int.

McConachie, Bruce. 2001. 'Doing Things with Image Schemas: The Cognitive Turn in Theatre Studies and the Problem of Experience for Historians.' *Theatre Journal*, 53: 569–94

McKay, Tom. 2009. Unpublished Correspondence with Ursula Canton. Received 22 July 2009

McKenna, John. 1993. *Clare: A Novel*. Belfast: Falstaff

McMillan, Joyce. 2009. 'Joyce McMillan on Theatre.' *Scotsman*, 30 April 2009, p. 43

Megson, Chris. 2007. '"The State We're In": Tribunal Theatre and British Politics in the 1990s.' In: Watt, Daniel and Daniel Meyer-Dinkgräfe (eds) *Theatres of Thought: Theatre, Performance and Philosophy*. Newcastle: Cambridge Scholars, pp. 110–26

Mergenthal, Silvia. 1999. 'The Dramatist as Reader: Liz Lochhead's Play *Blood and Ice*.' In: Huber, Werner and Martin Middeke (eds) *Biofictions: The Rewriting of Romantic Lives in Contemporary Fiction and Drama*. Rochester: Camden House, pp. 96–105

Meserve, Walter J. 1965. *An Outline History of American Drama*. Totowa, NJ: Littlefield, Adams

Meyer-Dinkgräfe, Daniel. 2003. 'The Artist as Character in Contemporary British Bio-Plays.' In: *The Professions in Contemporary Drama*. Bristol: intellect, pp. 87–100

Mitchell, Anthony. 1971. *Tyger*. London: Jonathan Cape

The Monthly Review. No Year. *History of Monthly Review* [online]. Available from: http://monthlyreview.org/aboutmr.htm. Accessed 25 February 2010

Moog-Grünewald, Maria. 1991. 'Descartes und Pascal im Dialog. Anmerkungen zu Brisvilles Bühnenstück.' In: Brunkhorst, Martin, Gerd Rohnmann and Konrad Scholl (eds) *Klassiker-Renaissance: Modelle der Gegenwartsliteratur*. Tübingen: Stauffenburg, pp. 67–74

Moran, Hiram. 2000. *O'Faoláin's The Great O'Neill* [online]. Paper presented at Sean O'Faolain Centenary Conference, University College Cork, 25 February 2000. Available from: http://www.ucc.ie/celt/OFaolain.pdf. Accessed 26 May 2009

Mulgrew, Gerry. 2010. Unpublished Correspondence with Ursula Canton. Received 9 April 2010

Mumford, Peter. 2009. Unpublished Correspondence with Ursula Canton. Received 2 September 2009

Munslow, Alun. 2000. *The Routledge Companion to Historical Studies*. London & New York: Routledge

Nadel, Ira Bruce. 1984. *Biography: Fiction, Fact and Form*. London: Macmillan

National Theatre. 2002. *Programme, Vincent in Brixton*

National Theatre. 2003. 'Vincent in Brixton.' *NT Homepage* [online]. Available from: http://www.nationaltheatre.org.uk/1193/productions/vincent-in-brixton. html. Accessed 12 April 2010

National Theatre of Scotland. 2009a. 'Trailer for *Mary Queen of Scots Got Her Head Chopped Off*.' *NTS Homepage* [online]. Available from: http://www. nationaltheatreofscotland.co.uk/content/default.asp?page=s515. Accessed 15 April 2010

National Theatre of Scotland. 2009b. 'Cast Interviews.' *NTS Homepage* [online]. Available from: http://www.nationaltheatreofscotland.co.uk/content/default. asp?page=s516. Accessed 15 April 2010

Nelson, Richard. 1996. *The General from America*. London: Faber

Network for Social Change. 2010. *Homepage* [online]. Available from: http://thenetworkforsocialchange.org.uk. Accessed 12 April 2010

Norton Taylor, Richard. 1999. *The Colour of Justice: The Lawrence Inquiry*. London: Oberon

Nzaramba, Ery. 2009. Unpublished Interview about *Rendition Monologues*. Conducted by Ursula Canton, Edinburgh, 19 August 2009

O'Kane, Patrick. 2009. Unpublished Interview about *Insignificance*. Conducted by Ursula Canton, 5 December 2009

Olsen, Christopher. 2000. 'Theatre Audience Surveys: Toward a Semiotic Approach.' *New Theatre Quarterly*, 18(3): 261–75

O'Reilly, Kate. 2006. *Reans Girls*. BBC Radio 4. 12 December 2006

Osborne, John. 1965. *Luther: A Play*. London: Faber

Osborne, John. 1983 [1966]. *A Patriot for Me and A Sense of Detachment*. London: Faber

Ottaviani, Jim and Leland Purvis. 2004. *Suspended in Language: Niels Bohr's Life Discoveries and the Century He Shaped*. Ann Arbor: General Tektroniks Labs

Paget, Derek. 1990. *True Stories? Documentary Drama on Radio, Screen and Stage*. Manchester: Manchester University Press

Palmer, Richard H. 1998. *The Contemporary British History Play*. Westport, CT: Greenwood

Panthaki, Ray. 2009. Unpublished Correspondence with Ursula Canton. Received 3 March 2009

Participations. Journal of Audience and Reception Studies [online]. Available from: http://www.participations.org/. Accessed 15 April 2010

Paterson, Erika. 1991. 'The Self-Determined Audience.' *Canadian Theatre Review* (CTR), Summer, 67: 49–53

Paulin, Tom. 2002. 'Comment and Analysis. Letters: Frayn and Heisenberg.' *Guardian*, 27 March 2002

Pavis, Patrice. 1985. *Voix et images de la scène*. Lille: Presses Universitaires

Peacock, Keith D. 1991. *Radical Stages: Alternative History in Modern British Drama*. New York: Greenwood

Pfister, Manfred. 1988. *The Theory and Analysis of Drama*, transl. John Halliday. Cambridge: Cambridge University Press

Pinnock, Winsome. 1989. *A Rock in the Water*. In: Brewster, Yvonne (ed.) *Black Plays 2*. London: Methuen

Portillo, Michael. 2006. 'History Lessons.' *New Statesman* [online]. Available from: http://www.newstatesman.com/200602200033. Accessed 5 March 2007

Postlewait, Thomas. 2003. 'Realism.' In: Kennedy, Dennis (ed.) *The Oxford Encyclopaedia of Theatre and Performance*. Oxford: Oxford University Press, p. 1114

Powell, James M. 1990. 'Introduction.' In: Iggers, Georg G. and James M. Powell (eds) *Leopold von Ranke and the Shaping of the Historical Discipline*. Syracuse, NY: University Press

Pownall, David. 1979. *An Audience Called Edouard*. London: Faber

Pownall, David. 1983. *Master Class*. London: Faber

Rattigan, Terence. 1950. *The Winslow Boy: with two other plays*. London: Pan Books

Raulff, Ulrich. 2002. 'Das Leben – buchstäblich. Über neuere Biographik und Geschichtswissenschaft.' In: Klein, Christian (ed.) *Grundlagen der Biographik. Theorie und Praxis des biographischen Schreibens*. Stuttgart: Metzler, pp. 55–68

Rebellato, Dan. 1999. *1956 and All That: The Making of Modern British Theatre.* London: Routledge

Reinelt, Janelle. 2006. 'Toward a Poetics of Theatre and Public Events: In the Case of Stephen Lawrence.' *The Drama Review*, 50:3(191): 69–87

Reinelt, Janelle. 2009. 'The Promise of Documentary.' In: Forsyth, Alison and Chris Megson (eds) *Get Real: Documentary Theatre Past and Present.* Basingstoke: Palgrave Macmillan, pp. 6–23

Reitz, Bernhard. 1999. 'Dangerous Enthusiasm: The Appropriations of William Blake in Adrian Mitchell's *Tyger.'* In: Huber, Werner and Martin Middeke (eds) *Biofictions: The Rewriting of Romantic Lives in Contemporary Fiction and Drama.* Rochester: Camden House, pp. 50–64

Richardson, Brian. 1997. 'Beyond Poststructuralism: Theory of Character, the Personae of Modern Drama and the Antimonies of Critical Theory.' *Modern Drama*, 40(1): 86–99

Rickman, Alan and Katherine Viner (eds) 2005. *My Name is Rachel Corrie.* London: NHB

Riffaterre, Michael. 1990. *Fictional Truth.* Baltimore: Johns Hopkins University Press

Roeg, Nicholas. 1985. *Insignificance.* Perf. Michael Emil, Theresa Russell, Tony Curtis, Gary Busey. Recorded Picture Company

Rokem, Freddie. 2000. *Performing History: Theatrical Representations of the Past in Contemporary Theatre.* Iowa: Iowa University Press

Ronen, Ruth. 1994. *Possible Worlds in Literary Theory.* Cambridge: Cambridge University Press

Rosenthal, Alan (ed.) 1999. *Why Docudrama: Fact and Fiction on Film and TV.* Carbondale: Southern Illinois University Press

Rosenthal, Alan. 2005. 'Staying Alive.' In: Rosenthal, Alan and John Corner (eds) *New Challenges for Documentary.* Manchester: Manchester University Press

Ruthrof, Horst. 1997. *Semantics and the Body: Meaning from Frege to the Postmodern.* Toronto: Toronto University Press

Saussure, Ferdinand de. 1979 [1916]. *Cours de linguistique générale*, eds Charles Bally and Albert Sechehaya. Paris: Payot

Sauter, Willmar. 2000. *The Theatrical Event: Dynamics of Performance and Perception.* Iowa City: University of Iowa Press

Sauter, Willmar. 2002. 'Who Reacts When, How and upon What: From Audience Surveys to the Theatrical Event.' *Contemporary Theatre Review: An International Journal*, 12(3): 115–29

Schabert, Ina. 1990. *In Quest of the Other Person: Fiction as Biography.* Tübingen: Franke

Schaff, Barbara. 1992. *Das zeitgenössische britische Künstlerdrama.* Passau: Stutz

Scheuer, Helmut. 1979. 'Kunst und Wissenschaft. Die moderne literarische Biographie.' In: Klingenstein, Grete, Heinrich Lutz and Gerald Stourzh (eds) *Biographie und Geschichtswissenschaft: Aufsätze zur Theorie und Praxis biographischer Arbeit.* München: Oldenbourg, pp. 81–110

Schoenmakers, Henri. 1992. *Performance Theory: Reception and Audience Research.* Advances in Reception and Audience Research 3. Amsterdam: Tijdschrift voor Theaterwetenschap

Searle, John R. 1979. *Expression and Meaning: Studies in the Theory of Speech Acts.* Cambridge: Cambridge University Press

Searle, John R. 1996 [1995]. *The Construction of Social Reality.* London: Penguin

Shaffer, Peter. 1978. *The Royal Hunt of the Sun*. London: Longman

Sheffield Lyceum. 2005. *Programme, Insignificance*

Shellard, Dominic. 2000. *British Theatre Since the War*. New Haven & London: Yale University Press

Shellard, Dominic and Steve Nicholson with Miriam Handley. 2004. *The Lord Chamberlain Regrets*. London: British Library

Shepherd-Barr, Kirsten. 2002. '*Copenhagen* and Beyond: The "Rich and Mentally Nourishing" Interplay of Science and Theatre.' *Gramma*, 10: 171–82

Shepherd-Barr, Kirsten. 2006. *Science on Stage: From Doctor Faustus to Copenhagen*. Princeton: Princeton University Press

Sierz, Aleks. 2009. Staging Interculturality, the 18th Annual Conference of the German Society for Contemporary Drama in English, held in Vienna. Substantial extract. Available from: http://www.theatrevoice.com/listen_now/player/?audioID=704. Accessed 16 September 2009

Sinfield, Alan. 1983. 'The Theatre and Its Audience.' In: Sinfield, Alan (ed.) *Society and Literature, 1945–1970*. New York: Holmes & Meier

Soto-Morettini, Donna. 2002. '"Disturbing the Spirits of the Past": The Uncertainty Principle in Michael Frayn's *Copenhagen*.' In: Maufort, Marc and Franca Bellarsi (eds) *Crucible of Cultures: Anglophone Drama at the Dawn of the New Millennium*. Brussels: Peter Lang, pp. 69–78

Sova, Dawn B. 2004. *Banned Plays: Censorship Histories of 125 Stage Dramas*. New York: Facts on File

Spencer, Charles. 1994. 'Daily Telegraph, 12 December 1994.' *Theatre Record*, 14(25–6): 1553

Stanislavski, Konstantin Sergeyevich. 1980 [1936]. *An Actor Prepares*, transl. Elizabeth Reynolds Hapgood. London: Methuen

Stanley, Liz. 1992. 'Process in Feminist Biography and Feminist Epistemology.' In: Iles, Theresa (ed.) *All Sides of the Subject – Women and Biography*. London & New York: Teachers College Press, pp. 109–25

States, Bert O. 1985. 'The Anatomy of Dramatic Character.' *Theatre Journal*, 37(1): 86–101

Stewart, Victoria. 1999. 'A Theatre of Uncertainties: Science and History in Michael Frayn's "Copenhagen".' *New Theatre Quarterly*, 15(3): 301–7

Stokes, Jane. 2003. *How To Do Media and Cultural Studies*. London: Sage

Stoppard, Tom. 1974. *Travesties*. London: Faber

Stoppard, Tom. 1997. *The Invention of Love*. London: Faber

Stoppard, Tom. 1999 [1993]. *Arcadia*. *Plays Five*. London: Faber

Stratton, Kate. 2002. 'Time Out, 14 August 2002.' *Theatre Record*, 22(16): 1051

Teale, Polly. 2003. *After Mrs. Rochester*. London: NHB

Teale, Polly. 2005. *Brontë*. London: NHB

Thaxter, John. 2002. 'What's On, 14 August 2002.' *Theatre Record*, 22(9): 551

Theatre Record, vol. 24, issues 1–10

Ubersfeld, Anne. 1982. *Lire le théâtre*, 4th edn. Paris: Editions Sociales

UK Government. 2010. 'Explaining the Role of the Witness.' *Criminal Justice System Website* [online]. Available from: http://www.cjsonline.gov.uk/witness/walkthrough/index.html. Accessed 7 April 2010

University of New York. 2005. 'More Copenhagen Events.' The Graduate Center. http://web.gc.cuny.edu/sciart/copenhagen/copenhagen.html. Accessed 24 August 2005

University of Reading. 2010. *Acting with Facts Project Website* [online]. Available from: http://www.reading.ac.uk/ftt/research/ftt-actingwithfacts.aspx. Accessed 3 August 2010

Upton, Carole-Anne. 2009. 'The Performance of Truth and Justice in Northern Ireland: The Case of Bloody Sunday.' In: Forsyth, Alison and Chris Megson (eds) *Get Real: Documentary Theatre Past and Present*. Basingstoke: Palgrave Macmillan, pp. 179–94

Van Gogh Bonger, Jo. 1913. 'Memoir of Vincent van Gogh.' *The Vincent van Gogh Gallery* [online]. Available from: http://www.vggallery.com/misc/archives/jo_memoir.htm. Accessed 12 April 2010

Wagner-Martin, Linda. 1994. *Telling Women's Lives: The New Biography*. New Brunswick, NJ: Rutgers University Press

Waugh, Patricia. 1984. *Metafiction: The Theory and Practice of Self-Conscious Fiction*. London & New York: Routledge

Weissmann, Philip. 1959/60. 'A Lively Theatre of Lives: Portraiture Versus Art.' *Modern Drama*, 2: 263–7

Wertenbaker, Timberlake. 1998. *After Darwin*. London: Faber

West, Samuel. 2005. Unpublished Correspondence with Ursula Canton

West, Timothy. 2005. Unpublished Correspondence with Ursula Canton

Westenra, Charlotte. 2009. Unpublished Interview about *Gladiator Games*. Conducted by Ursula Canton, 25 September 2009

White, Hayden. 1973. *Metahistory: The Historical Imagination in Nineteenth Century Europe*. Baltimore: Johns Hopkins University Press

Whitemore, Hugh. 1987. *Breaking the Code*. London: Samuel French

Wikander, Matthew H. 1986. *The Play of Truth and State: Historical Drama from Shakespeare to Brecht*. Baltimore: Johns Hopkins University Press

Willett, John (ed. and transl.) 1978. *Brecht on Theatre*. London: Methuen

Williams, Christopher (ed.) 1980. *Realism and the Cinema: A Reader*. London: Routledge and Kegan Paul

Wills, Paul. 2009. Unpublished Correspondence with Ursula Canton. Received 20 July 2009

Wolf, Matt. 2003. 'Michael Frayn on Democracy. NT Platform. Cottlesloe.' 19 September 2003. http://www.nationaltheatre.org.uk/?lid=7664. Accessed 27 February 2004

Wolfe, Welby B. 1977. *Matters of the Scene: An Introduction to Technical Theatre*. New York: Harper

Wright, Nicholas. 2002. *Vincent in Brixton*. London: Nick Hern Books

Wright, Nicholas. 2009. Unpublished Correspondence with Ursula Canton. Received 2 September 2009

Wu, Duncan. 2000. *Making Plays: Interviews with Contemporary British Dramatists and their Directors*. Basingstoke: Macmillan

Yeger, Sheila. 1990. *Self Portrait*. Charlbury: Amber Lane

Yeger, Sheila. 1991. *Variations on a Theme by Clara Schumann*. In: Castledine, Annie (ed.) *Plays by Women 9*. London: Methuen

Young, Toby. 2002. 'Spectator, 11 May 2002.' *Theatre Record*, 22(9): 551

Zimmermann, Christian von (ed.) 2000. *Fakten und Fiktionen: Strategien fiktionalbiographischer Dichterdarstellungen in Roman, Drama und Film seit 1970*. Tübingen: Narr

Index of Concepts

alienation / Verfremdung 8, 100
authenticity / authentical   3, 15,
  20, 21, 38, 43, 44, 46, 50, 55,
  58, 59, 67, 70, 97, 101, 147,
  155, 169

censorship   3, 4, 5, 6, 7, 8, 11, 13,
  14, 43

documentary theatre   2, 4, 5, 7, 12,
  14–8, 20, 38, 40, 41, 44, 47–50, 52,
  55–9, 67, 156, 164, 188

empiricism *see* reconstructionism
extra theatrical / extra-theatricality
  5, 8, 20, 21, 29, 34, 39, 44–8, 51–6,
  59–84, 88–98, 101, 106, 109, 133,
  135, 143, 147, 151–7, 161, 163,
  164, 169

feminism / feminist   12
fact / factual   4, 9, 10, 12, 15, 17–9,
  23, 25–32, 34, 38, 39–41, 44, 48, 51,
  52, 58, 59, 65, 67–9, 73, 74, 78, 80,
  82, 86, 88, 92, 93, 96–8, 101, 103,
  107, 120, 134, 143, 147–150, 153–5,
  157, 159, 163, 164, 166, 167, 172,
  174
fiction / fictional   9, 18, 19, 26–30,
  37, 38, 40, 41, 49, 96, 97, 101, 104,
  110, 115, 131, 134, 135, 143, 149,
  156, 166, 167, 173
functional approach   19–21, 23, 97,
  111, 167, 174

historical accuracy *see*
  reconstructionism

intra theatrical / intra Theatricality
  19, 29, 41, 45, 46, 69, 74, 75, 82–9,
  93–6, 100, 101, 104, 106, 117, 132,
  141, 143, 149, 157, 159–164, 166

Lord Chamberlain *see* censorship

modern / modernism   8, 24, 27, 30,
  32, 34–8, 42, 44, 97, 99

positivism / positivist   24, 32, 45
Postmodernism / Postmodernist   8,
  10, 11, 13, 15, 18, 24, 30, 33,
  35–42, 96, 111, 112, 122

realism *see* extra-theatrical
reconstructionism / reconstructionist
  4, 8, 9 11, 26, 27, 30, 32, 86, 87,
  95, 96, 110–12, 115, 118, 121, 134,
  159, 160

sociology of knowledge   38

theatricality / theatrical   5, 6, 9, 16,
  19–22, 27, 29, 33, 36, 37, 44–7,
  50–2, 57, 59, 62, 63, 69, 76, 77, 79,
  80, 83, 84, 89, 90, 93–102, 112–17,
  120, 126, 128–35, 138–41, 149–53,
  158–60, 162, 164, 166
truth / true   9, 17, 20, 25, 26, 28, 30–4,
  37, 38, 41, 43 48, 50, 55–9, 61, 63,
  67, 68, 74, 77, 110, 111, 134, 149,
  153, 156, 165, 168, 169, 173

verbatim theatre *see* documentary   4,
  15, 16, 20, 38, 44, 47–50, 52, 55–9,
  156

Index of Theatre Practitioners

Index of Plays and Biographical Characters

Note: excludes names mentioned in the titles.